TARGET

on our

BACKS

J.M. Darhower

ISBN-13: 978-1-942206-16-3

ISBN-10: 1-942206-16-X

To Leonardo DiCaprio...
I'm sorry for what I said.

Prologue

I'm going to tell you a story, a story about a lion that was killed by a callous hunter not long ago. This lion was the king of his pride, and this hunter? This hunter didn't even think twice about pulling the trigger, consequences be damned.

And consequences there were.

You see, when a king is killed, anarchy reigns as the next strongest male steps up to take his place. Sometimes that male is considerate, compassionate, but more likely he's a ruthless beast. To secure his place at the top of the food chain, to assert his dominance in a time of chaos, the lion annihilates anyone he considers competition, starting with his predecessor's cubs.

His offspring, the ones he created, the ones he raised to follow his lead... one-by-one they fell, victim to the new cruel tyrant, until the former king's pride was no more. In the hunter's mind, it was over the second he put down the gun, but in reality, that was when the real trouble began.

And trouble?

It came with a vengeance.

The pride lands were knee-deep in it.

Midtown Shooting Leaves One Dead

I stare through the darkness at the bold headline deep in the middle of yesterday's newspaper. It didn't make the front page. Not even close. It was tucked in along with the petty crimes that plague the city, like a shooting means nothing to these people nowadays.

Maybe it doesn't.

Who am I to judge?

Bullets certainly don't faze *me* anymore.

But this one stalled me. This one made me hesitate. My eyes drift from the vague headline to the lone victim's name: *Kelvin Russo*.

I know him.

Well, I *knew* him.

Kelvin is no more.

Once one of Ray's favorite street soldiers, Kelvin caught a bullet to the back of the skull. He was young, just starting out... couldn't have been any more than twenty-three or twenty-four. The paper doesn't say much about what happened, but I know an execution when I read about one.

Another of the former king's cubs has fallen.

I didn't pull the trigger this time, but when it comes down to it, I still shoulder the blame. He's dead because there's a new king of this concrete jungle, a king that's sending a message to everyone.

Bow down.

The thing is, though, I don't kneel for anyone. I get on my knees for no fucking man. I walked away a year ago, before pulling that fateful trigger, but that won't be good enough for someone like him.

It's only a matter of time before he comes for me.

Before he *wants* me.

Whoever he is...

Chapter One

Karissa

"A leopard doesn't change its spots."

Giuseppe Vitale isn't usually a man to mince words. He speaks in riddles a lot of the time, something his son inherited from him, but his point is always there, front and center. He knows what he knows and feels how he feels, and when it comes down to it, he won't hesitate to tell you how it is.

A leopard doesn't change its spots.

He's talking about Ignazio.

"But he's different," I say, my eyes drifting to the small wooden table between us, like maybe subconsciously I doubt my own words. He has been different, that's true, but I know that doesn't mean he has actually changed.

Can he change? I don't know.

Should I even want him to?

It has been over a year since a bullet tore through me in the foyer of the home in Brooklyn, although my chest still aches like it happened yesterday. The physical wound healed but my heart is another story.

Part of it remains broken.

It probably always will be that way.

Six weeks ago, Naz asked me to marry him. Really asked me, unlike before. This time, when I said yes, I knew exactly what I was committing to. I know what kind of man he is. I know the things he's done, the things he wanted to do. We said 'I do' that very night, in the chapel at the MGM Grand in Las Vegas, and I've spent every night since then convinced I'd made the right decision.

Because he's different.

He is.

But what exactly does *different* mean?

Giuseppe reaches over, placing his rough, calloused hand on top of mine, squeezing lightly to draw my attention back to him. He's got a smile on his lips, but it's not a smile of happiness. It borders somewhere on pity.

I can almost hear what he's thinking.

Poor little girl, you don't understand what you've gotten into.

"You know, they say if you put a frog in a pot of boiling water, it'll jump right back out," he says. "But if you put a frog in a pot of cool water and steadily raise the temperature, it'll stay right where it is, like nothing is happening. You get where I'm going with this?"

My brow furrows at the jump in conversation. "No."

"You're the frog, girl, and Ignazio? He's boiling you alive without you even noticing."

I want to argue against that. I want to tell him he's wrong. Because he is. He's wrong. But the only words I can come up with are 'he's different' and I'm not even entirely sure how to explain what that means. He's still Naz, still the same intimidating Ignazio, but Vitale hasn't shown his face... not around me, anyway.

I know Giuseppe can't differentiate between the masks, though. He looks at his son and only sees the monster he turned into over the years. He can't see the man he was, or the man he is, the man he swears he's trying to be.

He still disappears at night sometimes. There are still the occasional whispered phone calls. He's still paranoid, and overprotective, and extremely careful, but what he isn't is *cruel*. He isn't deceitful. I understand him. He understands me. He doesn't handle me with kid gloves, but he doesn't give me more than I can tolerate, either. He treats me like a person, not a possession, although, okay... his possessive streak can sometimes still be pretty fierce.

The man is an enigma. A beautiful, sometimes terrifying puzzle that I'm still piecing together, little by little.

Giuseppe, though, has no interest in his son's healing. He has no interest in him being different. As far as he's concerned, Naz is the kind of broken you just can't fix.

Before I can think of something to say to Giuseppe, something other than the usual 'but he's different' bit, the door to the deli opens, the bell loudly jiggling. I don't even have to look over to know it's him. There's something about the way he enters, a chill in the air, a heat in the stare, that tells me Naz is here.

Giuseppe doesn't turn to look, but I know he senses it, too.

"*Porca vacca*," he mutters, sighing loudly as he pulls his hands from mine and shoves the chair back, standing up. His eyes remain on my face, the pity now more frustration. "You want some cookies? How about some Snickerdoodles?"

He doesn't wait for me to respond before walking away.

A few seconds later, the chair across from me shifts again, another body planting in it. I glance up at him, smiling when he mutters under his breath, "just like a whore in church around here."

They're a lot alike, Naz and his father, but you won't catch me telling either of them that. *Stubborn men.*

"Of all places," he says, raising his eyebrows as he stares at me across the table. "I could've gotten a table at the last minute at Le Bernardin, could've even taken you to Paragone again, but no... you ask me to meet you for lunch at Vitale's Italian Delicatessen."

I shrug. "The food's good here."

"I won't argue with that, but the atmosphere leaves quite a bit to be desired."

Giuseppe returns then, sliding a small plate of cookies onto the table in front of me. They're so fresh I can smell the warm cinnamon sugar. "Uh, you are heaven-sent," I say, snatching up a cookie and taking a bite of it. Delicious.

Naz rolls his eyes. He *rolls* his eyes.

I don't think I've ever seen the man rolls his eyes before.

"Are you going to order some lunch?" Giuseppe asks impatiently, glaring at his only child. "Or are you planning to just loiter for a while?"

"Depends," Naz replies.

"On what?"

"On whether or not you're willing to serve me."

Giuseppe grumbles to himself as he stalks away, heading straight back behind the counter, roughly shoving the swinging door open.

He disappears into the kitchen.

"So, uh, does that mean we're eating?" I ask.

"It means I'm ordering," Naz says. "He's either gone back there to make the food for us, or he's calling the police because I'm trespassing again. But considering how hungry I am, I'd say it's probably worth the risk."

Getting up, Naz heads for the front counter, ordering two Italian specials.

After paying, he goes to return to the table but pauses. "You wouldn't happen to have today's newspaper, would you?" he asks the young guy running the cash register, one of only three employees Giuseppe pays to help him out around here. He tends to do the brunt of the work himself for whatever reason. Pride, maybe. Probably pigheadedness.

Before the guy can answer, Giuseppe hollers from the kitchen, "Buy your own damn paper!"

Shaking his head, Naz retakes his seat. "I suppose it's obvious by now where I got my asshole genes from."

"He's not an asshole," I say, still shoveling the cookie in my mouth. "Neither are you, for that matter. You're just, you know... a bit intense."

"Intense," Naz repeats. "That's one way to put it."

Intense, he is. His intensity is unrivaled. His bright blue eyes burn through me as they slowly, carefully, scan my face, watching me eat my cookie like he's getting off on it. I can feel my cheeks warming with blush. "Why are you staring at me?"

He leans a bit closer, a smirk tugging the corner of his lips, flashing his dimples. "Why not?"

It only takes a few minutes for our food to be ready. As it turns out, Giuseppe decided to serve him, after all. I dive right in the second mine is placed on the table, but Naz hesitates. He stares at the sandwich, picking it apart with his fingers, eyes slightly narrowed as he inspects the contents.

"For Christ's sake, Ignazio," Giuseppe shouts, coming out from the kitchen. "Just eat the damn thing!"

A second passes.

Then another.

And another.

I don't think he's going to eat it, but then... he does. He picks it up and takes a small bite, chewing carefully. *Holy fuck.*

I don't want to make a big deal out of the fact that he's eating at his father's deli, food that, not long ago, he wouldn't even touch. I don't want to rock the boat, so to speak, by pointing out that Giuseppe hasn't once actually threatened to throw his ass out on the street. I don't want to gloat, but I can't help it. I can feel myself smiling with satisfaction. He's different. He is.

'I told you so' is begging to come from my lips.

"See?" I say, almost giddy as I watch Naz eat. "I knew the two of you—"

I don't have a chance to finish whatever smug thing it is I'm planning to say. My words die on the tip of my tongue as loud bangs echo through the deli, one after another.

BANG

BANG

BANG

Before I even have a chance to react, Naz is on his feet, grabbing the table in front of us and flipping it over, shoving me to the checkered floor behind it. I hit the floor. Hard. Wincing, stunned, I peek around the table, watching in horror as the glass covering the front of the building cracks from the force of the flying bullets.

Bullets.

Fucking *bullets*.

Someone is shooting at the place.

Everyone else drops to the floor, scrambling away on instinct, everyone except for Naz... and his father, for that matter. Both men just stand there, staring straight ahead, as the tinted glass ripples and splinters between the metal bars but never breaks inside.

Bulletproof.

A few seconds. That's all it lasts. A dozen gunshots in quick succession before a car speeds away outside, the tires squealing, smoke flying. I can barely see it through the destruction, but I can tell the car is black, a shadowy mass of metal hauling ass to get away before it's caught.

My heart is hammering, my chest aching from the force of the thumps. Gasping, I try to catch my breath, but it's hard. *So damn hard.* Stark silence overtakes the deli in the wake of the gunfire. It seems to go on forever. We're all stunned. Eventually, Naz turns his head, calmly looking down at where I'm still crouching on the floor, carefully offering me his hand.

"Are you okay?" he asks, although he doesn't actually sound alarmed. I don't know if the man is just desensitized to this sort of thing, or if maybe he knew we were safe where we were.

"I, uh..." My voice shakes, my body trembling as I let him pull me to my feet. "Yeah, I think so."

He looks me over, still gripping onto my hand, before turning his attention to the window. People around us are getting to their feet, some fleeing from the fear of it all, while Giuseppe still just stands there, silent, staring.

He's in shock.

I don't know what to say. I don't know what to do.

Someone just shot up the fucking deli.

Something tells me there will be hell to pay from a Vitale for it.

I'm just not entirely sure which man at this point.

"*You*," Giuseppe growls, his voice laced with an anger I haven't heard since the first day Naz brought me to this place. It's the sound of simmering rage, of fury, of disgust. His head turns, his eyes going straight to his son. Naz turns to his father at the sound of the man's voice, his expression stoic. "Get out! Get out, and don't come back!"

I'm too stunned to do anything but stand there and watch. Naz, on the other hand, doesn't look surprised at all. He looks his father over for a moment before turning to me, pulling me toward him. He wraps his arms around me, and I hug him back, gripping tight.

"Next time," he whispers, "pick somewhere else to eat."

With that, he lets go of me.

With that, he's gone.

It happens in a blink. The bell over the door is jingling, and Naz is no longer beside me before I can even make sense of what's going on. Brow furrowing, body still trembling, I dash for the door, shocked my legs can even hold me up. I pull the door open and dart out onto the sidewalk, calling his name. "Naz? *Naz!*"

I turn around in circles, looking, but he's gone. That fast. He disappeared from the deli, leaving me there.

He just... left me here.

Like I said, he's different.

The old Naz would've never done that.

Sirens blare in the distance, coming closer as I stand there, my eyes drifting to the front of the deli. Shards of glass litter the sidewalk, as well as a few bullets that had ricocheted off. The glass kept them from getting inside, but it wasn't immune to destruction.

It's a mess.

People are running down the streets, shouting at one another, the neighborhood in utter chaos.

A drive-by shooting in broad daylight.

It's one of those things my mother warned me about, the horror stories of monsters that run these streets. Naz always told me never to be scared, that I had nothing to be scared of, but I am... I'm scared.

What the hell just happened?

I step back into the deli just as the police start to arrive. Giuseppe is finally moving around, helping people to their feet, trying to calm down his remaining customers. His voice is quiet, almost soothing as he talks, all traces of his anger gone out the door with his son.

Leaning back against the wall by the door, I slide down to the floor, wrapping my arms around my knees as the police descend upon the scene. I'm in a daze, listening but not hearing anything going on around me, the world just a big blur until someone calls for me.

"Miss Reed?"

I look up, seeing a familiar face staring down at me. He's so close his shadow covers me, swaddling me in a gloomy cocoon. It's ominous. *Detective Jameson.*

The last time I saw the man was when I'd been shot. He came to the hospital while I was in recovery, asking to hear my side of the story. It was as if he'd expected me to refute Naz's statement, to tell them he'd somehow done something wrong, but I couldn't. Naz, for as many times as he might've endangered me, saved me that day. The doctor had said it himself. Naz saved my life. The detective had gone away, saying his door would be open if I wanted to reconsider, but never once did I ever think about turning on the man I love.

Because even with everything that has happened, God help me, I *do* love him.

I love him more than I ever thought possible.

I clear my throat, surprised my voice works when I say, "Vitale."

Jameson's brow furrows as he squats down in front of me, like he thinks maybe if he's more on my level, I'll somehow make more sense. "What?"

Holding out my left hand, I show him the ring on my finger. "I'm not Miss Reed anymore."

I can see it in his face when it clicks, his cool demeanor dissolving. Reaching out, he snatches a hold of my hand, tilting it to get a better look at the ring. It's simple, relatively speaking... as simple as Naz gets, anyway. Just a gold band encrusted with a few small diamonds.

It had been his mother's wedding ring.

"You... you actually married him." His voice matches his expression. "When did that happen?"

"A few weeks ago," I say quietly, pulling my hand away, not liking him touching me, and I know for a fact Naz wouldn't like it, either. He wouldn't like the guy even talking to me.

"Well, then, Mrs. Vitale," he says, standing back up, his unruffled façade back as he towers over me once again. "I'd like to ask you a few quick questions, if you don't mind."

"She does mind," a voice chimes in, butting into the small space around us. *Giuseppe.* The man's got a few inches on the detective. "Got any questions, you can ask me. She doesn't know anything. She was just here, eating. Innocent bystander."

Jameson narrows his eyes at the intrusion. "If that's the case, I don't see why she can't just tell me that."

"She's traumatized enough, having to have her lunch busted up by some schmuck," Giuseppe says, motioning behind him, toward my now flipped-over table, the food scattered all over the checkered floor. "Last thing she needs is some pushy no-good detective breathing down her neck about it, like she did something wrong."

I still wouldn't call either man an asshole, but I definitely see where Naz gets his intensity. *Whoa.* Even the detective seems to balk for a moment, silently contemplating his next move. Before Jameson can say anything else, someone calls for him from outside the deli, and he excuses himself to go join whoever it is.

Giuseppe watches the man walk out, shaking his head, before turning back to me. "You all right?"

I nod. "Thank you."

"Ah, it was nothing. If Ignazio gets mad at anybody for squawking, let it be me."

I stand back up, grateful my legs seem more stable now. "I don't know why that guy's even here. He's a homicide detective. Nobody died, right?"

Oh God, nobody did, did they? We were all fine inside, thanks to the windows, but out on the streets might've been a different story...

"Nah, everyone's fine," Giuseppe says, brushing off my concern. "Shaken up, maybe, but no spilled blood today." He pauses, looking around. "Not here, anyway."

"So why's he here then?"

"Why do you think?" Giuseppe looks back at me, raising his eyebrows, his voice incredulous like I should probably know the answer to that question. And I do. The second our eyes meet, it clicks. He's here because of Naz. That's why he's *anywhere*. Doesn't matter if it's his jurisdiction or not... the man's got a personal vendetta against Naz. "Isn't the first time they've come sniffing around here and it won't be the last, not as long as Ignazio's out there, walking around scot-free. They come by with their questions, and I tell them the truth."

"Which is?"

"That I haven't seen him, and I don't intend to."

Something strikes me then, something I hadn't really considered before. Giuseppe constantly keeps his son at an arm's length, and Naz figures it's because the man hates his guts. And not to say he likes the things Naz is involved with, but maybe, just maybe, part of Giuseppe does it so he can claim ignorance.

So he can't be used to hurt his son in any way.

Plausible deniability.

It's selfless, in a sense, like he's sacrificing any sort of relationship with his son to do what he can to keep him safe, and while I don't know Giuseppe as well as I'd like to, it seems to me like something he just might do.

"You should get out of here," Giuseppe says then, not looking at me, his eyes fixed through the fractured glass of his deli. "Use the back door, through the kitchen, so they don't try to stop you."

I hesitate, but something about the tone of his voice tells me not to argue. I don't think Giuseppe is open to negotiation on these situations any more than Naz usually is. The cops are so busy collecting evidence along the street that nobody is bothering to cover the back of the deli. I slip into the alley easily, undetected, hugging my still-aching chest as I quickly make my way past the graffiti-ridden Dumpsters, away from the scene.

A cab sits on the corner, parked along the street. I hail it as soon as I get close enough, grateful nobody else beat me to it.

"Brooklyn, please," I tell the driver, rattling off our address, my voice strained. I settle in, snapping on my seatbelt, keeping my head down, afraid to look out, feeling almost like I'm running from the police. *Please don't come after me.* The driver's young, in his mid-twenties, maybe. He flashes a set of bright white teeth at me in the rearview mirror as he pulls out into traffic.

If Naz has taught me anything in our time together, it's to always be aware of my surroundings, to watch and learn. More is caught than taught. He's told me that a few times. My eyes instinctively gloss over the cab driver's license pinned to the dashboard of the car. Abele Abate.

Unfortunate name.

Naz doesn't like me taking cabs. He doesn't trust others to keep me safe from harm. But given the situation, I imagine he wouldn't have much to say about it right now.

My mind wanders during the drive, wondering where he might've run off to, what he might be doing right now.

Part of me is afraid to know.

It takes almost an hour to get home with traffic, and it costs sixty bucks for the trip. *Ugh.* I give the driver a hundred-dollar bill, telling him to keep the change. He seems surprised by the gesture, flashing me another smile and thanking me in a quiet voice.

He didn't try to talk to me the whole way here.

I appreciate it.

The house seems still, almost creepily so. I don't like being here much anymore, especially alone. The place is haunted by memories, a lot of them not-so-good... memories of times we fought, the time I drugged Naz's food... memories of the time he considered taking my life, the time I realized there was a monster inside of him. We both almost died in the foyer on separate nights, and although it was long ago cleaned up, sometimes, if I look just right, I think I can still see remnants of the blood.

We talk about moving... we talk about it all the time... but for some reason, we haven't pulled the trigger, so to speak, too caught up in every day life to make a decision.

Too caught up trying to adjust to our new realities.

Him, as out as someone like him can be.

Me, now his wife.

Crazy.

I use my keys to unlock the front door before stepping inside and relocking it behind me. Killer, my dog, is asleep in the living room. He looks up when I enter, on alert, before happily dodging toward me, wagging his tail, wanting to play. I rub his head, scratching his big ears, but I'm too exhausted to do much more today.

Sighing, I kick off my shoes right then and there and head for the den with the dog right on my heels. Maybe I'll take a nap on the couch, if I can even shut my mind off to fall asleep. God knows when Naz will get home. Could be hours. Could be days.

"Didn't take you long."

A scream rips out of me the second I hear the unexpected voice, startling me more than even the gunshots did. What the hell? My knees buckle and I almost drop to the floor, panicked, as my eyes seek out the source. Naz sits in the den at his desk, clutching a newspaper open, his eyes on it.

"Jesus Christ, Naz, what are you doing?"

"Reading today's paper."

"Reading today's paper," I repeat.

He's reading a fucking newspaper? Really?

"Yes," he says. "I picked one up on my way home."

"You picked one up," I say incredulously. "On your way home."

His eyes flicker to me then as he cocks an eyebrow. "Why are you repeating everything I say?"

"Why am I repeating everything you say?"

He can't be serious, can he?

Jesus Christ, he's actually serious.

Seriously?

Naz shakes his head, setting his newspaper down on the desk before leaning back in his chair, turning slightly to angle toward me. "Now I see why you hate it when I do that. It's quite annoying."

"I just..." Seriously, what the hell? "I don't even know what to say to that. I don't know what's happening. You just... what are you doing?"

His brow furrows, like I'm the one not making sense, and maybe I'm not, but I'm absolutely baffled. Why is he here? He disappeared from the deli, leaving me there to fend for myself, just to come straight home and read the goddamn newspaper?

It makes no sense.

"How did you get home?" he asks, eyeing me suspiciously.

"I took a cab."

"I thought I told you—"

"Yeah, well," I interject before he can even try to lecture me for not listening to him. "How the hell else was I supposed to get home?"

"You could've called for the car service," he says. "Would've taken them twenty minutes, tops, to get to Hell's Kitchen where you were."

"Well, it wouldn't have been an issue in the first place had you not just left."

"He told me to leave," Naz says casually, picking up his paper again as he turns back away. "What else was I supposed to do?"

"Uh... take me with you. You didn't have to just leave me there."

"You were safe."

"I was safe?" I scoff. "How do you know?"

"Because I wasn't there anymore."

His voice is matter-of-fact. I'm not entirely sure what to say to that. "But how do you know—?"

He sets down his paper again, this time with an exaggerated huff of annoyance, like he doesn't want to have to talk about this. I probably shouldn't press the matter, but I want to hear what he has to say.

I want some sort of explanation.

I deserve one.

"You're not dense, Karissa, so don't act like it," he says, staring at me pointedly. "You continue to refuse to look at the big picture when it's always *right there*. How do I know it was me they were gunning for? Tell me something, sweetheart... who else in the place has a target on their back? There's only one reason someone would do what they did, and you're looking at it." He motions to himself. "So, yeah, I knew you were safe, because I wasn't there. Is that a good enough answer?"

I want to say no, it isn't good enough, but I know he'll never accept that. Still, though, I can't help myself. "It's not your fault, you know."

"Then whose is it? Yours?"

"Why does it have to be anyone's fault?" I ask, walking over to where he sits, perching myself on the corner of his wooden desk. "Things just happen sometimes."

"Look, I appreciate what you're trying to do, but just... *don't*," he says. "I've made my bed, and I've long ago accepted that I'll someday have to lie in it. Nothing I do—or don't do—today will erase what I did yesterday."

"What did you do yesterday?"

He cuts his eyes at me, and I know I need to watch myself at this point, because he's not in the mood for my antics. He looks angry. He almost looks like Vitale. "You know what I mean, Karissa. The present doesn't make up for the past."

"Yeah, I get it," I say. "Just because you apologize doesn't mean you're automatically forgiven."

"Exactly," he says. "And in my case, I didn't even apologize."

"Are you sorry?"

"No."

I shouldn't laugh, because it's not funny, but I do. I laugh. Ever the blunt one. Naz looks at me, and he doesn't even crack a smile, but I see his expression soften a bit, his posture relaxing.

We sit in silence for a moment—me watching him, him looking at his newspaper—before it gets to be too much. "That still doesn't mean it's your fault, though."

He slaps his paper down on the desk with a groan before running his hands down his face. "Karissa…"

"Look, all I'm saying is we're responsible for our own actions. We're not responsible for what other people do." He doesn't look like he's at all buying what I'm saying, but I continue anyway. "So whatever you did yesterday, yeah, that's on you, but what someone does today because of it? That's on them, Naz. No one has ever been forced to retaliate."

"We'll have to agree to disagree on that."

"Pfft, I'm right and you know it," I continue. "Retaliation is a choice, plain and simple. You choose to get revenge. You always have the option of being the bigger man."

Naz stares at me like I've sprouted another head out of my neck. I don't know if I'm getting through to him or not, but I hope so. Because all of this? I really just want it to end. Maybe that's like asking for a miracle in our lives, but it doesn't hurt, I think, to just... ask.

"You know," he says after a moment, looking away from me. "You were a lot more submissive before I married you."

Again, I laugh.

Again, I probably shouldn't.

"Whatever," I say, rolling my eyes as he goes back to reading. I regard him curiously as he does, my words still bouncing around in my skull. *Retaliation*. Part of me figured that was what he'd been off doing, why he'd left the deli so quickly, leaving me behind. "How'd you get home, anyway?"

"Drove."

"Really? Your car wasn't in the driveway."

"I parked it in the garage."

My brow furrows. "Did you make any stops on the way home?"

He shakes his paper at me, continuing to read. He stopped for the newspaper... he said that earlier.

That's it? "You didn't go anywhere else?"

Carefully, his gaze slides my way, eyes narrowing slightly. "No."

I drop the subject then, knowing I'm pushing his buttons. We've got a policy now, one we both adhere to: I don't ask questions I can't handle the answers to, because he's not going to lie to me, no matter what it's about. Ignorance, he says, is most definitely bliss, but if I want to know, he's going to tell me.

Call it a perk of marriage.

It's bitten me in the ass before, though, especially with his bluntness.

Like when I brought up Professor Santino and he'd told me, point blank, the pointer stick broke off in the man's ribcage.

So if he says he didn't make any other stops, I'm choosing to believe him.

Choosing it, like I fear he's still choosing retaliation.

Chapter Two
Ignazio

Karissa's dreaming.

Or having a nightmare, rather.

I can hear her as she lays beside me, whimpering in her sleep. Her body is tense, jacked up like a live wire. I think if I try to wake her now, she might electrocute me.

I wonder, sometimes, if her dreams are about us. Are they ever the *happily ever after* variety? Or are they always about all the things I did? The hurt I caused, the pain she went through, the horror of falling in with a man like me. I wonder, but I don't ask her, because I'm not sure it matters.

I'm not sure she ever remembers.

She never mentions her dreams to me.

Besides, dreams mean nothing when it comes to reality.

Life is what it is.

You can't escape it.

The ceiling fan lightly spins, blowing her hair. Reaching over, I carefully brush the wayward hair away from her face, watching her for a moment, before leaning in to press a small kiss to her cheek. She sleeps right through it, deep in the throes of the dream, oblivious to my presence, hopefully just as ignorant to my upcoming absence.

I don't want her to worry about it.

As carefully as possible, I slide out of the bed, making sure not to disturb her. I grab a pair of black sweatpants on my way out the door, slipping them on out in the darkened hallway before making my way downstairs.

I'm grateful I manage to make my way past the mutt. He still doesn't like me... not that I blame him. I did shoot his owner right in front of him once. But he makes it hard to sneak around sometimes. Makes it hard to maintain peace in this house.

It's a warm, fall evening, nearing midnight, but the marble kitchen floor is cool against my bare feet. My footsteps falter as I near the sink, and I reach over, plucking the boning knife from the wooden block on the counter. The handle is black, the narrow blade eight-inches long, the point sharp enough to pull flesh from bone.

That's what it's meant for, after all.

I grab my keys from the hook near the side door before stepping out into the garage, mindful to close the door behind me again. Open doors are invitations I don't want to extend to anyone right now, but especially not Karissa.

I want her to stay right where she is, fast asleep.

Oblivious.

I pop the trunk on my Mercedes before shoving my keys in the pockets of my pants. The moment I do it, I hear whimpering as something shifts around inside the car. Pushing the lid open, I stare down at the form in the darkness, illuminated by the dull lights of the trunk.

Sweat covers him from the top of his bald head to the tips of his bare toes, his face drenched, dripping beads of it, his filthy white shirt clinging to him. And it stinks... Jesus, it fucking reeks. It'll take me a month to get the stench of piss out of my trunk after this. Anger surges inside of me at the very thought of him pissing himself, the spineless coward. He's lucky I don't plunge the knife into his neck, right here and right now. Lucky he might... *might*... live to see another day.

For his sake, I hope he does.

He looks like he wants to survive.

He stares at me, wide-eyed, panicked. The moment he catches sight of the knife, he breaks out into tears. He's hyperventilating, sucking air through his nose, trying to breathe but the duct tape covering his mouth, wrapped around his head, is damn near suffocating. His wrists and ankles, too, are bound, but it doesn't stop him from flailing around in the trunk, making a ruckus.

"What did I tell you, Armando?" I hold the knife to his throat, the action making him tense and stop moving so much, so not to cut himself. "You let my wife hear you and I'll have no choice but to slit your fucking throat."

He tries to quiet his cries, going mostly silent, but the tears continue to fall. I hate it, the sight of someone crying, be it man or woman, but especially men who are supposed to be a part of the *family*. Men who pledge to live by the gun shouldn't fall apart the second it's hinted they might die by it, too.

Or in this case, by knife, which arguably, when I'm wielding it, might hurt a hell of a lot more.

Armando Donati was one of Ray's street soldiers, the kind who did dirty work, who roamed in the trenches and wasn't opposed to bending rules off the books to win wars. Kidnapping, extortion, and assault were his specialties, as well as the average every day drive-by shooting. The parts of the life that had no honor. The parts of the life that none of them talked about. Armando had a knack for making a hit look more like a random act. Ray kept eyes and ears all over the street, and most of his information came straight from Armando and his band of bloody thieves.

So, naturally, the second gunfire lit up my father's business, I thought of him.

"No screaming," I tell him. "If you want any chance of going home, you'll listen. You got me?"

He nods frantically.

"Good."

Using the knife, I slit across the duct tape on his mouth, watching as blood flows around the hole, the blade slicing into his lip. He grunts, letting out a strangled cry as more tears fall, but he doesn't scream. He sucks in a large gulp of air through his mouth, immediately begging the second he exhales.

"Please, Vitale, it wasn't me! I swear to God! I swear on my wife, my children! I swear on the family! I didn't do it!"

I want to jab the knife into his larynx to shut him up, but instead I clamp my free hand down around his mouth and nose, squeezing. He starts to thrash, but settles down the second I say, "Don't."

He can't breathe now. I know he can't. His face is turning red, his eyes bugging out.

"I know it wasn't you," I say. "So don't waste your breath trying to explain that to me, or next time I'll take your breath away permanently."

I let go, and again, he gasps for air. His blood is on my hand and I absently rub it on my pant leg, not realizing what I've done until it's too late.

Shit.

I'll have to burn them now.

Get rid of the evidence.

He's quiet this time. Well, he's hyperventilating, and sobbing, but at least he isn't trying to *beg* anymore.

Armando lives in Hell's Kitchen, not far from my father's deli, in an apartment above the convenience store Ray used to own, the same one I stole from when I was sixteen years old. I stopped there on my way home to grab a newspaper... and I just happened to grab my old acquaintance while I was at it.

I know he didn't do it. I know, because he was sitting in a recliner, in his boxers, watching soap operas like the little bitch he is. But just because he didn't do it doesn't mean he wouldn't know who did. His kind are like wolves... they run in packs.

I'm gunning for the alpha.

The one brave enough to come after me.

"I want to know who shot up the block in Hell's Kitchen this afternoon," I say, continuing before he can give me the 'it wasn't me' spiel. "The streets talk, Armando, and you're about as close to a gutter rat as there is in this business. You hear it all. Ray's people are dropping like flies. Everyday, it's someone else. But somehow, you're still alive, and I can probably guess why. So I want to know who's behind it... I want to know who you're working for now."

"I'm not—" The words slip from his lips instinctively before he silences them with a gulp of air, swallowing back the lie he's trained to say. We're all taught to deny any involvement whatsoever, but he knows better. He knows giving me the lie will only get him killed. "Look, I haven't met the guy... he hasn't come to me yet, I swear! I'm nobody. I'm **nothing**. He probably doesn't even know who I am! But people talk, you know... they talk, just like you said. A guy came to me last week, came to me about some information, said he heard that I might know some things. He asked about you, but I didn't tell him anything he didn't already know!"

"Who was the guy?"

"I don't know his name."

As soon as the denial is out of his mouth, the knife slams down, right into the meaty part of his thigh. I yank it right back out, again clamping my hand down around his mouth and nose as he lets out a shriek of pain, muzzling the sound. His face turns bright red, and I let go, immediately regretting it when he screams, "Joe! They call him Fat Joe!"

He catches his mistake right away and starts pleading quietly, sobbing, as a stream of blood runs from the wound in his thigh. It's not much. Nothing he can't easily survive. I hold the knife up, telling him to be silent, as the damn dog starts barking in the kitchen, hearing us out here.

I listen for a moment, making sure Karissa hadn't been disturbed. The dog stops barking finally, giving up on finding out what's going on outside.

"Who does this Joe guy work for?" I ask when I'm sure we won't be interrupted. I need to get this over with and get my ass back upstairs. "And don't tell me you don't know, because next time, I'm aiming for the artery."

"There's a guy, he's new in town."

"I know that much."

"Joe, he didn't say who he was working for, and you know, Vitale... you know we're never supposed to ask! He kept saying 'my boss this, my boss that', but it's gotta be the new guy!"

"Does this new guy have a name?"

"They call him Scar, I think."

"You think," I repeat. "You better think right, or you'll come to regret giving me bad information, Armando."

"I'm sure," he corrects himself. "I'm positive that's it."

Scar. *Huh.*

"And Fat Joe's working for this Scar guy?"

I hate even asking that sentence.

My life has turned into a cliché Mafia movie.

"Has to be," Armando says. "Don't know who else would do it."

I stand there, trying to figure out what I'm supposed to do with this information, when Armando starts whimpering again, quietly begging for mercy. The sound grates on my nerves, and I step away, tossing the knife down on the top of my toolbox as I snatch up the roll of duct tape. I rip a chunk off and slap it over the bloody slit across his mouth, silencing him again.

"You're lucky, Armando," I say. "You see, I'm trying to do better these days, trying to be a better man, trying to be the man my wife thinks I can be, so I'm not going to kill you tonight. I'm going to give you a chance. If you survive until morning, I'll take you home; I'll drop you off right where I picked you up. You understand?"

He can't respond, not with his mouth taped again, but I take his muffled frantic mumbling for confirmation that he understands. Before, things would've been non-negotiable. Cross me, and you die. That was the way it was. But I can't do that anymore. I can't keep that up. If I'm not flexible, I'm not commendable.

And I'm trying to be commendable for her.

"But remember… you let my wife find you and the deal's off."

I slam the trunk closed, hearing his startled cry, but then he goes silent again.

The gutter rat wants to live.

Grabbing the knife, I head back into the house, making sure to lock up behind me. Killer retreats a few steps when he sees me, his chest rumbling as he starts growling.

In the kitchen, I reach up into the cabinet beside the sink, digging into the bag of pepperoni-flavored dog treats. I toss a few to the mutt, and he gobbles them up, too distracted by the treats to bother with me anymore.

I wash the blood from the blade and toss the knife in the dishwasher before heading toward the stairs, veering to the laundry room on my way. I pull off my sweatpants, burying them in a pile of dirty clothes, making a mental note to remember to do something about them later.

I head upstairs then, back to the bedroom.

Karissa is still asleep. It doesn't look like she's even moved an inch. I climb in the bed beside her, wrapping my arms around her and pulling her to me.

It worried me today.

Thank God she's safe.

I just need her to stay that way.

She stirs then, briefly waking up, before nuzzling against me and going right back to sleep in my arms.

She starts dreaming again.

This time, though, she's smiling.

She wouldn't be smiling if she knew what I was thinking, if she knew where my mind was venturing, the things I was yearning to do. I'm trying, for her, I'm trying my damndest, but I'm not sure how much more I can give. She says retaliation is a choice, and maybe she's right. Maybe it is a choice.

But maybe I want to choose retaliation.

Is it so wrong to want vengeance?

I don't think so.

"Good morning."

Karissa's voice is a sleepy mumble, her words broken around a yawn. I glance over toward the doorway as she steps into the kitchen. Her hair is a tangled mess. She's wearing nothing but a too-big black t-shirt that I'm guessing she stole from the back of my closet.

Half of her wardrobe comes out of there.

"Morning." I'm not sure yet if I'm willing to call it *good*. I haven't had a wink of sleep and I'm probably not getting any until sometime tomorrow. "You're up early."

It's seven, maybe eight in the morning. Clocks are still quite scarce around the house, and I don't feel like looking at my watch, so I'm not entirely sure. I'm dressed for the day and have been since around four.

"Yeah," she mumbles. "Had a hard time sleeping."

I consider pointing out how much she actually slept last night, but I think better of it. "Pity."

"I know, right?" Karissa tinkers with the coffee machine on the counter, brewing herself a cup, as I unload the dishwasher, making sure everything, including the boning knife, goes back where it belongs. She watches me as she waits on her coffee, rubbing Killer's head as he nudges against her, wanting her attention. "Looks like you've been busy this morning."

I've done a load of laundry, burned a pair of pants, and scrubbed the kitchen from top to bottom, all to distract me while waiting on her to wake up. "I suppose you're not the only one who had a hard time sleeping."

She regards me curiously, picking up her coffee cup when it's finished, blowing on the steaming liquid. "You know, it's still not your fault."

Pausing, I close my eyes, forcing myself to not react to that. I don't want to have this conversation again. She's starting to sound like a damn self-help tape with her constant reassurances. *It's not your fault.* After a moment, I press on with what I was doing and change the subject. "So, what are your plans for the day?"

"Oh, you know, a little of this, a little of that."

I shoot her a look as she sips on her coffee. She's purposely trying to provoke me. "Care to elaborate?"

"I've got class most of the day," she says, pausing before adding, "Which you already know. Other than that, nothing much... might stop by and see Melody later on. Been a while since we hung out. You?"

"Nothing."

"Nothing?"

"Nothing."

"Sounds exciting."

"I'm sure it will be as thrilling as it sounds," I reply. "Do you want me to drive you into the city?"

"No, it's okay. I can just grab a cab."

I pull my phone from my pocket as soon as she says that. "How about I call a car for you instead?"

She shrugs, like it doesn't matter, as she guzzles her coffee now that it's cool. It does matter, though. The drivers with the car service are vetted. I know their names and addresses.

I know where their parents live.

"Whatever you want to do," she says, pushing away from the counter to leave the kitchen. "I'll be ready in about forty-five minutes."

"I'll have them pick you up then."

An hour later, the car is sitting by the curb in front of the house, patiently waiting as Karissa dawdles around the house, feeding the dog and making herself another cup of coffee—this one to go. When she's finally ready, all of her things together, she rises up on her tiptoes and pecks a kiss against my lips before heading for the door.

"Have a good day doing *nothing*."

"I'm sure I will," I tell her, watching as she walks out, leaving me alone. I hate it, whenever she leaves, but I find myself relieved today to have her gone. I feel like I can breathe deeply without risking her realizing what I've been up to and having to see that look on her face.

The look that says I still terrify her sometimes, even to this day.

It's been a while since I've seen it.

I've certainly been trying to keep it at bay.

Sighing, I look around the spotless kitchen, smelling the harsh bleach scent that clings to everything, as I lean back against the counter near the sink. Killer stands in the doorway, ears laid back as he regards me. The second our eyes meet, I hear the grumble, a low growl resonating deep in his chest.

"Don't look at me that way," I say. "I do what I have to do."

He barks once without moving. Reaching up into the cabinet near my head, I grab a treat. I toss it to him, the growl instantly ceasing, his tail suddenly wagging as he gobbles up the treat, forgetting—at least momentarily—that I'm supposed to be the enemy.

He's easily trained.

Easily tricked.

If he keeps this up, I might eventually start to like him.

Or not.

Grabbing my keys, I leave, heading out into the garage. It's a little warmer now than last night. It's going to be a hot day.

Popping the trunk on the car, I grimace as the stench again hits me, waving it away as I recoil. Son of a bitch, it's even worse this morning. I'm going to need a ton of bleach to tackle this disaster.

Armando is out cold, but I can see his chest moving. He's still breathing. He survived the night.

Lucky bastard.

"Rise and shine," I say, slapping his cheek a few times, rousing him from his slumber. It's amazing… he got more sleep in a fucking trunk than I managed to find in my own bed. It takes him a moment to come around, a moment to realize where he is, to remember what I did to him. He balks when he sees me, blinking rapidly, his face contorting with pain. "Well, *nothing*, it seems you made it to morning. Congratulations."

He probably cried himself to sleep last night, thinking this was the end, thinking this was just me prolonging his death, torturing him a bit before taking his life. He probably passed out thinking it was the last time he'd see the dawning of a new day.

I still have half a mind to kill the bastard just on principle. *Don't leave witnesses.* He certainly witnessed what I was up to yesterday. But I'm not going to. Instead, I'm going to give him his second wind. "I won't kill you today, Armando. A deal is a deal, and I'm a man of my word. But that doesn't mean I won't kill you tomorrow. The first time you slip up or get in my way, I'm going to end you, and it's not going to be as merciful as a knife to the neck. You understand?"

He nods as he starts to cry again, tears streaming from his eyes. Disgusted, I slam the trunk closed and walk over, climbing in behind the wheel. I'll take him home, just like I said I would, and I'll let him go, like I said I would, too. I'm going to give him a chance to live out the rest of his days.

He better not disappoint me.

I'm already low on patience.

Chapter Three
Karissa

The café near NYU is pretty dead at two in the afternoon on a Tuesday, most students off in class somewhere or already headed home for the day. There are only a handful of tables occupied, nobody waiting in line for a drink. I sip on my chocolate mint tea as I glance around the place, tapping my foot on the dark linoleum floor. I've had a ton of caffeine already today, enough to revitalize a tranquilized horse, but that isn't what has me so antsy.

No, it's what happened at the deli.

I can't get it out of my mind.

I wonder how Giuseppe's feeling, wonder what he's thinking. His life's work shut down because of a hail of random gunfire in the middle of the afternoon. I remember Naz said his father added the extra security years ago, after his son fell in with Raymond Angelo, but for the first time, the precautions actually became necessary.

I can only imagine what it means for whatever sort of relationship the two of them were starting to form again.

Is there any coming back from this?

"Earth to Karissa!" Fingers snap right in my face, startling me.

"Are you having an episode?"

I flinch, my eyes meeting Melody's across the small, round table. "What?"

"Jesus, I thought you were having a psychotic break or something," she says, shaking her head as she regards me. "I've been talking to you for like, thirty goddamn minutes, and you haven't acknowledged the fact that I'm even here."

Ignoring the fact that we've been here for only ten minutes, tops, I lean back in my chair, gripping my drink with both hands, giving her my undivided attention. "What were you saying?"

"I don't even know anymore." She groans, her head dropping down right onto the open book on the table, her words muffled as she mumbles into the pages. "Why do I keep doing this to myself?"

"Maybe you're a masochist," I suggest. "You need a good sadist in your life."

That earns me a slightly raised head and one hell of a glare. Laughing, I shrug. Who knows? I never, in a million years, thought I'd be an exhibitionist, but Naz swears I might be, and I'm not going to deny the thrill I get at the idea of being watched. "Hey, you never know. We've all got our kinks."

"I'm an idiot," she counters, ignoring my suggestion. "I'm one-hundred percent a fucking dumbass. There's no other explanation. I'll never learn my lesson."

She dramatically bangs her head against the brand new textbook a few times before sitting back up. Another philosophy class, her fourth so far. This time it's *Philosophy of Mind*, whatever that means. I don't even know the difference.

Isn't all philosophy, you know, from the mind?

She's passed every single one of the classes, her grades just getting better and better, but that doesn't stop her from complaining every time.

Me? I gave up with the second one.

Philosophy is just not for me.

Melody, on the other hand, had the bright idea to make it her major. A degree in philosophy... what does one do with that?

"Don't be so hard on yourself," I say. "It's all just opinions, remember?"

That earns me yet another glare.

Man, I'm on fire today.

"Whatever," she says. "This is it. I'm not doing it any more. I'm drawing the line."

She literally uses her finger to draw a line across the table, her red-painted acrylic scraping against the whatever-the-hell-the-table-is-made-out-of.

"Yeah, right," I say, reaching over and snatching her book from her. She protests and tries to snatch it back, standing up like she's about to pounce and attack me over the damn thing, but I push her off as I look at it. *Functionalism.* I read the definition at the top of the chapter twice, but it's nothing but gibberish to me. "Whoa, is this even English?"

She rolls her eyes, once again trying to take the book, but I thwart her attempt as I flip pages. A few chapters in I run into a stack of papers—notes. I'm about to hand it back to her, not wanting to mess up whatever kind of chaotic system she has with the thing, when my eyes gloss over the top paper. It's a stream of definitions, notes written around them in the margins, but up top, front and center, is a little scribble, a boy's name is a lopsided heart.

Leo.

"Leo?" I squeak. I fucking *squeak.* "Who the hell is Leo?"

As soon as the words are out of my mouth, she forcefully removes the book from my hands, closing it and shoving it right into her backpack, like she hadn't needed to study in the first place. Functionalism be damned. I stare at her incredulously as her cheeks flush, turning bright red.

She's blushing.

Melody Carmichael, ever confident and controlling, is blushing.

Holy shit.

"Who is he?" I ask. "Oh my God, Melody, you better spill it right now, or I'm going to think you've got a thing for DiCaprio."

She shrugs. "He's not so bad."

"No, not *Titanic* DiCaprio," I tell her. "Not *Romeo and Juliet* DiCaprio. Not even *Wolf of Wall Street* DiCaprio. I'm talking *real* DiCaprio. On his yacht DiCaprio. Full beard DiCaprio."

Melody makes a face of horror, shuddering as she turns to me. "No way."

I cock an eyebrow at her. "You got a thing for dad-bod's?"

Laughing, she throws a balled up napkin across the table at me. "Oh, God, shut up!"

"Who is he?" I ask, grabbing the napkin and throwing it back. "Tell me!"

"Okay, okay!" She holds her hands up. "He's just... he's nobody, really."

"Nobody? You're drawing his name in hearts and he's nobody?"

"He's just a guy I met. We've been out for coffee a few times."

"Coffee?" I gasp, grabbing my chest in mock horror. "But coffee is our thing!"

She continues to blush. I'm absolutely baffled. First, Naz rolls his eyes, and now Melody is blushing. I woke up in the Twilight Zone yesterday, and I don't know how the hell to get out of it. I don't know if I even want to.

"It's not serious or anything," she explains. "I don't even know if that's something he's looking for."

"But you hope."

"But I hope," she admits, sighing as she leans closer to the table, smiling giddily. "He's just... *wow*. He's perfect in every way. Absolutely perfect."

Uh-oh. I've heard this before.

I heard this about Paul.

"Perfection isn't real," I point out.

"Puh-lease," she says, waving me off. "You married perfection, did you not?"

A sharp bark of laughter escapes me at that. "Hardly. Naz is... he's great. Naz is what I want in life. But perfect? No way."

I'm sure he'd agree with that.

"But he's perfect for you. You're both, you know..." She waves toward me, like that's supposed to make sense of it all. "In the words of Meredith Grey, you're dark and twisty, okay? He's all intense and you're all complex and you're frankly weird, okay? You both are. But it's a good weird; you know... it's a *mutual* weird. Sometimes he scares the hell out of me and sometimes you confuse the hell out of me, and together the two of you just... you make sense."

I stare at her as she finishes babbling. "We make sense."

"You do," she says. "And Leo... I don't even know how to explain it. He makes me feel like I'm the only other person in the world, like nothing matters more than me in the moment. He listens to me... really listens. And it's crazy, I know, because after what happened with Paul, I didn't think I'd ever feel this way again, but I do." She sighs. "I do."

I don't even know what to say. I'm happy for her, of course, but it worries me at the same time. Paul was the first guy she'd ever kept around for a while, and well, we all know how that turned out.

Well, I know how that turned out.

To most, he's just missing, vanished into thin air. They still hope he might someday come back.

I know better.

Another one of those bite-me-in-the-ass questions I asked Naz.

"That's great," I tell her, meaning it for the most part. I'm glad she's finally moving on with her life. "When do I get to meet the lucky guy?"

"Uh, I don't know," she says. "Maybe we could double sometime."

"Double? Like in a double date?" I ask. "I think me and Naz might be kind of beyond the whole double date thing."

Or rather, Naz is beyond dating.

"Yeah, you're right." She laughs. "Besides, I should probably get him to do more than take me for coffee before I start making plans."

"Probably," I agree, smiling as I watch her pack up her things. "I've got my fingers crossed."

"Me, too, girl... me, too."

"Leo," I muse over the name. "He's not like a, uh, tubby mountain man looking motherfucker, is he?"

"DiCaprio? Nah, he's not *that* bad."

"No," I laugh. "Your Leo."

"Oh, no way." Standing up, she slings her backpack on her back. "He's gorgeous, way out of my league."

"Nobody's out of your league, Melody."

She smiles, giving me an awkward one-armed hug, before planting a sloppy kiss right on my cheek. "And that's why you're my best friend, Kissimmee... you truly believe that. I'll see you later, okay?"

She's gone before I can even respond, jetting out the door to class so she isn't late for her Philosophy test. I sit there for a moment, sipping my tea, before getting up and heading outside with it. I'm done for the day and consider just grabbing a cab, as one is just sitting there, begging to be grabbed, but at the last second, I think better of it.

Pulling out my phone, I request a car instead.

They're there within a few minutes, a man I vaguely recognize. I've ridden with him before, but I don't know his name. He opens the back of the car for me and I climb in, settling into the seat for the trip back to Brooklyn.

When I arrive, I let him open the door for me again, because these guys get kind of angry when I do it myself. I don't know if it's policy or if they're just afraid of what Naz will do if they don't, so I oblige it, annoyingly, for the sake of keeping peace.

I watch as the car pulls away and turn to head for the house when I catch sight of another car parked in front of the place. The four-door unmarked black Ford sticks out like a sore thumb, with its darkly tinted windows and half a dozen antennas.

Detective Jameson is leaning against the bumper, his arms crossed over his chest. The moment I look his way, he pushes away from the thing, heading right for me.

Awesome.

"Miss Ree—uh," he says as he stops in front of me. "Mrs. Vitale."

"Detective," I say. "What are you doing here?"

"We didn't get a chance to really talk yesterday, so I thought I'd stop by."

"And what, interrogate me?"

"Hardly," he says, feigning offense. "I simply wanted to take a moment to offer my congratulations."

"For what?"

He nods his head toward my hand. "Your marriage."

"Oh." Absently, I tinker with the ring on my finger. "Yeah. Thanks, I guess."

"I would've said it yesterday, but you disappeared before I could. Your husband did, too, for that matter. He was gone before I even arrived. He was there with you, wasn't he?"

"You tell me," I say. "You'd know."

Turning, I start to leave when his voice stops me again. "Curious, though, how it all happened so fast."

I should keep walking. I know I should. But I want to know what he means by that. "What?"

"It's just that, well, the two of you rushed into marriage," he says. "So it's just a bit curious to me, you know… makes me wonder if it has anything to do with marital privilege, if maybe he made it so you'd never have to testify against him about anything."

I recoil when he says that, almost like he slapped me right in the face. How dare he belittle what we have? "Are you accusing him of something?"

"Should I be?"

"Naz didn't do anything," I say. "He was eating lunch like the

41

rest of us. Just another innocent bystander."

The detective shakes his head. "If that's the case—"

"If you'll excuse me, I'm done with this conversation," I say, moving to leave, not turning back around this time. "Goodbye, Detective. You can see yourself off our street."

I don't give the man a chance to try to goad me into more conversation. When I reach the front door of the house, I chance a peek back, seeing he's gaping at me. Guess he didn't like what I had to say. Going inside, I make sure to lock the door behind me, dropping my things right in the living room as I stomp through the house.

Jackass.

The moment I step into the kitchen, my footsteps falter. Naz is leaning back against the counter by the sink, exactly where he had been when I left hours ago. It's as if he hasn't moved an inch all day.

"So what did Jameson want today?" he asks right away.

"You knew he was out there?"

"Of course."

Of course he did.

I grab a bottle of water from the fridge, cracking it open to take a sip. "He wanted to know if we got married so I'd have some kind of immunity from testifying."

Naz seems genuinely surprised by that. "Oh really? What did you say?"

"I said I didn't need immunity because you weren't guilty of anything."

Immediately, Naz laughs, the kind of loud laughter that can't be contained.

"*This time,*" I elaborate, narrowing my eyes at him. I'm glad he finds this funny. "Regardless of what you think, you did nothing wrong yesterday."

"Whatever you say."

"Anyway..." I roll my eyes. "I can't believe you knew he was out there and you didn't do anything about it. You didn't even try to stop him from talking to me."

"You're a big girl. You can handle yourself."

I nearly choke on a drink of water when he says that. For the second day in a row, he let me fend for myself when it came to the police. Old Naz would've never risked it. Old Naz would've micromanaged that shit. "You're sure putting a lot of faith in me these days."

"I trust you," he says.

"You trust me?"

"Of course."

Those words stun me. Maybe they shouldn't after everything, but they do. Trust was always shaky between the two of us, and part of me figured it would just always be an issue, so to hear him say, point blank, that he trusts me, is almost mind blowing.

Although, truthfully, I suppose I've come to trust him, too.

"I married you, Karissa. I wouldn't have actually done that if I didn't trust you with my life. My faith in you was sealed the moment I put that ring on your finger."

"Because I belong to you now."

"No, because you belong *with* me. I decided to keep you that day, for better or for worse."

"And what happens if I decide someday to no longer keep you? What then?"

"Huh." He stares at me. "Haven't thought about it."

"You haven't?"

"No."

"You seriously haven't considered what would happen if I tried to leave?"

"Not at all," he says. "Back... before... I would've just dragged you right back. But now, if you walk away from me, I suppose I just hope I don't miss you."

"You hope you don't miss me?"

"Yeah, but I don't think it would be a problem," he says, pushing away from the counter, strolling toward me. "After all, I'm a pretty good shot."

I gasp when it strikes me what he's saying, and he grabs ahold of me, wrapping his arms around me, laughing. He's *laughing*.

"Not funny, Naz," I growl, trying to push him off, but he refuses to let go. "Not funny at all."

"Ah, come on," he says, kissing the top of my head before loosening his hold. "Admit it... it was a little funny."

I glare at him, not at all amused, which only makes him laugh even more.

"Look, you really want to leave me, Karissa? Then I suppose I just... watch you walk away." He shrugs, as if it's just as simple as that, as if he'd just let me go. "Are you trying to tell me something? Planning your escape?"

"No, of course not," I say, shaking my head. "I don't even know why I'm asking. I think the detective just threw me off with what he said."

"Well, it's nonsense," he says. "You've had ample opportunity to send me up the river... you could've easily gotten me locked up long ago just by opening your mouth. I didn't need to marry you to gain your silence. You've given it to me from the start. If you didn't turn on me then, when you had plenty of reason to, I trust that you won't do it now, ring or no ring. I married you, Karissa, because I love you. Nothing more, nothing less."

As many times as he's said those words... *I love you*... it still makes my stomach flutter to hear them come from him. The butterflies soar. He's not an outwardly emotional person, not at all, so when he says it, I know he means it.

Wrapping my arms around his neck, I reach up on my tiptoes and kiss him. His lips are soft, sweet. His tongue tastes like peppermint. "I love you, too, you know."

"I know."

My gaze shifts past him, out into the backyard. Killer is running around, excitedly chasing butterflies, wanting to play with them. He'd never dare hurt one. Naz usually puts him out there whenever it's just the two of them alone.

My guys, they still aren't quite fond of each other.

"So I guess you really did do nothing today," I say, turning back to Naz, looking him over, as my fingertips tinker with the hair at the nape of his neck. He's dressed nice. He smells like Heaven, woodsy and aquatic and so very him. He even shaved this morning. It's a rare occurrence, Naz being completely clean-shaven. "I don't know why you bothered to even put on a suit."

"I've told you before... I don't need to do anything to put on a suit. I'll put one on to answer the door, to order take-out, to sit at my desk... hell, I'll put one on just to fuck."

A chill rolls through me, tingling creeping up my spine. "That sounds nice."

"Which part?"

"Fucking."

"Huh." He leans down, his nose brushing mine. His cheek comes to rest against my cheek as he whispers in my ear, "Is that what you want? Me to take you upstairs and fuck you silly, Jailbird?"

It still gets to me whenever he calls me that. *Jailbird*. I can feel my body flushing, every inch of me warming in anticipation. "Uh-huh."

I can barely get the response out. My voice is breathy, needy. He chuckles quietly at my obvious reaction, his lips lightly skimming along my skin, his teeth grazing my earlobe. My eyes close, feeling his hands slip beneath my shirt, stroking the skin along the small of my back before his rough fingertips trail up my spine.

I lose myself in the moment, practically panting and close to just climbing him like a fucking mountain, when a loud noise echoes through the kitchen around us, startling me. My eyes snap open. I instantly pull away.

It's a song, I realize, after a second, as it continues blaring.

Hotline Bling.

What the ever-loving fuck?

Groaning at the interruption, Naz reaches into his pocket and pulls out his phone. The ruckus... the song... is coming from it.

Seriously. *What?*

He casts me a look as he presses a button on the phone, silencing the sound. I think he might've hung up on the caller, with the way he just stands there, but he brings the phone to his ear after a moment. "Hello."

I can't hear whoever is on the line, but Naz listens intently, his expression guarded. "Give me about twenty minutes and I'll be on my way."

He hangs up, slipping the phone back into his pocket, and advances toward me but I hold out my hands to stop him. "What the hell was that?"

He hesitates. "What?"

"That song," I say. "That ringtone."

"Oh, you don't like it?"

"I, uh..." What am I supposed to say? "I don't know, do you?"

He shrugs. "It's not the worst I've heard."

He tries to kiss me, leaning in, but I move my head out of the way. "No, seriously, Naz, what the hell? Where did it come from?"

He gives up, at least temporarily, and takes a step back, cocking an eyebrow at me. "I downloaded it today. Figured I could use a new ringtone."

"But *that?*"

"What's wrong with it?"

"Nothing, but..."

"But what?"

"But it's not you."

"Not me?"

"Besides, you don't even like music. You told me it was just noise, and pointless, and you didn't like it."

"True."

"So what the hell? Is this, like, some kind of mid-life crisis?"

"Ouch," he says, laughing. "I'm not that old."

"Okay, you're not, but really... what gives?"

Different.

So goddamn different.

He stares at me in silence for a solid minute, long enough to make me start to squirm under his gaze. Finally, he steps forward, his hand slipping around the back of my neck, gripping it as he steers me toward him.

"I'm down to fifteen minutes before I have to leave," he says, his voice stone cold serious. "So do you want to talk about Drake some more, or do you want to go upstairs and fuck?"

Well, when he puts it like that...

"Fifteen minutes," I say. "Is that long enough?"

His expression cracks at my question, a cocky smile turning his lips as the dimples come out. "Sweetheart, all I need is five."

"I'll take the second option, then," I tell him, "but I see no reason to have to go upstairs for it."

Naz's face hovers in front of mine, his mouth so close I can practically taste his breath. Softly, his lips brush against mine, as he whispers, "I like the way you think."

I go to kiss him, but before I can, he spins me around so my back is against him, his arm snaking around my waist, gripping me tight. He drags me across the room, shoving me against the kitchen counter so hard that it knocks the breath from my lungs.

I gasp, inhaling sharply, as he unbuttons my jeans and tugs on them, yanking them down my legs. I try to help, try to kick them off, and manage to get one leg free before he gives up. One of his hands slips down the front of my panties, his fingers roughly stroking my clit, as his other works on his own zipper, doing nothing more than yanking it down to free himself. He strokes his cock a few times before pushing my panties down my thighs, giving up when they reach my knees.

His hand is on my back then, pushing me down against the cold countertop. I brace myself, gripping the edge, as he pushes into me from behind. It's tight, since I can barely spread my legs apart, but he doesn't seem to mind a bit. I was ready the second he touched me, my body always reacting instantly to him.

The first thrust is gentle, careful, but after that all bets are off. He pulls out and shifts his hips forward so hard that I bang against the counter, almost knocking the damn coffee machine apart.

"Shit," I curse, but that's the last word I manage to speak, because he's driving into me so ferociously that I'm fucking lucky I can still breathe. I arch my back as one of his arms snakes around me, once again finding my clit, as his other hand still presses hard against my back, pinning me in position. He fucks me like he's sprinting toward a finish line, the bang-bang-bang of my body hitting the counter amplified in the otherwise silent house.

Fuck.

Fuck.

Fuck.

I'm gasping and moaning and groaning, grunting like a goddamn cavewoman who doesn't know how to speak.

Uh. Uh. Uh.

I'm barely holding on and my legs are shaky, but he's keeping me in place, like I'm not much more than a rag doll. I can feel the tightening in my stomach, can feel the tension taking over my muscles, gripping hold inside of me. It builds like I'm going up on a roller coaster before I hit the drop.

Whoosh.

A noise bursts from my chest, a growling scream. *Fuck.* My knees almost buckle from the intensity of the orgasm, but his strong grip keeps me up. He doesn't let up his movements at all, rubbing and thrusting, giving me all he's got, until my orgasm starts to taper off. My cries turn to whimpers, but he doesn't stop, grunting behind me as his body tenses.

I can feel it as he lets loose inside of me.

But in a blink, he's gone.

In a blink, he's out of me.

In a blink, he lets go.

His hands are no longer touching my body.

I instantly miss the warmth.

It's so quick I don't have a chance to adapt to the change. My legs give out on me, and I slip away from the counter, plopping my ass right down on the floor. There's a throbbing between my legs and a tightening in my chest, and I don't know how he did it, but I feel like I've gone twelve rounds in a ring and lost.

I stare up at him as he backs away.

"I've still got a few minutes," he says, his voice calm, composed, "if you want to go again."

I hold my hands up, waving him off. "I'm good."

His expression cracks with a smile as he tucks himself back away, zipping his pants up, straightening his belt. It takes him all of thirty seconds to pull himself together.

It's going to take me all night.

Stepping back toward me, he crouches down so we're eye-level. His hand gently rests on my knee as he slowly rubs circles on my skin with his thumb. He's quiet as he stares at me for a moment. I'm still trying to catch my breath… my panties are like shackles around my calves and my jeans are just fucking gone.

"Are you going to be alright?" he asks, looking me over, his smile growing as he does.

Smug son of a bitch.

"Fine," I say, nodding. "I'll be just fine."

Not if he doesn't stop stroking my knee, though.

Tingles are starting to course through the lower half of my body.

Is it possible to get off just from someone's touch?

Leaning over, he presses a brief, chaste kiss to my forehead, before he stands up.

"I don't know when I'll be home," he says. "You probably shouldn't wait up."

I want to ask him where he's going. I want to know what he's going to do.

I want to know exactly what he's up to.

I want to, but I don't ask, sitting in silence as he walks out.

He's right, you know... I'm not dense.

I could riddle out his plans if I really wanted to.

Chapter Four
Ignazio

It takes a lot to get a meeting with the five families in New York.

Once upon a time, they used to have this thing called the Commission, the organization above all organizations. Membership was limited to the heads of the New York families, as well as the leaders out of Chicago and Buffalo. The seven most powerful men in the country met in secret, making decisions, like delinquency was a democracy. Wanted someone murdered? Ask the Commission. Wanted to invite someone into the fold? The Commission was the only way to go.

Acting without permission would get you killed.

The Commission went the way of all flesh years ago. You're lucky to find two bosses willing to meet now, much less all of them. There are still rules, though… rules they insist we all follow.

Rules I broke when I killed the head of one of those families.

Raymond Angelo.

I stand on the front porch of an old brick mansion in Long Island. It's still light out, but dusk is creeping up. There's a hint of orange in the cloudless blue skyline. It looks almost like fire burns off in the distance somewhere.

The whole neighborhood can see me standing here, but I'm not ready to move yet, even if I am about to be late for the biggest meeting of my life. Because I know there's a chance, when I walk through that door, that it might be the last time I walk *anywhere*.

They might carry me back out, wrapped in a tarp.

Drop my body in the East River.

I'd never resurface.

The fact that they called me here during daylight doesn't mean a thing. I'm no fool. I never have been. Someone shot up my father's business while the sun was brightly shining.

These men don't let the earth's rotation dictate their schedules.

The white wooden door cracks open as I stand there. I turn toward it right away, slipping the peppermint in my mouth over against my cheek, still sucking on it, trying to calm my nerves. A young burly guy stands in front of me, his face rippled with craters. One of Genova's enforcers, I imagine. The guy has a type. *Beasts*. I'm not as versed in the inner-workings of the other families, although I've done business with all of them a few times in the past.

They had a job and I handled it, no questions asked.

That was how they knew how to get ahold of me this afternoon, how they knew how to call me in for this meeting. Apparently my number was still on speed dial.

I probably ought to do something about that.

"They're waiting for you," the guy says, his voice high-pitched, almost comically so, like his balls haven't dropped yet. *Or maybe they shoved them back inside whenever they fucked up his face.* "Follow me."

Should've known they were watching.

No need to knock.

I don't like taking orders from people. I never even liked taking orders from Ray. I'm inclined to resist, but I push back my instinct, following the guy instead.

Now's probably not the time to try to assert my dominance.

Someone shuts the door behind us. Glancing back, I see a guy standing guard right inside the foyer, trying to stay out of sight. *Huh.* I turn back around, following the burly guy through the house, turning down a long hallway. The second I round the corner, I see we're heading straight for a set of doors, two more guys standing guard outside of them.

The AK-47s over their shoulders tell me these ones are purposely trying to make themselves seen.

Guess they're trying to intimidate me.

They open the set of doors as we approach, and my footsteps almost falter. I don't let them see my hesitation, though.

The guy guiding me stops on the outskirts, but I keep walking. There's no backing out now. It's a dining room of sorts, or more like a meeting space. A long mahogany table runs through it, chairs surrounding it.

Only four of them are filled.

One of the men, boss Frank Genova, waves toward the doors behind me. "Leave us."

Right away, the man obeys. Not surprising that Genova's taking the lead. It's his house this meeting is in. I just stand here, awaiting something. I'm not entirely sure how this is going to go.

Like I said, these meetings are rare.

Once the man vacates the room, Genova motions toward the table between us. "Gun."

I hold up my hands. "I don't have one."

His brow furrows. "You came unarmed?"

"I never carry a gun," I say, "but that doesn't mean I'm unarmed."

Everything's a weapon if you look at it the right way.

"Knives, then."

"None of those, either."

"Then what do you got?"

"Not much." I consider it for a moment. "Some spare change, a peppermint, my wallet... oh, and I've got a pen in my pocket."

He looks at me with disbelief. "A pen."

Reaching into my pocket, I pull out a simple black ballpoint pen. Probably cost a dollar.

"You gonna kill somebody with that?" he asks.

I shrug, setting it on the table. "You never know."

That seems to confuse him for a moment, as he stares at the pen, before he shakes it off. "It's just a formality anyway. Doesn't really matter. Go ahead, take a seat. Join us."

I sit down right across from them and regard Genova, the chairman of this defunct board, prepared to speak for everyone. I don't like the way he worded that.

Join us.

"I'm sure you know why you were called here this afternoon," he says, diving right into it. "We need to discuss the murder of Raymond Angelo."

Ray's hypothetical seat at the table is glaringly vacant. I half expected the new guy in town to already be filling his shoes, so to speak, but no... the chair's empty. Guess the fabled Scar has yet to be invited in.

Pity. I would've liked to meet him.

"I wouldn't call it a murder," I say. "It was more of an untimely death."

"That's an interesting way to look at it, Vitale, but it doesn't change the fact that a boss was killed. We can't have those kinds of things happening, you know. It's bad for business. Bad for order. People start forgetting where their place is and we're all in trouble. You get me?"

I nod.

"So you see how this is a problem for us," he continues. "You see how you killing a boss is bad news. See how we can't really tolerate it happening on our watch. It's nothing personal, you know, but..."

He trails off with a casual shrug of the shoulder, as if to say 'no hard feelings when we kill you for it'.

"With all due respect," I say. If I'm going to die today, I'm going to die. Nothing I do in this room will change their minds. "You call me here to talk about these rules, but where are you when rules are being broken every other day?"

One of the other bosses chimes in then. *Michael Grillo.* "What are you talking about?"

"Forgive me if I'm wrong, as I've never personally taken the vows, but don't you gentlemen lecture your men when they're brought in that women and children are never to be harmed? So where was the meeting when Raymond Angelo was out there hunting someone's wife and daughter?"

Grillo scowls. "And forgive me if *I'm* wrong, Vitale, but wasn't it *you* actually doing that hunting?"

He's got me there.

"I wasn't the one who gave the order," I say. "Ray was the one who planted that seed. If you put a man in charge that turns out to be a monster, you shouldn't be surprised when someone makes the monster go away. I killed Ray, and I don't regret it. I won't. He shot the woman I love right in front of my face."

Genova chimes in now. "Wasn't it Johnny Rita who did that?"

Anger surges through me, and maybe it's irrational, but I want to ring the man's neck for saying that name. "Karissa. Ray shot Karissa."

I don't know if he's truly dumb or he's just feigning ignorance, but a look of surprise passes over his face. "That's the woman you love, is it?"

"Are we here to discuss my relationship, Genova, or can we get back to business?"

My voice is sharp, but he laughs it off. "Yeah, you're right. I can't keep up with you kids. Hate 'em one day, love 'em the next. But I digress... I'll agree that Angelo, too, took some questionable action, so I can't say I blame you for what you did. Still... we can't tolerate those kinds of things, Vitale, so I'm warning you now: if you forget your place again, you'll have to be dealt with."

I don't like being threatened.

Talk is cheap.

I'd rather a man try to kill me than threaten my life.

At least in that case I can defend myself. Here, I just have to sit down and take it, nod my head like the submissive little soldier I don't have it in me to be.

The submissive little soldier they want me to be.

The one I've never been.

"And what about Ray's replacement?" I ask. "I can't help but notice he's absent from the meeting."

"Angelo hasn't been replaced yet."

I almost laugh at that.

The full metal jacket ammo from the AR-15 that lit up my father's deli just days ago tells me otherwise. Family in New York is dropping like flies. So what he means to say is they haven't voted, but Ray's most definitely been replaced.

And whoever he is, he's probably worse than the rest of them.

He doesn't ask permission.

He doesn't care about these rules.

Voting doesn't mean shit to him.

"Who is he, the new guy?" I ask. "Nobody seems to know much about him."

They look like they don't want to talk about this. The other three remain stone cold silent, while Genova at least pretends to humor me. "Scar, they call him. Young guy. Ruthless."

"How young?"

"About your age," he says. "Came from the south."

"Philadelphia?"

"Nah, much further south."

There isn't much of a family presence past the Mason-Dixon Line, so I'm not sure how southern he can be. I don't press it, though. I can tell I've already pried too much.

We don't ask questions in this business.

It's probably the biggest rule.

"Is that all?" I ask. "Am I free to leave?"

"Not yet," Genova says, folding his hands on the table in front of him. "Before you go, I want to talk to you about some business. Got a couple of jobs I need you to do for me."

Jobs.

Things I told Karissa I wasn't doing anymore.

"What kind of jobs?"

"Oh, you know... the usual."

The usual. "I'm not doing that anymore."

The men mutter amongst themselves. You see, when a man with a penchant for killing anyone who denies him asks you for a favor, well, it's kind of ballsy to say no to that... especially when that man just gave you a pass.

"And why's that?" Genova asks. "Decided to go straight? Get a life? Get a real job?"

They laugh at that, laughing at my expense.

"Or maybe you're retiring," Genova continues. "Next thing you know, you're wearing penny loafers and got a house down in Boca Raton. Is that what you're going for?"

I say nothing.

I take the ridicule.

He thinks he can break me with it, bend me to his will, get me to do what he wants me to do.

I won't do it.

By the time the meeting finally concludes, it's pitch black outside, darkness long ago setting in. Genova waves me away from the table, sneering. "Get out of my face, Vitale. Think about it. Come back when you finally come to your senses."

The same guy from earlier shows me to the door, the armed soldiers trailing behind us, not a single man at ease.

I guess my reputation precedes me.

It isn't until I'm in my car and driving down the street, away from that house, somehow still breathing, that I allow myself to sigh with relief.

It always pays to be worth more than you take.

I may have denied him tonight, but Genova isn't done.

He won't give up.

When I get home much later, the house is still lit, even though it's nearing midnight. I head straight for the den, finding Karissa fast asleep on the couch. Schoolwork is scattered all around her. I told her not to wait up for me, but she was never very good at listening.

It would've been a long night for her had I not made it out of that house alive.

Kicking off my shoes, I grab her legs, picking them up so I can slip beneath them, sitting down on the end of the couch. She stirs from the movement, eyes opening. Blinking rapidly, she looks my way, a sleepy smile overcoming her face. She shifts onto her back as I place her legs back down, her feet right in my lap.

"You're home," she says, her voice gritty from sleep.

"I am," I say, running my hands along the tops of her feet before my thumbs graze the soles. She squirms, like she's about to yank her feet away, when I start massaging one of them. That stalls her, her toes curling as she lets out a sigh.

She likes it when I do this.

I learned that back in Italy.

It's quiet, except for the sound of the television she'd left on when she passed out. Food Network, as usual. She still spends her free time studying that nonsense.

"Really?" she says after a while, an incredulous note to her voice. "Of all things? Hotline Bling?"

"We're going to talk about this again?"

"Of course. I mean, I just expected if you ever got down with any music, it would be something else... something like, I don't know... Frank Sinatra?"

"How stereotypical." I shoot her a look. "Maybe I should've chosen the Godfather theme."

"Yes!"

I shake my head, continuing to rub her feet. "I just wanted something different."

Something that didn't make me think about *that* time of my life.

Something that didn't remind me of working for Ray, of being *that* man, every time my phone rang. Karissa loves music. The way she describes it, it's almost like it owns a piece of her soul.

Part of me wanted to know what that felt like.

Wanted to know if I had it in me to by that kind of person.

To feel that kind of thing.

"So you went with Drake?"

Reaching into my pocket, I pull out my phone and toss it to her. It lands right on her chest, and she huffs as she picks it up.

"Find me something else," I say. "But so help me God, Karissa, if you choose that Bieber twit…"

"Ugh, gross." She grimaces. "I would never."

She browses music as I continue to rub her feet.

It only takes a minute before a loud ruckus breaks the silence, high-pitched piano notes mingling with what sounds like kids shouting over a drum beat. It's obnoxious. Karissa tosses my phone back, and it bounces off my lap, hitting the floor.

Instinct takes over, and I almost step on it.

I almost stomp on the fucking thing just to get it to be quiet.

"What is *that*?" I ask, reaching down and snatching it up, pressing the button on the side to silence it right away.

"One Direction," she says.

"Seriously?" I shove her feet off of my lap. "That's even worse!"

She gasps as she sits up, grabbing her chest. "No! Take it back!"

"Please stop."

"You're crazy! One Direction is the greatest band to ever grace the stage!"

"You're being ridiculous."

"They're utterly brilliant, the best thing to ever come out of the UK," she says, grabbing ahold of me when I try to stand up. Before I can move, she pushes herself across the couch and climbs into my lap, straddling me. "Rolling Stones, what? Beatles, who?"

My hands find their way to her hips, holding onto her, as I stare at her pointedly. "You're embarrassing yourself, Karissa."

She laughs, like I'm not being dead serious, and presses her lips to mine before I can say anything else. She kisses me passionately, deeply, tongue gliding out and meeting mine. After the night I've had, it's a welcome change. I couldn't think of a better distraction. She hums against my lips as my hands move from her hips, sliding around the curve of her ass. I groan when she shifts in my lap, rubbing herself right against my crotch. It doesn't take much, just a warm brush against my cock for it to stir, standing right at attention for her.

I shift my hips up, slowly grinding against her, eliciting a gasp from her as she breaks the kiss. My lips trail down her jawline, making their way to her neck, as she whispers something.

Something I don't quite hear.

"What was that?" I ask, my teeth grazing the sensitive spot just below her ear.

She repeats herself again, and again, her voice breathy, almost melodic. It takes a moment before the words strike me, for me to realize what she's doing.

She's singing the fucking song my phone was just playing.

"That'll be about enough of that," I say, grabbing her hips and shifting her right off of me, back onto the couch, as I get to my feet. She tries to cling to me, laughing, but I peel her off and walk away.

"Wait, where are you going?" she asks, turning to watch me.

"To take a shower."

"But your, uh, situation," she says, motioning right toward the crotch of my pants. "Don't you wanna take care of that first?"

"I'll handle it myself."

I walk out, and all I hear is laughter... loud, carefree laughter. Shaking my head, I can't help the smile that fights to break free. It's completely ridiculous. It's probably the most absurd few minutes of my life. But the sound of her laughter, of her happiness, does to me something nothing else can.

It cuts straight through my darkness.

With her, I almost feel *light*.

I head upstairs and strip out of my suit as soon as I reach the bathroom. I don't bother to turn the light on, navigating it in the darkness. A small nightlight is plugged in above the sink. It's really all I need. My eyes fix on my reflection in the mirror as the water warms up for my shower.

I'm not sure if it's just my perception, but I look older than my thirty-eight years.

I certainly feel older, too.

I feel like I've lived more than one lifetime, each of them lasting an eternity. An eternity of rage, and resentment, and wrongdoing... it takes its toll on a man, that's for certain. But none of it had half as much effect on me as this past year. Something I learned was sentiment can take it out of you. I used to have no regard for myself—or anybody, for that matter. I had no reason to live anymore. But now that I care about what happens to her—and for her sake, *me*—I'm growing exhausted from the constant worry.

Worry my past will catch up to us.

Worry that she'll be the one to pay for those sins.

It's the consequence, I think, of loving me.

The consequence of being with someone who lived so carelessly.

As steam starts to fill the bathroom, I step into the shower, letting the scalding spray wash away today. It can't be more than a minute or two later when a sudden blast of cold air surrounds me.

Somebody opened the bathroom door.

The shower curtain is pushed aside, and I glance that way, my eyes meeting Karissa's. She's not laughing anymore, but the amusement is still etched all over her face. Without a word, she starts to strip, flinging her clothes behind her onto the floor.

"Is there something you need?" I ask, raising an eyebrow as my gaze trails along her exposed skin. Brave woman she's turned out to be. "Something I can do for you?"

"Maybe," she says, climbing into the shower with me, flinging the curtain closed again. It's so dark I can barely see her. "Or maybe it's something I can do for you."

She drops to her knees in front of me, right there, under the water. Her hand wraps around my cock, stroking it, her grip firm. A voice in the back of my mind tells me to stop her, reminds me she doesn't belong on her knees, reminds me that after everything I've done, I should be the one worshiping her. She deserves it. But her mouth is on me before I can say anything, her lips wrapping around my cock as she takes me in, and I forget.

I fucking forget.

I forget I've ever had a worry in the world.

It's just that good.

"Jesus, Karissa," I groan, running my fingers through the wet locks of her hair. "I wish I knew what I did to deserve you."

Chapter Five

Karissa

"Today, ladies and gents, we're going to dive into the topic of war."

Adjunct Professor Rowan Adams stands in the middle of the classroom, his hands absently drumming against his pants legs, as he looks around at all of us. We're in a familiar classroom... the same classroom I once took philosophy in. They seem to think enough time has passed that people wouldn't be affected anymore, and maybe they're right, I don't know. All of the makeshift memorials that popped up after his death are long gone. But what I do know is that I'm freaked out by it, even if nobody else around here is.

Three weeks into the semester and it still gives me the heebie-jeebies.

Professor Adams, who insists we call him Rowan, is a far cry from the kind of teacher Santino had been. He's open, and kind, and patient. I've never heard him belittle anyone. He's also young, late 20s at most, barely out of college himself with a degree in something or other. Okay, I hadn't exactly paid attention, but I'm guessing History, since that's what he's teaching. So maybe it's his age, or maybe it's just his temperament, but he runs this room vastly different than Santino had.

"Give me some reasons why people go to war."

Answers are shouted out all around me.

"Revenge."

"Pride."

"Stupidity."

"Fear."

"Protection."

"Love."

Rowan acknowledges the answers one by one, smiling as he points toward the source of it, before zeroing in on that last one. He swings toward the guy who shouted it... a guy who happens to be sitting right behind me. *Ugh.* "Ah, yes, love. But the love of what specifically?"

"Country."

"God."

"Women."

Again, it's the guy behind me who shouts out the last one, the one that gets the professor's attention. He turns back to him, grinning. Most eyes in the room shoot that direction, almost like it's instinct, and I slouch down further in my seat, not wanting them to notice me. I learned my lesson last time. I'll never draw attention to myself again.

"The love of a woman," Rowan says. "There's no more valiant reason, is there? Whether it's to defend her honor or prove their own worth, men have been fighting wars since the dawn of time all because of the love of a woman. Cleopatra... Helen of Troy... we all know their stories... but today we're going to talk about Bathsheba."

He wanders by the desk at the front of the classroom—a desk he never sits at—and snatches a Bible off the top of it.

"During the fight for the Holy Lands, King David found himself transfixed by a woman named Bathsheba. Problem was, Bathsheba was married to one of his soldiers—Uriah. That troubled King David, but not enough to keep him from sleeping with her. The two had an affair, but King David, deep in love, wanted her all to himself, especially... *especially*... after she became pregnant. Imagine the scandal! So come the Battle of Rabbah, David ordered Uriah to the most dangerous position on the battlefield, knowing the soldier wouldn't make it out alive. His enemies took care of his rival for him. Problem solved."

Rowan pauses, looking around to see if we're getting the point.

"Pride, revenge, protection, fear, love," he continues. "Probably a healthy dose of stupidity on top of it. It's all right here in this book. King David married Bathsheba when it was all over, and she gave birth to their son, but the child died afterward. Punishment, he thought. You see, there are always consequences to war, even after we think we've won."

He tosses the Bible back down on the desk. A few people throw out questions that he happily answers. He's got a 'don't bother raising your hand' policy on top of an 'I'm not going to call on you if you don't want to speak' philosophy that makes for a fairly peaceful class period.

If only we weren't in this damn room.

I wait out the rest of the hour, jotting down a few notes, waiting until we're dismissed to haul ass out of my seat. I'm the first one to the door, the first one out of there. It's my third year at NYU, although I'm technically still a sophomore.

I missed a semester while in recovery.

Wandering outside, I pause and look around, not sure what to do. I've got about an hour before I have my next class, and usually I'd just head over to the library, but for the first time in quite a while I'm caught up on everything.

Down the block, I cross the street, heading over to Washington Square Park. It's a nice day out, the summer weather insisting on lingering. I find an empty cement bench along the path and plop down on it, dropping my bag on the ground by my feet. I slip in my pink earbuds and plug them into my phone, pressing play on some music, as I look around.

Enjoying the view.

Enjoying the sense of solitude.

It's somewhat busy out here, with students coming and going, but nobody bothers me. Nobody even seems to notice me, for that matter.

It's nice, surprisingly, feeling invisible.

I used to yearn for someone to look at me, to see me.

Some days I wish I could just disappear again.

Not to say I don't love my life, because I do. I love it. But I don't love some of the things that happened. I don't love all of the memories that haunt me here.

I just always wanted a normal life.

None of this is normal.

I've been sitting here for about twenty minutes when something catches my eye. Familiar blonde hair bounces my direction as people weave along the path. Melody. Smiling, I tug an earbud out and am about to call for her when someone beats me to it, someone standing nearby. The voice is all male with a strange sort of accent, almost like they don't really have one. *Weird.*

Turning my head, I spot a young guy.

A gorgeous young guy.

Holy shit.

I watch as Melody turns to him, her expression brightening, eyes lighting up like the Forth of July. And I know it instantly, just by the look on her face... that smitten, speechless, one of a kind expression.

Leo.

Tubby mountain man motherfucker he is not.

He looks like something off of a runway.

He's tall, and skinny, but not lankily so. Broad shoulders and tanned skinned, a sharp jawline and dark, dark features. His hair is as black as midnight, and his eyebrows might be a tad bit bushy, but he rocks them like it's the latest thing in fashion.

And hell, what do I know?

Maybe it is.

His teeth are so white they're dazzling as he flashes a smile at her. He's wearing jeans and a black button down, the sleeves shoved up to his elbow, which come on, is the hottest thing imaginable.

I love Naz. I do. I love him more than anything in this world. The first time I laid eyes on him, the man left me speechless, and looking back, I knew that moment that life as I knew it had been over. Naz is the kind of guy that, once he walks into your world, he throws it off its axis, so even if he walks back out, nothing spins the same anymore.

I love him, despite everything, with every fiber of my being.

But Leo.

Whoa.

I can appreciate beauty when I see it.

That's the kind of face women would go to war for, I think.

They approach each other, and he wraps an arm around her, pulling her to him for a hug. It's brief, but I can see the blush on her cheeks from him doing it. When he pulls back, he says something to her, chatting for a moment, but they're too far away for me to hear any of their words. The more he talks, though, the more her eyes light up, before she eventually nods enthusiastically. He kisses his fingertips and presses them to her lips. The action is so quick I barely catch it.

He's gone then, walking away, looking back at her once and smiling before disappearing into a crowd of people. Melody stares at him, waiting until he's out of sight before she lets out a loud squeal.

She jumps up and down in place, like she's having a fucking fit.

"Melody?" I call out.

The sound of my voice stalls her. She swings my way so fast she nearly falls over. "Karissa!"

She jogs over to where I'm sitting, wordlessly shoving me over on the bench. I make room for her, shifting my bag out of the way so she can drop hers by our feet.

"That must've been the infamous Leo," I say, motioning the direction he disappeared. "Gotta say, Mel, I totally get it now."

She grins, shoving me excitedly. "Told you! Isn't he everything?"

"Yeah, he's something, all right."

"He just asked me out," she continues. "Like, really asked me out, and not just for coffee. I'm talking dinner and a movie. A real date."

"That's awesome! When is it happening?"

"Tonight." The moment she says it, her expression drops. "Oh my god, it's tonight! What time is it? I gotta go! I've got my hair to do, and makeup, and oh shit... what am I gonna wear?"

"Whoa, calm down. It's like, one in the afternoon right now."

"That only gives me six hours to get ready!"

I laugh to myself, amused by her panic, before she grabs ahold of my arm and yanks me out of my seat. Reaching down, she grabs both of our bags, pulling me along with her. "Let's go!"

"Whoa, wait, I've got class in a bit."

"Jesus Christ, Karissa, class can wait! Didn't you hear me? I have a date!"

I'm not sure if she realizes she rhymed there. Usually she'd point it out, like she's some kind of rapper in training, but I think she's too frazzled to find the humor in it right now. "Okay, okay, relax, Dr. Seuss. I'll go with you. Just... give me a second."

She stops pulling on me, and I take my bag from her, situating it on my back before motioning toward the path. "After you."

Melody still lives in the dorms, the same room we used to share together, back before I moved out and, you know, got married. A sense of nostalgia hits me when we reach the thirteenth floor, and I stare at the door as she unlocks it, smiling. **1313**.

So many memories happened here, but unlike the classroom, these are mostly all happy.

My smile dims, though, the moment she pushes open the door and my eyes fall right upon her latest roommate. It's her fourth since me... they never last long. The new girl turns, her eyes narrowing, and she glares at us as we enter, the kind of hostility you shouldn't ever get from a stranger. Slamming her book closed, she snatches it up and storms from the room, brushing right past us without saying a word.

Melody seems, for the most part, unaffected. I watch as the girl goes straight for the elevators, slapping the button for it like the damn thing offended her. She's a pretty girl—ginger with green eyes and freckles—but the scowl on her face is kind of ugly.

"Trouble in paradise?" I ask, stepping into the room behind Melody and shutting the door.

She sighs dramatically. "They can't all be as understanding as you were."

"Uh-oh, you didn't pick up a guy in a flight suit at Timbers and bring him home to screw, did you?"

Shit. Shit. Shit.

The moment the words come from my lips, I instantly regret them. I'm an idiot. Of course I'd bring up Paul at a moment like this.

She frowns, flopping down on her bed... or what appears to be just a gigantic pile of clothes currently. "She says I'm messy."

"Yeah," I say, looking around. Melody's side of the room is, as usual, akin to a natural disaster. "So?"

"So she says I'm careless, and loud, and ugh, she says I snore. Can you believe that? Me? Snore?"

"Well, uh... only when you've been drinking."

"I haven't been, though. I've done nothing to that girl! But all she wants to do is sit here in silence and eat her frickin' protein bars and meditate. Do you know she's never been to Timbers? Who hasn't been to Timbers?"

"I guess she hasn't, whatever her name is."

"Kimberly," Melody says, her face scrunching up. "Kimberly Anne Vanderbilt. Rich snob of a name if I've ever heard one."

I refrain from pointing out that she's a *Melody Priscilla*

Carmichael, which isn't any more common-folk sounding. I can tell she's getting in a funk now, though, so I change the subject. "Now, about this date..."

It's like a switch is flipped. That quick. The spark is back in her eyes as she lets out another squeal.

Man, I still envy how she bounces back so easily.

She's off the bed again, digging through her closet, flinging more clothes onto the mountain on the bed.

I'm not much help. I mean, come on... does anybody expect anything different? I have more stuff now than I ever could've imagined, but I'm still wearing my favorite pair of old jeans, black boots, and a black top, one I'm about ninety-percent certain I found in Naz's closet. It's way too big for me. So I just sit there, trying to distract her from her panic, as she strips willy-nilly in front of me, trying on half of what she owns.

An hour passes, and I miss my class, but it's nice to just hang out and laugh with my friend again.

Besides, it's just math.

Who really needs to know how to do that?

The door to the room opens, and Melody is standing there in a bra and her panties, not giving any sort of fucks when her roommate walks in. The girl lets out a noise of disgust as she plops down at her desk, her back to us.

"I have nothing to wear," Melody say, shaking her head, ignoring that I've given the thumb's up to at least a dozen outfits. "Like... nothing."

"Well, where's he taking you?"

"I don't know," she says, pulling on a pair of leggings. "But he said something about reservations, so I'm pretty sure it isn't **Wendy's**."

"Huh, is there even a Wendy's here in the city?"

"There are a few." She shoots me a look. "That's not important here."

Some fries dipped in a chocolate Frosty sound pretty damn

important to me at the moment, but I let her slide on that.

"Look, come on," I say, standing up from the bed. "It's obvious we're not getting anywhere here so let's go somewhere else."

"Thank God," Kimberly mutters, not even under her breath, obviously not caring if we hear.

Melody shoots daggers at her roommate before turning to me. "Like where?"

"My closet."

She scoffs, looking me over, judging my outfit, before something seems to strike her. "Oh! That's right! Naz updated your wardrobe! I mean, can't really tell it…" She scowls at my shirt, reaching over and tugging on it. "I was about to say, ain't no way I'm wearing one of your scarf-y ensembles on my date tonight. You can keep your damn Crocs."

I roll my eyes. "I don't wear Crocs."

"But you own some."

I have half a mind to come to my own defense, but what's the point, really?

Besides, I'm pretty sure she's right, so I let her slide on that too.

She throws on a long shirt and slips into her shoes, not saying a single word to her roommate as she stalks out the door.

"Uh, bye," I mumble, giving an awkward wave, but the girl doesn't even look at me, much less say anything back.

When we step outside, I pull my phone out to call for a car, but Melody waves me off. "Look, come on, there's a cab right there."

She flags it down.

Who am I to argue?

I'm not taking it alone.

That means it doesn't count as breaking Naz's rule, right?

I slide in beside her and she rattles off the address, flubbing up the street numbers, but I correct them. As the cab pulls into traffic, I glance in the front out of habit.

It takes a moment, but recognition strikes me.

Abele Abate.

Man with the unfortunate name.

He drove me home just the other day from the deli.

He glances in the rear view mirror, smiling just like last time. I don't know if he recognizes me, but it's doubtful. He certainly doesn't say anything. He probably drives hundreds of people around every day.

When we get to the house, the first thing I notice is it's empty. Naz is gone. Killer greets me as soon as I open the front door, wagging his tail excitedly.

"Hey boy," I say, rubbing his head. "You all alone?"

Melody skirts right past the dog, holding her hands up. "Oh my God, don't jump on me or I might smell like you."

I laugh. "He doesn't smell that bad."

"Really, Karissa? When's the last time you bathed the poor thing?"

"Uh, it's been a while."

I have a hell of a time doing it myself, and Naz is no help. He's nice enough to drive him to the groomers for me in the Mercedes when I ask him, but Killer doesn't like getting in that car.

"Seriously, hose the poor puppy off out back if you've got to," she says. "He's starting to smell like my roommate's feet. Ugh, they reek."

Rolling my eyes, I head to the back door of the house, opening it to let him run out. The yard isn't very big, but that never seems to bother him. I've tried to take him to the park before, but that requires getting in the car, and well... like I said, that doesn't make him happy, so the backyard it is.

"I'm sure you can figure out which one's my closet," I tell her. "Upstairs, first door on the right."

Melody disappears while I put out some food for Killer, making sure he's satisfied before I join her upstairs. Less than ten minutes have passed, but half of my clothes are already scattered around the bedroom. She slips on a little black dress, one I've never had a reason to wear. "God, this thing is gorgeous. Who's the designer?"

She glances at me like I'm supposed to have an answer to that. "Uh, that guy, you know... the one who did that thing that time. *Him*."

She cracks a smile. "You're so full of shit."

I am.

"It looks great on you," I tell her. "You should wear it."

She squeals, dashing for the closet again. "Got any shoes to go with this thing?"

Five minutes later, she's standing in the bathroom, fixing her hair in the mirror and borrowing my little bit of makeup. I leave her to her primping and head back downstairs. Man, just watching her get ready makes me all frazzled. It's exhausting.

"You're home early today."

The unexpected voice startles me. Grabbing my chest, I take a step back, looking toward the front door. Naz stands in the foyer, hands in his pockets, newspaper tucked beneath his right arm. After all this time, how does he still sneak up on me?

"Jesus, Naz, I didn't hear you come in."

"I didn't think you did," he replies, his voice flat. "You seem to be quite busy."

"I was just... I mean, we were... you know."

I motion behind me, up the stairs. I don't know if that's enough for him to go on, for him to riddle out what I'm saying. But my nerves are suddenly completely shot, waves of nervousness running through my body, as I look at him. He's not moving, not at all. He stands there like he's standing guard.

I wouldn't say he looks angry, because he doesn't, but something feels off.

"Yes," he says. "I know."

"Melody has a date tonight," I tell him, as if he actually cares, but if he's upset that she's here, maybe he'll understand if I explain why. He's always been weird about people being inside the house. "She needed something to wear, and well, she didn't have anything. I mean, she had stuff, but nothing, you know... to wear. So we came here, to see if I had anything, and I did, so she's wearing it, because, well, she didn't have anything."

As I babble like an idiot, his expression shifts, his brow creasing. "Why are you nervous?"

"I'm not."

"You're lying."

I sigh. I am.

He breaks his stance, stepping toward me. "What's wrong?"

"Nothing."

"Another lie."

"Ugh, okay," I say, waving his way. "You're just, you're being all you and it's throwing me off."

"I'm being me," he says, "and it's throwing you off."

"Yes! I didn't expect to see you here."

"You didn't expect to see—"

"Ugh, and there you go!" I say, cutting him off. "You're doing it!"

"I'm doing it."

"You're repeating everything I say."

That stalls him for a moment.

Yeah, he knows now how annoying that is.

"I'm just trying to understand what's got you nervous," he says. "Other than me being me, whatever that means."

"I don't know." Not a lie this time. "You're just standing there and it caught me off guard because you weren't here and then suddenly there you were."

"Ah." He steps closer as his posture relaxes a bit. "I was just off getting the car detailed. I didn't expect you home until later. Thought you had classes."

"I did," I say. "Or I *do*. I skipped them."

After Math was English, but really, who needs that either? I already speak it pretty good.

Or... *well*?

I speak it well?

Who knows?

He steps even closer, pausing right in front of me. He nudges my chin with his hand, tilting my face up. "Skipping classes? How very delinquent of you, Jailbird."

After kissing me, a simple peck on the lips, he steps back, snatching hold of the newspaper he's carrying, lightly tapping me with it as he walks away, heading for the den. I stand there for a moment before following, stopping in the doorway. I lean against the doorframe, watching him as he sits down at his desk and opens the newspaper in front of him. He skims through pages quickly, stopping somewhere in the middle, and stares down at it. I don't know if he's reading or what, but he's certainly transfixed by something he sees.

Curiosity gets the best of me.

Carefully, I stroll over to him, half expecting him to close the newspaper and throw it aside when I approach. That's what Old Naz would've done, anyway. Old Naz kept secrets. Old Naz sometimes shut me out. Instead, though, he simply pushes his chair back, putting a bit of room between him and the desk, as he looks away from it. His eyes turn to me, and he opens his arms, inviting me into his space.

I don't know if I'll ever get used to the openness.

I perch myself right on the arm of his office chair.

My gaze goes straight to the newspaper.

Fire Destroys Historic West Village Building
Seven reported injured, two dead in the blaze.

I'm not sure what I expected to see, but that certainly wasn't it. There's not much in the way of details, just that it happened the day before and the cause was still under investigation. I turn my head, glancing at Naz. He's staring at a fixed point on his bookshelf along the wall, that expression again on his face, the same one from the foyer.

Not angry, no... more troubled.

"You didn't?" I ask quietly. Okay, I shouldn't be asking at all, but

I can't help it. This is bothering him. "I mean, did you...?"

"No."

"I didn't think so, but you know..."

"But I wasn't home when it happened." It was when he'd left, telling me not to wait up because he had things do to. "I was somewhere else then."

I turn back to the paper. If he says it, I believe him. "Did you know the people?"

"Yes."

"Were they friends of yours?"

He lets out what sounds like a sharp bark of laughter, but there's no humor to it. "I wouldn't exactly say I have any friends, Karissa."

"Then maybe you need to make some."

I'm serious, but he laughs again, this time like it's the funniest thing he's ever heard. "I'm afraid my days of finding friends out on the playground are long over."

"Well, what about the neighbors?" I ask. "This is a nice neighborhood. They look like they might be the dinner-party-on-the-weekend types. I could hang out with the Stepford wives while you, I don't know, go golfing or something."

"Golfing."

"Yeah, I bet you have a killer swing."

He shakes his head. "With as many times as the police have visited this house, Karissa, I don't think that's going to work. I step one foot on their property and I guarantee they're already calling 911."

"Well... then I'll go golfing with you."

Raising his eyebrows, he glances at me. "You want to go golfing?"

"No."

"Me, either."

Thank God.

"We could always double with Melody and her new guy sometime."

Naz reacts to that just as I expected he would the first time

Melody suggested it. He stands up, laughing again, as he shuts his newspaper, balling it up and throwing it in the trashcan. "I've seen her taste in men, so I'll have to pass on befriending anybody she takes up with."

"I don't know," I say. "This new one might be different."

"Have you met him?"

"Yes," I say, quickly correcting myself. "Well, not technically, but I've seen him."

"You've seen him."

"Yep."

"Looks can be deceiving."

"I know that," I say defensively. "I've just got a good feeling about this one."

"Did you have a good feeling about me when we met?"

"No." I hesitate. "I don't know, maybe? You were kind of intimidating, but I didn't have bad feelings about you, if that's what you mean."

Naz strolls across the room, over to his bookshelf. His fingers graze the spines of a few books before he pulls one out. He turns back to me as he clutches hold of it, and I catch a glimpse at the cover. *War & Peace*. He pauses in front of me, tilting his head slightly as he studies my face. "This new guy, he's what? Nineteen? Twenty? Probably not even old enough to legally drink."

"Probably."

"And you think I'd have something in common with him?"

His question is serious.

He thinks I'm being ridiculous.

Hell, maybe I am.

But not for the reasons he thinks.

"I'm only twenty, you know," I remind him. "My age didn't stop you from getting to know me."

I think it's a goddamn good argument, personally, but I can tell he still thinks I'm just being ridiculous.

"Karissa, baby, I love you. You know that. But do you honestly think, if I hadn't had other reasons, I would've even given you a second look?"

I blanch. "Ouch."

I stand up from the arm of the chair and attempt to walk away—because *ouch*—when he grabs my arm. "Don't act like that's anything more than it is. You're beautiful and wise beyond your years. But I'm pushing forty here, sweetheart. It wouldn't have even crossed my mind to pursue you. You're everything I'm not. Everything I'll probably never be. And just the simple fact that you honestly think it's possible for me to make friends in this city, after the things I've been involved in, proves what I'm saying."

I almost do it, because part of me thinks he wants it. I almost bring up moving, the possibility of getting away from New York, like we've talked about before, when Melody shouts my name from somewhere near the foyer.

Now's not the time for this conversation, I realize.

"I'm in here," I yell back as Naz lets go of my arm. It only takes Melody a moment to appear, bounding into the doorway, her hair pinned up.

"How do I look?" she asks, spinning, showing off the getup.

"You're wearing the Moreau," Naz says.

Melody looks down at herself as she stops. "The what?"

"Moreau," he says. "He designed the dress."

She looks at him with surprise. Hell, I do, too.

"How do you know that?" I ask.

He shrugs. "I know the guy. He owed me."

"He owed you."

Okay, now I'm doing the repeating thing, which Naz notices and narrows his eyes at me for. "Yes, he owed me, and that was his repayment."

He motions toward the dress.

"Oh shit," Melody says, swishing the bottom part of the dress.

"Should I take it off?"

"No," Naz and I say at the same time. I glance at him as he shrugs, continuing. "Karissa will never wear it, so you might as well. I just made sure he paid. That was all that mattered."

Melody shoots him a questioning look but doesn't ask what making him pay means. We never broach the subject of what Naz does for a living. I'm pretty sure she's got most of it figured out, considering everything that happened last year. His name hit the newspaper when he killed Ray. Even though it had been done in self-defense, it didn't stop the reporters from speculating, dragging up every nitty-gritty detail they could get their hands on to insinuate he wasn't, exactly, the hero in the situation.

She read the article. I know she did.

The girl has probably never bought a newspaper in her life, but she certainly knows how to use Google. She would've sought out information.

"Thanks," Melody says, smiling. "I hope Leo likes it."

Before I can tell her I'm sure he'll love it, Naz chimes in. "Leo?"

"Makes you think of DiCaprio, doesn't it?" I ask.

He shakes his head. "I thought of the lion."

That gets Melody's attention. "You believe in astrology?"

"No."

Her expression falls. Melody's a horoscope-in-the-inbox kind of gal, the one who doesn't do shit when Mercury is in retrograde, whatever that means. She cheered herself up after Paul's disappearance by reminding herself that their signs weren't compatible, anyway, so it never would've worked.

Naz and I?

Total soul mates, she says.

I thought it was all bullshit hocus-pocus until she said that.

"I have some errands to run in the city," Naz says, tucking the book under his arm, his gaze flickering to me before settling on Melody. "Do you need a ride back home?"

Melody shrugs. "Sure."

"Do you, uh... do you want me to ride along?" I ask curiously.

"Nonsense," Naz says, leaning over and kissing my cheek before heading for the door. "I won't be gone long."

Melody grabs her things, waving goodbye. "Coffee in the morning?"

"Sure."

She jets toward the door behind Naz. I just stand there in the den, listening as they head outside.

I don't think the two of them have ever been alone together before.

And I trust them both, of course, but to be a fly on the wall of the car during that drive...

Chapter Six
Ignazio

It's only six miles from the house in Brooklyn to the dorms of NYU where Karissa used to live, but it takes more than a half hour to get there with traffic.

Sometimes it's even an hour.

I know, because I've clocked the drive numerous times.

And traffic, at this hour, is on the heavy side, the Manhattan Bridge packed almost bumper to bumper. For the first time in as far back as I can remember, I actually turn on the radio.

If there's noise to fill the silence, maybe Melody won't feel compelled to try to talk to me.

It's a trick I learned from Karissa.

I've transported plenty of people in this car, but other than Karissa, Melody's the first person to climb into it of her own free will. And I didn't necessarily want to invite her to, but I was heading that way and it would've been wrong of me not to offer.

I'm trying to be better, remember?

Besides, I might not have friends anymore, but Karissa does, and it would probably suit me well to at least be civilized to them. Things at home are much more agreeable when I'm not making a big deal about her having people over.

Still, I don't like it.

I never will.

"This is a nice car," Melody says, slouching in the passenger seat as she tugs on the seatbelt. She's been fidgeting the entire drive so far, staring out the side window. She's nervous. I'm not sure if it's the impending date or me that's getting to her at the moment.

"Thank you," I reply, impatiently drumming my fingers against the steering wheel. I'm not sure what kind of music is playing, some current top 40 nonsense. I just pressed the button on the thing, stopping on the first station that came in. I want to shut it back off, but it might be doing the trick, since we've been in traffic for thirty minutes already and that's the first time she bothered to speak.

"What does one of these run someone? Sixty, seventy grand?"

I smile at that. "Add a hundred to it."

"A hundred and seventy grand?" She gasps. "Are you serious?"

She turns her head, looking at me like I'm out of my mind.

"That's the starting price," I say. "I paid quite a bit more for mine."

"Why?"

Why? I hate that word.

Karissa never asks it.

"Because it's armored," I say. "It costs to stay safe."

"I could eat for my entire life on what you spent on this car."

Now she sounds like Karissa.

I'm pretty sure she's said that same thing to me before.

"About a dozen lifetimes if you only eat Ramen noodles."

"Ugh, who would do that?"

"Karissa, if I let her."

Melody laughs. "Yeah, she probably would. Wouldn't even complain about it, either. You're good for her that way, you know. Not saying you aren't good in other ways, but definitely that. She never had anything really, I guess. Her mother... hell, I don't even know what to say about Mama Reed. Not to talk ill of the dead, but she was a bit of a whack-a-doodle. Karissa couldn't even breathe without the woman questioning it, and she just... accepted it, you know? Karissa acted like that was normal. So it's good, seeing her be happy and have things and do things."

I could say a lot to that, but I keep my mouth shut, grateful when the traffic starts to loosen and we can go more than ten miles an hour.

"So basically, what I'm saying," Melody continues, "is that Karissa could do worse."

"She could," I agree.

Probably not much worse than the man who killed her parents, but I think the extenuating circumstances count for something to my benefit.

Melody turns back to the window, looking out of it again, still shifting around in the seat like she can't quite get comfortable. The music seems to do the trick again, as she quietly mouths the lyrics to whatever is playing on the radio, as I weave through the streets toward NYU. When we approach her dorm, she lets out a dramatic sigh, glancing back my way, like she's struggling hard to think of something to say.

I guess it's normal, chitchat with people, small talk, but I hate it.

"*War & Peace*, huh? Isn't that, like, a billion pages?"

I take my eyes off the road for a second, glancing down at my lap where the book rests. "It's around thirteen hundred, give or take."

"Favorite of yours?"

"I wouldn't exactly call it my favorite, but it's been there for me in times of need."

She smiles like she knows what I mean. "I've read stuff like that."

"Like?"

I almost expect her to say the Bible, when she spouts off with, "Cosmopolitan."

Pulling into the entrance of the parking garage beside the dorms, I put the car in park as I turn to her. She gets out, not hesitating, and while I really want to just let her go, I feel compelled to say something. "Be careful on your date, Miss Carmichael. Not everyone is worthy of your time and attention."

She seems taken aback as she pauses beside the car, the door still open. Leaning back in, she smiles. "You sound like my dad, you know."

I try not to grimace.

I'm quite aware of who her father is, and I'm nothing like that man. *Wall Street schmuck*. He's more of a crook than I am.

She shuts the door, jogging away, toward her dorm, as I put the car in reverse and swing back out into traffic, ignoring the blowing horns from the intrusion.

I head toward West Village.

It's only a few blocks away.

The Cobalt Room.

Once upon a time, this was where dreams were made. Deals were concocted in the office in the back, schemes that netted more money than most people would ever see in a lifetime. I spent more nights than I can count within those walls, plotting my revenge, questioning my future.

The Cobalt Room was like my home away from home, back when my home was nothing more to me than a shell, but the Cobalt Room is nothing now.

Yellow police caution tape flaps in the wind as it surrounds the building, once the greatest structure on the block, now a burned out slab of nothing. The shell of it still stands, the outside charred, but it's easy to see, even from a distance, that the inside is gutted. Whatever flowed through it burned hot and fast... so fast that two people couldn't even get out.

Seven others had been burned, some of them damn near unrecognizable.

It melted their skin off, like they'd personally been doused in gasoline. And maybe they had been, I don't know. The ones capable haven't uttered a word about what went on. All any of them have said is, "I don't know what happened."

But I know... or well, I have an inking.

Because this kind of fire?

This was done by someone who knew what they were doing.

I park my car in the first spot I find down the street and reach down, opening up *War & Peace*, pulling the small silver handgun from the well created in the cut out pages. I slip it in my coat. I don't anticipate needing it, and I don't even like carrying it, but I'm not about to take any risks today. Reaching into the glove box, I pull out my black leather gloves and put them on.

Getting out of the car, I keep my head down as I make the trek back toward Cobalt. I slip beneath the flimsy caution tape that blocks the alley beside the place, making my way to the back of the building where passer-byers can't see.

It isn't hard to break in. What's left of the back door is locked, but a simple push against it knocks it right off the hinges. Grimacing, I lean back, turning my head away to avoid the puff of ash that rises up when the door hits the floor. It reeks, like fire usually does. It smells like smoke and accelerant, a hint of sulfur, like a lit match slapping me right in the face. And I know it's not safe... barely safe enough for me to even step inside, but I do, treading carefully.

I only make it a few feet before I stop, not really needing to go further. I can faintly make out what I'm looking for. Holes litter the floor, but not ones caused by the fire. These are man-made, drilled in the foundation, probably when everyone was asleep. They would've been covered during the daylight, so nobody would've been any the wiser, before a fire was started down in the cellar.

In the cellar, where all the alcohol is stored.

I'd guarantee all of the windows were shoved open, to let even more oxygen in, but there's no way to tell that, not from where I'm standing. Still, I'd guarantee it.

Because that's what I would've done, had it been me.

It's peculiar. I almost would've said it was my doing, looking at it, but I was in Long Island with the Five Families when the fire started.

Or well, I was with *four* of them.

I suspect number five was right here.

Lingering is pointless. I saw what I came to see. I don't trust police reports or what I read in the newspaper. Those are skewed by human error, tainted by perception. I needed to see with my own eyes that this was what I suspected it to be.

Another attack.

Another message.

I slip back out of the building and make my way to my car, my eyes studiously scanning the neighborhood. It wouldn't surprise me if someone were watching, if eyes weren't still on the building.

I never looked back.

I didn't loiter.

But I know others like to watch.

They like to stick around and bask in their destruction, to oversee the aftermath.

The sun is starting to set as I head back to Brooklyn. By the time I reach the house, it's dark outside. It has only been about two hours since I left her, but Karissa is already in her pajamas, like she's ready for bed. When I walk in, she's standing in the kitchen, leaning against the counter, holding a bowl of something in her hand.

"You're back already," she says, sounding surprised.

"I told you I wouldn't be long."

She blows into her bowl, stirring whatever it is with a fork.

"What are you eating?"

I can't remember the last time I actually sat down and ate something.

It has been a long week.

Too damn long.

"Noodles," she says, holding up a forkful. "Want some?"

"I'd rather starve."

She laughs, shrugging, and takes a bite. "I saw some recipes on the Internet of how to jazz them up with like, cream of chicken soup and cheese or whatever. Thought I'd give it a try."

She's jazzing up noodles that cost a quarter.

What am I going to do with her?

"Is that what you plan to make for these hypothetical dinner parties when you miraculously befriend people in this neighborhood?"

"Pfft, no. They're doing the cooking. We're just going to eat."

"Eat their cooking."

"Yes."

"Food prepared by strangers."

"No, they're going to be our friends, remember?"

"Even worse," I say. "You've got to watch the people you let near you. They can't stick a knife in your back if you don't let them get close enough to do it."

She doesn't say anything to that, just staring at me as she takes another bite of noodles. She's staring hard, like she's looking for something.

"What?"

"There's soot on your shirt."

I glance down when she says that, seeing the smudge. Shit. I try to brush it off, which is impossible. The shirt is white and it only extends the black streak.

"Or at least I think it's soot," she says. "Either that or it's makeup, like dark eye shadow or maybe mascara, and if that's the case then I think you have some other kind of explaining to do."

"It's not makeup."

"Yeah, I didn't think so."

She's staring at me again.

When did this woman get so fearless?

The minute I convince her I'm never going to kill her, suddenly she's the one trying to intimidate me.

"I didn't do it," I tell her, knowing what she's thinking, "but I went to see."

"Did you find what you were looking for?"

"Yes."

"Well, that's good." She pauses. "I think."

She shovels another bite into her mouth.

As much as I don't want to admit it, it's making me hungry.

But I'm not eating what she's eating.

Never doing that again.

"Look, let's go out for dinner."

"I'm wearing pajamas," she says. "Besides, I'm already eating."

"You can't change?"

"I could," she says, "but why can't we just stay in? I have class in the morning, and I'm already kind of tired, and the last time you and I ate somewhere... well, look what happened. I'm just not in the mood for another shoot out tonight."

"It wasn't a shoot out."

"What was it?"

"A drive-by."

She sighs loudly. "What's the difference, honestly?"

"I didn't shoot back."

She shakes her head, muttering, "Maybe you should've."

It takes a moment for those words to register.

I almost don't believe my own ears.

"What did you just say?"

"Nothing, just ignore me... I don't know what I'm saying." Sighing again, she tosses her bowl of noodles onto the counter, ignoring when some of them splash out, making a mess. "Maybe we should go get some food, but I get to pick the place."

Reaching into my pocket, I pull out my keys. "That's fine by me. Just let me put on a different shirt."

"Don't bother," she says. "I'm not changing."

I think she's joking.

Really, I do, because she's wearing a pair of my plaid lounge pants that are about three sizes too big for her. But instead of changing, she just slips on a pair of shoes and says, "Okay, let's go now."

I look her over before motioning toward the door. "After you."

Who am I to tell her what to wear?

We get in the car and I pull away from the house, waiting until I reach the end of the street before asking her which way I'm supposed to turn.

"Uh, depends," she says, looking both ways, her brow furrowed.

"On what?"

"On which way the closest *Wendy's* is. You don't happen know, do you?"

I just look at her.

Sighing dramatically, like I'm being irrational by not answering that question, she pulls out her phone and asks Siri, hitting a button when Siri answers to open up a map. "There, just follow those directions."

I do it, because I agreed to let her pick.

I don't like to go back on my word, not if I can help it.

So that's how, ten minutes later, I end up standing inside a busy little *Wendy's*, ordering French fries and a Frosty for Karissa and some kind of chicken sandwich for myself.

After I order, I stand there.

And I wait.

And I wait.

And I wait.

Karissa is sitting at a small plastic table, as I continue to stand here, about to lose my patience. I'm three seconds away from snapping when they slap my food down on a tray, shoving it toward the edge of the counter. I grab the tray and join Karissa at the table, watching as she snatches up the Frosty and immediately, without hesitation, dips a fry into it.

She eats it then.

I don't know what to say.

"What?" she says, noticing my expression. "Come on, you can't tell me you've never done it."

"I haven't," I say. "But then again, I don't make a habit of ordering ice cream with my dinner."

"You should. You don't know what you're missing." She grabs another fry and dips it into her Frosty before holding it out to me. "Here, try it."

My natural instinct is to deny her, not because I think it might be tampered with, but because it frankly sounds disgusting. But I'm turning over a new leaf here, and I've already ended up at a fast food restaurant with my wife in her pajamas.

Why not humor her?

I take a small bite, chewing slowly, as she pops the rest of it in her mouth.

It's not terrible.

It's just... chocolate.

And cold.

A chocolate, cold potato.

Okay.

I don't like it.

She laughs at my expression.

"You're such a snob," she says. "It's good!"

"Whatever you say."

I eat half of my sandwich before throwing the rest out. It's not that great, either. I could go for a steak, or maybe some lobster, or even some real chicken, but Karissa seems quite content with what she's eating.

It makes me think of what Melody said in the car.

When you've got nothing, I suppose you appreciate the little things so much more.

We head back to the car after she's finished, and once we're inside, she reaches over and grabs my hand. "Thank you."

"You're welcome," I say, "but next time, I pick."

Chapter Seven
Karissa

Security at the dorms was always worthless.

I can't count how many times Naz slipped in and out of the place undetected when I lived there. So I'm not at all surprised that I'm able to just walk right inside, bypassing check-in to head upstairs.

It's late morning and people are steadily coming and going. I've called Melody a few times only to get her voicemail. The damn thing doesn't even ring. She was supposed to meet me for coffee this morning, but she never showed up at the café.

Late night, I'm guessing, considering she was out on her date.

I pause in front of room 1313, quietly listening, but there are no sounds inside that I can hear. Tapping on the door, I hear some shuffling before it's opened, someone appearing in front of me. Red hair, dozens of freckles, and the angriest scowl I've ever seen greet me. The second she lays eyes on me, she literally grimaces, letting out a sound of disgust like she's actually repulsed by me.

What the fuck?

"Uh, hey... Kimberly." I think that's her name. "Is Melody here?"

"No."

No.

That's it.

No greeting.

No explanation.

Before I can say anything else, the door slams right in my face. I stare at it for a moment before shaking my head, turning to leave.

"Karissa?"

I glance up at the sound of the voice, locking eyes with Melody as she steps onto the floor from the elevator. Her hair is a rat's nest on top of her head. Old makeup streaks her face. She's still rocking my black dress.

Good ol' walk of shame.

"What are you doing here?" she asks, smiling sheepishly as she tugs on the dress, knowing damn well I notice she hasn't changed.

"I came to check on you," I say. "You stood me up this morning."

"Oh, shit!" Her eyes widen. "Coffee! I'm so sorry! I forgot!"

"No big deal." I motion toward her. "I can tell you were, uh... otherwise occupied."

Blushing... yet again... she grabs my arm and drags me back to the room, not offering a word in the way of explanation. She unlocks the door and waltzes in, yanking me inside behind her before shutting the door again. Kimberly is sitting at her desk and doesn't bother turning around as we enter, but I can see her back straighten like she's preparing for an attack or something. I plop down on Melody's messy bed, relaxing back on a pile of clothes, as Melody whips the dress off over her head, tossing it at me.

"I'm seriously so sorry," she says, rooting through her dresser drawers. "I would've never stood you up like that. It completely slipped my mind."

"It's fine. I just wanted to make sure you were all right."

"I'm more than all right," she says, snatching up a shirt and a pair of pants before turning to me. "I'm perfect. He's just... wow. He's perfect. He took me to dinner last night at Paragone... you know, that fancy ass place over near Central Park? Can you believe it? I've always wanted to eat there!"

Can I believe it?

I don't know.

I ate there once before.

Naz took me on our first date, I guess you could call it. He dropped thousands on tiny plates of food and crazy overpriced champagne. He had to intimidate the staff to get a table because they book up weeks in advance.

"Wow," I say. "How'd he get a reservation?"

"Who knows," she says, "but we showed up and there was one in his name! We ate and talked and laughed... and then we went back to his place and we slept."

"You... slept."

"Yes." She turns to look at me. "We both fell asleep. It was the first time in my life I just slept with a guy all night long, you know? No hanky-panky."

I seriously don't know what to say.

Boy crazy Melody Carmichael is standing in front of me, half naked, telling me she kept her clothes on last night?

"So you guys didn't, you know... do it?"

"Oh, pfft, of course. Fucked his brains out first thing this morning."

She laughs.

I just shake my head.

Kimberly, across the room, slams a book closed and runs her hands down her face.

Melody shoots her roommate a look, rolling her eyes, before focusing on me again. "So that was my night. I had to make the trek back here from Brooklyn looking just like this."

"Brooklyn?"

"Yeah, like, Bensonhurst or something. Took forever. Anyway, I'm going to take a quick shower. Don't go anywhere, okay?"

She doesn't give me time to respond before jetting off to the bathroom, leaving me here. I sit in silence, absently smoothing and folding the dress to occupy my time, as Kimberly shifts things around on her desk, arranging her books. She pulls one out of her bag, and I catch sight of the black and white cover. *History: A Definitive Guide.*

I have that book, too.

"Are you taking Rowan's class?"

The question is out of my mouth before I can even talk myself out of asking it. Kimberly continues what she's doing as she answers flippantly, "You sit three rows behind me."

"Oh."

I didn't notice.

I don't pay attention to my classmates.

I've been too busy trying to fly under the radar.

"He's a nice professor," I say, not sure what else I can say in response to that. "Better than most, anyway. I've definitely had worse."

She shoves her chair back, turning to look at me. The screech of the legs against the floor silences my babbling. The scowl is still on her face, but it's deeper now, etched with a stark sort of anger.

"Can we not do this?" she asks, motioning between us. "Can you stop trying to engage me in conversation like we're friends so I can pretend you're not here? It would make my life so much easier."

I blink a few times, balking at her tone. "Excuse me?"

"You heard me. It's bad enough I have to live in this hellhole with that… girl. I don't need whatever bad karma you bring on top of it."

I'm utterly flabbergasted.

Did she really just say that?

"Look, you don't even know me, so I'm not sure what I've done to make you—"

She laughs, cutting me off, but it's sort of a maniacal laugh, like the girl has a bit of Joker in her that's dying to come out. She's three seconds away from painting her fucking face and going after Batman.

"You can't be that stupid," she says. "Maybe you're a nice person, I don't know, but stuff happens when you're around, stuff I'd rather not happen in my life. Maybe it's all a coincidence, but maybe it's not. And people talk. The Reed girl, the last person to see Professor Santino alive. The girl whose roommate's boyfriend disappeared. The girl who was shot by a frickin' gangster last year. That stuff... it's not normal. It doesn't happen to normal people. So please, take whatever baggage you have elsewhere, because I'd rather not help you carry it."

She swings back around, going right back to her books, as if she hadn't just raked me over the damn coals. I stare at her, my stomach tied up in knots. I feel like I'm going to throw up.

Melody waltzes back in then, returning from the quickest shower she's ever taken, and is yammering away about something. I don't know. I'm not listening. I can't focus. My mind keeps replaying Kimberly's words.

People talk.

People talk about me?

"Earth to Karissa!" Melody snaps her fingers in my face. "Jesus, girl, what's been wrong with you lately? You always seem so far away!"

I glance at her.

I still don't know what to say.

A ringing shatters the silence, though, saving me from having to come up with some words yet. The room phone. Kimberly huffs, standing up and storming out, while Melody grabs the phone to answer it. "Room 1313."

The call only lasts a minute before she hangs up, telling whoever it is she'll be there in a minute.

"Package or something," she tells me, even though I didn't ask. She quickly finishes dressing and brushes her hair. "Walk with me downstairs?"

"Uh, yeah... I should get going, anyway."

"Right, you've got class."

"Yeah."

Melody continues her yammering on the way down to the lobby. I catch a few of the words—she's gushing about Leo. I smile and nod, trying to be a good friend. But is that even possible?

I don't know, honestly.

Because all those things Kimberly mentioned?

Definitely not a coincidence.

"Are you okay?" Melody asks, grabbing my arm to stop me when we reach the first floor and step off the elevator.

"Yeah, uh... I don't know." I shrug, because really, I don't know. I'm not an idiot. I'm not stupid. I know people gossip. But I've ever had someone blatantly bring it up. "Have you heard...? I mean, do people really talk about me?"

Melody stares at me in confusion before her expression shifts, a knowing look overcoming her face. I wouldn't call it pity. Melody isn't the kind of person to pity anybody. But it is sympathetic, like she knows exactly what I mean.

Like she's heard rumors.

"People are assholes," she says, waving it off. "They like to make up stories like this is *General Hospital* and Sonny Corinthos is out there running the streets. I don't even pay them any attention and you shouldn't either."

Easier said than done, I think.

She smiles, like she means what she says, and I smile back, because maybe she does. Regardless, I know I don't deserve a friend like Melody. She's better off without Paul in her life, sure, but that doesn't forgive me for my part in his absence. I didn't lay a finger on him, personally, but that doesn't make me innocent.

I walk with Melody to the front desk, where she flashes her school ID. The lady working, in turn, hands over a bouquet of white lilies. Melody squeals excitedly, flashing me the tag. No message written on it, just the words: *x, Leo*.

"What did I tell you?" Melody clutches them to her. "Perfect."

I leave her still basking in her post-date glow, telling her I need to get to class, but I stroll the opposite way instead, heading for the subway. I rarely take it home, because it's always so crowded, but I'm so much in my head I barely notice the others.

The front door is locked when I get home, but Naz's car is in its usual place in the driveway, so I'm guessing he didn't go anywhere. I let myself in, heading to the den, and find him sitting behind his desk, reading today's newspaper.

I'm starting to sense a pattern.

He looks up when I enter. "You're home early again."

I plop down on the couch, dropping my bag by my feet. "Is that a problem?"

"For me? No. For you? Maybe."

"Why?"

"All this skipping class can't be good for your grades," he says. "So I guess we'll see if it's a problem when report cards come in."

I laugh at that. "What are you going to do, ground me?"

"No, but I might spank you."

"Promise?"

He stares at me.

He's not laughing.

His eyes search my face, looking for something. I'm not sure what, but I don't think he sees it, because he folds his paper and sets it aside, leaning back in his chair to regard me. "Come here."

"Why?"

He cocks an eyebrow before repeating himself. "Come here."

Part of me wants to resist, simply because he ignored my question, but I don't have it in me at the moment. I get up and walk over to where he sits, scooting between him and the desk. I climb up on it, sitting down, my legs dangling. He continues to stare at me, like he knows something's wrong.

He probably does.

He doesn't ask me if I'm okay.

He doesn't have to.

"You're beautiful," he says, "even when you're not smiling."

It's so out of the blue that I can't help but smile at the

compliment. "Thank you."

He nods, his hands coming to rest on my calves. He strokes my legs through my jeans. "Do you want to talk about it?"

"Not particularly."

He nods, yet again, and that's the end of it.

His hands roam further up, caressing my thighs, before he reaches for the button of my jeans, easily undoing it. I wordlessly watch as he tugs down the zipper, his hand slipping right inside. My jeans are tight, barely giving him any access, but his fingertips still somehow manage to stumble upon my clit.

His fingers are magnetic, drawn right to it.

He rubs, and strokes, working instant magic, the kind that makes my toes curl and my skin tingle, setting my insides on fire. I close my eyes, tilting my head back, as the tiny jolts of pleasure ripple through my body, coursing up my spine. I don't know how the man does it, taking my body from zero-to-sixty in half a second flat. I lay back on the desk, almost falling off the thing when he yanks on my jeans, pulling them down.

One second it's his hand, the next it's his tongue, pressing flat against my aching clit, tasting me as he rids me of my clothes. I help him out, pulling them off and tossing them across the room, not caring when I'm completely naked and he's still fully clothed in his suit. I reach for his coat, to try to help him out of his, when he grabs my wrists and pins them to the desk.

"Relax," he whispers. "I've got this."

Who am I to argue?

I forgot what the hell I was about to do, anyway.

Because his mouth is on me once again, licking and sucking, his teeth grazing my skin. I'm writhing and moaning as he increases his pace. It takes me forever to get myself off, but somehow this man can accomplish it in seconds, like my body just knows it's all for him. I can feel the pressure building and building, faster than I know how to deal with. My heart is racing. My fists are clenching. My back is arching. A scream is building in my chest that I try to swallow back, to keep down, but I can't. I *can't*. I let it out, a rough, strangled cry, as orgasm rips through me, making my legs shake from the intensity of it.

I'm panting, clutching my breasts, my muscles like jelly beneath my skin. Opening my eyes, I instantly meet Naz's gaze as he stands there, leaning over me.

It's almost instinct as I wrap my legs around his waist, trying to draw him closer as my hands reach for him. His serious expression cracks with a small smile, and he grabs ahold of me, pulling me off the desk and onto his lap as he sits back down in his chair.

I'm straddling him.

He still has all of his clothes on.

Mine are God-knows-where.

His hands start at my hips and slowly run up my back before slipping around to the front. He palms my breasts, his thumbs stroking the nipples, as he stares at me. *Again*.

He makes no move to take it any further.

No indication that this is going anywhere.

"What was that for?" I ask, my voice still breathless.

He shrugs. "You looked like you could relieve a bit of stress."

That's an understatement, I think, but it certainly did the trick. The tension I've felt all morning has lessened. I almost feel at ease sitting here with him. Just the two of us. Just me and him. It's all still there, though, in the back of my mind, but for the moment I let go of the guilt over it all.

Guilt is an ugly thing.

It slowly eats away at your insides.

I wonder how Naz does it, how he makes it through his days without feeling the nagging sensation deep within him, the ugly reality of regret. Because he's done things... a hell of a lot more than I ever did. He ended lives. He took away futures. He destroyed dreams.

Hell, he almost murdered *me*.

But yet he gets up every morning and goes to bed again every night, and he survives the hours in between without ever buckling.

He's trying to be better, yeah, but I think, when it comes down to it, he's doing it for me. He's not doing it because he wants to repent for his actions. He's not doing it to make up for his sins. He's doing it not because he's tired of being the man he has been. He's doing it because he thinks it's what I need.

He wants to be a better man to ease my guilt for loving someone like him.

A leopard doesn't change its spots.

That's what Giuseppe said.

You can dress a wolf up in sheep's clothing, but the son of a bitch will still eat you alive if you let it.

Naz's hand shifts to the necklace around my neck. The pendant lies low, almost between my breasts. He rolls the small, round encased crystal between his fingertips, gazing at it. "You never take it off."

"No," I whisper, even though he hadn't actually asked it as a question. He knows I don't. He sees it on me every day. "Well, I mean, I take it off to shower, and when I go to sleep, but I put it right back on in the morning."

He's given me a lot, but the necklace has special meaning. I still remember the day vividly, the words he said to me after he fastened the necklace around my neck.

It could be like this all the time, Karissa, every moment of every day. I can give you the best of everything. You just have to let me.

Those words have stuck with me. Even when we were at odds with each other, I never forgot what he said. Because that night, for the first time in my life, I felt truly worth something. I felt like I mattered, like maybe I was somebody. And it's not because of a silly piece of jewelry, although, okay... it's gorgeous. It's because, even if he hadn't said the words that night, I truly felt loved.

Carpe Diem. The words are etched along the pendant. Tomorrow isn't a guarantee. Nothing's promised. So today? *Seize the Day.*

That's how Naz lives his life.

That's how I want to live it with him.

He glances at me, letting go of the necklace. "Let's go upstairs."

"Why?"

He cocks an eyebrow at me... again... but this time he answers that question. "Because you still feel a little tense. I think you've got some kinks we can work out, if you know what I mean."

I laugh, gripping onto him tightly as he stands up, clutching hold of me. Once he's upright, I drop down to my feet, pushing away from him.

"I could've carried you," he protests.

"Pfft, and have you throw out your back, old man? I don't think so."

"Ha-ha," he says, trying to grab a hold of me, but I slip away from his grasp. Laughing, I dodge through the doorway, heading for the stairs. I take them two at a time, grasping my breasts so the damn things don't bounce, almost out of breath when I reach the bedroom.

I can hear Naz as he comes upstairs, his footsteps measured, methodical, intentionally loud. The man is damn good at sneaking around, but he's making sure I hear him. He's taunting me.

Anticipation is a bitch.

He heads down the hallway, right for the bedroom, and pauses in the doorway.

Instinctively, I back up a few steps, toward the bed.

"You think you're funny, don't you?" he asks, taking a step toward me, not hesitating when I retreat some more.

"Maybe."

"Maybe," he repeats, pausing in front of the dresser, opening up the top drawer. Every muscle inside of me freezes up, my stomach in knots when he pulls out a thick leather belt. He wraps it around his fist as he turns back to me.

The look is on his face.

That look.

It has been a while since I've seen it, since he's looked at me that way. Since he let his guard down and let the monster come out to play.

It's thrilling.

Titillating.

Terrifying.

Maybe it's sick that I've missed this side of him, but I have. I've missed it. I haven't admitted that even to myself until now. There's something exciting about living on the edge, about inciting what I know he keeps buried inside of him. He's not going to hurt me. I know he isn't. But he's passionate and primal. *Ferocious.*

He steps closer.

And closer.

And closer.

I back up until I run into the nightstand, wedged right beside the bed. Naz stops in front of me, the tips of his black shoes against my bare unpainted toes, his body almost pressing against mine as he towers over me. He leans toward me, his face coming close to mine, the slight stubble of his jaw rubbing against my skin.

It's dead silent.

My heart is racing.

The thump-thump-thumping is all I hear.

"I was going to take it easy on you," he says, his voice low. "Lay you down on the bed and worship you, all day and all night. Kiss and caress every inch of you. Taste you with my tongue until you can't take anymore. And then I was going to give it to you, deep and slow... make you come over and over again, until all you can do is whimper, cry my name." His free hand, the one not clutching the belt, slowly ghosts along the front of my body, his fingertips brushing against my flushed skin. He runs the hand along my breasts before settling on my chest, over my heart. "You like it that way, don't you? Like when I make you feel all of my love."

I nod, tingles erupting all over. "Uh-huh."

"And I was going to love you right, remind you what it feels like to be cherished, to be idolized, to be treated like the queen you are. I was going to make *serious* love to you, baby." I let out a shaky breath, and before I can even inhale again, his hand shifts. It's a split second, barely a blink. His hand is around my neck, tightly squeezing, as he yanks me toward him, flush against him. "But now I think I'll just fuck you instead."

I gasp as he shoves me onto the bed, flipping me so I'm on my stomach. He easily pushes me around like I weigh nothing, an arm snaking around me, beneath me, and pulling my ass up into the air. I try to adapt quickly, my vision blurring from the adrenaline rushing through my veins. I push up on my hands and turn my head to look at him in just enough time to see him loop the belt together.

His eyes meet mine.

It can't be more than a few seconds.

Before I even realize what he's doing, he slips the belt down over my head. Gripping the end of it, he tugs, tightening it around my neck like a collar.

I gasp.

He tightens it more.

Oh fuck.

I can't breathe.

I can't breathe.

I try to grasp my neck, to loosen the belt, to give myself some fucking air, but it just tightens more every time I move. Five seconds. Ten seconds. A minute. A fucking eternity. My chest is burning, my eyes are watering, and I viciously start bucking, raising up on my knees. Before I can do much to fight him, Naz is shoving me back down against the bed, his grip on the belt loosening. I inhale sharply, desperately, barely able to take a breath before he pushes inside of me hard, knocking the air right out of me again.

I cry out as the force of his thrusts shove my face into the mattress. He holds onto the belt loosely, so I can feel it pressing on my throat, but he doesn't cut my airflow as he starts to fuck me brutally. He's still wearing his suit, and he tries to pull it off between thrusts, yanking his shirt open but not getting very far before giving up. His hand that isn't holding the belt digs into my hip as he holds me in place, keeping me from moving away.

Not that I would.

No, not today.

I'm pushing back against him, meeting his thrusts, grunting as he goes deeper and deeper, annihilating a part of me while still, he builds me up.

"You fucking love this, too, don't you?" he asks, his voice low, strained. "You don't need me to treat you like royalty to know what you mean to me. I can fuck you like this, fuck you like you're *nothing*, and you still know you're everything to me."

I want to answer him.

I want to tell him that's true.

But the words are lodged deep in my chest, blocked by the belt pressing against my throat. All that seems to make it through the barrier are grunts and cries, screams that sound like his name, as he fucks me.

And fucks me.

And fucks me so much I'm on the verge of trying to beg.

Beg for him to stop.

Beg for him to keep going.

Beg for him to fuck me into oblivion.

Beg for him to give me more... more... more.

I don't know how much time passes, or how many orgasms rip through me, before my entire body starts to tremble, while he continues to push inside of me. My breathing is labored, my heart hammering hard, as something inside of me seems to break and I give up. I stop fighting. I stop bucking. I give in and let him do what he wants. My body goes limp on the bed, while Naz's body grows taut.

The belt tightens around my neck, cutting off my airflow once more, as another orgasm tears through my spent body. Naz thrusts hard a few times before coming himself, growls echoing from his chest as he lets loose. The second he finishes, he completely stops, dropping the belt, letting it fall.

I inhale sharply, collapsing into the bed when he pulls out.

He sits there behind me, on his knees, not making a sound or even moving. I'm panting, still catching my breath, as I drown myself in the soft comforter. Holy shit, I can't move. I can't do anything but lay here.

My body is nothing but an aching ball of tingles.

I'm thoroughly fucked.

Literally.

Figuratively.

Who really knows?

After a moment, Naz tucks himself away before reaching over and undoing the belt, pulling it from around my neck. He climbs off the bed, and I hear his quiet footsteps crossing the room.

Rolling over, I look at him.

It baffles me how he looks so unruffled.

His shirt is open, sure, but that's all that's askew. I don't even think he broke a sweat. How the hell is that possible?

He puts the belt away before carefully stripping out of his clothes, tossing them aside, before joining me in bed again. Lying beside me, his hand makes its way to my neck, and I tense, but he doesn't squeeze.

He rough fingertips gently caress the skin.

"Probably shouldn't have done that," he says, thumb stroking my throat.

"Why?"

My voice is hoarse, laced with confusion.

"Because," he says, eyes meeting mine, "you're probably going to have to wear a turtleneck tomorrow."

I laugh lightly, reaching up to lay my hand on top of his. "Yeah, well, I'm afraid I don't own any of those. I don't think anybody does."

"I do."

I gape at him. "You do?"

He nods. "A black one."

"I, uh... what? How come I've never seen it?"

"Because I don't wear it," he says. "It's in my closet somewhere."

I've scoured that closet and stolen clothes.

I can't believe I've never noticed it before.

"Why am I not surprised?" I mutter. "I mean turtlenecks were all the rage long ago... you know, when you were my age."

He squeezes my neck playfully as he glowers at me, and I laugh. He gets so worked up when I pick on his age.

"Keep it up," he says, "and I might end up spanking you before this day is over."

Rolling my eyes, I scoot over in the bed, moving closer to him. He wraps his arms around me, pulling my head onto his chest. Neither of us says anything else for a while. Silence overtakes the room. It isn't long before I'm lost in my head again, thinking about everything.

"Do you ever feel guilty?" I ask eventually, curiosity getting the best of me. Okay, maybe I do want to talk about it.

"Guilty about what?"

"Everything," I say. "*Anything*."

He pauses before saying, "Why are you asking?"

"I don't know," I say. "I guess I'm just wondering."

"You're wondering if I feel bad about the things I've done."

"Yes."

He's quiet again.

I don't really need him to answer.

That silence tells me everything.

"If I had the chance, I might do some things different," he says finally. "But most of it, I'd probably still do. Do I feel guilty? No, not really. I don't think I have it in me to feel that kind of remorse."

That response doesn't surprise me.

It's about what I expected to hear.

Chapter Eight
Ignazio

Joseph Gladstone.

They call him Fat Joe.

That's all I really know about the man in front of me—his name—but it's more than enough. Armando dug up an address where I could find the guy, which—lucky for him—turned out to be credible. I don't know when he was born or where he's from, don't know if he has a family or if he lives alone, don't know how much money he makes or if he even has any in the bank. Don't know, and don't care, because at the end of the day, it doesn't make a difference.

All that matters, frankly, is that he somehow crossed the wrong path, walked the wrong line, and offended the wrong man.

Me, namely.

But poor Joe doesn't know that yet.

He doesn't know I'm watching him.

He doesn't know I've been following him.

Waiting for the perfect moment to strike.

He walks leisurely, like he's got nowhere to be, like he isn't afraid of anything out on these streets. And maybe he isn't. I'm certainly not. But he should be.

It's nearing midnight on a Wednesday. Karissa is at home, in bed, asleep, oblivious that I'm even out here, picking up old habits, prowling the streets. If I'm lucky, she won't wake up until morning, won't even know I left the comfort of our bed to come out here and do this.

Do something I told her I wasn't doing anymore.

The kind of thing good men don't do to other people.

Stepping out of my car, I quietly shut the door, keeping my head down as I follow Joe down the mostly barren street. He walks this route almost every night at this time... every time I've been out here, anyway. I'm not sure where he's going. I never stick around that long to see. He leaves a shitty little apartment above a small grocer in the Lower Eastside and cuts down a few side streets on his way to a park over by the East River.

Tonight, he's not going to make it there.

He cuts down the first alley, and I'm right on his heels. He doesn't notice me in the shadows, doesn't hear my footsteps until it's too late. He starts to turn around, sensing my presence, words on the tip of his tongue that barely break through from his lips when I hit him.

I punch him.

Son of a bitch, his face hurts my fist.

It stuns him but he doesn't drop. Not fat, like his nickname suggests, but the man is massive. It catches him off guard enough to give me the upper hand. I put him in a chokehold, cutting his airflow, strangling him.

He fights.

He's strong.

I can barely keep my grip on him.

He claws at my clothes, trying to hit me, trying to break free. His eyes bulge, his face turning bright red as he panics. He knows he's in trouble. *A lot* of trouble.

"You're lucky I don't feel like killing anyone today," I tell him as he starts to fade.

Once he's out cold, I let him drop.

He hits the alley hard, banging his head on the asphalt. A nagging feeling claws at me, taunting me, urging me to finish it. To kill him. I should. I could. Part of me obviously wants to. And as I stare down at him, I almost do it. Wouldn't be hard.

It's never that hard.

I'm just here to send a message. To let them know I'm not just rolling over and taking it. If I wanted him, I could have him, but this pathetic coward isn't worth getting more blood on my hands.

Less than a minute and I'm turning to stroll away, heading back out of the alley. I make it a few steps, no more than ten, before I hear something behind me, the sound of a running engine.

A car is pulling into the alley at the other end.

I toss a quick look that way. It's all black, small... looks like a BMW. I can't make out much of it in the darkness. The lights are blacked out.

It's trying not to be seen.

I hurry my steps as I turn back around, needing to leave.

I make it barely another five, almost to the end of the alley, when another car whips in right in front of me, so close I have to make a quick retreat, a few steps back, to keep it from ramming me. My heart stalls in my chest, stalls at the identical black car with the blacked out lights and tinted windows facing me.

I'm blocked in.

I know it instantly then.

And I'm pissed. I'm fucking *pissed*.

Because I wasn't the only one sneaking around tonight.

Wasn't the only one watching, stalking, waiting for the perfect moment.

I'm pissed I didn't catch it sooner, that I didn't realize I was being followed, too.

I freeze right where I am, slipping my hands into my pockets as I stare down the car, not letting the fact that I'm alarmed show.

Never let them see your fear... it's rule number one. And it's not that I'm afraid. No, I'm not.

I don't fear death.

I've already died too many times before.

I'm a cat with nine lives and I'm already on number twelve. I'm living on borrowed time. When death wants to take me, it'll take me.

But I'm so pissed that I'm off my game, pissed that I might not be able to kill whoever is in that car before they can kill me, and that's just unacceptable. If I die, you can be goddamn sure I'm taking everyone around me out, too.

Everyone that might ever try to go after *her*.

Three of the car doors open—both front and the rear passenger. Three men step out, stalling right where they stand, shielded by the doors. I don't recognize any of them, not that I expected to. They look like the typical roughnecks who run in our circles, dressed in all black, a leather jacket thrown in here and there. Dark hair, dark features... Italian, obviously, or close enough to pass as one. I don't see any weapons, but that doesn't mean they're not carrying.

Men like that don't leave home without a gun.

The fourth door opens after a moment, another man appearing. The second I lay my eyes on him, a sense of familiarity hits me.

Son of a bitch.

I know him.

He's older than I remember, but I suppose I'm much older now, too. It's been almost two decades since we crossed paths, an entire lifetime, but I would never forget a face that fucked up.

I get it now, why they call him *Scar*.

I almost laugh at the absurdity of it.

A grotesque jagged scar runs the whole way down the right side of his face, slicing through his eye. It's discolored, a lighter shade of blue than the other. He's blind in it, has been for as long as I've known him, but it has never gotten in his way. His other senses make up for it. He's a stealthy motherfucker.

He ought to be.

I taught him a lot of what he knows.

He learned how to survive by watching me.

He strolls toward me... saunters, really. The bastard has not an ounce of fear or alarm written on him anywhere. His eyes burrow right through me as he approaches, and he pauses a foot to my right, hesitating, as his gaze trails over me, like he's sizing me up. He's assessing.

He steps past then, walking down the alley behind me. I don't move my body, but I do turn my head, watching as he approaches Joe lying on the asphalt, bleeding from where he hit his head.

"Friend of yours?" I ask.

Lorenzo shakes his head as he kneels down beside the guy. "He's still alive."

He glances at me as he says that, raising his eyebrow.

"For now," I say.

"For now," he repeats, turning back to Joe. Shaking his head again, he stands back up and starts toward me. "It's been a long time, Ignazio."

"It has."

"It's good to see you."

"I wish I could say the same."

He laughs at that.

I'm not surprised.

Most people probably find him charming, even alluring, despite the scar on his face. He can be so charismatic, so manipulative, that they overlook it. But me? I know a predator when I see one. I can spot one a mile away. There's nothing innocent about the guy, nothing harmless about his intentions. He draws you right into his web with every intention of trapping you for life.

For however long, it is, he decides to let you live.

I told Karissa before that I wasn't the most dangerous thing out there, and I hadn't been lying. Because him? The one they call Scar?

He might just be the worst of the bunch.

Lorenzo Gambini.

When Genova said he was from the south, he'd meant it.

Florida.

Kissimmee.

"Oh, don't be that way," Lorenzo says, stopping beside me again. "We're friends, are we not?"

"I have no friends."

"None at all?"

"None, and you know that," I say. "There are no friends in this business. There are only people who need you, until the day comes when they don't need you anymore."

He smiles at that. "Ever the cynical one."

"More like realistic."

"It's nice to see you haven't changed," he says, slapping me on the back, hard, making me take a step from the force of it. My hair bristles in response, my hands clenched into fists in my pockets. If he doesn't stop touching me... "But I still think you and I could be friends... or at least the kind of people who need each other for the long haul. You get me?"

I get him.

I get exactly what he's saying.

He can dress it up in pretty words like 'friends' but I'm not stupid.

He wants me to do something for him.

I knew it was only a matter of time.

"I'm of no use to you," I say. "I'm not in the business anymore."

He laughs yet again as he motions down the alley. "Looks to me like you're still hard at work. Or, wait, is this personal? More quests for revenge? Pray tell, who killed your wife this time?"

I don't even think about it.

The second I hear those words, I react.

I lunge toward him, but he's quick, like he expected this reaction from me. Hell, he probably did. He takes a step back, holding his hands up defensively, as I grab the front of his shirt, yanking him back toward me. In an instant, guns are cocked, all three guys standing guard whipping them out and aiming. Lorenzo stares at me, looking more amused than anything, while I fight to keep from pummeling him in the face.

"Testy," he says, prying my hands off of him. He straightens his shirt, smoothing the wrinkles from it. He's not dressed like the rest of them. He's dressed like he's nobody. Jeans and a t-shirt. Makes it easier to blend into crowds that way. Casually, Lorenzo motions toward the guys, telling them to lower their guns. They listen to his silent order, no hesitation. "You always did have a bit of a temper, Ignazio."

"Cut the bullshit," I tell him. "Tell me what you want from me."

He shrugs, taking a few steps back. "I told you... I just want to be friends, but if you don't want to be my friend, so be it."

"So, what, you're going to kill me? If that's your end game, Lorenzo, I'm right here. There's no reason to put it off. You got me. But do it now, if you're going to do it, because I'm not playing these games with you."

He ignores that, turning around to walk back to the car. Pausing by the door, he glances at me, his expression serious for the first time since stepping out of the thing minutes ago. "You told me something a long time ago, something that stuck with me. You said, 'if you're not standing by my side, you're just standing in my way.' So I stood by your side then, Ignazio, and it'll do you well to remember that."

He gets in the car, shutting the door. Seconds later, the others follow suit. The car pulls out of the alley, gunning it to speed down the street as the car on the opposite side of the alley does the same, disappearing.

I don't hesitate.

I've already been here for far too long.

Any longer and Joe will be awake.

Ducking my head, I make a speedy exit, heading back toward my car. I leave the neighborhood, my gloved hands clutching the steering wheel tightly, my knuckles hurting from the strain. I have half a mind to track Lorenzo down right now, to kill him in his sleep for even thinking of talking to me that way, to even think of sneaking up on me, but I know I can't. I shouldn't.

He's on guard. He's surrounded.

There's no way I'm getting close to him.

Not tonight, anyway.

Besides, he could've killed me, but he didn't, which means he wants something from me, something to make him value my existence, but I'm not deluded to think it has anything to do with sentiment. Despite what he might claim, Lorenzo doesn't have friends, either.

He wouldn't bat an eyelash if I died.

He wouldn't even hesitate to pull the trigger.

It's after one in the morning when I make it home. I tread lightly heading inside, making sure to be quiet, but the dog hears me the second I step through the door. He appears right there in the foyer, his hair bristling, a low growl rumbling his chest.

"Don't start with me," I mutter as I head to the den, pulling off my gloves, tossing them on my desk. He follows me, stalling in the doorway. "I've dealt with enough shit tonight. I don't need you hassling me on top of it."

"Me or the dog?"

Her voice is close.

Too damn close.

I didn't even notice her in here.

My eyes glance across the room, at where Karissa sits on the couch in the darkness. Her bare feet are propped up on the coffee table as she eats from a small carton of Ben & Jerry's ice cream, wearing nothing but a too-big t-shirt.

"The mutt," I say, strolling over and sitting down beside her. "I married you, so it's sort of your job to give me a hard time."

"Good to know." She points her spoon at me before scooping up a big chunk of whatever the chocolaty flavor is she's eating. "You were gone for a while. I woke up and you know... you weren't here. Wasn't sure where you ran off to."

"I didn't expect you to wake up," I admit. "Had something to take care of."

"And did you get it taken care of?"

"I did."

She nods and continues to eat her ice cream.

She doesn't ask me to elaborate.

Doesn't ask anything else about where I've been.

I can feel the tension, though. I've felt it coming off of her since yesterday when she got home. It's like a wall surrounding her, one I'm not sure how I'm supposed to break through.

"I'll tell you," I say, "if you really want to know."

She pauses eating, slowly pulling the spoon from between her lips. "I know you will."

She still doesn't ask.

Smart girl.

Sighing, she discards the spoon in the nearly empty carton and sets it down on the coffee table. Tugging the shirt down over her knees, she tucks her legs up toward her on the couch, wrapping her arms around them. She lays her head down on her knees, facing my way. Her eyes are cautious as they scan me. "Maybe we should move."

"If that's what you want."

"But I want you to want it, too."

"I've got what I want," I say. "I've got you. I couldn't care less where we live, whether it's here in New York or halfway around the world. So if you want to move, we'll move. I go where you go."

I don't know if she likes my answer.

It's true, yeah, but it's no help with her decision.

"Is there anywhere we can even go where I'll be able to sleep all night without you slipping out to *handle things*?"

I shrug. "Alaska."

"Alaska?"

"I'd never leave the house. It's too cold up there. My balls might shrivel up."

She laughs.

Her laugh is one I love.

It's soft and feminine and completely genuine.

"That would be tragic."

"Tell me about it. I kind of need those things."

"Well, there's always Nevada. California. Ohio. Florida."

"Not Florida."

"No?"

"I'm not a fan."

She regards me cautiously again. "Maybe we should just stay right here."

"If that's what you want."

"I don't know," she says. "I don't know what I want."

"Let me know when you figure it out."

She rolls her eyes, standing up and grabbing her carton. "I'll be sure to do that."

Reaching out, I grasp her arm, stopping her before she can walk away from me. "I'm trying, Karissa. I don't know what more I can do."

"I know," she says. "It's not that."

"Then what is it?"

She hesitates, like she's considering not answering, before she lets out a resigned sigh. "Do you think I'm a bad person?"

Out of everything in the world she could've said, that wasn't even on my list of possibilities. I'm stunned to even hear her ask that. Her? A bad person? "Of course not. Why would you even think that?"

"Because I'm here."

Her answer is automatic. Her panicked expression tells me she didn't mean to say it out loud.

"Because you're with me," I elaborate for her, "and because I'm a bad man."

"No, I didn't mean—"

I pull her to me, silencing her before she can even try to explain herself away. It's pointless. I know what she means. I don't need her to backtrack about her feelings. "Look, I make no apologies for who I am, or for what I've done, but none of that is a reflection on you. The fact that you love me doesn't make you like me."

"But what if I am like you?"

"You're not."

"But—"

"You're not," I say again. "You love a sinner. If anything, that makes you a saint."

She smiles, leaning down to kiss me softly. "I'm heading to bed, Naz."

"Is that your way of getting out of this conversation?"

"Maybe," she says, before whispering, "good night."

Chapter Nine
Karissa

"Did you know... and this might be shocking... but Napoleon Bonaparte wasn't short at all?"

A few people murmur in response to Rowan's declaration, but most, like me, are just listening in silence. While I'll give him credit, he's a more interesting professor than most, there's only so much he can do to excite us about the Napoleonic Wars.

"He was actually, by modern measurements, just shy of five feet seven inches, so he was as tall as I am," he continues. "The rumor likely got started for a few reasons, one being he's listed at only five-two on his death certificate, but those were French increments. He was actually above average height of his time, but he surrounded himself with much taller guards, which just made him look smaller. Fascinating, isn't it?"

Fascinating?

Not the word I'd use, but whatever floats his boat.

Class is over, technically, and people around me are packing up to leave, but the professor is still speaking, clearly passionate about the subject.

"For next Tuesday, I'd like a paper on why his height even matters. Two pages, double spaced!"

That gets a reaction from everyone, but it isn't a good one.

Honestly, I don't know why any of it matters.

Short, tall, big, small... it doesn't make him any less of a dick.

People are already jetting out the door when I slip my history book into my bag. My attention is fixed three rows in front of me, to the redheaded nightmare packing up her things. She looks all around me, making a point to never look at me, like maybe if ours eyes don't meet she can pretend I don't exist on the same plane as her. It's childish. Ridiculous. *Rude*.

It's probably exactly what I'd do in her shoes.

I'm almost the last one out of the classroom today. It's uncharacteristically warm, and I've been sweating all morning.

It probably doesn't help that I'm wearing a thick black scarf.

It was the only thing I had to cover the faint bruise along my throat. I tried using makeup, but well, I've never been good at matching skin tones. It was like drawing a freaking bull's-eye right on my neck.

So scarf it was.

Strolling outside, I pause in front of the building, considering my options. I've got another class in a little over an hour, so as usual, I've got a bit of time to waste.

Honestly, I kind of want to just go home and say to hell with it.

I'm not really sure what's gotten into me, if people are all up in my head or if I'm just too exhausted to really care. I feel like I'm just going through the motions with no real direction, having no idea what I want to do when I grow up.

I'm supposed to declare a major soon.

I'm nowhere near ready for that kind of responsibility.

Getting married was an easier commitment.

I start to walk away, to do just that—leave—when I catch sight of Melody in the distance, heading this way from class. She's not alone today, no... someone's right beside her, holding her hand.

Leo.

I stay right where I am, waiting, as they approach.

Jesus, he's even prettier up close.

Melody notices me standing here and dodges right for me, dragging Leo behind her. He laughs, seeming confused for a moment, before he notices me, too. The confusion melts from his face, replaced with some sort of understanding that tells me he knows exactly who I am without needing an introduction.

He gets one, though… Melody makes sure of it.

"Kissimmee!" She yanks me into a hug, still holding onto Leo, so we're in some awkward ass triangle embrace that only Melody would think is acceptable. "This is Leo… Leo, this is my best friend, Karissa."

"Nice to meet you," Leo says, holding his free hand out toward me. I stare at it for a moment before shaking it weakly. "I've heard a lot about you."

"I was afraid of that," I mutter, pulling away.

Melody laughs, nudging me. "It was all good, promise."

"It was," Leo agrees.

"Well, in that case, it's nice to meet you, too."

"We were just heading to grab some coffee," Melody says, smiling radiantly. "You want to join us?"

"I shouldn't…"

"You should," Leo chimes in.

I shrug, conceding, not wanting to be rude. "Sure, I guess."

I walk with them the few blocks to the café, feeling like one hell of third wheel, as the two of them stroll hand-in-hand, touchy-feely the entire way.

It's nice, though, seeing her look so happy.

"I'll grab the drinks," Leo says as soon as we arrive, pulling his hand away from Melody's. "You two find us some seats."

"I can get my own," I say.

"Nonsense," he replies.

Nonsense.

I hear that word all the damn time.

It's one of Naz's favorites.

I start to protest some more, because he doesn't need to buy my coffee when he doesn't even know me, and besides, I'm not entirely sure how Naz would feel about another guy fronting a bill for me, but Melody yanks on my arm, pulling me toward a small table over along the side, not letting me fight it. I grumble, sliding into the chair across from her, saying something about paying him back that she completely ignores.

Typical.

"By the way, I totally nailed the test the other day," she says. "Only fucked up one question."

"The philosophy one?"

"Yep."

"See? You were worried for nothing."

She shrugs, nodding at the same time, like she's agreeing but doesn't want to admit I was right. Leo returns then, juggling two coffees and a small chocolate mint tea. He sets the warm tea in front of me and I glare at it while he settles into his seat beside Melody.

"Problem?" he asks hesitantly. "That's what you drink, right?"

"Yeah, it is." I glance at him suspiciously. "How did you know?"

He seems taken aback by my question and just stares at me, while Melody chimes in, waving it off. "He just said like two minutes ago that he's heard a lot about you, which means he's probably heard everything about you by now. We've come here a few times. I've mentioned how you drink that pissy chocolate thing."

"Oh."

"I may have also mentioned how scarf-y you usually are," she says, motioning my way. "Jesus, it's like, eighty fucking degrees out today. Aren't you hot?"

Reaching up, I run my fingertips along the scarf. "No."

I'm lying. Obviously.

I'm sweating like a pig.

The heat radiating from my drink sure isn't helping.

It feels like a sauna in this place.

Ugh, I think I might be running a fever...

She shrugs it off, like she believes what I'm saying, and turns her attention on Leo. *Thank God.* I sit in silence, watching the two of them converse, a natural ease between them as they talk and laugh. I don't drink my drink. I don't really know why. The thought of doing so almost nauseates me.

Five.

Ten.

Fifteen minutes.

I don't know.

They're encased in a bubble of whatever the hell it is that's radiating off the two of them. I don't know that I'd call it love, since it's still so brand new, but there's certainly a healthy dose of lust mingling with something bigger. Something more.

Hell, maybe it *is* love.

What do I know?

I fell in love the moment I laid eyes on Naz outside of Santino's classroom.

I didn't know it then, but it happened.

It happens.

So maybe it happened to them, too.

A ringing phone shatters the moment, the sound of Tupac blaring through the café. *Amitionz Az a Ridah.* My eyes instantly settle on Melody, but she makes no move to answer whatever's ringing. No, beside her Leo fumbles in his pocket instead, pulling out a gold iPhone. He glances at the screen of it, frowning, before pressing a button on the front. The song instantly cuts off as he brings the phone to his ear. "Yeah."

I'm stunned.

Absolutely flabbergasted.

Somebody other than Melody is still rocking Tupac.

That was always her thing.

"Did you do that?" I ask quietly, waving toward his phone, as he turns away from us, not getting up, but definitely muffling his conversation. Not that it matters, you know, considering all he's doing is a lot of agreeing with whatever the person on the line is saying. *Uh-huh. Yeah. Okay. Sure.*

He's so damn... agreeable.

"What?" Melody asks, glancing at me before laughing. "Oh, no... wasn't me. It's actually how we met, if you can believe it. I was walking by him one day over in Washington Square. His phone started ringing. I started signing. The rest is sort of history."

"Oh, I figured you met him in class or something."

"Nah, he doesn't go to NYU."

"Where does he go?"

"Wherever he wants to go, I guess, since he isn't in school."

"He's not? What does he do, then?"

"Whatever he wants," she says. "Right now, he's sort of just working with his brother."

"What does his brother do?"

"Oh, uh... I don't know. It's a family business or something. He's just doing odd jobs for him to make a bit of money."

So many red flags are going up I'm surprised I can see past them.

This all sounds familiar... so, so familiar.

He's practically unemployed, doing odd jobs to help out family, yet he can afford a meal at Paragone? Either he's a trust fund baby with a heart of gold or his dealings aren't exactly above board.

Ugh, I don't know what to think.

He couldn't be, could he?

"Alright, alright, yeah... give me a few minutes." Leo hangs up his phone, slipping it in his pocket. His focus turns back to us, and he smiles, but there's something off about it. I don't know if I'm just being paranoid, after everything that has happened, or if he's really acting the way I think. Either way, my hair bristles when I look at him. "Ladies, I hate to jet, but I have some things I need to go handle for my brother."

Melody frowns. "Will I see you later?"

"Of course," he says as he stands, leaning over to press a quick kiss to her forehead. "I'll call you." He turns to me, nodding. "Nice finally meeting you, Karissa. We'll have to hang out again sometime."

"Yeah," I say. "I'm sure it'll happen."

He's gone, just like that, giving a brief look back before disappearing.

Melody sighs once he's out of sight. "So?"

"So?"

"So what do you think?"

What do I think?

I'm not sure that's something she's open to hearing.

Not yet, anyway.

"I think you like him," I say, "a lot more than I've ever seen you like anybody."

Her smile grows. "I think you're right."

"How much do you really know about him, though? I mean... who is he, really?"

A cloud of confusion takes over her face. "What?"

"I'm just saying, you know, you haven't known him long..."

"It feels like I have, though," she says, shrugging. "It feels like I've known him my whole life. There's just so much about him that seems... familiar."

"I know the feeling," I mutter.

"I'm not trying to sound cliché or whatever, but when I look at him, I feel like I'm looking at myself... like, a part of me. You know?" She laughs. "Ugh, I sound like a damn Nicholas Sparks romance novel."

"He actually writes tragedies," I point out. "They call it romance, but someone usually always dies, and that's sure as shit not where this is going..."

I don't think, anyway.

Ugh, God, please don't let it be.

I don't want our lives to be a damn Nicholas Sparks story.

"Really?" She grimaces. "How is that romantic?"

"I don't know. I guess it can be, if you're dying for someone you love, or someone loves you even knowing you're going to die. It's selfless, sacrificing yourself for someone else, so someone you love doesn't have to suffer as much as they might otherwise."

"Wow, that's..." She pauses. *Loving? Compassionate? Noble?* "Morbid."

Morbid.

"That's one way to put it." I laugh. "It's kind of like the Plank of Carneades."

"The plankton of *what*?"

"The Plank of Carneades," I repeat. "Jesus, you're in your fourth semester of philosophy and I still know more than you do about it."

She makes a face, sticking her tongue out.

"It's a thought experiment," I continue. "If two people are shipwrecked and there's one board floating in the water, big enough to hold only one person, so only one of them lives, who gets it?"

"Kate Winslet," she says right away. "Didn't you see the movie? Hello! Pre-Dad Bod DiCaprio, remember?"

I laugh. *Titanic.* Of course her mind went there. Mine had, too.

"And didn't you think that was romantic?" I ask. "The fact that he gave it to her, that he let her have it, knowing he was going to die in the water because he did?"

"It was stupid," she says. "I would've pushed that bitch right off and took it."

"No, you wouldn't have."

"Uh, yeah, have you seen *You, Me, & Dupree*? The movie? Absolutely terrible. We'd all have been better had she not been around to make it."

I stare at her. Is she serious? I can't tell if she's being serious. "You know that wasn't her, right?"

"Of course it was."

"No, that was Kate Hudson, not Kate Winslet."

She waves me off. "What's the difference?"

What's the difference?

Seriously?

"They're different people," I say. "Like, they're not even the same person at all."

"Are you sure?"

"Uh, yeah... positive."

"Huh... and which one was in *Almost Famous*?"

"Hudson."

"Well, what the hell has Winslet done?"

"Plenty," I say. "*Eternal Sunshine of the Spotless Mind*, for one."

Her brow furrows. "Isn't that a Dr. Seuss book?"

"I just..." I think she's serious. Like, honestly serious. "I don't even know what to say to that."

"Me, either," she says. "But you know, like Dr. Seuss said, we all make mistakes, so I guess we can forgive hers."

"I don't think he said that," I point out. "I don't think Dr. Seuss said *we all make mistakes*."

"How do you know? He's been alive for like, a hundred years... I'm sure he probably said it at some point."

There's so much wrong with what she's saying that I'm not sure where to begin, so I don't even bother trying to correct her. It's not like it matters, anyway. We've gotten so off topic that I can't remember what the hell we were talking about to begin with.

"I should get going," I tell her, shoving my chair back to stand up. "I'm going to be late for class if I don't get out of here."

"Boo... you sure you can't skip? We hardly get to hang out anymore."

"I skipped it last time," I say, "and one day last week."

"Well, what are you doing this weekend?"

"I don't know... the usual, I guess."

Sitting at home.

Doing nothing.

"Let's go out," she says, her expression brightening. "We can go to Timbers. It'll be just like old times! Oh my God, I think it's even eighties night!"

I want to argue.

I try to argue.

I try to tell her it's the worst idea in the world, the two of us going to Timbers again, especially on eighties night. I remember what happened last time, and although things have worked out since then, I certainly don't want a repeat of that night. But she doesn't give me a chance, doesn't let me get in a word edgewise. She's already on her feet, planning, giving me a quick hug as she rushes toward the exit.

"I'll call you," she says excitedly. "I can't wait!"

Sighing, I watch her disappear from the café. Picking up my still warm, untouched drink, I walk over to the trashcan, dumping the thing in. Pity, you know, wasting it, but I've got a feeling in the pit of my stomach I can't quite shake.

If Naz taught me anything, it's that sometimes coincidences aren't really coincidences.

Sometimes they're orchestrated.

My entire life was chaos growing up.

New places, new faces, never the same thing twice. We were on the run from the day I was born until the day I finally put my foot down and moved to the city, wanting nothing more than to actually experience New York. I craved stability. I was desperate to find something of my own.

I have it now.

I have those things.

I have permanency. I have somewhere to call home.

I have a routine.

But sometimes, I realize, that's really fucking boring.

Don't get me wrong... I love the life we're building.

And, God help me, I certainly love Naz, too.

But there's something to be said about predictability, about rarely being surprised anymore. Naz has become a creature of habit. Hell, maybe he was always this way. I don't know. But when I come home from class, he's always here, sitting in the den, reading the day's newspaper. He's always wearing the same black suit. His hair always looks the same. He never has the TV on, never listens to music, which okay, is probably a good thing if what he'd listen to is Hotline Bling.

But doesn't he get bored of things just always being the same?

It's like I'm living out *Groundhog Day*.

"Anything interesting today?"

His gaze flickers to me when I ask that question before he turns back to his newspaper.

"More of the same," he says. "Corrupt politicians... tax evaders... bomb threat in a school. A pub caught on fire in the meatpacking district. The New York Rangers are actually doing good. A man shot his lover's husband in Harlem. Oh, and a guy was found unconscious near the East River."

"Awesome," I deadpan.

He closes the newspaper, folding it up, and tosses it right in the trashcan beside his desk. "What about you? Anything interesting happen today?"

I drop my bag to the floor beside the couch. "I met Melody's new boyfriend."

"She has a new boyfriend?"

I look at him incredulously.

And he accuses me of not paying attention.

"Uh, yeah, remember? She was here getting ready for her date."

"I remember," he says. "I was just unaware it was that serious. You can date without being in a relationship. In fact, I took you out a few times before you were anything more to me than just a date."

"I was never a date," I tell him as I plop down on the couch. "I was more of a target."

"And I hit my mark, didn't I?"

"Depends on who you ask."

"I'm asking you."

"Then sure." I unzip my bag to pull my work out. "You hit it."

"Over and over again."

I shake my head, deciding not to respond to that.

I know a sexual innuendo when I hear one.

Turning on the TV for some kind of background noise, I grab my things for History class and settle in to write my paper, to get it over with, before I forget about it. Napoleon Bonaparte, average-sized dictator with one hell of a complex. I skim through some sections in my book, nearly dozing off at the boring text, before resorting to searching him on my phone, looking for something even remotely interesting.

"So, tell me about him."

"Uh, he probably wasn't afraid of cats, even though some people seem to think so," I mumble, scrolling through some Wikidepia-esque website, "and God help us, but apparently he wrote a romance novel or something."

Naz is silent for a moment. "He wrote a romance novel."

"Yeah," I say. "Or I guess it's more of a short story, since it's only like, twenty pages. I don't know. I don't even know what to do with that information."

"Me, either," Naz says. "And is this literal cats you're talking about, or are you speaking metaphorically about pussy?"

Whoa. That gets my attention.

I blink a few times, glancing over at Naz. "What?"

"Is he afraid of pussy?"

"Oh, uh…" I grimace. "I'm gonna say no, since he had some kids."

That seems to surprise him. "He has children?"

"Yeah, a couple."

"And Melody's okay with that?"

"Melody? Why would she care?"

"Well, he is her boyfriend, isn't he?"

My brow furrows. "What are you talking about?"

"The fact that children are a big deal," he says. "No offense, but that doesn't seem like the type of responsibility your friend is prepared to take on."

I just stare at him.

He stares right back, waiting for some kind of response about Melody raising children. *Yeah, right.* I don't even know how she keeps up with herself.

"I think we're talking about two different people here," I say eventually. "I'm talking about Napoleon Bonaparte. I'm thinking that isn't who you mean."

He laughs. "No. You said you met her boyfriend today."

"Oh, yeah, right…"

"Why are you talking about Napoleon?"

I hold up my book and the blank piece of paper, showing it to him. "I have to write a paper about why anyone gives a crap about how tall he was."

"Huh."

Huh.

That word can get so annoying.

"You got a theory on why that is?" I ask. "If so, I'm all ears."

He shrugs. "It's all about perception."

"Perception."

"Yes," he says, getting up from his desk and strolling across the room, to his bookshelves. "His short stature sort of made him a joke, a caricature in a sense… a tiny man compensating for his shortcomings by trying to take over the world. It's hard to take him seriously when he's viewed that way. It's emasculating. Is he really that intimidating if he's characterized as looking like a child? *Hardly.*" He pauses, scanning the spines of a row of books. "But it's vastly different when you find out he was just an average guy. Because that makes him less of a toddler throwing a tantrum and more of a mastermind hiding in plain sight. His enemies didn't want that. They didn't want him taken seriously, and still, to this day, he often isn't. But the fact is, Napoleon was one of the greatest military leaders of all time, but that's often overshadowed by the debate about his height."

Tossing my phone down on the cushion beside me, I dig in my bag for a pen. "You want to repeat all that so I can write it down?"

"I'm sure you got the gist of it."

He pulls a small book off of his shelf before walking over to where I'm sitting. He taps me on the head with it, smiling, and drops it onto my lap, right on top of my paper.

I glance down at the cover.

Clisson and Eugénie

Napoleon Bonaparte

He owns the book. *Unbelievable.*

"It's actually decent," Naz says, picking up my phone from the cushion to move it out of his way so he can sit down beside me. "You should give it a read."

"I'll keep that in mind," I say, setting it on the arm of the couch as I focus on my paper. I can't even lie—I write down exactly what Naz just said, having no shame that I'm using his words. It makes sense, after all... reality is all a matter of perception. We see what we want to see.

"He's good looking," I say after a while.

"We said he wasn't short," Naz says. "Good looking might be pushing it."

"No, I mean Melody's boyfriend." I laugh. "He's good looking... like, *really* good looking. I'm talking cover of GQ kind of good looking. It's like, *wow...*"

"If you're trying to get me to kill him, all you have to do is ask."

Gasping, I elbow Naz. "Not funny. I would never. I'm just saying..."

132

"You're saying he's good looking." He waves me off, like he doesn't really care what I think about the guy's looks, but I can tell by his expression that he does. Holy shit, is that jealousy I see? "Like I said, it's all about perception."

"Yeah, it is," I agree quietly. "And yeah, he's good looking, but he's almost too good looking, you know? And he's smart, and nice... really nice... generous..."

His tone is clipped as he cuts in. "I get the picture, Karissa."

A smile tugs my lips. Definitely jealous.

"I mean, I just met him, so I don't really know him," I continue, "but there's something about him... something that feels familiar."

Naz perks up at that, raising his eyebrows. "How so?"

"He took her to Paragone for their first date."

"Nice place."

"I know... that's where you took me and spent an ungodly amount on overpriced food. Like, way more than a person should ever pay. It's insane. And he took her there at the last minute, just like you did, somehow managing to get a table... like you did."

"Maybe he knows somebody."

"Like you did?" I shake my head. "And he works for family. That's what Melody said. *Family*. And today he got a call and had to leave quick, had to slip away to handle some things. Sound familiar?"

"Somewhat."

"Somewhat, my ass. He's practically you."

"Nonsense," Naz says right away. "There's only one of me."

"Maybe so, but there are plenty like you," I counter.

"Are you insinuating he's in the mob?"

His blatant question stalls me.

Am I?

That's a serious accusation.

"I'm not insinuating anything. I'm just saying, you know... I think it's all kind of weird, how he comes out of nowhere and does these things that are so familiar to me. Like, he sent her flowers after their first date, just like you did. He insists on paying the tab, just like you do. She sees him around, near campus, even though he's not a student, just like I used to see you."

"You know, Karissa, there's a reason I did all those things. It's because they're natural things someone in those circumstances might do. Not everyone has ulterior motives."

"But sometimes they do."

"Sometimes," he agrees. "And sometimes we're just being needlessly paranoid."

He sounds so calm, matter of fact, like I'm being ridiculous. And, hell... maybe I am. But it's hard to shake the feeling that there's more to this all than meets the eye.

"His name's Leo," I point out. "As in, Leonardo. That's Italian, right?"

A slight smile turns Naz's lips. "Yes. So are Michelangelo and Donatello. He's more than likely a Ninja Turtle in disguise."

"Ha-ha. *Funny*. I'm just saying..."

"You're saying you think he's in the mob," Naz says. "Look, what's his last name? Maybe this family of his is a family I know."

"I, uh..." *Shit*. "I don't know."

"You didn't think to ask?"

"No."

"Can't be too worried about it, then."

"I'm not worried," I say, rolling my eyes and elaborating when Naz shoots me a look of disbelief. "I don't think it makes him a threat, or that he really has ulterior motives, or anything. I'm not worried about that part. I'm just a little concerned about Melody. She's been through enough with guys. After what happened with Paul, I don't want her to get hurt anymore."

"I hate to break it to you, sweetheart, but that's not something you can control."

"I know," I say. "I just think she should know what she's getting into, you know? And if he is in the mob..."

"Then, what? You sit her down for a heart-to-heart?"

"I don't know... maybe?" I shrug. I have no idea what I'll do if my suspicions are true. "Maybe you could talk to him, scare the guy straight, so he doesn't hurt my friend?"

Naz's earlier smile erupts again, with it a laugh this time. He shakes his head, toying with my phone, running his fingers along the edges of the pink glittery case, but says nothing.

"Something funny about what I said?"

"There's a lot funny about it."

"Like what?"

"Like the fact that you want me to warn a guy away from Melody. And not just any guy... someone you suspect is connected."

"So?"

"So you say you supported me walking away, but you still think I have the same kind of pull I had when I was in. I hate to break it to you, but it just doesn't work that way. People listened to me because they were afraid of the consequences if they didn't. The downside of that is, in order to get my point across, sometimes those consequences had to happen. I have to be a man of my word. So you want me to scare him? Sure, I will. But if he doesn't listen, I'll have to take him out."

I flinch.

He notices.

A look of disappointment crosses his face.

"Empty threats will only get me killed," he explains. "It's one thing to go radio silent in the business. It's another to make the kind of promises I'm not planning to keep."

I get it.

I do.

I don't like talking about it, but I know it's true.

He's out... as out as someone like him can be. But that doesn't mean he's free of his own consequences. Doesn't mean the rules don't still apply to him.

It's a dangerous game he used to play.

I guess, in a way, he'll always have to play it.

"Yeah, I guess we don't want that," I mumble.

"I'm quite positive we don't," he says. "Besides, Melody's an adult. She doesn't need anyone meddling in her affairs. So unless this guy in any way endangers your life, what he does for a living is none of our business."

I scowl but don't respond to that assertion, even though I whole-heartedly disagree with it. She's my friend. Sure, she has to make her own decisions, but that doesn't mean it's not my business who she's hooking up with.

Friends look out for each other.

I turn my focus back to my paper, scribbling some more about perception, before packing my stuff up and putting it all away. I grab the book off the arm of the couch, the romance story written by Napoleon. "What's this about, anyway?"

"A soldier falls in love with a woman."

"Does it have a happy ending?"

He glances at me. "What do you think?"

I think not, because Naz would enjoy tragedy a hell of a lot more than he'd enjoy a happily ever after. *Fictionally, of course.*

I flip through the pages before settling in, tucking my feet beneath me as I open it at the beginning. It'll only take me like half an hour to read it, so why not?

"You don't happen to have any Nicholas Sparks on your bookshelf, do you?" I ask curiously.

"Of course not," he says, his voice tinged with disgust. "Although, *A Walk to Remember* was a decent film, so I might consider reading that book."

"Seriously?"

"Sure."

Shaking my head, I mutter, "I don't even know who you are anymore."

"I'm the same man I always was," he says, standing up. "Just a little less preoccupied with murder."

I scowl.

Again.

Naz starts to walk out but pauses in the doorway of the den. "A word of advice?"

"Uh, sure."

"Judge him by his actions and not your suspicions," he says. "Because if the only measure of a man's worth is what he does to make money, a lot of good men would be judged unfairly."

"Like you?"

"Not like me," he says. "Not sure how many times I have to tell you... I'm not a good man, Karissa, and try as I might, I probably never will be."

Chapter Ten

Ignazio

The deli is once again open.

In fact, it only really closed for one day.

Repairs are underway, what looks like a decent remodel, but that's as far as it has gotten. The glass has been replaced, new locks and bars installed. There's no florescent neon sign out front, beckoning people in, but lights shine from back in the kitchen, so I know my father's here.

He probably never left, frankly.

Ever since my mother died a few months ago, her heart stopping in her sleep, he's stayed away from the home they shared as much as possible.

I have no idea where the man sleeps, if he even does.

He always said he'd sleep when he was dead.

The way he's going, I can see that happening.

I linger in front of the place for a moment, checking out the repairs, before heading for the alley that leads behind the building.

I shouldn't bother him.

I know I shouldn't.

He doesn't want to see my face anymore.

Can't say I blame him.

But something drew me here, early this morning, the sun barely starting to rise. Maybe it's some form of masochism where I get off on my father berating me on sight. It's probably sick, but I almost find it refreshing these days, someone not afraid to tell me what they truly think about me. Especially when Karissa is always in my ear, trying to convince me I'm a better man than I believe.

My father? He certainly doesn't think so.

He thinks I'm a callous, menial piece of shit.

He sees the ugly that still bleeds from me.

The ugly that Karissa just doesn't see.

He makes me feel like *me*.

"I thought I told you to leave."

His voice is flat, emotionless. He's leaning against the graffiti-riddled brick wall beside the propped open back door, a dirty white apron tied around his waist. Cigarette smoke surrounds him like fog as he breathes it in before letting it back out. Not sure when he traded the cinnamon toothpicks back in for the Marlboros... same kind he smoked when I was a kid. Maybe it was when he lost the love of his life.

Maybe it was when I started coming back around here.

"You did," I say, stalling in the alley near him. "I'm not very good at listening."

He lets out a bitter laugh. "You never were."

"Yeah, my mother used to say I inherited that from my father."

"You got a lot from me," he agrees. "Shame it was all of the bad and none of the good."

I nod, not disagreeing with that, and watch him as he continues to smoke. He draws the smoke in deep, holding it in his lungs before letting go of it, savoring every breath, cherishing the nicotine. I never understood it... picking up a habit that would kill you so easily.

But hey, what do I know?

I killed people for a living.

There's no quicker way to get you on Death's guest list than by meddling in his affairs and taking part in his game.

"So, when did you start smoking again?" I ask curiously.

"When someone tried to destroy my life's work," he says, motioning beside him, toward the back of the deli. "You figure out who that was?"

I'm surprised he's asking me that.

"I've got an idea."

He takes another drag of his cigarette before tossing it down and stamping it out. "Yeah, well, when you catch up to them, tell them they owe me ten grand. Had to wipe out my savings to get everything fixed."

"I—"

I would've paid for it.

Those words stall on my lips.

I know better than to offer.

He doesn't want my money.

He'd be offended by the offer, and I've offended the man enough.

"I'll be sure to tell them."

He nods before turning, yanking open the deli door to go inside. It bangs against the cement block propping it open when it closes again. He didn't offer an invitation to join him. I didn't expect one. But that doesn't stop me from doing it anyway, from grabbing the door and stepping inside the kitchen where he is.

He's gotten straight to work, slicing tomatoes. I'm quiet, as I join him, but he hears me.

Senses me.

Knows me.

"Something you need from me, Ignazio?" he asks, frustration tingeing his voice. "Because I don't remember inviting you to come hang out this morning."

Or any morning.

"I just wanted to check to see how you were."

He laughs at that.

Laughs.

"You didn't come around here for years. *Years.* You didn't care how I was doing when you were out running these streets, causing problems. Didn't care how it affected anyone else when you were making these enemies. Why should I believe you suddenly care now?"

"I've always cared."

He turns around, using the knife to point at me. "Bullshit. The only people you ever cared about were the people who could do things for you, so tell me, Ignazio... what do you need from me?"

My skin prickles at that accusation.

I don't like it.

It might be the truth, I don't know, but it *feels* like a lie.

I certainly care about Karissa. Maybe, at the start, it had been about what she could do for me, but it's more than that now. A lot more. Even when she wasn't giving me the time of day, when she wanted nothing to do with me, I cared about what happened to her. I worried about her. And not because I knew it would destroy me to lose her... because it would. There would be no coming back from that. But when it came down to it, I worried for her, because of her. I didn't want her to get hurt. I would've sacrificed myself to make sure she walked away unscathed.

And I did.

I let her go.

I told her to walk away.

But she came back.

"She says you're different, you know," he continues, turning back around to continue slicing his tomatoes. "I've been trying to see it... to see what she sees... but you don't seem any different to me."

I want to tell him it's because he's not looking hard enough, but that's a lie and I know it. The problem is, he's looking harder than Karissa is. She thinks I'm different because she wants me to be. And I'm trying to be. But I'm still me.

I can't be anybody but me.

At some point, every part of me became every part of *that*. The life isn't just something I lived... it was how I survived. It infused itself into every one of my cells, infecting every mitochondrion. It's in my blood and my bones, and unless you drain me dry and rip me to pieces, you'll never rid me of all of it.

It's like expecting a man to survive without a beating heart in his chest. Expecting him to breathe without lungs.

Expecting him to fight when he has no reason to live.

It's like expecting a man to still be a man after taking away everything that makes him who he is.

I can be good to her.

I might even be good *for* her.

But that doesn't mean I'm good.

My father knows that.

"I love her."

"I know you do."

That wasn't the response I expected from him. Figured he'd fight me on that, say I wasn't capable of loving anybody.

"You do?"

He nods. "Figure you must, since she's still alive."

Hearing him say that makes my chest tighten. "What makes you think I ever planned to kill her?"

He shoots a look over his shoulder, his eyes narrowed. "I never said you did."

Huh. I suppose he didn't.

I can tell by the look of disgust that crosses his face that I just gave a key piece of information away. He thought I'd get her killed. Hell, he still thinks I'll get her killed. But until now, he never realized I'd sunk so low that I would've killed her myself.

"People started shooting and the first thing you did was throw her out of harms way," he continues, turning back away from me. "Then you stood there, where they could see you, because you knew who they were after. You knew you were the target."

"We were safe," I say. "I knew the glass was bulletproof."

"Doesn't matter," he says. "It was instinct, and it wasn't the first time that kicked in. You killed Angelo last year. You always said he was a father to you... more of a father than me. But you killed him, for her... you chose her over who you called family. You and me... we love differently. But that doesn't mean you don't love her, in your own twisted way."

That almost sounds like a compliment.

Almost.

"I got myself in something," I say, "something I can't get out of."

He's quiet for a moment, continuing what he's doing. I almost want to fill the silence, to try to explain, even know I know there's no point in elaborating. He knows what I mean. But something about the man makes me feel like a kid again, a kid trying to ward off a whipping by explaining it all away.

Never worked then.

Wouldn't work now.

I could try to make him feel sympathy for what I'm going through, but I'd never succeed. The only thing I might rouse is a tad bit of pity.

Pity that I'm pathetic, probably.

Pity that I can't save my own ass.

"Is that what you came here for, Ignazio? Some fatherly advice?"

"Maybe."

"Then I'll tell you the same thing I told Johnny all those years ago," he says. "Run."

Coldness rushes through my body at those words, starting at the top of my head and flowing straight toward the tip of my toes. My fingers tingle, my skin prickles, pins and needles all over my body. "You told him to run?"

"I did," he says calmly, matter of fact, like those words are no more potent than as if he were recounting yesterday's deli special.

"He came to me, scared, said he was in too deep to ever get out, and he was worried... not for himself, but for her. The girl."

Carmela.

"Did you know?" My voice is low, so low I don't even know if those words even come out. The cold rage that flows through me makes my body shake. "Did you know what he'd done to me? To my wife? To my baby?"

"I had an idea," he admits. "You were still in the hospital. You weren't talking yet. I didn't think he'd pulled the trigger. I didn't think he could've. But I thought... I suspected maybe he knew. Maybe he knew too much. Maybe he was somehow involved."

"So you helped him?"

"No, I was trying to help *you*."

"How? How was telling him to run helping me?"

He turns around, his expression blank, like he's not at all affected by the anger in my voice, the anger I'm fighting really hard to contain. My mother, God rest her soul, would never forgive me if I stole that knife from his hand and jammed it through his throat. "Because I didn't want my son to become a murderer. It was bad enough, thinking maybe Johnny fell that far, but you? My kid? I still had hope for you then. I hoped you'd wake up, and you'd realize what that life did to you, what being *Angelo's son* got you, and you'd walk away before it was too late."

He turns back around, yet again, returning to his tomatoes, yet again. Like that's his biggest priority here. Tomatoes.

"Lot of good that did," he says. "Look at you now."

Bitter tension hangs in the air.

I have no idea what to say.

What to do.

Ray tried to induct me into his organization after what happened. He said I'd earned my place. He said I belonged with them. In another life, I probably wouldn't have hesitated, but in the world I woke up in after losing my family? None of that mattered. All I cared about was revenge.

I tracked Johnny to Florida eventually, found him and Carmela staying at an orange grove. I knew the place. Knew it, because we'd gone there before. The two of them looked happy, planning their lives together, settling in with the help of a *family friend*. Edoardo Accardi, former enforcer for the Genova crime family. He'd moved on to bigger things: the black market. If you wanted something, you went to Accardi.

I told him I wanted Johnny.

He refused my request.

I realized, quickly, that there were no friends in this business.

So I killed Accardi for it... among other things.

A sense of betrayal carves into me as I stand there, stewing on the memory. It slices me apart like my father slices those damn tomatoes. "You should've convinced him to turn himself in."

"Like that would've ever worked."

"You never know."

He stops what he's doing. "Tell me something, Ignazio... are you going to turn yourself in? Johnny killed one person in his entire life. *One.*"

"It was my wife! And our baby... he killed our child!"

He looks at me. "Two, then. And I get it. It wasn't right. But how many people have you killed? How many lives have you ruined? How many families have you torn apart? I'm venturing to guess it's a lot more than him."

"But this was my life he ruined. My life he tore apart!"

"He killed your family, and that's unforgivable, but your life, Ignazio? You ruined that yourself. You ruined it by doing exactly what I hoped you wouldn't do. I told him to run, and he listened, because it was the only way to save his family. So I'm telling you the same thing... you in something you can't get out of? *Run.*"

My head hurts.

It really fucking hurts.

I don't even know what to say anymore.

"It didn't work for him. What makes you think it would work for me?"

"It probably won't," he says. "But it gave him quite a few years, didn't it?"

I shake my head—not that I'm disagreeing, because running did give him almost two decades, but because I can't believe what he's saying. I came here for... hell, I don't know, but it wasn't for this conversation.

"I'm not a coward," I say. "I don't run."

"Then walk."

I laugh, despite the seriousness of his voice. This conversation? It's not funny. It's downright ridiculous. But that? That was funny. "How is that any different?"

"It's not," he says, "but walking away doesn't make you a coward. It makes you smart. You keep it up, you're going to die, and she might die, too. You leave, you'll still die... someday. But it probably won't be as soon. That's reality... the reality you created."

I think I've had about enough of this back-and-forth.

"Well, it's nice to know where you stand," I say. "I should probably be going."

"You should," he agrees.

There are no *goodbyes*, no *see you laters*, nothing but the sound of his knife hitting the cutting board as I turn around and walk out. It's a cool morning, like fall might finally be upon us, although the sun is shining bright. Karissa's probably up by now, probably wondering where I ran off to while she was asleep.

Being lectured by my father is the last thing she'd suspect.

For the second time in such a short amount of time, I find myself at this place, this old brick mansion over in Long Island, once more uneasy about it. When did I become this person? What turned me into this kind of man?

The kind of man who is hesitant to knock on a door.

This isn't me.

I step up on the porch, giving a brief glance around the quiet neighborhood.

Steeling myself, I knock.

The door is opened almost at once, a young guy appearing. He's big, somewhat muscular, and ugly to boot. A street soldier, I'm guessing. I was that kid once. I remember hanging around Ray's house, running errands, answering doors.

"I need to talk to Genova."

The kid says nothing, merely nodding before shutting the door again. I stare at it, my eyes scanning the chipped white paint of the wood as I wait.

A minute later, the door opens again.

This time Genova himself greets me.

"Vitale," he says, his voice hesitant. It's still so early he's wearing what I suppose are his pajamas, but it looks more like something Hugh Hefner might lounge around in—white undershirt, silk pants, and matching robe. He's even barefoot. I caught him before he was ready for company. "Nice of you to drop by... unexpected, but still... nice. What can I do for you?"

His voice tells me my dropping by unannounced is anything but nice, but he's tolerating it, like I figured he would, because his curiosity is piqued. "I was hoping you could spare a few minutes to talk."

"About?"

"Things."

I don't have to elaborate.

Not right here, anyway.

He knows *things* are the kind of things we don't talk about in public, so he doesn't have much choice but to invite me in. Stepping aside, he wordlessly motions his head for me to come in. The sound of some type of Italian opera music wafts through the downstairs as I follow him not to the room we met in days ago, but instead to a small den on the same floor. It's the source of the music... it's much louder in here. Genova turns it down a bit before taking a seat in a black leather chair.

"Join me," he says, motioning to another chair a few feet across from him. *Join.* There's that word from him again. "Tell me what kind of things you want to talk about this morning."

"My father has a deli," I tell him. "It's over in Hell's Kitchen."

His expression lights up. "Oh, of course! I know all about Vitale's. Best mozzarella I've ever tasted. Great place."

"Yeah, well, the other day we had an incident there."

All at once, his expression shifts. "What kind of incident?"

"Somebody shot up the place."

"Ah."

Ah. That's all he says. That's his only reaction.

"I talked to some people who steered me in the direction of a guy they thought was capable of doing it, so I confronted him—"

"You confronted him."

He sounds almost alarmed by that word.

"He's still alive," I elaborate, not wanting him to think I'm in any way back in or wanting to play his game. "But after our little confrontation, I had another encounter... this time with the guy you call *Scar.*"

I stare at him when I say that, hoping to gauge his reaction, but his expression stays blank. No surprise. No fear. No intrigue. *Nothing.*

"What kind of encounter are we talking here?"

"Just more or less an introduction."

Or rather, a reintroduction, but I leave that part off.

I'm not ready to give away all of my cards.

"First impression?"

First impression? Same one I got so many years ago. "Curious."

"Curious," he echoes, reaching into a humidor on a table beside him, pulling out a cigar. It's long, deep tan in color, with a brown label. Cubans, I'm guessing. He wordlessly offers me one but I wave him off, declining. He lights his, taking a deep puff before continuing. "He's not going to be a problem, is he?"

Maybe.

"For me? Not at all."

"And for the rest of us?"

Knowing Lorenzo like I think I do? The rest of them are screwed. It all depends, though... depends on what I do about him. Depends on how hard he makes life for me.

"Hard to say," I reply. "He's determined; I'll give him that."

"Seems that way," he says, puffing away on his cigar. It has a strong smell to it. It makes my nose twitch. "He's been wreaking a lot of havoc, the kind of havoc that draws attention to us all."

That he has.

Genova stares off in the distance, like he's pondering that. He flicks his ashes right onto the floor, letting them drop to the tan carpet. I pity his housekeeper.

"Tell me, Vitale," he says after a moment. "You planning to do something about him?"

"I'm thinking about it," I reply. "Is that going to be a problem?"

"For me? Not at all."

It doesn't escape my notice that he's using my exact words. Genova's a smart man. You can't just take him at what he says... you have to consider how he says it.

Standing up, I brush the wrinkles from my suit coat. I came to test the waters. That was all I really wanted. I hold my hand out toward him. "Been a pleasure."

He takes my hand, shaking it. "Pleasure's been all mine. If you decide to handle your little problem, I'd be happy to offer—"

I cut him off before he can finish what he's saying. I don't want anything from him. "Don't worry about it."

He looks surprised. "You're certain?"

"Handling it will benefit everyone. Call it a parting gift."

The surprise on his face only deepens at those words. "Oh? Going somewhere after all?"

I half-shrug. "I'm getting too old for it all."

"Nonsense, Vitale... you're still young. Get to be my age and then we'll talk."

I don't respond to that. There's no point. Nodding my goodbye, I turn to walk out, finding the young guy lingering in the hallway right outside. He trails me, a few steps behind, following me to the front door of the house.

He locks it up the moment I step outside. I can hear the clanging as he secures the door, keeping anyone from being able to come in. Genova always was more paranoid than the others. More locks. More security.

It's probably why he lives alone, why he has never been married. He doesn't trust anyone enough to lie beside him when he's asleep.

Stepping off the porch, I head to my car, but my footsteps stall as I approach. The muscles in my body grow tense. A few feet away, I pause, hands in the pockets of my black pants, clutching my keys.

Someone is perched on the hood of my car.

Not just any *someone*, either.

Lorenzo.

Unbelievable.

He sits there, relaxed, right foot propped up on the corner of the front bumper, his arms resting on his knee. He's peeling an orange, pulling it apart and tossing his scraps right into the street.

My eyes scan the neighborhood, looking for any black sedans that might account for the cars I encountered last night, but the street is quiet, nothing out of the ordinary. He seems to be alone.

Huh.

"Littering's illegal, you know."

He glances my way when I say that, raising his eyebrows. "Assaulting men in alleys is illegal, too... or so I've heard."

"It is, but the trick is to be careful. The cops in this city are always looking for a reason to take us down. One dropped receipt on the sidewalk can earn someone like us ten days in lockup."

"You spend many days in lockup?"

"No," I say. "I'm careful."

He laughs, turning back to his orange, and peels another piece, again tossing the scraps into the street. He's not worried, not a bit. Fearless. "Ah, life's too short to always be cautious, Ignazio. Sometimes you've got to put yourself out there and take risks."

"True, but you have to be smart about what risks you take."

He pops a wedge of the orange in his mouth, chewing slowly as he regards me. I don't know why he's here or what he wants, and I'm pretty sure I'm not going to get a straight answer out of him about it if I ask. He's playing some sort of game, a game I have no desire to play, but he's going to force me to, anyway.

"You've got balls," I tell him. "It takes them, to be sitting out here, in front of this house, in broad daylight."

"Oh, you mean old man Genova's place?" Lorenzo motions toward the brick mansion. "He's not going to do anything to me."

"How can you be so sure?"

"Because he swore it himself," he says. "Had a meeting with the five families late last night. Or well, the four that are left." He shoots a look my way that tells me he knows exactly what happened to number five. "It was... enlightening, I guess you could call it. Temperamental bunch. Burn down one silly little building and they get their panties all twisted, but I managed to straighten them out... for now."

My hair bristles at the casual way he says that.

A meeting with the families?

I'm not sure what to make of it.

I'm not sure if I believe it.

Genova certainly didn't mention it when suggesting I kill the guy.

"Come on, Lorenzo... we both know that's not *all* you've done."

"What makes you say that?"

"The streets talk."

He ponders that for a moment, continuing to eat his orange, dripping juice all over the hood of my car. I want to snatch a hold of him and rip him off of it, slam his face against the mess and make him lick it up, but I'd also like to go home today. And even though I can't see any recognizable cars around us, I'm not entirely convinced he's out here alone.

Is he really that brazen?

"How'd you get here?" I ask curiously.

"Friend dropped me off."

"Friend," I muse. "You got a lot of those? Friends?"

"I've got ten of them," he says. "Eleven, if we're counting you."

"We're not."

"Ten, then."

"And you're sure one of them isn't Fat Joe?"

His response is immediate. "The rapper?"

"The man in the alley."

His eyes seek me out when I say that. He's still sitting casually, like he's not bothered at all, but there's something in his eyes now, a deep kind of suspicion, like he knows I'm on the tip of an accusation. "You got something you're trying to get at here, Ignazio? Never thought you'd be one to beat around the bush. Just spit it out."

"You had someone shoot up my father's deli."

He shakes his head. "Wasn't me."

I take a step toward him, reacting on instinct, but I manage to stop myself before doing something. His denial grates at me, though, burrowing under my skin. It's cowardice. *Ridiculous.* If you're going to attack a man so personally, the least you can do is take credit for the act.

"So I guess none of it was you, huh? Ray's men being picked off, one-by-one?"

"Nope."

"Not even the men who died at Cobalt? The ones who burned alive that night? Still not your fault?"

"Now, okay, that *was* me," he says, pushing away from the car to stand up, popping another wedge of orange in his mouth. "I warned them first, though. Not my fault they didn't take me seriously. Guess they will now."

"Yeah, the ones who survived."

His brow furrows as he steps around my car, toward the passenger door. "Don't tell me you had some sort of emotional attachment to that place."

"I spent a lot of time there," I say. "I wouldn't say I was attached, but it hit a little too close to home for my liking."

"Oh, well, then in that case..." He holds up his hands, smirking. "Innocent."

He's a lying son of a bitch.

I know he's being sarcastic, but by no means do I find it funny.

"In my defense," he continues, lowering his hands, "well, you know, there's really no defending it. You know as well as I do that sometimes things just have to be done. You've been there."

I have.

He knows it.

I know it.

I've done more than my fair share of bad because I felt it was just what had to be done. I never bothered trying to defend my actions.

I'm not surprised he isn't bothering, either.

"And yeah, okay, maybe I picked off a guy or two," he says, holding his hand up like a gun and shooting. *Pew-pew.* "But I have no reason to target you, Ignazio."

He doesn't need a reason, I think, and I start to point that out, when a loud, obnoxious ruckus shatters the air around us. My pocket vibrates, and I reach into it, grabbing my phone. The song... it's coming from it. *Shit.*

The fucking boy band.

I silence it, pressing the button on the side, just to stop the annoying blaring. Karissa's face is plastered on the screen, and as much as I hate doing it, I ignore her call.

Now's not the time for it.

Slipping the phone back away, I glance at Lorenzo. His eyes are wide, the orange halfway to his mouth, like he's forgotten about everything else for the moment.

"Was that...?" He gapes at me. "What *was* that? Do I even want to know?"

"No," I admit, "you don't."

He shakes his head before tossing what's left of his orange right into the gutter beside my car. He wipes his hands on his black pants like they just don't matter. He's dressed casual, his light blue button down halfway open, exposing part of his chest.

At least it's not jeans and a t-shirt today.

"Great seeing you, as always," he says, just as a black car whips around the corner of the block, heading our direction. *Bingo*. "We should get together again soon. I'd love to meet this wife of yours. I've heard so much about her."

"From who?"

"The streets talk, remember?" He steps off the curb behind my car just as the black sedan pulls up beside us, blocking me in. "Besides, you seem to forget I once knew her parents. You aren't the only one."

With that, he's gone, yanking open the passenger door and ducking inside before it drives away. I stare at it as it accelerates, my eyes scanning the Florida license plate.

No, I haven't forgotten he knew her parents.

I was just hoping like hell it wouldn't come up.

Chapter Eleven
Karissa

High-waist jean shorts.

Pastel pink leg warmers.

Matching distressed sweatshirt, hanging off my right shoulder.

I feel utterly ridiculous and completely out of place, even though, okay, I just bought this outfit today. It was all there, in the store, waiting on the rack. Apparently the eighties are making a comeback.

Who knew?

I certainly didn't.

Clothes surround me in my bedroom, some with the tags still on, others dragged here from Melody's closet... or her floor... or bed... or whenever they'd last been. Enough crazy outfits to dress a dozen people.

I'd managed to nab the most modest get-up of the bunch.

The faint bruise around my neck has mostly faded. I can barely see it anymore. Nobody around me has mentioned it, not even Melody, who I know for a fact would've rang the alarm had she noticed.

I'm looking myself over in the full-length mirror beside the dresser—another one of my purchases today. The only mirror Naz ever had in this place was the small one in the bathroom, and well, let's just say Melody noticed last time she tried getting ready here. "Ugh, no wonder you're always so... you," she'd said, motioning at me. "How do you pick out pants in the morning without, you know, checking out your ass?"

Wasn't sure how to answer that question.

Wasn't sure there was even an answer for it.

But still, I bought a mirror this afternoon, because she had a point somewhere in there, I think.

And okay, I have to admit... my ass does look kind of nice in these shorts.

Looks bigger than it used to be.

"You got anything lace?" Melody asks, walking right over to my drawers to scour through my things. She starts with the top drawer, shooting me a smirk as she yanks out a pair of my underwear. "Anything other than this thong?"

She shoots it at me, like it's a damn slingshot, before turning back to the rest of my drawers and opening them to find nothing she wants.

"Don't wear much lace," I admit. "It itches."

"So?"

"So I like to be comfortable."

She looks at me again, closing the last drawer. "Sometimes we have to suffer for fashion, Kissimmee."

I grimace. "You, maybe. I'll pass."

Rolling her eyes, she gives up her search for lace and dives into the pile of clothes strewn around my bed, finding a pair of leggings with a stich of lace on the bottom of them. "Ha!"

Apparently leggings are back, too.

And harem pants.

Hammer pants.

Melody bought a pair of them today.

I don't know what's wrong with her, honestly.

She shimmies out of said pants right where she stands beside the bed, tossing them onto the pile, already regretting that purchase, I think. She's situating the leggings, about to pull them on, when a voice calls out through the room.

A voice that isn't ours.

"Do you—?"

Naz steps into the doorway, cutting off mid-question. His reaction is automatic, his expression shifting to one of surprise as he turns his head, away from us, and closes his eyes, raising his hands as if to ward of whatever the hell he'd just seen.

Melody is in her underwear.

I don't know why, but I find it pretty damn funny.

I laugh, seeing his distress over walking in on that, especially when Melody groans. "Geez, Ignazio, never took you for a voyeur."

"I can assure you," he says, "that was the last thing I wanted to look at."

Melody scoffs, leggings finally on, and playfully nudges him with her elbow as she jets out of the bedroom, heading for the bathroom down the hall. Naz cautiously turns back my way when she's gone, his eyebrows raised as he approaches. His eyes scan the room around me, taking in the utter mess, before settling on the mirror. He regards my reflection as he pauses beside me, eventually turning right to where I stand. "Another venture into the eighties, I gather."

"How'd you guess?"

"You look like someone I used to masturbate to when I was in my teens."

My face heats at that, blush taking over my cheeks.

Naz's eyes scan me, from my head to my toes, before settling on the piece of black lace by my feet. He reaches down and picks it up. It isn't until it's in his hand that he realizes exactly what it is. His face pales just a bit as he whispers, "Please tell me this is yours."

"Of course it is."

He breathes a sigh of relief, smirking, as he takes a step back, wordlessly shoving the thong in his pocket. I laugh and am about to say something about it when Melody waltzes back in, brush in hand, steadily teasing her blonde hair. Naz looks her over quickly, not at all the same way he looked at me.

He almost looks confused.

"You know, we didn't really dress like that in the eighties," he tells her... same thing he once told me. "I don't know where you girls got that idea from."

Melody looks down at her outfit, her black lacy leggings and what looks like a neon pink sports bra with matching tutu. She's even got on a pair of jelly sandals... something else we found today at the store.

She said she wouldn't be caught dead in a pair any other time.

They shouldn't make them for anyone over the age of nine.

"Really?" she says. "What did you wear?"

"Acid-wash jeans," I chime in. "The also really liked shoulder pads for some reason."

Melody pretends to gag. "Even I'm not crazy enough to go down that path."

Naz shakes his head, like he disagrees, and turns back to me without commenting. Melody disappears again after grabbing her bag full of make-up, as usual the last to ever be ready.

"Do I, what?" I ask, running my hands over my hair. It's poufy from being crimped. Another thing we stumbled upon at the store— a hair crimper. I didn't even hesitate before grabbing that one.

"Excuse me?"

"When you walked in," I say. "You were asking something."

"I was wondering if you had any plans tonight," he says, glancing around. "Sort of already answered my question."

"Oh, yeah... Melody wanted to go to Timbers, and I mean, I didn't think it was a good idea... I still don't know, but I figured, well... no harm, right?"

I'm babbling, because I'm not sure how to explain it or what I'm supposed to say, if I'm supposed to ask how he feels about me going out. I'm barely twenty, and this is prime 'going out' age, but we're married now.

I've never exactly seen an example of how normal married life is supposed to be.

"Right," he says. "You don't need my permission. If you want to go dancing, by all means, go dancing. I'm not going to tell you *no*."

"Are you going to follow me, though?"

A slow smile spreads across his face.

Of course he is.

I'm not surprised, and it's not like I planned to do anything he wouldn't approve of, but still, I roll my eyes. Now that is old Naz. As much as I might hate it, I've got to admit—it's good to see him being himself again.

"I would," he says, "but I have a few other things I need to do tonight."

"Like?"

"Like," he says, stepping closer, so close our toes touch, as he leans down slightly toward me. "*Things.*"

He leans in to kiss me, closing the distance, but I turn my head, trying to contain my smile when he groans because of my rejection. I glance at him in the mirror. "Promise me something."

"What?"

"Just… something."

"You want me to promise something without knowing what the something is?"

"Yes."

"It doesn't work like that," he says. "I can promise to always try my damnedest to come home to you at night… I can promise to love you for the rest of my life… but I can't promise whatever this something is without knowing more about it."

"Why?"

"Because I don't break promises," he says. "I have to know it's something I can keep."

I glare at his reflection. "If you follow me tonight, after you're done with your things, promise me you'll at least come in."

"You want me to come inside the club?"

"Yes," I say. "If you follow me."

He hesitates. I can tell by his conflicted expression that he wants to say no. Timbers is hardly his kind of scene. It's loud, and crowded, filled with drunken college kids. I know he used to go to that place called The Cobalt Room to drink, but I'm pretty sure that place was like a nursing home compared to the nursery room of Timbers.

"Fine," he concedes, his voice strained, like he had to force the word for his lips. "If I show up tonight, I'll come in."

"Promise."

"I promise," he says, grabbing my hips and turning my body, forcing me to look at him and not his reflection. "But I need you to promise me some things. No drugs, no drinking, no flirting, no fighting, and for god's sake, no fucking."

"Uh, no fun," Melody says, appearing in the doorway. "Way to be a spoil-sport."

He ignores her, staring at me, his expression dead serious. He's waiting for my promise. He already knows he has nothing to worry about with the last few, and I'm certainly not one to do any drugs, but drinking?

Ugh.

"One drink."

"None."

"Just a sip."

"No."

Ugh. Ugh. Ugh.

Compromise sucks.

"Fine," I mutter. "I promise."

He kisses me then. This time I don't turn my head. It's soft, and sweet, and way too brief.

"What about me?" Melody chimes in.

"You can do whatever you want," Naz says, turning toward her. "As long as you don't get my wife caught up in it, that is."

Melody playfully salutes him. "Got it, boss."

Naz walks out. I can hear his footsteps on the stairs, and then he's just gone. I'm not sure where he's off to, what sort of the things he has planned tonight, but I'm hoping he's safe, wherever he is, and not doing anything that can get him hurt.

"I swear, the two of you..." Melody says, shaking her head. "I still can't get over it. You're both just so cool about everything, like, *whatever* about it all."

I know what she means. It's hard to explain, but I guess when you jump over a hurdle like the murder of your parents, everything else sort of just pales in comparison. It's been a while since we've fought about anything, since I've been genuinely angry with him. He's frustrating, sure, but I understand him.

And I like to think, after everything, he understands me.

"Are you ready?" I ask, looking at Melody. It's well after dark, and we've still got to make the trek to Manhattan.

"Ugh, just like, five more minutes," she says, swinging around to jet out of the bedroom. "I'm almost done."

Five minutes turn to ten, which turn to twenty. Half an hour later, she's finally done. We take the subway back into the city, and Melody seems to enjoy the attention she gets on it, wearing her ridiculous outfit. The eighties are back, yeah, but I guess most of New York hasn't gotten the memo yet. She stands in front of me, clutching the bar, while I slink down on a bench beside two seat-hogging businessmen.

The line outside of Timbers is long when we arrive, but it only takes us a few minutes to make it inside. I hand my driver's license to the guy working the door, a beefy guy that looks like he's carrying a pack of hot dogs on the back of his neck, and scowl when he draws a big black 'x' in permanent marker on the back of my hand.

Melody, as usual, gets her lime green wristband complimentary of the fake ID she carries. Pretty soon, she won't need it. She'll be twenty-one in just a few weeks. The bouncer glowers at it, though, bending it and studying it, like he knows the thing isn't real.

"You remember that other guy that used to work the door here?" she asks once we're inside. "You know, the hot guy... Kevin or something?"

It was Kelvin.

I remember.

He worked with Naz.

"What about him?"

"I heard he died," she says. "Some of the girls in my class were talking about it a few weeks ago. He got shot or something. Nobody knows who did it."

"That's... *wow*."

"Right? He seemed like such a nice guy."

I don't have a response for that, but her words nag at me.

Kelvin. Shot.

I don't think that's something Naz would've done.

I don't have a chance to dwell on it, though, as Melody grabs my hand and drags me through the club. Madonna blasts from the speakers, vibrating the floor as energy hums in the air. It's muggy, crowded out on the dance floor, but Melody doesn't hesitate to pull me deep in the crowd, wedging us into a small space in the center. It's some techno remix of *Like a Prayer*, the bass thumping through my body as I start to move, like it's almost instinct. Melody and I are jumping around, singing at the top of our lungs, screaming the lyrics like our lives depend on it.

Madonna turns to New Kids on the Block, which turns to Michael Jackson somewhere in there, before Madonna comes right back around again. Over and over, a continuous pouring of old songs.

It all blurs together in a mix of bass thumping and eighties loving hysteria. Melody disappears to get herself a drink but by then I'm to the point I just don't care.

Bad idea? *Pfft, fuck that.*

It's been a while since I've had some carefree fun.

I'm dancing on my own, **voguing**, laughing as I sing along.

Sweat drips down my face.

Jesus Christ, it's hot in here.

Melody's there and back and then there again, guzzling drinks and giggling as she shakes her ass on anybody who comes near her. At one point, she appears, shoving a clear plastic cup at me. "Here."

I take it, stalling as I look at the thing. It's filled halfway with something. Bringing it to my nose, I sniff the liquid, earning a laugh from her as she dances against some gangly boy that probably looks nice with her beer goggles.

"It's just water," she says. "I promise."

Shrugging, I guzzle it down, my throat dry.

It tastes like water to me.

She's busy grinding on the guy, so I slip away, squeezing through the crowd to the nearest trashcan, tossing the empty cup in. I turn around, still signing at the top of my lungs—Paula Abdul now—when I run right into someone standing there, almost knocking them over. "Shit! Sorry!"

Hands grab my arms as whoever it is steadies himself and laughs. I glance up at his face, about to apologize again, when somebody I know greets me.

Well, sort of. I recognize him.

Leo.

Conflicted feelings run through me. I smile kindly in acknowledgment, because holy shit, Melody's going to be happy, but another part of me bristles at his presence. Because no matter what Naz said, I still can't just shake the weird feeling, especially with him being here.

"Hey!" I say, motioning to the dance floor. "Melody's over there."

He glances back that way the same time I look. We've got a perfect viewpoint of his girlfriend... backing it right up on the weird dude. *Ugh.* Not good.

I expect some sort of angry reaction from him, an intense surge of jealousy, but instead he just laughs and shakes his head.

Okay, that's not like Naz, not at all.

He pushes his way over to her, and I follow his path. Melody looks up, spotting us, and squeals, instantly abandoning the guy she was dancing with, thrusting herself at her boyfriend. She wraps her arms around him, jumping, so the only thing keeping her from hitting the ground is his grip.

Shit, she's really drunk.

He almost falls trying to hold her, but he doesn't seem to mind.

They start dancing together, slowly, not at all on beat to the music playing. I turn away from them, shrugging it off, and start dancing, too. I don't know what song's playing but I remember it from *The Breakfast Club*, so I sing what I know and just go with it all.

Time passes.

I'm pouring sweat.

My feet hurt and my muscles burn, but it doesn't stop me from dancing.

Melody drinks more.

Leo drinks nothing at all.

Another cup of water is forced in my hand, and I'm grateful for it, because I'm parched. I don't know how many songs have passed, how many hours we've been here, but the crowd has thinned just a bit, giving me more room to move. I'm singing the last verse of *Tainted Love* when I turn around, my footsteps faltering, lyrics stalling on my lips.

Holy shit.

He's here.

I have to blink a few times, because I can't believe my own eyes.

Naz.

He promised. He did. But I never actually expected him to show up, to walk his ass on inside the club.

He's not at all dressed for the place, but he's toned it down a bit, taking off the jacket and tie, loosening his collar. His sleeves are rolled up to his elbows, which, once again, is the hottest thing there is.

He's looking around, looking for me.

He's looking at everybody, dressed in their fake eighties clothing.

He looks utterly disturbed by it.

Carefully, I slip to the edge of the dance floor, watching him, waiting for him to approach. When he's within earshot, I raise my voice, so he can hear me over the music. "Come here often, stranger?"

He turns toward me right away, and all at once I can see the tension leave his shoulders as relief replaces it. Wow, I don't think I've ever seen him look so uncomfortable.

Talk about stepping out of the box.

"Can't say I do," he says, looking past me, at the dance floor, before focusing on me again. "Can't say I'll ever come here again, either."

"But you came," I point out as he steps closer, pausing right in front of me.

"I did," he says. "I made a promise."

The song changes again.

"Dance with me," I say, grinning as I grab his hand and try to pull him onto the dance floor. It doesn't work. He doesn't budge at all. He's a hell of a lot stronger than me and he's infinitely more stubborn.

"Nobody said anything about dancing."

I stall, glaring at him as I let go of his hand. "You remember that time you took me to that dinner party-slash-political fundraiser-slash-whatever the fuck that was at the hotel in Manhattan?" I reach into my shirt, pulling out the necklace concealed in it. "It was the same night you gave me *this*."

"Of course I remember."

"You told me to dance with you that night, and I hesitated, and

167

do you remember what you said to me? You told me to stop being chicken shit."

He laughs, loud and genuine, when I say that. "I'm not sure I used those words, sweetheart."

"Whatever," I say. "I danced with you that night, so now it's your turn to pay me back."

"Fair enough." He motions for me to go out on the dance floor, but I just gape at him. He conceded way too quickly. I was prepared for more of a fight. I was conjuring a whole argument to win that one. I was prepared to bring out the tears. "Go on, then."

Shaking it off, I turn around and slip out onto the dance floor, him right behind me. I start to turn around when we reach an open space, but his hands grasp my hips tightly from behind, pulling me back against him.

I dance.

Naz mostly stands there, but I can feel him slightly swaying along, in tune with the beat. Two songs pass, or maybe it's three, before the sound of Bell Biv DeVoe rocks through the speakers.

Poison.

I'm surprised he's giving me this much, but I know it won't last, and I'll probably never get a repeat, so I'm going to make the most of it. Pulling from his grip, I turn around in his arms, glancing at him.

He's singing.

Holy shit, he's singing.

Okay, so not really, because not a sound is coming from his lips, but he's damn sure mouthing the lyrics, which means he knows them. He stops when he realizes I've seen it, and he just stares down at me, but it's too damn late.

I caught him.

"Ignazio Michele Vitale," I say playfully, intentionally flubbing the middle name, just to get more of a rise out of him. "I can't believe you were singing a song from the eighties."

"You were seeing things."

"I don't think so," I say. "I think maybe you like that song. I mean, I know it's no *Hotline Bling*, but..."

His eyes narrow slightly as his hands slip down, around, resting on my ass. "It's also not from the eighties."

"Of course it is."

"No," he says. "It came out in 1990. I was in middle school. I remember it."

I want to argue but he's probably right, and well, I hadn't been born yet, so I certainly don't remember it. "Well, whatever... doesn't change the fact that you were singing, old man."

His eyes darken when I say that.

It sends a chill down my spine.

"Keep talking to me like that," he says, "and I'll fuck your throat so hard you'll never speak again."

There's no emotion in his voice.

It's matter of fact.

Jesus Christ, that's almost terrifying, but for some reason, I get a thrill out of it. "What if I like that idea?"

"Me destroying your voice box?"

"No, you fucking my throat," I say. "Sounds like it could be a good time."

I don't know what's come over me.

Hell, I'm turned on by the thought of it. Goose bumps cover every inch of my sweaty skin. He's always been one to turn away from a blowjob. I've never had him take initiative in that department.

He stops moving and stares at me, eyes scanning my face, like maybe he isn't sure what to say. After a moment, he pulls away, snatching the drink from my hand. He sniffs it just like I did before taking a sip.

"Water," he says, like he thought maybe I'd broken my promise and had been drinking tonight.

"Yep."

Nodding, he downs the rest of it, before grabbing my hand and pulling me off the dance floor, tossing the empty cup in the trashcan as we pass it. I think maybe we're leaving, like he decided it was time for me to go home, and I look around for Melody, to say goodbye, having no idea where she ran off to with Leo.

But once outside, Naz diverts a surprising direction, veering away from the street, instead into a small nearby alley. Oh my god, he can't be serious. He stops about halfway down it, but I've still got a wide-open view of the street, where anyone can walk by anytime and see me.

"Are you...?" I stare at him incredulously as he starts undoing his pants, unbuckling them. "You're *serious*. You want to, I mean... *here*?"

"Figured it wouldn't be a problem," he says, "since you like the idea of being watched and all."

Somewhere, deep inside of me, resides a prim and proper lady, one with a sense of modesty, one who doesn't say 'fuck' very much... if ever at all. She's pretty, and kind, and blushes like a virgin at the very idea of ever dirtying her reputation. That girl is frantically shaking her head, shouting that this is preposterous. We can't just do that here. It's completely insane.

But another is holding that girl captive.

This one has a bit of a wild streak.

This one says, "Fuck it."

"You sure about this?" he asks. "I need you to tell me."

"Uh, sure," I say. "I'm sure."

He gets his pants unbuttoned and grabs my arm, pulling me around, pushing me back against the side of the brick building, into the shadows. He's rough as he shoves me down to the ground, and I hiss when my bare knees hit the filthy asphalt.

Shit, that hurts.

He grabs my head, wrapping crimped hair around his fist, jerking my head toward him as I cringe.

"Open your mouth," he growls, and I'm so damn surprised I can do nothing but oblige. He pulls himself free with his other hand, stroking it, before guiding my open mouth at him.

Whoa.

One thrust, one stroke, and I'm already struggling as he forces me down onto him, sliding the whole way down my throat. I'm trying not to gag... trying... and *trying*... but he's too big and a hell of a lot harder than I remember him being. I choke as he bucks his hips, fucking my throat, his balls slapping against my chin. I don't want to bite him but my jaw clenches in response, and I can feel my teeth grazing against him, over and over. He growls at the sensation, and I know it has to hurt, but instead of easing up on me, it just sends him into a bigger frenzy.

Fuck.

Fuck.

Fuck.

He's watching me the whole time. I can feel his eyes on my face. I peek up curiously, meeting his stern gaze. There's something in his expression, darkness I can't shake. His grip on my hair tightens as he pulls my head up, forcing it back, opening my throat more to him.

"Relax," he whispers. "Relax your throat."

I try to listen to him, but well, how? How the fuck can I relax when I can barely breathe, when my eyes are starting to water because of it. He looks almost angry, like I'm disappointing him, but I don't know what to do.

I've never done this.

It's only a minute.

Maybe two.

I don't know.

He yanks me off of him, and I inhale sharply, sucking in a gulp of air. I'm breathing heavily, frantically, as he strokes himself, fast and hard.

He's not messing around.

His hand is still tangled in my hair. I watch in awe as he pleasures himself. It can't be more than another minute before he pulls me back to him, again thrusting down my throat.

One stroke, and that's it.

I can feel it when he spills in my mouth. The bitterness gags me, but I force it down. Tilting his head back, Naz groans, loosening his hold and pausing his movements as I suck him.

There's a noise near the alley. Movement. *Voices*. Naz moves away from me, and before I can even get a grip on what's happening, he pulls me to my feet. He's tucking himself back away, fixing his pants, while I just stand there, startled, unsure what to do about anything. I run my fingers through my hair... not like it'll make a difference.

Before I can stress over any of it too much, Naz pulls me toward him, putting his arm around my shoulder as he steers me down the alley, toward the disruption. The club is getting out already.

Where did this night go?

I'm nervous, maybe irrationally. I don't know. My body is trembling as I tuck in at his side, almost like I'm shrinking away. Did he even enjoy that?

"You did good," he whispers, like he can sense my worries. Naz was always good at reading me.

I peek up at him, seeing a lazy smile on his lips. It's like a burden was lifted from the man's shoulders. Okay, maybe he did enjoy it.

"Yeah?" I ask, surprised. "I wasn't sure. Never had my throat fucked before..."

He laughs quietly, pausing at the end of the alley as a crowd of Cyndi Lauper look-a-likes starts to form. He pulls me around, so I'm in front of him, and it's almost like instinct, but I wrap my arms around him, hugging him. I lay my head against his chest, feeling his warmth, smiling when I feel his hands on my back, holding me to him.

It's like being wrapped in a cocoon.

Public displays of affection aren't really Naz's thing, but he seems at ease—for the moment, at least.

"So you like it like that? You've never tried to do it to me before."

His hands rub my back. "You know I like it when you struggle."

I should probably be worried about that statement, but I get it. I do. He likes pushing me to the brink before pulling me back, shoving me under before letting me resurface. It's like it gives him life again, being there, watching me breathe.

"Yeah, you like that damsel in distress routine," I mumble. "Get your rocks off being my hero."

His hand snakes up my spine, grabbing my hair, and he pulls on it, playfully jerking my head back so I'll look up at him.

"You're no damsel in distress, sweetheart," he says. "And I'm the furthest thing there is from a hero."

"Whatever," I say. "How about for your birthday this year, I let you hog-tie me, maybe even ball-gag me, and have your way with me all night long?"

"That's not going to happen."

"Why not?"

"Because it isn't safe." He looks at me, dead serious, almost admonishing, like somehow I should already know this. "If you're tied up, you can't fight me. If you're gagged, you can't use your safe word. If you're completely incapacitated, Karissa, you're liable to get hurt. The only reason we play around as much as we do is because I know, if it's too much for you, you'll find a way to stop me."

"You wouldn't really hurt me."

"Not intentionally," he agrees. "But just because you call me a good guy doesn't mean I am one. It just means I've sufficiently *Stockholm'ed* you."

Laughing, I elbow him, just as someone calls my name. *Melody.* Turning around, I settle back against Naz, his arm still wrapped around me as she approaches, staggering, dragging Leo along. He looks hesitant, like he's trying to pull her the other direction, but she's not having it.

"Karissa!" she screeches, looking me over. At this point, I'd be surprised if she weren't seeing double. "My God, what happened to you?"

173

I glance down at where her eyes have settled, feeling blush rising through me, settling in my cheeks. My knees are skinned from the alley.

"She fell," Naz says, tucking me further into his side, as he turns from Melody, instead settling on her boyfriend. I can practically feel him as he puffs out his chest, like he's trying to be intimidating, but okay... he doesn't have to try. Leo senses it, too, it seems, because he keeps a bit of distance between them, damn near flinching when Naz holds out his hand. "Ignazio Vitale."

Whoa.

He's introducing himself.

I'm kind of proud.

I don't know if this is some ridiculous show of arms or something, or if this is his way of trying to make friends to appease me, but either way, it's nice to see.

Leo reaches out, taking his hand, shaking it. "Nice to meet you. I'm Leo."

"You got a last name, Leo?"

Leo nods, and I think maybe that's the only answer he's supplying, before he clears his throat. "Accardi."

"Like Bacardi!" Melody chimes in, giggling. "Which is totally what I've been drinking tonight!"

I laugh at her.

Naz nods before tugging on me. "If you'll excuse us, we should get going."

He pulls me away before I can even say goodbye to my friend.

Not that she notices, really.

A quick glance back tells me she's already too wrapped up in Leo.

She's nuzzled into his neck, while he's whispering something, something I imagine is probably scandalous based on the way she reacts to it.

It's sweet, I have to admit.

Even kind of cute.

Okay, maybe I'm being ridiculous with this whole *weird feeling*.

Leo seems really good for her.

Shrugging it off, I follow Naz just down the block, to where his Mercedes is parked. He unlocks it, opening my door for me. I start to get in but pause, looking at him. He senses my attention and looks at me, wordlessly raising his eyebrows.

"Thank you," I tell him, "for coming tonight."

A sly smile takes over his lips.

"You're welcome," he says, "for both meanings of that word."

Rolling my eyes, I climb in the car. I watch out of the windshield, down the block, as Leo leads Melody away from the club. A black car pulls up, coming to a stop, double-parking the cars right out front. Leo opens the back door to the car, motioning for Melody to get in, and she does without hesitation. He gets in after her, closing the door before the car again takes off.

Naz is about to get in but pauses, watching them. He stands there, not moving, his eyes fixed to the black car as it slowly drives by us. It isn't until then that he finally gets in beside me, but something is wrong.

I know it is the second I look at him.

His posture is tense, his expression blank. Anger, sadness, and happiness are one thing with this man, but when he goes completely blank, I know we've got a problem.

"What's wrong?"

"Nothing."

His tone is clipped.

Before I can question it any more, he turns the car on, shoving it in drive. He gives a quick glance at the mirrors before pulling out in traffic, instantly making a U-turn in the middle of the street, eliciting some car horns as people slam on their brakes to keep from hitting us.

I don't question it, though.

Not to him.

No, I clip on my seatbelt instead as my heart hammers hard in my chest. He passes cars, weaving through traffic, driving in a way Naz usually doesn't drive. It isn't until we pull up to a stoplight a few blocks away, right beside a black car, that I realize exactly what he'd been doing.

He was following the car Melody got in.

The light stays red for what feels like forever, the glow of it bathing us in the car. I'm watching Naz, on edge, while Naz is turned to the side, watching the other car. It's a BMW from what I can gather from the emblem on the hood. The windows are blacked out, darkly tinted, illegally so. New York has laws. You have to be able to see in.

I can see *nothing*.

The red turns to green, and the car takes off, heading straight through the intersection. I stare at it as it does, seeing a Florida license plate.

Naz sits there for a second, until the car behind us blows the horn. The sound seems to jar him back to reality as he turns, facing straight ahead, and hits the gas, heading the direction of Brooklyn.

"What's wrong?" I ask again, my voice hesitant, when he says nothing by way of explanation for whatever just happened.

I need to know, though, if it involves my friend.

"Nothing," he says again, glancing my way. "Just thought I recognized the car."

Chapter Twelve
Ignazio

It's a small, two story house in Bensonhurst, a neighborhood in the southern part of Brooklyn, not too far from where I live. Brick with pale pink trimming, it appears unassuming, bright and airy, surrounded by a white railing, the closest we get to a white picket fence around here. There's a small driveway right off the sidewalk, barely big enough for one car to fit.

And there it is.

The black BMW.

It wasn't hard to track down. One unannounced visit to Armando and not only did I have an address, but I was given directions right to it. It's amazing to me, the information a man can produce, when you stick a knife to his throat and threaten to slice if he doesn't tell you exactly what you want to hear.

I walk around the car, surveying it, before leaning back against the passenger door and crossing my arms over my chest.

I wait.

Ten minutes pass, then twenty, but it doesn't matter. Patience has always been a strong suit of mine. I'll stand here all day if I have to, but I know I won't.

He'll come out sometime.

It's been about thirty minutes when the front door to the house opens and out he waltzes. *Lorenzo.* Dressed down, in jeans and a black t-shirt, clutching an orange as he hums to himself. He looks up out of habit, glancing toward the car. His footsteps falter, a look of surprise passing across his face that he quickly straightens out.

I caught him off guard, but he's good at this game, because he didn't let it show for long.

Carefully, he steps off the porch and heads toward me, pausing on the other side of the white railing. Only a few feet separate us. I could reach him if I wanted to.

We both know that.

"Ignazio," he says, nodding in greeting. "What can I do for you?"

"I'm just curious what you're up to."

"Uh, checking the mail," he says, motioning toward the mailbox. "Thinking about what to eat for lunch."

"You know what I mean, Lorenzo. You blow into town and start making waves. You've got people nervous."

"You wouldn't be one of those people, would you?" he asks. "Nervous I might spill some of your secrets?"

"You don't worry me. I have no secrets left for you to spill."

He stares at me hard for a moment before his expression cracks and he laughs. "Right, right... so you want to know what I want, Ignazio?"

"Yes."

"I want the entire world," he says, "but I've decided to settle for New York."

He says that like it's just that simple, like all of New York can just be his if he wants it. That's not how this works, though.

"That won't be easy," I say. "You'll find resistance here."

"So I've learned," he says. "It's curious, though, considering I haven't gone after any of their territory. Everything I've done has

178

been fair game."

He's right, technically. He's done nothing but take over Ray's old stomping grounds, places that were ripe for the picking. Anybody could've claimed them. He's messed with nobody except Ray's men.

"You planning to stop there?" I ask.

"Of course not," he says.

I'm not surprised by that answer.

I can only imagine what he's planning.

"It's a problem, because they don't like outsiders. You're a stranger to them."

"Maybe you should vouch for me, then."

"I'm afraid that's not happening."

Not now.

Not ever.

I won't vouch for anybody.

Not anymore.

Because once upon a time, I made a grave mistake and vouched for a man that I thought was my best friend. A few months later, he paid me back for that gesture with a shotgun blast to the chest.

"Didn't think it would," he says. "I can't even get you to admit to yourself that we're friends."

I ignore that.

I'm not going to be goaded into that conversation.

There's movement in the house behind him, something dropping in the front room, a curtain shifting. It's just a brief flicker as a face appears before vanishing again. Lorenzo glances that way, frowning, before turning back to me.

He nods his head toward the house. "You remember Leo?"

I do, but I don't. I never knew his name. Never cared to learn it. They called him *Pretty Boy* back then. He was nothing more than a whiny little toddler the last time I saw him.

Lorenzo's little brother.

They shared a mother.

"Somewhat," I admit. "He's grown a bit."

"Yeah, a bit. He's still a pretty boy, though. He's soft. This life... his heart ain't in it like mine is."

"If that's true, why's he here?"

"Because I'm all he's got," Lorenzo says.

That's the only explanation he gives me.

It's probably the only explanation he's got.

I'm not sure if it's enough, though, not in this situation. Because he's tangled up in something dangerous and he's getting too damn close to my personal life.

I don't like it.

He's dragging me back in.

"Look, I'm only going to tell you this once," I say, pushing away from the car, taking a step toward the railing. I'm already tired of this conversation. It's exhausting. "If my wife gets hurt in any way, I'll kill you, and I can promise it won't be merciful."

He knows I mean it. He's seen me do it before. He stood beside me, in his stepfather's home, and watched as I took the man's life without an ounce of sympathy or remorse.

He nods. "Understood."

"Good."

I start to turn, to leave, until his voice stalls me.

"But I've already told you, Ignazio... I have nothing against you, no reason to target you, no reason to hurt this wife of yours."

"I heard you."

"Yet you don't believe me."

No, I don't.

I don't have to verbalize that.

He knows.

"He means her no harm, either," Lorenzo continues. "My brother, he's smitten by the Carmichael girl. I assure you, it's purely coincidental. Has nothing to do with me or you. So I'm asking you not to mess that up for him. A favor for a favor. Leave my brother out of this, and I'll make sure nobody hurts what's yours."

"Fair enough."

He smiles the second I agree and tosses me his orange. I damn near drop it, not expecting it, and grip the fruit tightly in my palm. Lorenzo backs up a few steps, pointing at me. "Have it... it's yours. Straight from the grove in Kissimmee. I'm sure you remember. Best oranges in the world."

I glance down at the orange, squeezing it, and nod in gratitude. It's an olive branch he's extending. I don't trust him, but I know how to play this game.

I'll give him something, too. "Piece of advice, Lorenzo?"

"Yeah?"

"Do something about your car," I tell him. "You still have Florida plates. It sticks out like a sore thumb. Made it easy for me to find you."

He glances at the car, that look of surprise returning, like he hadn't even considered that. "How *did* you find me?"

I shrug, turning to leave. "Streets talk, remember?"

The second I open the front door of my house I hear the growl.

It's a low rumble, completely menacing. I don't have to look at him to know he's baring his teeth. It's the same greeting, every single time. He remembers what I did.

Unlike Karissa, he hasn't forgiven me yet.

Although, *forgiveness* may not be the word for it. More like she's choosing not to hold it against me when it comes to our relationship. It's complicated. Doesn't make much sense.

It is what it is.

But Killer?

He's holding it against me still.

For the moment, anyway.

181

Stepping into the foyer, I pause there, taking off my jacket as I stare at the mutt. Rolling my sleeves up, I waltz right past him, eliciting a small retreat out of panic. He follows me, though, still lightly growling, as I head into the kitchen and fix myself something to drink. I take a few swallows of ice water before reaching up into the cabinet, grabbing a dog treat.

I toss it at him.

All at once, the growling ceases. He gobbles it up, suddenly wagging his tail, before looking at me like he wants another.

In all, I toss him three.

Walking out of the kitchen with my water, still clutching the orange Lorenzo gave to me, I make my way into the den where the television plays.

It's the middle of the afternoon, but Karissa is fast asleep.

Sprawled out on the couch, huddled under a fuzzy black blanket, the remote lying on her chest as she snores quietly. I snatch up the remote before settling in on the edge of the couch cushion near her feet, careful not to disturb her.

Food Network.

Shaking my head, I quickly flip through the channels, stalling when I come across *The Godfather* on one of the cable stations. It's cut down and edited, diluted for the masses, but it's a hell of a lot better than what she'd been watching.

Setting my water down on the coffee table, I start peeling the orange, my eyes on the screen. Sonny Corleone's black car speeds up to the toll plaza, blocked in by another. The tollbooth worker? He ducks and hides.

Even he knows it's an ambush.

BANG

BANG

BANG

BANG

BANG

A rapid succession of gunfire lights up the screen, annihilating the car with Sonny still in it. He climbs out, prepared to fight back, but he knows he's in over his head. Men like Sonny? Men like me? We know when it's too late.

Help comes, but not soon enough.

Spoiler alert: Sonny's dead.

If I ruined it for you, well, that's your own fault. The movie has been out longer than I've been alive. I've watched it a few times, mostly fueled by curiosity, picking out the shreds of accuracy that relate to my life. It might be cliché, but it's not all bullshit.

I've considered that might be how I die someday.

Wouldn't exactly be surprising, would it?

Except, unlike Sonny, I don't think I'd have a father show up to mourn me afterward.

Laughing to myself, I look away from the television as Sonny's father, the Don, weeps over him in the morgue. Yeah, not in *my* lifetime...

"You know, most people find this part sad, not funny."

As soon as I hear Karissa's voice, I glance her way, meeting her eyes as she regards me warily from where she lays. She's awake now, but barely. Her face is flushed, eyes bloodshot, with sleep-lines marking her cheek.

"It's not funny," I say, continuing to peel the orange. "I was just thinking about how, if that were me, Giuseppe would probably be dancing."

She rolls her eyes and shifts around on the couch, pushing the blanket off of herself. "He would *not*."

"Yeah, you're probably right," I mutter. "He's told me a few times that I'm already dead to him. I died two decades go. *This*?" I motion toward the television, where they've all already moved on, the plot moving forward. "This would probably just be a relief."

"You dying wouldn't be a relief to anybody." She pauses, her face scrunching up. She's not stupid. She knows I have enemies. "Well, I mean except for, you know, anybody who truly hates you, but that's not your father."

"If you say so."

"I do," she says, her voice stern. "So no dying. I forbid it. You've gotta stick around and grow old."

I wait for it, as soon as she says that.

As usual, she doesn't disappoint.

"Well, older, anyway," she mumbles. "You're already kind of old."

Smiling, I pull the orange apart, breaking off a wedge to eat. It's sweet and juicy. You can find navel oranges in any grocery store, but there's nothing quite like one pulled straight from a tree in Florida.

"I didn't know we had oranges," Karissa says, still eyeing me. "Hell, I didn't know you *liked* oranges."

"I do, but we don't," I say, pulling off a wedge and holding it out to her. "Got this while I was out."

She doesn't hesitate to snatch it right from my hand, eating it before motioning toward me, silently asking for another piece. Or more like demanding it, since she knows I'll give it to her. She doesn't need to ask. I break what's left in half, forfeiting part to her, as my attention turns back to the movie.

I'm not paying her any attention.

That's why it catches me off guard when she throws her part of the orange down and jumps up from the couch, accidentally kicking me to get around where I'm sitting. I jolt, startled, and turn to her, but she's gone.

She's already out of the room.

She's running.

I'm not one to fall victim to herd mentality, but I'm on my feet without a thought, following her. She's up the stairs and down the hallway.

I catch up to her in the bathroom.

The door is wide open, and she's on her knees in front of the toilet, losing everything in her stomach. Panic sweeps through me. It's a rare sensation. It makes me sick to my stomach.

That's all it is, isn't it?

I look at my hand, at the remnants of the orange that I'm clutching. **Son of a bitch.** I should've known better than to actually eat something he gave me. The thought didn't even cross my mind that it might not be safe.

I'm getting soft.

Too soft.

This isn't like me.

This soft, flawed idiot I've become is nothing like the strong-willed man I always prided myself as being. That man didn't take candy from strangers and just fucking *eat it* like he had no reason to be worried. That man knew the cost of being soft.

I toss what's left of the fruit in the trashcan before crouching beside Karissa, my hand on her back. It seems to have let up already, and now she's just laying there, against the toilet, her head down, like she's planning to go to sleep.

I'm trying hard not to be disturbed by that.

I scrubbed it not long ago, one night when I couldn't sleep.

But, still... I piss in that thing.

"Karissa, baby..." My voice is quiet. I'm not trying to alarm her. "Talk to me."

She turns her head, opening her eyes. "I think I'm coming down with something."

"What makes you think that?"

Her face contorts at that question. "Other than the fact that I'm laying halfway in the toilet?"

"Other than that."

"I've felt like crap all day. I'm queasy. Exhausted. I almost feel hung-over, but I didn't drink last night, so..."

"So you're coming down with something."

"Yep."

I rub her back a moment longer before standing up, offering her

185

a hand. She lets me help her stand up, not at all arguing when I grab her, sweeping her right off of her feet, and carry her down the hall to the bedroom. Yeah, must be coming down with something to not put up a fight over that.

I get her settled into the bed and run my hand along her forehead. She's clammy but not hot. "How about some soup?"

"You going to have some delivered?"

"No, I'm going to cook."

"We don't have any *Campbell's.*"

"I don't need any," I tell her. "I know how to make soup from scratch."

She stares at me with disbelief as she throws the covers off that I just got on her. "If you're cooking, I'm watching."

Laughing, I force her back into the bed and once again put the covers over her. "Relax. You can watch some other time. Right now you need to take it easy."

She pouts but again doesn't argue, staying put. I plug my phone in to charge, laying it on the bedside stand, as I leave the bedroom.

Killer stands in the hallway between the bedroom and the stairs, watching me. He growls a bit as I pass, but I ignore him, heading downstairs.

The pantry is loaded with ingredients, thanks to her incessant desire to learn how to cook everything she sees on television. I want to make her my mother's Italian Chicken Soup, and pull out everything I remember her using for it when I was a kid, but I'm drawing a blank and having to wing some of it.

Or most of it, rather.

It has been a long time since she last made it for me.

I spend a while getting it together and letting it simmer on the stove before heading back into the den, this time alone. The theme from The Godfather echoes through the room as the credits roll on the television screen. Grabbing the remote again, I flip through channels, stalling when I reach the local news, catching a breaking report about a small corner store in Hell's Kitchen exploding, taking out the entire apartment building above it.

Gas leak, they're calling it, but I know better.

Because I know that store. I know those apartments.

I was just inside them, visiting Armando, threatening him for information.

I'm staring at the live feed playing from the site, barely listening to what the reporter's saying, but I catch a few of her words, the tail end of her segment.

A black car seen lurking near the business, missing a license plate.

I wonder why that is.

I turn off the television and sit in silence for a moment, letting that sink in.

I didn't give up any names, but I wouldn't be surprised if Lorenzo riddled it out. If he figured out where I got my information and decided to silence the source.

I may have very well gotten Armando killed this afternoon.

And I might've even helped Lorenzo get away with it.

When the soup's finished, I carry a bowl of it upstairs, finding Karissa lying in bed, playing on a phone. *My* phone.

The sight of it stalls me.

Not that I've got anything to hide from her. I try not to keep any secrets. If she wants to know, I'll tell her. But still, my natural instinct is to balk. "What are you doing?"

She looks up at me, smiling, and sets the phone down. She doesn't look alarmed, like she's been caught doing anything she shouldn't have been doing. "Just changing your ringtone to something more *you*."

"More boy bands?"

"Does it count if they're boys in a band?"

"Pretty sure that's the definition."

"Then yep," she says, as I hand her the soup. "But hey, at least it's still not Bieber."

"Thank God," I say, taking the phone from her and again plugging it in. "I'd hate to have to divorce you."

"You'd *divorce* me?"

"Or worse."

Chapter Thirteen
Karissa

"Miss Vitale? A word?"

It's still strange to me, going by that last name. So strange I don't respond to it sometimes, because it doesn't click it's me they want until they say it again.

"Miss Vitale?"

Glancing up, stalling the packing up of my backpack, I look at Rowan as he stands at the end of the aisle, beside my desk. Most of my classmates have already jetted out of here, but I'm running a little behind the crowd today.

Like an idiot, I fell asleep in class.

I dozed right through his entire lecture, missing all of it. I remember siting down and well... here I am, an hour later, getting ready to leave again.

Oops.

I clear my throat. "It's Mrs."

That takes him aback. "Excuse me?"

"There's a Mister, so I'm not a Miss."

"Oh. You're married."

"Yeah."

He seems genuinely surprised by that tidbit.

Must not have read my file.

Thank God.

"Oh, well, Mrs. Vitale, I was hoping to have a word with you."

I want to say no, because having a word with me leads to more words, which leads to me saying words back, and judging by how the last conversation I had with a professor in this room ended up being one of his last, I'm going to go out on a limb and say having a word with me probably isn't wise. Another thing he'd know if he read my file. But how can I explain that without actually explaining anything?

I don't know.

I can't.

So I merely shrug and continue packing up my things to leave, figuring if he wants to have a word with me, there's really nothing I can do to stop him.

"I just wanted to tell you that I graded your Napoleon paper."

"Oh?" Putting on my backpack, I eye him warily, feeling this strange sense of déjà vu about this conversation. "Let me guess... unimaginative? Mediocre? *Pretentious?*"

That's what Professor Santino always said about my papers.

His brow furrows as he pulls the paper out of a folder he's carrying, holding it out to me. "I actually found it to be refreshing."

That word stalls me for a moment. *Refreshing.* I take the paper from him, glancing at it, seeing the red **A+** written on the top of it.

Whoa.

"Thanks," I say, unsure what I'm supposed to say in this situation. "I wasn't sure..."

"Most people were literal about the assignment," he says, like he knows where I'm going with what I'm saying. "But you explored the concept deeper, and it's appreciated. I know history, to most people, is rather boring, so it's refreshing to have a student actually attempt to analyze things. That's how we learn from history, so we don't find ourselves repeating it... if you know what I mean."

"Yeah..." I know exactly what he means. "Thanks again."

He smiles kindly. "I should be thanking you."

"Well... you're welcome, I guess," I say with a laugh, turning to leave. He's right beside me, walking along with me. "I don't really have a good track record when it comes to writing analytical essays. I sort of bombed my first philosophy class because of it."

"Daniel Santino's class?"

"Uh... yeah. That's the one."

"I never met the guy, but I heard he could be quite difficult."

Difficult. Hell of an understatement.

"I wasn't exactly his favorite person," I tell him as we head outside. "We had some issues, so that probably had something to do with it, too."

"Probably," he agrees. "Because I doubt your essays did you in, especially if they were anything like *this*."

Reaching over, he shakes the paper I'm holding onto, giving me another smile before walking away. I stand there, in front of the building, watching him.

Weird.

"Friend of yours?"

I jump at the unexpected voice behind me... *right* behind me. So damn close I can practically feel the warm breath against my neck. Swinging around, I look at Naz. "Oh, hey! What are you doing here?"

"Came to see you," he says casually before motioning down the street, in the direction Rowan jetted off to, repeating his question. "Friend of yours?"

"Rowan's my history professor, actually."

"Huh. On a first name basis with a professor, are we? And what exactly did *Rowan* want?"

"He was just talking to me about my paper."

I shake it in his face, showing off the fat, red **A+** on top of it. Naz snatches it from my hand, eyes glossing over the paper. "You

191

wrote down exactly what I said."

"Yep," I say, absolutely no shame.

He laughs, handing it back. "It's nice to know I've still got it."

Taking my bag off, I fold up my paper and shove it in. I try to put the bag back on then, but Naz grabs a hold of it, taking it from me.

"I can carry my own stuff, you know."

"Nonsense."

Nonsense.

That's his response.

I almost take offense to it.

Reaching over, I snatch my bag back, ignoring him as I put it on.

Nonsense, my ass.

He laughs again, reaching for me, pulling me toward him. "I'm glad to see you're feeling better."

I roll my eyes at that.

I was feeling queasy earlier, and I still feel like I could sleep for a damn year straight, but at least I haven't thrown up today.

"So do you have any classes this afternoon?"

"Math... English..." I eye him warily. He knows my schedule. He had it memorized before me. "Why?"

"Thought we could spend some time together this afternoon," he says, "if you weren't too busy."

I'm equal parts flattered and suspicious. I love when he wants to spend time with me, but I'm not an idiot. I know when Naz is up to something. I have enough practice at this point to tell it.

"Never too busy for you. Do you want to grab some lunch or something? Hang out? Maybe take a walk?"

"A walk is perfect."

Yep, definitely up to something.

We don't take walks.

I motion past us, down the sidewalk, toward Washington Square Park on the corner near the school. It's as good of a place as any to walk to. Naz takes my hand, something that surprises me, even though it probably shouldn't. We're married, for Christ's sake, but still... he takes my breath away sometimes with the little things.

It's busy in the park, as it usually is at this hour, as students come and go between classes. We find an empty bench near the entrance and sit down on it. I drop my bag by my feet, kicking it to the side, away from Naz, so he doesn't get any bright ideas about trying to carry it again.

He takes care of me enough as it is.

"Have you thought about it any more?"

His question catches me off guard.

I'm not sure what he means.

"Have I thought about what?"

"About leaving New York."

"Oh." My insides twist at that. Have I thought about leaving? Sure. I think about it at least once a day, sometimes more. But have I made up my mind about whether or not I want to? Well, that's where I'm just not as sure...

Memories haunt me here. Every time I turn a corner, they're there, lingering, lurking, a reminder of everything that happened, the things he did, the things I caused. I know it's not all my fault, not at all, but I'm not blameless. *Silence implies consent.* I've heard that said so many times. If you don't speak up about something, you're letting it happen. *Acquiescence.* Living here, there's no way we can ever really have a fresh start. We're covered in permanent marker. We can't erase our black marks... not in New York.

But to actually leave means walking away from the only place I've ever thought of as *home.* It means leaving the people I care about, leaving my best friend, saying goodbye to Naz's father. Am I ready for that? It means leaving behind the good memories I've had here along with all of the bad. Because there's been a lot of bad, yes... but there was still so much good.

"Oh," he repeats after a moment. "Should I take that as a no?"

"I don't know," I say. "I just... is it a mistake? I don't want it to be like we're just running away from our problems, because eventually they'll catch up to us whenever we stop running, you know?"

"Yeah," he says. "I know."

"I just wish someone would give me some sort of sign so I know what the right thing to do is."

"The right thing, Karissa, is whatever you want to do. There's no wrong decision here."

I want to believe that.

But it doesn't feel that way.

"I don't know," I say. "I don't know what I want. I'm happy here, but I just wonder if maybe we'd be happier somewhere else."

He says nothing to that.

I don't know what he's thinking.

I wish he'd be the one to make this decision.

But he puts it on me, and that's a lot of pressure, because despite what he says, I fear there might be a wrong decision here.

And knowing me?

I'd be the one to make it.

"Hey! Guys!"

Melody's voice is unmistakable. By the time I look up, she's already right in front of me, dragging a flustered looking Leo along with her, her hand locked in his so tightly he nails dig into his skin. He doesn't put up a fight, but he doesn't seem very enthusiastic about it for some reason.

"Miss Carmichael," Naz says casually. "Nice to see you again."

"You, too." She gives him a brief once-over. "Stylin' and profilin' as usual, I see."

Naz glances down at himself, brow furrowed slightly, like maybe he doesn't know what the hell she means.

"Hey, Mel," I chime in, to spare him from that conversation. If he asks, she'll only confuse him more. "What are you guys up to?"

"Heading to grab some lunch," she says. "Oh! Why don't you join us? That would be awesome, wouldn't it?"

I start to decline, as Leo nervously rubs his neck with his free hand, but Naz interjects before anyone else can say anything. "I think that's a wonderful idea."

Uh... okay.

Not the response I was expecting, especially after the conversation we'd had about him making friends. He glances at me, raising his eyebrows, awaiting agreement. I shrug, because really, who am I to decline at this point? He's already said yes.

"Sure," I say. "Where are we going?"

Melody turns to Leo, smiling proudly, knowing she accomplished one hell of a feat getting Naz to agree. "Where to?"

He hesitates, glancing between Melody and me, his eyes never greeting Naz. "Wherever you want to eat, love."

"I know a place," Naz says, getting to his feet. He stands right in front of Leo, a mere few feet between them. He casually fixes his tie, eyes right on the boy, not once looking away. Leo still doesn't look at him, but it's obvious he notices, with the way he fidgets, pulling Melody closer, trying to look unflustered, but man... he's a mess.

Naz says I'm not intuitive, that I'm terrible at reading people, and it's obvious to even me that Leo is uncomfortable around my husband.

"The deli?" I ask, hopeful. I haven't seen Giuseppe since the incident. I miss the guy. Would be nice to see him again.

Naz laughs. "No, the pizzeria in Brooklyn."

"Oh, uh..." I look to Melody for her reaction, knowing we ate there before with Paul, but she merely shrugs, like that doesn't bother her at all.

"Sounds great to me," she says, looking to Leo for his reaction, but he says nothing. No objections. No confirmations. *Nothing.*

"Wonderful," Naz says, reaching into his pocket for his keys. "I'll drive."

I see it then, the panic in Leo's eyes. The color drains from his face as he quickly shakes his head, locked in place, tugging Melody's hand to stop her when she tries to walk away. "We'll just meet you guys there."

Naz raises his eyebrows. "Nonsense, my car's right over there."

"Yeah, but, you know..." Leo stammers, like he's searching for a reason not to get in that car. "It's just that, well..."

"Come on," Melody says. "We'll get there faster if we just ride with him. Besides, ugh, I don't really feel like taking the subway today."

"But..." Leo stalls, taking a deep breath, before shaking it off. "Okay, I guess."

Naz doesn't seem offended by the boy's hesitance.

I think I get it, though.

He's intimidating.

He still makes me nervous sometimes.

The Mercedes is parked less than a block away. We climb in it, and Naz starts the engine, the locks automatically clicking in place the second he puts the car in drive. My eyes are fixed to the side mirror, and from my peripheral I see Leo flinch in the backseat, his gaze on the door. He looks like he wants to jump out, like he's already considering tucking and rolling in the middle of the road, when Naz pulls into traffic.

Melody seems oblivious, though.

When we reach the first stoplight, Naz reaches up, adjusting his rearview mirror, angling it so he can look in the backseat.

Melody talks incessantly during the drive. I haven't seen her so carefree in a long, long time...

Leo, on the other hand, looks wound tight.

Naz's eyes flicker between the road and the rearview mirror the entire way to Brooklyn. I try to humor my friend, chatting back to her, but my attention is on *him*.

A sinking feeling is settling in the pit of my stomach.

I'm starting to think this was a bad idea.

A terrible fucking idea.

And I'm absolutely sure of it the second we make it to the pizzeria and Naz, as usual, secures a table right away. We follow the hostess to the small, round table in the back, isolated away from the other diners. Naz pulls my chair out for me, eyeing Leo as the boy does the same for Melody.

"Bottle of your best wine," Naz tells the woman.

She brings it promptly, preceded by the owner of the restaurant. Andretti, I think his name was. He approaches the table, a wide smile on his face, greeting Naz like Giuseppe greets, well... everyone *except* for Naz.

"Ah, Vitale!" the man says, grinning as he squeezes Naz's shoulder affectionately. "*Che piacere vederti!*"

Naz responds with something I don't comprehend, and they go back and forth for a minute, spouting off Italian, as the cork is popped on the bottle of wine. I listen, even though I have absolutely no idea what either of them are saying, and can feel my face heating when both men look my way.

"*Ciao, bella,*" the owner says, reaching over and grabbing my hand, kissing the back of it. "*Come stai,* uh... *special someone?*"

"Karissa," Naz says. "Her name's Karissa."

"Karissa," the man repeats, raising his eyebrows as he waits for me to answer whatever the hell he'd just asked me.

"Uh... hey," I say, pulling my hand away.

I have no idea what I'm supposed to say.

"He asked how you're doing," Naz interjects, pouring wine into his own glass.

"Oh, I'm good," I say. "Great, really. Wonderful."

The man's eyes narrow as he starts firing stuff off, fast and fluent and right over my fucking head. I stare at him as he animatedly talks with his hands, motioning toward me, before stalling, eyebrows raised, like he again expects me to answer some kind of question that was in there.

"He said you're lying," Naz chimes in, pouring a bit of wine in the other three glasses. "He says you look... how can I put this nicely? Run down."

"Nice," I mutter. "Tell him I said thanks for the compliment. I appreciate it."

Before Naz can say anything, the man continues, spouting out something that makes Naz choke on thin air. He coughs, laughing, and shakes his head. "No, no... she's just been under the weather."

The man eyes me for a moment before shrugging it off, looking to Melody. He greets her warmly in Italian, also taking her hand and kissing the back of it, before his eyes gloss over Leo. It's subtle, the shift in the man's demeanor.

He says nothing to him.

No hello.

No nice to have you.

Nothing.

Instead, he turns to Naz, leaning closer, mumbling something I can't hear. Not that I'd understand it, anyway, but the man is intentionally trying to conceal it from prying ears. Naz nods in confirmation to whatever it is, and the owner again squeezes his shoulder before simply walking away.

"Tell me something, Leo," Naz says, picking up his glass and swirling the red wine around before taking a sip. "Are you fluent, or do you just know a bit?"

Leo looks over at him, for the first time meeting his eyes. "What?"

"*Mi avete sentito,*" Naz says, his tone clipped. "*Tu parli Italiano.*"

Leo hesitates before mumbling, "Just a bit."

Naz nods, like he's not surprised by that answer, but I am. I know enough to grasp where this conversation is going and son of a bitch... Leo speaks Italian?

I glance at Melody. She seems just as surprised by that. "You know Italian?"

Leo looks at her, a slight flush on his cheeks, like he's

embarrassed to be having this conversation. "Some... the basics, I guess, but not much more than that."

"Wow." Melody leans toward him. "Say something dirty to me."

I laugh at that, as does Naz, but Leo's flush only deepens.

"Drink," Naz says, shoving Leo's glass toward him. "You'll probably need to with that one there."

Melody rolls her eyes at that, grabbing her glass, and guzzles down all of her drink before reaching out, asking for more. Naz obliges, pouring her some wine, before setting the bottle in the middle of the table, telling her to help herself to as much as she wants.

It's strange, seeing him so... nice.

He's nice to me, sure. He spoils me. And he's always tolerated Melody, to an extent, for my sake. But right now he's being hospitable, like maybe he is actually trying to make friends. He's trying.

We order food.

They drink wine.

I take a sip, but it's too bitter for my taste buds, and I'm not really feeling it, whatever it is. So I drink water instead, watching as they grow at ease, Leo's posture not as tense, but it doesn't escape my notice that he still tries not to look at my husband.

"Tell me, Leo," Naz says when the food arrives. "You got any goals for the future?"

Goals.

For the future.

Is this a job interview?

"Uh... I'm not sure, really. Still trying to get used to living here," Leo says. "It's so fast-paced compared to where I grew up."

Naz doesn't ask where that is, and starts to question him some more about the future, but I chime in. Call me curious. "Where did you grow up?"

Leo looks at me and hesitates. "Florida."

"Where at in Florida?"

He doesn't answer, but Melody jumps in, her voice raised with excitement. "Oh my God, I can't believe I forgot to tell you... he's from Kissimmee! Isn't that crazy? Kissimmee..." She points at me. "Kissimmee!"

That sinking feeling from the car settles back in. I glance at Naz, and he doesn't react to that. He doesn't look surprised at all, like he already knows all of this.

He probably does.

After all, he knew who I was before I even did, so why wouldn't he learn Leo's life story the second they were introduced?

"That is crazy," I say. "Small world."

Naz puts his arm around me. "Small world, indeed."

Lunch is awkward, as Naz fires off question after question, all of them aimed at Leo. He asks about his family (one brother, no parents... been an orphan since he was just a kid). He asks about his work (right now washing dishes at Paragone... his brother knew a guy who knew a guy who got him the gig). He asks about his living situation (staying in a house in Bensonhurst with his family).

He all but asks, 'what are your intentions with this woman?'

Although, okay, I kind of want to ask that, so I wish he would.

Leo takes it all in stride. Or, well, he tolerates it, really. He doesn't look happy to be getting interrogated, but he answers everything Naz throws at him.

I eat a few slices of pizza, my appetite somewhat returning, as the three of them finish off the bottle of wine. Melody and Leo chat quietly to themselves as Naz relaxes back in his chair, having not touched a bite of food.

"I'm ashamed, Jailbird," he says, grabbing my glass from the table. "You're letting the wine go to waste."

"Then drink it," I say. "Really... you should drink it. It probably costs as much as my tuition for the year."

Smiling, he sips from my glass. "Not quite."

"Ugh, don't even tell me," I say. "You know, there are people starving in America, people with unclean drinking water, who barely have heat in their homes to stay warm. There are people in frickin' New York who are out there freezing because they can't even afford clothes."

"Maybe we should give them yours," he says playfully, his hand drifting down my chest, fingers dipping below the neckline of my shirt, stroking the skin around my bra. "I'll keep you warm all by myself."

I smack his hand when he tries to cup a breast. "Jesus Christ, Naz, keep it in your pants. We're in public."

"Thought that was how you liked it."

Rolling my eyes, I grab my glass of water and take a sip, trying to conceal the ferocious blush on my cheeks. Melody clears her throat then, thankfully distracting Naz, as she checks her watch. "We should get going. We've been here a while now."

Naz nods. "I can drive you back to the city."

"Don't worry about it," Melody says, waving him off. "You guys live, like, right down the street from here."

More like across the borough, but close enough.

"Besides, we're going to go to Leo's for a bit, so he's just going to have his brother pick us up in a few minutes. No biggie."

Naz stares at her.

He says nothing.

Something tells me, to him, for some reason, that is a **biggie**.

"What do we owe you?" Melody asks, standing up.

"Nothing," Naz says, holding out a hand and stopping Leo when he pulls out his wallet. "Your money's no good with me."

I expect a fight on that. I expect these two men to have a pissing contest over the check. Instead, Leo hesitates before putting his wallet away, nodding.

"You're a cool dude, Ignazio," Melody says. "I don't care what anybody says."

Naz blinks a few times. I see his lips move as he incredulously mouths the words **cool dude**.

Melody walks away, and Leo starts to follow, but Naz's hand

darts out, tightly gripping Leo's arm, stopping him. They stare at each other in silence for a moment... a moment that feels like it lasts forever... before Naz loosens his grip.

Gone is his casual demeanor.

For the first time, in a while, I'm seeing Vitale again.

"Send my regards to your brother," Naz says, his voice hard.

Leo pulls his arm away, saying nothing as he rushes away, disappearing from the pizzeria without a word in response to that. I gape at Naz as he relaxes again, finishing the wine from my glass.

Send my regards to your brother.

Holy shit.

"I'm right, aren't I?" My voice is low, like the words don't want to come out. "I was right about him. He's a... you know... he's like you."

"He's nothing like me."

I don't know if he means that.

I don't know what to think.

Naz wouldn't lie to me, but something is off about this.

"Promise me something," Naz says.

I glance at him. "What?"

"Just promise me," he says. "Whatever I'm about to say, you'll listen. Promise you'll trust me on this."

Ugh. "I promise."

"Keep your distance from him."

My brow furrows. "What?"

"I'm not saying you can't be friends with Melody," he says. "All I'm asking is you keep your distance from her boyfriend. No more dates with them."

"Why?"

He looks at me, pausing as his eyes survey my face, studying me again like there's going to be another test. He'll pass this one, too, just like he aced the last.

He knows me.

He knows me better than anyone.

"Because I don't want to have to kill another boyfriend of hers."

Those words stall me.

He says it so matter-of-fact, like it's actually a prospect. Like he actually might kill him, and it might be my fault for not listening to him. "But—"

His hand darts up, covering my mouth, silencing my protest. "You promised."

Reaching up, I yank his hand away. "But you said he wasn't like you"

"He's not," he says. "But that doesn't mean he's harmless, sweetheart. Some of the most dangerous people are only dangerous because of what they mean to others, not because of who they are."

Like you.

He doesn't say those words, but I know he means them. I'm dangerous because of Naz. Naz would kill for me. He'd kill because of me. I know he would.

He's done it before.

And he's telling me now, if I don't keep my distance, he might have to do it again.

Chapter Fourteen

Ignazio

There's a difference between a fight and a battle. A fight is isolated, usually over as quickly as it started. But a battle? A battle is part of a bigger war.

Battles can go on *forever*.

Long, drawn out, bloody, and merciless... it's the kind of battle we find ourselves in the middle of now. The city is burning and people are falling as the devastation spreads through the boroughs, touching places it hadn't infected before.

The new king decided it was time to claim more than just the pride lands. He wants those shadowy bits that don't belong to him. He wants the entire kingdom.

The problem, you see, is that most people don't seem to notice. They go about their days like nothing has changed. The casualties barely make a blip in the newspaper, treated as isolated incidents, like they're not even connected.

But they are.

They all add up to a fucked up situation.

One I'm caught smack dab in the middle of.

"He's got to go."

Genova sits across from me in the den of his brick house, frantically puffing away at one of his cigars. Smoke permeates the room. It's locked up tight and has no place to go. My eyes sting from the haze, my chest tightening with every breath. I can feel it scorching my lungs and I'm not even the one smoking.

"Who?" I ask, not entirely sure why I'm here. He asked me to meet him on short notice, saying he had something important to discuss with me.

"The guy," he says. "Scar."

Ah.

Scar.

"He hit one of my safe houses this week," he continues. "Robbed me of a whole gun supply. Took out three of my guys!"

Pity, I think, but I don't say that.

Don't want to piss off a boss any more than I already have.

"He's certainly persistent," I say.

I wish I could say that I was surprised.

I'm not.

"He's a pain in my ass," Genova counters. "He's a fuckin' cockroach I wanna squash! He's got to go, there's no away around it. So I need you to take care of that for me, like you said you were gonna."

I just stare at the man after he says that.

"I never said—"

"You said you were gonna handle the problem."

"I handled it."

"Yeah? So why the fuck is he still breathing?"

Good question.

"He's a boss now," I point out. If what Lorenzo said is true, that he'd been called in to meet with the families, like it or not, he's now one of them. He's off limits. "I can't kill a boss without permission from the others."

I did it once and got away with it.

I won't be so lucky if I do it again.

There are three other families out there who would need to give permission before I could ever touch a man in his position. They're unwritten rules, ones they've admonished me on before.

I can't risk it.

I would.

But I can't.

Not while staying out of it all.

"He's nothing," Genova spats, flicking the ashes from his cigar right onto the floor. "He's nobody! *Nobody!* He'll never be a boss!"

I don't know if he means what he's saying or if it's the anger talking, so I nod noncommittally and just hope that's enough to get him off my case about this.

"So?" he asks. "You going to take care of this for me or not?"

Or not.

"I'm out," I say. "I've told you that."

He scoffs. "The only out in this life is in a fuckin' wooden box. You've been in for as long as I've known you. Just because you belonged to Angelo—"

"I didn't belong to anybody," I say, cutting him off. "I'm not a made man, Genova. I never took an oath. Never said those vows. Never swore myself to anybody."

"Except your wife, right?" He laughs bitterly. "Or wives, I guess it is. Took oaths for them, didn't you? Swore yourself to them. They're good enough for your loyalty, but what, none of us are?"

He's twisting shit, trying to manipulate me. "It's different."

"As far as I'm concerned, Vitale, it's all the same. It's all love, and respect, and family. You make a vow to a piece of pussy to worship it forever, but you never were man enough to take a vow to commit yourself to the brotherhood with us. After all Angelo did for you, after all he lost... gotta say, that always rubbed me the wrong way."

I can hear the anger in his words, the deep-seeded resentment I always suspected he felt. I declined their sacred invitation, probably the only one who ever did it.

The only one who lived to tell about it.

I got a pass for the rejection because of who I am.

Or rather, who I was.

But I'm not that person anymore.

I'm no longer Angelo's golden boy, the bloodthirsty son-in-law eager to take on the entire world for the cause. I've said it before... there are no friends in this business. There are just people who need you until they don't need you anymore. Either you're on their side or you're standing in their way, and the last place you want to be is in the way of a war.

And I'm standing in the middle of the battleground with nowhere to go.

Pick a side, they're all screaming.

It's a tug-of-war I can't win.

"What would you do now?" he asks. "If I invited you to join us, to be one of us, to vow your loyalty to us after all these years, would you deny the family again?"

"I'm not your enemy," I tell him, evading that question, because he wouldn't like my answer to it. I'm not joining.

"You're not my friend either," he says, "not if you turn your back on us."

Silence permeates the room then. Guards stand in the corners of the space, falling into the darkened shadows, watching, waiting, protecting the man they swore themselves to, a man I'm very clearly pissing off by refusing to join them. But that just wasn't me, despite what they all might've thought. I wasn't made to be a street soldier. I wasn't built to follow orders. I'm not afraid of a man with a gun. Giuseppe Vitale's blood pumps through my veins. As much as the man might hate it, that's an undeniable fact. There's nothing coded in my DNA that makes me a passive pushover... nothing that makes me one of his brainwashed monkeys.

"I knew him," I say.

Genova stares at me. "Who?"

"Scar." I stare back at the man, waiting for a reaction, to see if he knew that. His expression remains blank. I'm not sure if he's just that damn good at wearing a mask to hide his surprise or if he did his homework, too, if he made the connection. It couldn't have been that hard. You see, while Lorenzo's blood came straight from the Gambini family, an Accardi raised him, and the Accardis were always loyal to Genova. That's got to burn. This is personal. "I knew him, long ago. I knew him, and I saw something in him, something that reminded me of myself."

"Why are you telling me this?"

"Because it won't be easy to squash him, Genova," I say, "not when I helped make him the monster he is."

Genova nods.

No, he's not surprised at all.

"That's why I'm asking for your help, Vitale." He leans toward me, flicking even more ashes onto the floor. "Join us. Help us. Let's put all of this animosity behind us, and let's finally embrace each other as *friends*."

I stare at him for a moment, considering how to answer, before I just say the words. "I have no friends."

There's somebody at my front door.

Scratch that. Two somebodies—a woman and a little girl. The woman is dressed in a pantsuit with heels, tall and blonde and too attractive to be natural. The child, maybe seven, is pulling a red wagon, wearing a green vest.

A Girl Scout.

They're easily recognizable.

I whip my car into my driveway and pause for a moment, watching as they talk to Karissa. She stands on the porch with them, the front door wide open behind her, Killer wagging his tail excitedly in the yard, being doted on by the little girl.

I'm not sure how long they've been here, but I'm guessing a while. They all look so comfortable.

The moment I step out of the car, though, that changes. The visitors quickly depart, heading the opposite direction, while Killer's stance turns defensive.

Karissa turns my way. "Where'd you run off to this morning?"

It's afternoon already.

She's still in her pajamas.

It's obvious she hasn't gone anywhere.

Huh. "Didn't you have class today?"

"I asked you first."

"Had stuff to do."

"Well, me, too," she says, waving behind her, into the open house. "Lots to do like… sleep."

I laugh at that, stepping up onto the porch with her. My gaze drifts down the street in the direction the people scurried off. "So you had some visitors today?"

"Uh, yeah… they were selling cookies. I bought a few boxes."

Shaking my head, I step past her into the foyer and freeze. At least a dozen boxes of cookies are stacked up inside the front door.

"A few boxes," I repeat as Karissa joins me, ushering Killer inside.

She shuts the door. "Yeah, I mean, I would've gotten more, but this was all they had left."

"More?" I ask incredulously. "You bought them out."

She pushes past me, grabbing the box from on top, and rolls her eyes dramatically, making sure I see it. Opening the box, she tears into it, pulling out one of the peanut butter Tagalongs, not even hesitating before eating the thing. "You know these things are hot commodities, and they only sell them, like, once a year. We need to be stockpiling them like it's the fucking apocalypse."

I glance at her. "I don't think they're that serious."

"Come on, don't even act like those people on *The Walking Dead* wouldn't be a billion times happier if they had some Thin Mints."

"I think they'd rather have showers, and clean clothing, and maybe even the occasional steak to eat."

"Well, then, they're stupid," she says, pulling out another cookie and pointing at me with it. "These things are the key to survival. Mark my words... the Girl Scouts are geniuses. They're saving the world, one Samoa at a time."

Grabbing some boxes, I take them into the kitchen, finding room in a cabinet to shove them in. Karissa follows me, carrying the rest of the boxes, but she doesn't bother trying to help me put them away. She guards the open box, devouring the things, as she hops up on the counter beside me, just sitting there, swinging her legs.

"I always wanted to be a Girl Scout," she says. "Really, I think it was just for the damn cookies, but still... it's as good a reason as any.

"Why didn't you do it?"

"My mom wouldn't let me."

"Huh."

"Yeah, something about it being too dangerous," she says. "Guess she thought the boogeyman might've found me easier if I wore that green vest."

"He might've," I offer, not sure if my honesty will make her feel better about that. "Would've been another piece in a paper trail."

"So basically, what you're saying is, it's *your* fault I'm hoarding cookies."

I close the cabinet and look at her. She's being playful about it. There's nothing accusatory in her tone. "You seem to be in a good mood today."

"Yeah, I'm feeling better," she says. "I think I was burned out, you know? Between school and life and you... it's just been a lot of stress."

"Nice of you to include me."

She kicks her foot out, hitting me with it. "You know what I'm saying."

"I do. And I'm glad you're feeling better."

"Me, too," she says. "And Cherry and Destiny bringing me cookies was just the icing on the cake."

Cherry.

Destiny.

What the hell?

"Cherry and Destiny," I repeat.

"Yeah, the Montgomerys," she says. "They live just down the block. Cherry's a stay-at-home mom. Her husband, David, is an investment banker. Isn't that cool? I told her you do all that stuff, too."

"All *what* stuff?"

"Like trade stocks and portfolios or whatever."

"You're thinking of a stockbroker. An investment banker helps companies raise money."

"Same difference," she says, waving me off as she grabs another cookie. "It's all about money, isn't it? You know about *money*."

"So, you talked about me?"

"Of course," she says, like that's not a big deal at all. "She asked what my husband did for a living."

"And what did you tell her?"

"Same thing you told me."

"Which is?"

"Freelancing."

I laugh. *Freelancing*. I remember telling her that. It was true, albeit misleading, I'll admit. I left off the part that what I was doing was illegal.

I suppose she left that off, too.

"You know, her husband goes to a club," she says. "One of those men-only, non-stripper kind of clubs that you used to go to. Bunch of rich guys drinking liquor and having pissing contests or something, I don't know... whatever you do at those places. I told her you might be interested—"

"Karissa, just... *don't*." Stepping to her, I cradle her face in my hands and stare at her pointedly. "I love you, I do, but so help me God, the next person who talks to me about *making friends* is going to have their tongue ripped out for it. You got me?"

She clamps her lips closed.

"I'm not interested in hanging out with investment bankers," I say, letting go of her. "I'd rather spend my time with you."

She opens her mouth, like she's going to say something to that, but instead she just shrugs and finishes her cookie.

Once it's gone, she closes the box up and sets it aside before hopping down onto her feet. "Ugh, I'm starving... you want to head into the city and grab something to eat?"

I grab her hips, pulling her to me. "I've had a long day and I'm tired. Why don't we just order some delivery, instead?" My hands travel down the curve of her ass as I press myself against her. Dipping my head, my lips find her neck. Her skin is soft and warm, slightly tangy, as my tongue makes its way along her throat. "We can eat and then I can... *eat*."

My teeth nip the base of her throat, and she hisses, pushing away from me. "Thought you were tired?"

"Never too tired for you, sweetheart."

As soon as those words are out, I'm yawning.

"Ugh, as great as that sounds, I've got a meeting with my advisor a little later, so I've got no choice but to head to the city."

I sigh, letting go of her. "You can't skip it?"

"Afraid not. The time has come to declare a major finally."

Huh.

I'm not exactly surprised. She's been in school for quite a while now and she's running out of time. But she hasn't mentioned it before this moment.

Hasn't brought it up at all.

"So what are you declaring?"

"Dunno."

"You don't know."

"Nope."

"No idea at all?"

She shakes her head. "Thinking about playing eeny-meeny-miny-moe at this point."

I don't know what to tell her.

She's been indecisive for as long as I've known her.

"You shouldn't do something just for the sake of doing *something*," I tell her.

"Says the guy who just a few weeks ago told me he needed a hobby for something to do."

I guess she got me there.

I'm still trying to figure out my something.

Because this life? This tug-of-war? It isn't it.

"Get dressed and I'll drive you into the city," I say, motioning toward the stairs.

She heads upstairs, to the bedroom, and I make my way to the den, taking a seat on the couch to wait. My chest is still tight from my visit to Genova's. My lungs feel like flames have charred them. Someone punched holes in me before setting my insides on fire, making sure that every inch of me burns.

I'm in a daze, staring at the wall, going over the conversation this morning, again and again stewing over his words. My eyes sting, and I close them as I lay my head back, stealing a moment of darkness to try to find some peace.

Peace.

Peace.

All I fucking want is some *peace*.

"Naz?"

My eyes open at the sound of my name, meeting Karissa's gaze. She stands right in front of me, already dressed, her hair fixed and a bit of makeup on her face.

Sitting up, I groan, rubbing my eyes. "That was quick."

"Uh, not really... it took me like forty-five minutes."

I look at her with confusion. Forty-five minutes? "I must've dozed off."

I start to stand up when she presses her hands to my chest, shoving me back against the couch. "Why don't you get some sleep?"

"What about lunch?"

She scoffs. "I can feed myself."

"I told you I'd give you a ride to the city."

"I can find my own way there."

I debate that, and almost refute it, but truth is, I'm exhausted and could use some rest. "Call a car."

"I will," she says. "I'll look both ways before I cross the street, and I won't even take candy from strangers, even if it's chocolate."

Grabbing her, I pull her down toward me, giving her a kiss. "Good girl."

Chapter Fifteen

Karissa

The moment I open the door to the deli, I'm greeted by a sound.

Whistling.

It's loud and enthusiastic, downright cheerful, echoing overtop of the usual chatter. The sound makes me pause, my eyes seeking out the source over behind the long counter.

Giuseppe.

He's cutting meat at the slicer, his back to everyone. It's like he's in his own world... a world full of rainbows, and sunshine, and whatever else makes people happy.

Puppies?

I don't know.

Happiness to me these days is orgasms.

Weeks have passed since the last time I came here, since the day gunfire tried to rain on the man's parade. I'm not sure when Giuseppe reopened the deli, but my fears of it hurting his business were obviously unfounded.

The place is chaotic.

People pack the tables, eating lunch, as the boy working the cash register helps customers, orders piling up. Giuseppe doesn't at all seem concerned about that, though. He's not rushing in any way.

He's enjoying it.

The cashier glances at me as I approach and smiles warmly. "Your usual?"

I have a *usual*.

Naz would lecture me about that.

"Sure," I say, pulling out some cash to pay, leaving the change with him at the register, like usual, for them to keep as a tip.

There's only one small table empty, a two-seater along the wall that somebody just vacated, leaving their scraps just lying there. Ugh. I clean it off, throwing the trash in a nearby trashcan, and turn back around to take a seat when one of the chairs pulls out and somebody plops down in it.

Un-fucking-believable.

"Excuse me," I say, approaching the table. "I was sitting there."

The guy looks up, and something inside of me twists. I blanch. It's wrong, I know it, and I feel terrible right away, but I physically recoil. I don't know him, have never seen him before, but he's got a one-of-a-kind face. A horrid scar cuts down the whole side of it, right through his eye. The color of it is milky, cloudy, the blue sort of like a murky lake. It seems to stare right through me.

Vacant.

He notices my reaction. *Ugh, he notices.* I can tell it in his expression, the way his lips draw into a hard, thin line. It's like he toughened up in just those few seconds, like he's steeling himself because of my reaction to his face.

God, I suck.

I'm a horrible person.

"Apologies," he says. "There was nowhere else to sit."

He roughly shoves the chair back to stand up, but I stop him as I sit down across from him. "No, wait, it's totally okay."

He pauses, halfway out of the seat, and raises his eyebrows.

"There's no reason you can't sit here, too," I say. "I mean, I don't need that chair, and you're right... there's nowhere else to sit. So, really... have a seat."

He looks like he might still leave, and just stares at me in silence, his expression strained, before he settles back into the chair.

Digging through my bag, I pull out a beat-up catalogue of NYU. It'll probably be a while before I get my food, so I might as well go through it again and try to make some kind of decision about what I'm doing.

"So, I'm guessing you're a student?"

He says it quietly as he tinkers with a watch on his wrist, running his fingers along the metal band. It looks crazy expensive, like it might even be a Rolex, but he isn't exactly dressed like a wealthy businessman. Jeans, and a t-shirt, with a pair of white sneakers on his feet. He almost looks like he could be a student, except he's a bit older than me.

Thirty, maybe even older... I don't know.

I'm not good at judging age.

"Yeah, I am."

"What are you studying?"

"Uh, I'm not sure. I've just been kind of taking whatever. I'm actually supposed to declare a major in like, two hours, and I still have no idea what I want to do."

He laughs, the sound low and casual, like that genuinely amuses him. "Not easy deciding your future, is it?"

"Not in the least," I mutter, flipping through the pages of majors. "I've always sucked at making decisions, though, so this really is nothing new. It's just... I guess I have a hard time imagining myself doing any of this forever."

"That's because *forever* could be a very long time," he says. "Nobody wants to do the same thing forever. Nobody I know, anyway."

"That's what worries me," I say. "I like going to school, and learning, but I'm just not sure where it's going, and if I don't know where it's going, I'm worried there's no point, you know?"

Does he know?

I don't even know this guy and I'm asking him personal existential questions.

"Nah, there's always a point," he says. "So what if you don't do it forever? That's what's great about life... you can always change your mind and do something else instead. So don't think about forever. Think about today. Today might be all the forever you get, anyway."

"Is that how you decided a major?"

"Ah, no... never found myself in that position," he says. "Never went to college. Never even graduated from high school."

"Really? Why not?"

"There was nothing school could teach me that I cared to know," he says. "I found a better teacher out in the real world. I learned how to survive... how to thrive... and that was what mattered to me."

"So what do you do for a living? If you don't mind me asking..."

"I took over the family business."

"And what exactly is your family's business?"

He hesitates, a small smile tugging the corner of his lips. I think maybe he doesn't intent to tell me, but after a moment he simply says, "Produce."

Produce.

Like... farming?

"So, you grow things?"

"Sure. Well, the workers do... I more so just sit back and enjoy the fruits of their labor, so to speak. Not a bad position to be in."

"I bet," I say, turning back to my catalogue. "Sadly, I'm a bit lacking on the family front, so I wasn't lucky enough to inherit any business... or anything, really... so I'm on my own here."

From the corner of my eye, I see his face cloud with confusion. "No family?"

"Well, I mean, I have a husband." Holding my hand up, I wiggle my ring toward him. "And I've got a father-in-law now. He actually owns this place. Otherwise, no... I had a mother, but she died over a year ago, and my father, well, he was a real piece of work. I never knew him, and he's dead now, anyway, so it doesn't really matter. I heard he had a mother that was still around, but I'm pretty sure she wants nothing to do with me considering she wanted nothing to do with him."

"And that's it? No brothers or sisters? No aunts or uncles? No cousins?"

"Nope, no nothing. Not that I know of, anyway. I mean, it's hard to say, considering until a year ago I didn't even know my own last name."

"How did you not know your own last name?"

"Long story," I tell him. "But it boils down to my parents changing their names."

"Like, witness protection or something?"

"Or something," I mumble. "Like I said, long story, but it doesn't really matter, since I'm a Vitale now. I don't have to worry about whether or not I was ever a Rita to begin with. Family's about more than blood, anyway. That's what my husband says."

He stares at me.

And stares at me.

And stares at me some more.

He stares at me like he can't quite understand what the hell I'm going on about, and really, I can't blame him. It's certainly a convoluted story. I'm not even sure why I bothered to tell him that much, why I'm even talking to this guy, except that I feel bad for the way I reacted to him earlier.

Ugh, does it make me an even worse person that I'm humoring his company out of guilt?

"Fascinating." He holds his hand out toward me. "I'm Lorenzo, by the way, and you are...?"

I take his hand, shaking it. "Karissa."

"Pleasure to meet you, Karissa," he says. "You're certainly one interesting girl."

He lets go, pulling his hand away, and sits back in his chair, tinkering with his watch again when my food is finally delivered. The boy slides it onto the table in front of me, giving me a small smile, before scampering away to deal with others. I look down at my sandwich, my stomach growling, before I glance at the guy across from me.

I debate for a moment before saying 'fuck it' and pick up my sandwich, taking a bite of it. It's rude to eat before everyone else is served, but it's not like we're here *together*. We're just sharing a table.

The food is good, so good I damn near moan. It's an Italian sub, yeah, and maybe you can get them all over the city, but nothing tastes quite like the ones here. Giuseppe cooks with love, and that always rings through with his food.

I devour it in just a few minutes. Not even five, and the damn thing is gone. Lorenzo sits across from me, not paying attention, acting like I'm not even at the table with him anymore. He pulls out a phone and is typing away on it, texting or emailing or doing whatever the hell it is people who work in produce do on their phones. Getting up, I walk over to the trashcan, throwing my trash away, when the door to the place opens, a breeze filtering through. My eyes look that way just as the door closes, and I see the back of Lorenzo as he disappears outside.

Guess he got his food to go.

Sitting back down, I shove the catalogue back into my bag, as the whistling in the deli grows louder, closer to me. Standing up, I put my bag on my back when Giuseppe pops up in front of me. "Did you finally get smart?"

My brow furrows at the question. "What?"

"Did you finally get your wits about you and leave my son?"

"What? No, of course not... why would I?"

He shrugs. "Saw you sitting here with someone who certainly didn't look like Ignazio."

"Oh." I'm almost embarrassed and feel my face heat at what he might've thought when he saw that. "No, the guy just needed somewhere to sit, you know, since it's packed in here, so we shared a table."

"Huh."

Huh.

Jesus Christ, I hate that word.

I hate it when Naz uses it, and it's even worse when Giuseppe does. He sounds like maybe he doesn't believe me, like he thinks I'm lying about that. "I'm serious... he just said he needed somewhere to sit."

"I believe you," he says, holding up his hands. "It's just kind of funny."

"What's funny?"

"The fact that he needed to sit, yet he didn't even eat."

"Oh, I guess he decided to take it to go or something. Nothing weird about that."

"No, except he didn't order anything. He just came in, sat down, and then he left again. That's why I figured he was with you... wouldn't be the first time you brought someone in who refused to eat."

Giuseppe reaches over, patting my back, and offers me a smile before moving on to some other customer, the conversation dropped. I glance at the table, confused by that, before shrugging it off.

Guess he just needed to take a load off for a few minutes.

Doesn't really matter, so I shove it from my mind, heading outside. Cabs linger in the neighborhood, but I ignore them, heading for the subway to take it to Greenwich Village, using the time to think.

I've got a decision to make, and I've only got an hour left to make it.

"And you're absolutely sure about this?"

The advisor's voice is skeptical as she regards me across the small, brightly lit office. The fluorescents makes my head hurt, and I squint a bit as I look at her. It feels almost like I'm caught in a pair of headlights and I'm not sure which way to run.

"I'm sure," I lie, because truthfully? I'm not sure at all. I could be making the biggest mistake of my life. Hell, I probably am making the biggest mistake of my life. I should probably feel shame... I should probably be ashamed... but I feel nothing but a strange sense of relief.

And, ugh, annoyance at the bright ass lights.

Really, is this a goddamn interrogation?

"Well, if you change your mind, Karissa, it can easily be reversed in registration," she says, rearranging my paperwork in a folder before handing it to me, "but otherwise, I suppose we're done here."

"Thank you."

I don't wait to hear if she says I'm welcome.

It has been a weird day, and honestly, at this point, I'm just ready to go home.

It's five o'clock on the dot, probably the worst time in existence to try to get home to Brooklyn. The streets are crowded, and the subway will be packed. I call the car service as I stroll down the block, toward the nearest intersection.

"It'll be about a thirty-minute wait," the dispatcher says.

I sigh, pausing, and glance around at the sea of cabs flying by all around me, most of them darkened, not in service. I'm about to tell her that's fine, that I'll just wait, when a cab suddenly flips its light on right in front of me.

"Never mind," I tell the dispatcher, hanging up the phone, as I throw my arm out. The cab halts suddenly and whips over toward me. I jump in the back of it before someone can try to steal the damn thing. Thank God.

"Brooklyn," I mumble, before rattling off the address, settling into the back. It whips back into traffic, and I glance up toward the front, my brow furrowing. It takes only a second, as my eye gloss over the license hanging from the dashboard, for recognition to dawn.

Abele Abate.

I catch his gaze in the rearview mirror, and he smiles but says nothing, weaving in and out of lanes as we head south. Traffic is heavy, so I settle into the seat, opening my folder to look over the paperwork.

Term Withdrawal
Leave of Absence

No, I'm not sure about this at all...

But I've been struggling, ever since everything that happened... struggling to find my footing, to find meaning in any of it anymore. It's hard to walk into those classrooms, to face those people, to know they look at me and think those things about me. So maybe I'm not sure about leaving New York... yet... but I think I'm right about leaving NYU.

It left its mark on me in the best way possible, but I've left my mark on it, too, and the mark I've left hasn't been beautiful. There's a story I heard, right after I moved into the dorm, about the ghost of a young artist haunting one of the university buildings after he died in it, and I'm not a fool to think I haven't had a part in creating more legends for the future.

The kind meant to scare others.

The kind that taints the image of the school I love.

The kind that turns good things dark.

Sighing, I glance out the side window as we pass through an intersection. I get a glimpse of the street sign, barely a blurry glance, but my brow furrows at what I see. **E. Broadway**. We're heading east, through the Lower Eastside, when we should've stayed south, toward the Manhattan Bridge.

My stomach twists and my heart seems to drop, my chest tightening from that knowledge. I try to keep calm as I glance toward the front of the cab, but panic is surging through me when I meet Abele's eyes.

"Heavy traffic," he says right away. "Bad accident on Canal, so I'm taking a different route."

That's logical, I guess.

Maybe?

I don't know.

Fuck, how am I supposed to know?

What I do know is Brooklyn is south from here, and the cab is pointed in a different direction. And that, Naz would say, is nonsense. Especially considering the driver doesn't look sure about any of this, himself. His eyes are darting between the road and the rearview mirror as he weaves through lanes, looking like he doesn't plan to turn south again anytime soon.

Glancing behind me, I see a black BMW right on our bumper. There's another one a few cars back. I don't know if they're related, but I know enough to say that being tailgated for any reason is never good.

Spinning back around, I watch as we near the end of the road.

Right or left. They're his options. Left, north, will take us up toward the Williamsburg Bridge, while right, south, will take us down to the Manhattan one, where we should've gone to begin with. At this point, both directions put us out of our way, but at least, over one of them, I might make it to Brooklyn today.

We reach the intersection and I hold my breath.

Right. Left.

Right. Left.

Right. Left.

He looks like he's going to go left, and swings over into the lane, but at the last second abandons his path and cuts cars off, ignoring the incessant horn blowing as he takes a right. I grip onto the seat, my heart hammering erratically, and look behind me, out the back window. The BMW hesitates, coming damn near to a complete stop in the middle of the intersection. The cab cuts down another street, doing a loop, before driving right toward Corlears Hook Park. He jumps a small curb, driving onto a path, going where I'm pretty fucking sure cars aren't supposed to go. He makes a few turns, cursing under his breath. "Shit, shit, shit..."

"Look, whatever's happening, I've got nothing to do with it... so please, just let me out... slow down and I'll jump out... just, please..."

"Shut the fuck up," he growls, whipping the car around. "I'm thinking!"

He heads right for a concrete building. It's small, but big enough that he can pull behind it, out of view. He throws the car in park, and I go to say something, but there's no time.

He's not quick enough.

He's not slick enough.

Whoever was after him, found him.

Oh God.

Before either of us can say another word, before I can try to run, to escape, a car whips around the building behind us, slamming right into the cab. **BAM**. I jolt, slamming into the back of the seat in front of me, my folder falling, papers scattering all over the cab floor, as my phone goes flying toward the front seat. I blink a few times as my vision goes black. It's only a few seconds before it all comes back to me. My head is pounding... pounding... pounding... and sounds are muffled... but I can see again.

And what I see nearly makes me pass out.

Men, dressed in all black, wearing ski masks surround us. Abele, frantic, cursing, locks the cab doors, but it's pointless. It's fucking pointless. A gun aims right at the window, pressing against the glass.

Abele cries out, but it's barely half a word before they silence him.

BANG

BANG

BANG

Three shots, right to the head, no hesitation, the trigger pulled in quick succession. Glass shatters and blood flies, and I duck my head, curling up in the backseat, letting out a scream. It originates in my chest, and I try to be silent. I try to be compliant. I don't want to die. Fuck, I didn't do anything to deserve this, whatever the hell this is. But it's too hard, and I'm too weak to keep it inside. I scream, and the window above me is shattered, a gloved hand reaching inside, undoing the lock, before ripping the door open so hard he almost tears it off the hinges.

Strong arms grab ahold of me, pulling me right from the back of the cab, yanking me around like I weigh nothing. Tears stream down my cheeks, and I can't seem to breathe. I'm hyperventilating, as he pulls me back against him, his hand wrapping around my neck, pinning me there, his gun pointed to my temple.

Another car pulls up behind us. I can't see it, but I hear it... can hear the engine, the doors open, and footsteps against the concrete before a door slams. The guy holding me turns, and I squeeze my eyes shut, my vision blurring.

I can barely stand on my own two feet.

"Easy-peasy, boss," the guy holding me says with a laugh. "Told you it wouldn't be a problem."

I open my eyes, blinking to clear my vision, even though I'm terrified to see. And the first thing I see, beyond the masked gunmen, is a familiar face regarding me. He looks me over casually as he approaches. There have to be maybe five, six guys dressed in all black, but he's still looking laid-back... jeans, t-shirt, sneakers.

Lorenzo.

The guy from the deli.

He says nothing, stepping past me, glancing in the car at the dead cab driver.

It's gruesome, but Lorenzo doesn't seem bothered by that.

He turns back to me, looking me over again, and steps closer, so close that I can feel the warmth from his body. It's suffocating. He raises his hand, and I flinch, thinking he's about to hit me, when instead he brushes the hair back from my face. His hand cups my chin, his thumb stroking my cheek. I wince, his finger grazing over what feels like a cut.

"She's injured," he says simply.

"Yeah, guess some glass got her when I pulled her out," the guy holding me says. "Not a problem."

"I told you not to get the girl hurt," Lorenzo says. "*Problem*."

Before the man can respond, Lorenzo pulls out a gun from beneath his shirt, aiming it right past me. No hesitation. No second-guessing. He pulls the trigger.

BANG

I let out another scream as the masked guy drops. I drop. He takes me down with him, hard. I can feel the blood splatter hitting me as I collapse to the ground in sobs. Oh, God... I'm so stupid. So fucking stupid. How could I not see him for what he was?

What the fuck is wrong with me?

Naz taught me better than this.

"Please," I cry, the word breaking when I force it out. *Please... please... oh, God, please...* "Please don't hurt me."

"You shouldn't beg," Lorenzo says.

I can't help it. The word comes bursting out of me again. "Please."

Lorenzo stares down at me, still clutching his gun. After a moment of silence, he raises a hand motioning past him. All at once, the men disperse. They rush back into the car, and Lorenzo stares at me for another moment, before putting his gun away and kneeling down.

"I knew your parents," he says. "Carmela and Johnny... I knew them both, once upon a time. And I've got to tell you, sunshine... not having them around? You're definitely better off." He stands up then and steps past me. "Send my regards to your husband, Mrs. Vitale."

I hold my breath, staring straight ahead, as the cars speed away, leaving me there crouching on the ground, beside a bleeding body. Trembling, I push away from the guy, crawling along the concrete back toward the cab. My legs are weak. There's no way I can stand. I look in the back of the cab, shoving my strewn-about papers around, blood from my hands smearing all over them.

"Don't look," I whisper to myself, trying to ignore the blood. So much blood. *Don't look. Don't look. Don't look.* I reach under seat, wincing as shattered glass jabs me, and start crying harder.

I can't find my fucking phone.

Pulling myself up, I take a deep breath, trying to steady myself on my feet, as I reach around, unlocking the passenger side front door. I move to the front seat, opening the door, and lose it the second I glance inside.

Dropping to my knees, I heave. It's violent, and my stomach churns, purging everything inside of me. Oh God. Oh God.

Jesus, fuck, don't look.

Don't look.

Don't look at the guy with his head blown off.

Glancing at the floorboard, relief mixes with the adrenaline in my system when I see the hint of glittery pink peeking out from under the seat. My phone. Snatching it up, I crawl around to the front of the car, away from them, away from it, away from everything, and plant myself in the grass.

My hands are shaking so hard I can barely hold onto the phone.

Blood covers my hands and it smears all over my phone. I can't get the fingerprint authentication to work to open it, and the fucking numbers just don't want to work. Why won't they work? I punch them frantically but it keeps saying it's wrong, they're wrong, so I hit the 'emergency call' button.

Because this?

This is an emergency if I've ever seen one.

Chapter Sixteen
Ignazio

The blaring of an old, familiar pop song rouses me from my nap. The second I hear it, I jolt upright, startled. Poison. Bell Biv DeVoe. Groaning, I dig around in my pockets.

The ringtone's a lot better than the last one, but I'm already sick of hearing it.

Grabbing the phone, I pull it out and glance at the screen, sighing. *Karissa.*

I hit the button to answer the call. "Why aren't you home yet? I'm starting to get lonely here."

Silence. Sniffling.

Men are talking in the background.

There's a siren in the distance.

I hear a police radio.

Shit.

"Karissa?" Panic brews inside of me. "Answer me, sweetheart."

There's a ruffling, the phone moving, before a voice breaks in. "Mr. Vitale?"

"Yes," I say. "Who the fuck is this?"

"Detective Jameson," he says, "with the NYPD—"

"Homicide division. I know. Why do you have my wife's phone?"

I can feel it, can feel it pecking at my core, the anger, the devastation, the goddamn fear.

No. No. *No.*

"I want to notify you that there was an incident this evening—"

"Don't do it," I say, my voice cracking, interrupting him.

Don't you do it.

Don't you say it.

Don't make a notification over the phone.

Don't make a notification, period, because I refuse to believe you need to notify me about anything. Tell me this is all a mistake, tell me you just happened upon her phone, but don't you tell me the one thing... *the one fucking thing...* a homicide detective would notify someone for.

"Don't tell me something happened to her," I say, "not unless you want the world to burn."

He hesitates.

He knows I mean it.

He's dealt with me enough.

He made the notification twenty years ago in the hospital.

Showed up in that room, as I lay in that bed, and told me Maria was gone.

I knew it already then, knew I lost her.

But I refuse to believe that will ever happen again.

I refuse to *let* it.

"Your wife's being seen by a medic right now, but she seems to be just fine," he says. "As I said, though, there was an incident, and she asked that you be notified."

"Where are you?"

"Well, we're at Corlears Hook Park but—"

I don't let him finish, hanging up and shoving my phone in my pocket before running out the door. Corlears Hook. What the hell was she doing there? It's not near NYU. It's not on her path home. It's nowhere she should've been.

Traffic is a mess.

A nightmare.

I speed around cars, cutting through lanes and running red lights, even driving the wrong direction, all in the name of getting there faster. I sideswipe a parked car but keep going, cursing under my breath, hoping nobody got my license plate number for it. For most, it would be nothing more than a fine, a slap on the wrist, but they'd find a way to send my ass upstate for life for it.

Corlears Hook Park runs along the shoreline. It's a small park, compared to some of the others in the city, so it isn't hard to find where I need to be. Dozens of cop cars surround the area, lights on, a section quartered off by crime scene tape. I pull my car up toward the entrance, jumping the curb and just leaving it there.

They're lucky I bother to shut the damn thing off.

"Sir? Sir! That's not a parking spot!"

"Tow it, then," I say, walking right past him, grabbing the police tape and ducking under it, heading right for the crime scene. I can see an ambulance not far from me, near a small concrete building. The officer tries to stop me, grabbing my arm, but I yank away from him, continuing on.

He radios for help. I hear him, desperately shrieking that someone's entered the perimeter, and I see others turning their focus my direction, like they're about to come after me. Detective Jameson steps around the side of the building then, directly in my line of sight, right in my path, and calls them down. "It's fine, gentlemen. He's the victim's husband."

Victim.

"Where is she?" I ask.

"Like I said, she's fine." He motions toward the ambulances. I can make out two, which tells me she wasn't the only victim here. "She's still being seen."

I walk right past him, but he jumps in front of me. "Wait."

"So help me God, Jameson, don't try to stop me from seeing her."

He holds his hands up defensively. "I'm not. I'm only asking you go that way."

He points the long way, around the other side of the building, and I start to argue, but I get it. If I keep going, I'm going to trample right through his crime scene, and he still pretends to care about *integrity* and *justice.*

So I do it, this small concession, because he's well within his right to throw me to the ground and arrest me right now for interfering, and I've got more important things to worry about.

The first ambulance is locked up tight, the lights off. The one right beside it is wide open, officers surrounding it. Dead center, standing in front of the back door is Jameson's partner, Andrews. I can't see Karissa past all the cops and medics, but I'm guessing that's where I'll find here, so I head right there.

They part when they see me coming, like they're afraid of what I'll do if they don't. They all move out of my way except for Andrews, but it doesn't matter, because I shove right past him. The moment he moves, the moment I get a good look at the ambulance, my heart drops right to my fucking toes.

She's sitting there with her feet dangling, a dazed look on her face. Blood stains her clothes. Her hair's even matted with it, but I don't think it's hers. *Thank God it isn't hers.* There's a bandage on her cheek, and her eyes are bloodshot as they seek me out.

The moment she sees me, she closes her eyes.

She closes them, and breathes deeply, like she's overwhelmed with relief.

I don't hesitate. I grab her. I yank her off the back of the ambulance and pull her right into my arms. Her feet can't touch the ground, and I'm probably going to break her back with as hard as I'm squeezing, but I can't help it. Because I feel it, the relief she's feeling. I feel the deep breath she took. I feel it in my soul.

She starts sobbing as she nuzzles into my neck, clinging to me right back.

"It's okay," I whisper. "Just keep breathing and you'll be all right."

"Mr. Vitale?" Andrews chimes in. "If you don't mind, we still have a few questions for your, uh... wife."

"Does she look like she's in any condition to answer your questions?"

Karissa pushes away from me, and I loosen my hold, setting her on her feet.

"It's okay," she says, her voice strained as she tries to pull herself together. She wipes her tears away with the back of her hand, grimacing as it tugs on the bandage. "It's fine. I just... I don't know what else I can tell you. I was in the cab, I was taking it home from school, and I wasn't really paying attention... next thing I know, we're going the wrong direction, and a car is following us. He came here; I don't know why... to hide, maybe? But there they were, and here we are, and there he is, and here I am."

I glance over toward the building, seeing the yellow cab, windows busted out with blood surrounding it. A body lays on the ground beside it, covered in a sheet, the crisp white material soaked with red.

"And the other deceased gentleman?" Andrews asks. "Where did he come from?"

"Other guy?" I chime in. "What other guy?"

"The cab driver is still in the car," Andrews offers. "The second was found deceased beside the cab when we arrived."

Karissa's eyes dart my way nervously. "He was one of them... one of the guys following us. There were five of them, maybe six. I'm not sure. He pulled me out of the back of the cab, and he had a gun to me, and I thought he was going to shoot me." She lets out a cry, but holds her hands up to stop me when I try to pull her into my arms again. "No, it's okay, I'm okay... he had me and then he said something to another guy, something about it not being a problem, it being easy, and then the guy shot him. He just *shot* him!"

"So his own friend shot him," Andrews says, jotting that down. "Why would he do that?"

"How's she supposed to know?" I ask. "She's not psychic."

"How about you let her answer, Vitale."

I step toward him. "How about you stop interrogating her while she's distraught."

"And how about you don't tell me how to do my job."

"Your job is to get justice, not traumatize women... unless, of course, you get off on that sort of thing."

He doesn't like that. His cheek twitches, eyes glazing over with anger. "You want to talk to me about traumatizing people? Let's talk about the things you've done! In fact, it wouldn't surprise me a bit if you were involved in this!"

"Me?" I glare at him, raising my voice. "You think I'd do this? That I'd hurt my own wife? I'd *never*."

"How am I supposed to know?" he asks, throwing my words right back at me. "Not a psychic."

I almost swing.

I almost hit him.

If Karissa weren't standing between us, I would.

"Guys, guys... can't we all just get along here?" Jameson asks, coming around the side of the building, approaching the ambulance.

Andrews mutters something, something I can't make out.

"What was that?" I ask him. "Couldn't quite hear you."

"I said we'll get along when your ass is finally behind bars." He closes his notebook, shoving it in his coat pocket. "Your wife, too, if she's withholding evidence."

"Relax," Jameson says, slapping his partner on the back. "I'm sure she has told us everything she knows. Isn't that right, Mrs. Vitale?"

"Yes," Karissa says quietly. "There's nothing else I can say."

"So is she free to go?" I ask, "or is your partner going to hound her some more?"

"She actually needs to be transferred to the hospital," Jameson says. "Tried to send her earlier, but she was insistent we wait for you."

"The hospital?" I look her over. "Are you feeling all right?"

"Yeah, I, ugh..." She makes a face, motioning to herself. "Body fluids all over me. They need to collect them. Evidence or whatever."

Ah.

"Which you're contaminating," Andrews says.

"Also," Jameson interjects, "it's always better to be safe than sorry. They'll want to run some tests, maybe give her some booster shots, just to be safe."

I appreciate Jameson trying to keep the peace.

Appreciate him cutting in.

Because if his partner keeps running his mouth, Karissa won't be the only one visiting the hospital.

"Can I take her," I ask, "or do you have to?"

"You can take her in," Jameson says. "Lower Manhattan... I'll meet you there."

Andrews starts to object. "But—"

"Like you said, it's already been contaminated," Jameson says. "She'll be more comfortable going in with him."

I don't waste any time getting her out of there. I don't want to risk Jameson changing his mind and deciding to be a dick.

"You okay to walk?" I ask quietly, taking Karissa's hand.

"Sure," she says, even though she doesn't sound sure, but I'm going to take her at her word. I lead her around the side of the building, and she almost keeps in step with me as we approach my car, still parked on the curb. "Um, Naz?"

"Yeah, sweetheart?"

"What happened to your shoes?"

I glance down at my feet... at my black socks. "I wasn't wearing any when they called."

"So you just came in your bare feet?"

"I'm wearing socks."

"Uh... okay. I've just... never really seen you without shoes like this before."

I pause beside my car, opening the passenger door for her. "Yeah, well, when I get a call from a homicide detective wanting to notify me about something happening to my wife, shoes aren't really what's on my mind."

The color drains from her face.

Whatever color she had left, anyway.

"I didn't think," she says. "I didn't want *you* to think..."

"But I did," I tell her, "and you could've been. Jesus Christ, Karissa... how many times have I told you not to take a cab from the city? How many times? *Too many*. But you didn't listen. Why couldn't you have just listened?"

"I did." Her voice cracks as tears fill her eyes. I shouldn't be yelling at her, not now, not here, but fuck, this is serious. She could've *died*. "I called for a car but they were too busy, and the cab was there, so I didn't think it was a problem. I thought you were just being paranoid."

"And yet here we are," I say. "A double homicide, in broad daylight, with you caught in the middle of it."

She starts crying, the tears breaking free, streaming down her cheeks as she looks away from me.

My chest tightens, and I'm nauseated from the anger and adrenaline overdose in my system. "Don't cry, okay? You're okay. *We're okay*. I just need you to understand how serious this is."

I motion to the open door of the car, and wordlessly, she climbs in. I close it, walking around to the driver's side, starting the car up and pulling it back off the curb.

She's quiet for a moment, staring out the side window, as I head the direction of the hospital. She waits until I pull into the parking lot, the car coming to a stop, before she lets out a deep sigh. "He said he knew my parents."

Her voice is so low I barely understand what she's saying, but I get it. She's telling me what she didn't tell the detectives. "Your parents."

She nods.

Huh.

"Did he say anything else?"

"Just to tell you that he sends his regards."

The moment she says that, I know.

I know.

I know who did it, who attacked them, who damn near put my wife in a grave this afternoon. "Lorenzo."

"You know him," she says, or asks... I'm not sure. I guess it's a logical conclusion, if he knew her parents...

"Come on," I say. "Let's get you checked out."

Usually people can wait around hours at the emergency room to be seen, but Jameson must've called ahead, because the second they lay eyes on Karissa, they know who she is.

They know what happened.

They know why she's here.

They jump into procedure, whisking her into the back to clean her up and run some tests. Time passes as I sit in the waiting room, stewing. That son of a bitch made a big mistake. He messed with the wrong person. He should've known better. I could look the other way when he attacked my father's business, and when he attacked other people, but my wife?

He knew she was off limits.

He fucking *knew* it.

Jameson shows up eventually, but he doesn't stay long, heading to the back and returning with a paper bag full of what I assume are Karissa's clothes. He approaches me carefully, pausing out of arm's reach. I'm angry, fuming, and I think he can tell it.

"We're going to—"

He starts to talk, but I cut him off. "Don't tell me you're going to catch whoever did this, because I know better, Jameson. You didn't catch them last time. You won't do it now."

He pauses, frowning, before speaking again. "I was going to say, we're going to need her to come down to the station when she gets the chance to make an official statement."

I nod. "Our lawyer will be in touch."

He leaves then.

Leaves me alone.

Alone to stew some more.

To let my anger flourish.

I'm damn near jumping out of my own skin, too anxious to just sit here, waiting.

Standing up, I walk over to the desk, to the nurse in charge of this place. "Look, any chance I can go check on my wife? She's been back there for a while."

She looks torn and picks up the phone to make a call, asking whoever answers if it's fine if I'm allowed back. She buzzes me through then, offering a sympathetic smile. "Down the hall, take the first left, and it'll be the second door on the right. They're just finishing up."

I follow her directions, and approach the door just as the doctor exists. He glances at me before averting his eyes, grumbling a greeting as he hurries past.

I don't bother to knock, instead walking right in. Karissa doesn't even look up when I enter. The nurse is finishing whatever she's doing and glances my way before turning to leave. "We're done here, so you're free to leave. We'll call in that prescription for you."

Karissa mouths the words 'thank you' but I certainly don't hear it. She's pale, almost ghostly white. It's like she's trapped in her own world.

"Prescription?" I ask. "Is there a problem?"

She shakes her head. "It's just a vitamin or whatever. I told them I hadn't been feeling well. The doctor thought... well, I mean, said I should take something."

Vitamins.

After what she went through, that's the least of our worries. "Otherwise?"

"I'm okay. They'll probably have to run more tests later, just in case, but he assured me everything was fine. Got a few shots, and you know... a pair of these."

She motions down at herself.

She's wearing some oversize paper scrubs, flimsy plastic looking things. Guess they're tired of people stealing their real ones. "I can almost see through them."

"Yeah, well, the alternative was the backless gown."

She stares at the floor.

Something's wrong.

I can sense it.

She won't even look at me.

"What's wrong?"

"You're angry."

I pause. "Is that what's wrong?"

"Just an observation."

I walk over to her, cupping her chin, tilting her face so she'll look up at me. Her eyes look all around me for a moment before finally meeting my gaze. Sadness, along with a healthy dose of fear. That's what greets me.

I hate it.

She should be happy.

She certainly deserves it.

This was supposed to be her happy ending.

What happened to it?

"I'm not mad at you," I say. "I'm mad this happened to you, that I have to be paranoid about you going places. I'm mad that I have to be mad, Karissa, but I'm trying to not take my anger out on you, because it's not your fault. It's mine."

It's my fault without a doubt. I got her into this.

It's my job to get her out of it.

I don't know if that matters to her right now, though.

If that even makes a difference.

It sure didn't alleviate any of that sadness or fear.

"Can we get out of here?" she asks. "I'd like to really be anywhere but here."

Can't argue with that.

I hate hospitals more than most people.

I'd like to be anywhere but here, too.

She doesn't say anything as she's discharged and we head out to the car, but she notices right away when I start driving the wrong direction. She tenses, staring out the side mirror. "Brooklyn isn't north of here."

"No, but NYU is."

"So?"

"So you should pay a visit to Melody."

"What?" She turns to me, eyes wide. "Why?"

"Because right now, you could really use a friend."

Tears brim her eyes again.

She's trying not to cry.

I can tell it.

And I don't want to leave her, I *don't*, but there's something I need to handle. And I can't leave her at home alone, not tonight, so that leaves us with Melody.

She'll be safe there.

Because Lorenzo would never do anything to harm his little brother, not directly, so if he's going to go after Karissa again, it won't be when she's with his brother's girlfriend.

"You're going to do something, aren't you?" she asks. "You're taking me there so you can go after him."

"You'll be okay there," I say, avoiding that question. "I don't want you to worry."

"Don't want me to worry, Naz? What if I don't see you again? What if you never come back?"

I whip the car into the parking garage beside the dorms, and cut the engine before turning to her. "Don't think like that."

"How can I not?"

"I'll always come for you," I tell her. "The fucking devil himself couldn't stop me. It'll just be a few hours, morning at the latest. I promise you, I'll be back."

"But I thought you said I should keep my distance. You made me promise."

"I just wanted to know when you were around Leo, so I could keep an eye on things."

She ponders that for a moment before her eyes narrow, something seeming to strike her. "That's his brother, isn't it? *Send my regards to your brother.* That's what you said to Leo. That's what the guy said to me today. *Send my regards.*"

"It is."

"That *thing* is his brother? Seriously? And Melody's dating him?"

"Don't take it out on your friend. Once upon a time, you fell for a monster. These things happen."

"That's different."

"Maybe so," I admit. "And in that case, what you did was worse. Because Leo? He's just lightly treading through a sticky situation. Me? I'm knee-deep in it."

"But you're out," she says. "Aren't you?"

"As out as I can be."

It's what I tell her every time.

I'm not sure if she gets it.

Out only means I can sit on the sidelines, waiting until I get called back into the game. And they've been calling for me, pretty incessantly... both teams.

So I'm out, yeah, which means I'm reluctantly still in.

That's just the way it is.

"Come on," I tell her. "I'll walk you inside."

It's not hard to get into the dorms.

It's not hard to get in anywhere, honestly.

The trick is just to look like you belong.

If you act like you're supposed to be there, nobody questions your presence. It's all a matter of confidence.

We make our way right through the joke of a checkpoint and head right upstairs, to floor number thirteen. Karissa trails behind me.

I can tell she doesn't want to be here.

She doesn't want me to leave.

As soon as I reach room 1313, I raise my fist and pound on the door. It's so loud that Karissa flinches, looking at me with concern.

It does the trick, though.

It only takes a few seconds for the door to fly open.

In front of me stands a startled redheaded girl. Her eyes grow wide as she looks at me, and she retreats a few steps, away from the door, as I waltz right in.

"Sorry," Karissa mumbles, stepping in behind me.

Melody is sitting on her bed and looks up with confusion. "Ignazio?" She glances around me, at her friend. "Jesus, Kissimmee, what happened?"

"I, uh..." She slips around me to point at her cheek. "Just a cut."

That's putting it lightly.

Melody stares at her like she's crazy as she gets to her feet. "Is everything okay? What are you guys doing here?"

Karissa stammers, saying nothing coherent.

"She's had a bit of a rough day," I say. "I'm hoping it's okay if she stays with you for a few hours while I handle a bit of business."

"Oh, absolutely!" Melody smiles, feigning cheerfulness, but her concern hasn't wavered. "Karissa can stay here as long as she wants."

The redhead across the room sighs loudly.

I turn to Karissa as she just stands there, arms wrapped around her chest. Nothing I can say will make her feel better at the moment, so I just press a kiss to her forehead before walking out.

Places to go.

People to see.

Blood to spill.

You know how it is.

Music thumps from the pink-trimmed house in Bensonhurst.

It's not loud enough to rattle the windows, not loud enough to disturb the neighbors, but I hear it when I approach the house, hear it coming from the front room. Voices carry over the sound, mindless chatter, even a bit of laughter.

The sound grates at me.

I wouldn't call it a party, but people are here.

They're here, and they're hanging out.

It's almost like they're celebrating.

Two cars, including the BMW I'm looking for, now without a license plate. They both can't fit in the driveway, so they're spilling out onto the curb. I swing right into a neighbor's vacant driveway, stealing someone else's spot.

It doesn't matter. I don't plan to be here long.

In. Out. Gone.

I hop over the white railing, not bothering to open the gate, and head right around to the back of the small lot, to the opposite side of the house from where the people are gathered. The back door is unlocked. I'm not surprised. Lorenzo thinks he's invincible. *Untouchable*. No reason to lock the doors if nobody is stupid enough to try to rob him, right?

Right.

I open the back door and walk right into the kitchen, no hesitation at all in my footsteps.

Like I said, the key is to act like you belong somewhere.

It's dark in here.

In fact, most of the house is dark.

The only light is dim and shining somewhere down the hallway.

The front room.

I give a quick glance around, assessing, contemplating, before stepping over to the kitchen drawers and rifling through them, looking for something. It's pretty bare in here, and I come up short in the way of weapons, but I manage to find an old steak knife tucked in with the silverware.

Fuck it. A knife is a knife.

If it's sharp enough to cut meat, it's good enough for me.

Before I can move, the door to the kitchen swings open and someone waltzes right in. The guy is dressed in black, from head-to-toe, and he's too preoccupied with something on his phone to notice I'm here. I don't know him, but I've seen him before. I saw him get out of the car that day in the alley.

Right now, he's unarmed.

I move right toward him. By the time he senses me it's too late. He's too late. He looks up, brow furrowing, eyes squinting as he tries to make sense of what he's seeing. But it's dark, and he's slow, and I don't have time to try to negotiate and convince him to keep his mouth shut.

So I shut it for him.

"Hey—"

That's the only word he gets.

Grabbing a hold of him, I pull him around, the blade of the knife going right to his neck. I cut, hard, slicing through the skin, slitting him almost from ear to ear. He gurgles, dropping the phone, and tries to scream, but there's no way anyone can hear his cries over the music in the front room.

He drops to the floor with a thud, struggling.

I move around him, past him, and head for the hallway, my steps quiet. Benefit of not having shoes on... it's easier to sneak. But I'm not trying to go undetected. There's no point to it.

In ten seconds, they'll all know I'm here.

Ten.

Nine.

Eight.

I step into the hallway, and somebody's there.

Somebody's walking right toward me.

Seven.

Six.

Five.

I grip tightly to the knife, now covered in blood.

It drips from the tip, splattering on the floor.

Four.

Three.

Two.

He pauses and looks up.

Suddenly, I know there's a God.

I've doubted it, a time or two. Doubted one could exist. Doubted one would ever create someone like me. But in that one second, when those eyes meet mine, I know it... there's a God... and He just handed me the miracle I need.

One.

Leo freezes right there in the hallway. It's like a deer in headlights. He stops and just stands there and stares. Horror fills his eyes, the rawest kind of fear. His brother might not be afraid of me, but Leo certainly is.

Good.

He should be.

I'm out of time now. I know it then.

My seconds are up.

I've only got one play here, and I have to take it.

Leo's senses kick in just as I reach the boy, snatching ahold of him. I spin him around, facing him away from me, so his back is to my chest. My left hand pins him close as I drag him right to the front room, my grip tight. He struggles, and tries to break loose, but he's not nearly strong enough. I have him subdued the second we step into the doorway.

It's weak.

Pathetic.

Karissa puts up more of a fight when we're fucking.

"Lorenzo!" Leo screeches his brother's name, his voice an octave higher than any guy's voice should be.

That gets their attention.

They react instantly. Three guys, dressed in all black, scramble for weapons. They aim at me. Fingers touch triggers. The only reason they hesitate is because of Leo. I won't think twice about using him as a shield if I have to. Maybe he's an innocent, but he's still a part of this.

A *big* part of this.

Casualty of war.

I don't want to have to do it, but I will.

Reaching up, I place the blade of the bloody knife against his Adam's apple.

The air is cloudy with marijuana smoke. I can smell it, feel it, as I inhale. It's not as bad as Genova's cigars, but my eyes still burn from the thick haze.

I can make out Lorenzo, though, clear as a bell. He sits across the room on a small black couch.

He's the only one who didn't reach for a gun.

He hasn't moved at all.

Silence befalls the room, except for the music pouring from the speakers.

Ten more seconds pass before Lorenzo reacts.

He sits forward, and I grip Leo tighter. The boy yelps, starting to cry, while the others seem to be struck with panic over that. The men are on their feet and yelling, throwing out threats they can't follow through with unless they plan to also kill Leo. It's chaos, and my heart races in my chest as I take it in. I'm banking on this man truly still loving his brother.

If he doesn't, I'm fucked.

"Relax, relax," Lorenzo says casually, grabbing a small remote from the table right in front of him. Pressing a button, he silences the music. "Why don't we all just take a deep breath?"

The men stay on guard, but they stop yelling. They stop threatening, but I know they'll still make good on those words. They stand there and stare, waiting for permission.

Lorenzo looks around at them before he again rests back against the couch.

Confidence.

It oozes from him.

I wonder how much of it is real.

"Ignazio, what's going on?" he asks. "What are you even doing?"

"Thought I'd pay you a visit."

"By sneaking in? Taking hostages?" He shakes his head. "If you wanted to talk about something, if you wanted to meet up, all you had to do was ask. I always make time for my friends."

"Friends," I repeat. "You keep insisting on using that word."

"Because it's true," he says, "and I always speak the truth."

A sharp, bitter laugh stabs at my chest. "Truth? You speak the truth, Lorenzo?"

"Always."

"That's funny," I say, raising my voice, that anger refusing to stay at bay. "Funny, because I remember you telling me you wouldn't *harm my wife!*"

His brow furrows. "Is she not all right?"

"*Don't,*" I growl. "Don't even sit there and pretend you weren't involved. Be a man, Lorenzo. Admit it."

"Oh, I'm not denying anything." He raises a hand, a smile on his lips. A fucking *smile.* Does he think this is a joke? "Guilty. But you're overreacting."

"I'm overreacting?"

"You are," he insists. "You should be thanking me, honestly."

"Thanking you?" I take a step closer, shoving Leo along with me. The boy whimpers, the knife pressing harder against him. Every sound he makes sends the others closer to the brink. I'm damn lucky nobody has popped a shot off accidentally. "We had a deal. You don't hurt her, and I leave your brother alone. But it's obvious you're no longer a man of your word, so I guess our deal's off, Lorenzo."

He's starting to sweat.

I can see it.

It's building along his brow, but he doesn't let his stress otherwise show. His eyes scan us, slowly, like he's considering his options, trying to riddle out what to do here. His gaze settles on my feet eventually, and he lets out a dramatic sigh as he pushes away from the couch, standing up, muttering, "I'm not high enough for this."

He takes a measured step toward me, then another. The third step is too close for my comfort. I yank Leo back, away from his brother, the knife slicing into his neck. It's just a cut, just a small gash. A trickle of blood flows down the center of his throat. It's not much at all.

But they react.

They don't wait for permission anymore.

I guess blood gave them what they needed.

The men lunge, coming for me, but Lorenzo stops it before anything happens. "Whoa, whoa, whoa! *Down, boys!* Did I say attack?"

He physically creates a barrier between us, and I pull Leo away from the doorway, away from his brother, before they can get their hands on him.

"Get out, all of you!" Lorenzo orders. "Leave Ignazio and I alone."

He doesn't have to say it twice. The men vacate the house, heading right out the front door. I stand there, watching as he shakes his head, before he turns to me. "You gonna let my brother go now?"

"Give me a reason why I should."

"Because I asked nicely."

"Not good enough."

"You want me to say *please*? I'm not really one to beg."

"I want you to tell me why you thought it was smart to attack my wife."

"I didn't attack her."

"Don't deny—"

"Again, not denying anything." Lorenzo runs his hands down his face. "Look, let my brother go, and you and I will talk about this. I'll tell you everything that happened. But it's kind of hard to focus when you've got a knife to his neck."

Slowly, I lower the knife, using my free hand to shove Leo right at his brother.

Lorenzo grabs him by the chin, lifting his face, checking out the boy's neck, making sure the cut isn't too deep. He shoots me a look as he does.

Clapping his brother on the back, he ruffles his hair, treating him like he's still a little kid. "You'll be just fine. No harm done. Look at it this way... you survived an attack by Vitale. Not many people are able to say that."

He laughs about it then. He *laughs*.

It's not often I'm caught off guard, but he's got me here.

Lorenzo turns my way then, walking right toward me. I tense, preparing to react, but he walks around me.

"Come on," he says, hitting me on the chest with the back of his hand as he passes. "I need a drink."

He heads for the kitchen.

Call it curiosity.

Call it stupidity.

Call it whatever you want.

I follow him.

Lorenzo swings the kitchen door open and hesitates before stepping over the guy I left in here. He's on the floor, in a puddle of blood, although he's still breathing. I tread carefully, slipping into the kitchen behind him, every inch of me still on guard.

I watch Lorenzo as he strolls over to the counter, grabbing a bottle of Cuban rum and unscrewing the lid. He takes a drink right out of the bottle and hisses as swallows.

Leaning back against the counter, he looks at me.

He looks disgruntled.

Disappointed.

"What is this?" I ask, using his earlier words on him. "What are you even doing?"

"Drinking," he says, holding out the bottle. "Do you want some?"

"I'll pass."

"Suit yourself," he says, taking another swig. "For whatever it's worth, and I don't know if it makes a difference, but I told them not to hurt her."

"You told them not to hurt her."

"Yeah."

"They didn't listen."

He ponders that before taking another drink. "I know."

Does that make a difference? *No.*

"Wrong place, wrong time," he says, shrugging it off. "You know how it is."

"I'm not interested in your excuses, Lorenzo."

"Aren't you?" he asks. "I know you, Ignazio. I know your methods. I know what makes you tick. And if you aren't interested in somebody's excuses, you don't give them a chance to speak. You didn't come here to kill me. You came here to get to the bottom of things."

He says that nonchalantly.

I don't like that he thinks he knows me.

And maybe he's right.

Maybe I didn't come here to kill him.

But that doesn't mean I'm buying his bullshit.

"So," he says, "did she tell you what happened?"

"She told me everything."

"Everything." Lorenzo says that with a laugh. "Did she tell you the name of the man driving the cab?"

"What does it matter? He's dead."

"Precisely," Lorenzo says, pointing the bottle of rum at me. "I told you, you should be thanking me."

I narrow my eyes at that. "What was his name?"

"Abele Abate," he says. "Ring a bell?"

It does.

He knows it does.

"He was one of Ray's guys."

He nods. "Did she tell you she's taken this particular cab a few times? That this wasn't the first time he drove her somewhere? That whenever she needed a ride, he just happened to be in the area? Did she tell you that?"

No, she didn't.

"I caught him sniffing around her a couple weeks ago," he continues. "It was entirely coincidental, you see, because I just happened to be sniffing around her, too."

"Why?"

"Why?" he asks incredulously. "Come on, I ask around when I get to town and the first thing I find out is you're married. *Again*. And to not just anybody. You're married to *her*. Never in my wildest dreams. So call me curious... I wanted to see the girl who finally thawed that frozen heart of yours."

He smiles, but I don't find it amusing.

"So, what... thought you'd hit two birds with one stone? Take out another one of Ray's men while going after her?"

"Never went after her." He sounds adamant. "And Abele? Seems he's been working for someone else these days, someone who took a special interest in your girl."

"Who?"

He hesitates. "Hard to say."

Hard to say.

Either he doesn't know or he doesn't want to tell me.

"Cut the bullshit, Lorenzo."

"Look, all I'm saying is I stopped your wife from being truly harmed. You're welcome for that, by the way."

I don't thank him.

I don't know if I believe it.

It feels too convenient.

I look around the room, my eyes skimming over the man on the floor. He's moaning, still moving around.

"He's still alive," Lorenzo points out.

"For now," I say. "What happens to him depends on if you plan to help him out."

"Oh, I'll help him out, don't you worry about that."

I glance at Lorenzo.

He takes another swig of the liquor, staring at the man on the floor. "When was the last time you actually killed someone, Ignazio?"

It's a question I don't want to answer.

It's one I really don't have to think about.

The last life I ended was Raymond Angelo's.

Everyone since then, I've left alive.

I hesitate so long he knows I'm not going to answer, but that, I suppose, is answer enough for him. "That long ago, huh?"

"It doesn't matter," I tell him. "Whether it was a year ago or an hour ago, it doesn't make a difference. There's so much blood on my hands they'll never get clean."

"It doesn't matter, but yet you're trying."

"For her."

"Well, don't worry," he says, motioning toward the writhing man on the floor. "I'll make sure he's taken care of, so the last blood on your hands won't be today."

I don't know if he expects me to thank him, but I don't. I don't say anything.

I just slip right out the back door.

Heading around the house, I go toward my car in the neighbor's driveway, when I hear it. I hear the lone gunshot from the back of the house.

BANG

Chapter Seventeen
Karissa

Sometimes, when I can't sleep, I just lay in bed and wonder.

I wonder what my life would be like if Naz hadn't happened.

If I hadn't walked into that philosophy classroom, maybe nobody would've ever noticed me. Maybe I would've continued on, undetected, building a life for myself right under their noses, living out my days oblivious and happy. Maybe I would've never known the truth of my parentage, and I could've existed in an eternal ignorant bliss. Maybe I'd be an art major, or maybe even do something in science. Maybe I'd still be living in this very room with Melody. Maybe I'd forever be eating ramen noodles while fielding a dozen messages from my mom every afternoon.

Maybe she'd still be alive.

Maybe.

Maybe.

Maybe.

I imagine myself having another life, in another place, surrounded by other people... people I haven't met yet, people maybe I'll never actually meet. And so much feels right about it, so much feels freeing, but there's always this pang in my stomach, a tightening in my chest, like there's a big, gaping void that's growing and growing.

Something's missing.

Him.

When I think about a life without Naz, I start to feel lonely. It's like I'm standing in a crowded room, screaming, but nobody is even listening. That day, outside of the classroom, when he handed me my phone, was probably the first time in my life I felt like someone truly noticed. That someone paid attention. I like to think he heard me screaming, even if, at the time, it was for the wrong reasons.

And as I lay on the dirty floor in Melody's dorm room, a room that holds so many memories, I'm doing it again... I'm imagining a life without him.

A world where he doesn't exist.

It's dark. I don't know what time it is. I don't have it in me to look. I feel like I've been here forever, each tick of the clock taunting me. I'm silently screaming and tonight, nobody's listening, nobody's hearing me, nobody's coming to save me from this heartache.

Tick.

Tick.

Tick.

The longer he's gone, the greater the chance he's never coming back. He promised he would, but he's not indestructible. He's human. He's flawed. He has a heart that beats in his chest, just like me. All it would take is a twist of a knife to rip it apart. I know. I know.

I feel it.

The void.

The part of me that's missing.

I feel it.

Tears fill my eyes as bile burns my throat, forced up by the expanding mass in my chest, the vicious darkness that's eating away at me. "Oh God," I whisper, shoving myself up, my vision blurring from a sudden rush of dizziness. "I'm going to be sick."

I run to the bathroom, tripping over shit in the darkness, grateful to find it empty. Collapsing to the floor, I start gagging, but nothing's coming out. There's nothing left in me to give.

Please.

Please come back to me.

I need you.

The light flicks on, harsh and blinding, and I squeeze my eyes shut tightly as I continue pleading.

Please.

"Karissa?" Melody's voice is hesitant as she steps into the connected bathroom. "Are you okay?"

Am I okay? No. I'm not okay at all.

Words have been scarce from her since I showed up an hour... a day... a year ago. I don't know. I told her what happened to me, the Cliff Notes version, leaving out the parts having to do with Leo, but spilling secrets that even Naz doesn't yet know.

Naz.

Oh God... *Naz.*

What if he never knows?

The shock of it all rendered her speechless, and if I hadn't felt lonely enough before, now I certainly do. Nobody understands. Nobody hears me. Melody tried to listen, tried to rationalize what was going on, but no amount of 'everything happens for a reason' will ever be enough to keep me calm.

Instead of answering, I squeeze my eyes shut tighter, trying to imagine another world again. A world where we're happy, where we're together, where we're away from all of this.

A world without a target on our backs.

A world where Naz comes home.

A world where we can live in peace.

A world that's just ours.

"It'll be okay," Melody says, switching her course of action. "He's Ignazio, you know? He's, like... he's just *him*. He'll be all right."

I really want to believe that's true.

But sometimes, people don't come back.

And Melody knows that.

She knows that more than a lot of people.

And she's trying to be positive, being the best friend she can possibly be, but I can hear the apprehension in her voice. I can sense the shred of fear. This is heavy, way too heavy for such a naturally cheery girl. But it's always a possibility, every time somebody leaves, that it might be the last time you ever see them. It might be the last time they grace your world.

"If he doesn't come back—"

"Don't think that way," she says, cutting me off. "You can't think that way, Karissa."

Pushing away, I sit back on the floor and pull my legs up, wrapping my arms around my knees. Silent tears stream from my eyes. I don't even know I'm crying until I feel them on my cheeks. "I'm just... I'm just so tired of never having the ground under me. I feel like we're free falling, and everything around us just keeps moving in a blur, and I don't know how to make it slow down so we can land on our feet."

"I know," she says quietly, "but that's what happens when you fall in love with a force of nature."

I tilt my face, looking up at her.

She smiles sadly. "Look, I get it... I don't know really what Ignazio is like. I know the guy he wants me to know, and really, I don't think he wants me to know any part of him, but he tolerates me... because of you. So I know that side of him. And he's... intense. I'm not saying he's not nice, because he's never been *not nice*, but he's overwhelming. Honestly, Karissa, the man scares the shit out of me. But you love him, and I know you do... I can *tell* you do... because he's all consuming. It was like he got inside of you, and he gripped tight, and there's no way to get him out again unless we rip half of you out along with it. He's a force of nature. So it's really no surprise a shitstorm follows him, you know?"

I don't know what to say as I stare at her, absorbing those words. She's never made quite so much sense before. She does heavy better than I thought.

"Guess all those classes are paying off," I mumble. "You'll be the greatest philosopher of our generation."

She laughs. "I'm pretty sure Kanye already holds that title. Haven't you heard?"

I smile at that. "I'm sure we've all heard."

"So, yeah, I know you're fed up or whatever," she says, holding her hand out to me, to help me up, "but you gotta keep your head up."

I get to my feet, shaking my head. "Tupac."

"Who happens to be the greatest philosopher of the twentieth century," she says. "Screw Wittgenstein and Sellers and Rawl... Pac is where it's at."

I appreciate her trying to lighten the mood, and it almost works, almost distracts me from reality, but a loud banging coming from the dorm room overshadows everything.

Oh my God.

I push right past Melody, darting into the room, almost knocking Kimberly over as the girl heads for the door. She backs up, hands up, muttering angrily, but I don't listen to what she's saying.

Yanking the door open, my heart stops.

It stops for just a second.

It's the worst pain I've ever felt.

It's like the world stopped turning, nothing more existing, before everything kick-starts back into gear. It nearly knocks the breath from my lungs when I see him standing right there.

Naz.

He doesn't move. I don't give him a chance to come inside. The rush of emotions, of adrenaline, of *hormones*, is just too much to bottle up. I let out a cry as I fling myself at him, knocking into him hard, shoving him further out into the hallway.

He's here.

He's alive.

He laughs softly, wrapping his arms around me.

He holds me tight.

"California," I mumble against his chest.

He's quiet for a moment before asking, "What about it?"

"That's where I wanna go."

Another moment of silence. His hand comes to rest in my hair, pinning me against him as he kisses the top of my head. "If that's what you want."

It is.

It's all a blur after that. Naz thanks Melody. I'm too much of a mess to say anything. We leave and walk right out of the dorms, his hands never leaving me. His car is haphazardly double parked out front. It's pitch black out. Midnight? Maybe later.

The clock keeps on continuing to tick.

It brought him back to me this time.

He opens the passenger door but I stall there, clutching tightly to his hand, not getting in. Tears continue to stream from my eyes, and I really want to stop them, but son of a bitch... I can't.

He pauses, too, using his free hand to brush the tears from my face. "Hey, now... it's okay. I told you I'd be back."

"I know, but—"

I can't even finish.

I just cry harder.

My chest hurts just as much with that void again filled. Now it feels like it's going to burst, like there is not enough of me to contain all of this. My world is shipwrecked and I'm clinging to that goddamn plank, desperate to believe there's enough room for both of us to hold on. But my shoulders are heavy, too much weight pressing on my chest, and if I don't unburden myself really fucking quickly, I'm going to drown.

"But—?"

"I'm pregnant."

I blurt it so fast that it sounds like one jumbled word, a word that carries the weight of the world. *Pregnant*. I can feel the pressure on me lessening. Secrets are hard to keep. I've only known for a few hours myself, but every second that passed it ate away at me.

This isn't how I wanted to tell him.

I didn't know how to tell him, period, but this? This isn't how it's supposed to be. I'm not supposed to blurt it out in a bout of frightened tears.

I don't know how he's going to react. Don't know if he'll be happy, or angry, or just as shocked as me. We weren't trying. We haven't really talked about it. I was still on the pill, but I kept forgetting to take it, and I'd try to catch up later, but a lot of good *that* did.

Pregnant.

A baby.

Ugh, I'm gonna be sick again.

He stares at me.

And stares at me.

And stares at me some more.

I really need him to say something, but he just keeps staring, like maybe he didn't hear me. Did he? I almost blurt it out again, but I'm still crying, and the words just aren't forming like I want them to.

He stares so hard I think he burned right through to my soul, before he tugs on my hand, pulling me closer, and says, "Get in the car."

That's it.

That's all the reaction I get.

I listen and finally let go of his hand, climbing in the car. This isn't the place for it. He shuts the door for me, and I put on my seatbelt, my hands shaking. Ugh, I wish they'd stop. I wipe away my tears and try to pull myself together, expecting we'll have a conversation any second, but instead he just gets in and drives away without a word.

I'm trembling the whole way to Brooklyn.

I don't know what to make of anything.

He pulls into the garage when we arrive, locking the car up, and ushers me through the side door, into the kitchen. Killer starts barking excitedly when he sees me, jumping up and down, nearly knocking me on my ass. I head to the back door, letting him out into the yard, and am considering heading right upstairs when Naz appears behind me. I see his reflection in the glass. "How sure are you?"

Turning, I eye him warily. "On a scale of one to ten?"

He studies my face before saying again, "How sure are you, Karissa?"

"Uh, pretty sure, I guess... as sure as I can be. I haven't, like, peed on a stick or anything..."

"Then how do you know?"

There's a hint of anger in his voice then. He's trying to restrain it, but it's coming out.

"Because the doctor said I was."

"The doctor."

"Yeah, when we were at the hospital."

"At the hospital."

"He ran some tests or whatever, and I guess he kind of just happened upon it."

"He happened upon it."

He's doing it again.

Repeating my words.

"Yes," I say. "He happened upon it."

Naz nods, crossing his arms over his chest, his stance almost defensive, like he's trying to keep me from getting in. His face is still passive, even stoic, but his eyes are blazing. "How far along?"

"Eight weeks."

"So... two months."

He looks away from me, taking a deep breath, like he's trying to steady himself.

"You're angry."

"I am."

Ugh, he's not denying it.

"Yeah, well, maybe you're not the *only* one."

I try to storm away, but he grabs ahold of me, pulling me to him instead. My instinct kicks in, and I start to fight him, shoving and trying to get around him, but he just tightens his hold, pinning me there.

I give in right away.

When Naz wants something, he gets it, and truthfully, I feel better in his arms. He might be angry for whatever reason, but I'm terrified.

"A month ago," he says quietly. "I choked you."

"So?"

"You were already pregnant."

My stomach drops.

That hadn't even crossed my mind.

Leave it to Naz to fixate on that out of everything going on.

"You didn't hurt me... or *us*... or whatever."

Us. There's an us.

There's me and this... **baby**.

"I could've," he says. "I haven't been easy on you."

"That's because I can take it. And this... uh, you know..."

"Baby," he says quietly.

Baby.

Jesus Christ, I can feel the tears coming on again.

"It has your DNA," I say. "So obviously it's stubborn as shit and gonna be resilient."

He doesn't say anything to that.

I don't know if I'm making a difference in how he feels.

Probably not.

Naz already lost a family once. He lost a baby he never got the chance to know, so I'm not really surprised by his overbearing worry.

I just don't want him to beat himself up about it.

People tend to get hurt when that happens.

He lets out a resigned sigh. "So, California, huh?"

"Yes," I whisper.

One of the last conversations I had with my mother, she mentioned running away there. Maybe she was onto something. It's about as far away from New York as we're going to get without leaving the country.

"Well," he says, "better start packing then."

∽∾

Most of my life was spent living out of boxes. No reason to unpack when, sooner or later, I'd just have to pack it all up again.

I never had much as a child, or even as a teenager, so it wasn't hard, living such a life of simplicity, to pick up in the middle of the night and just walk away. It's easier to disappear, to slip into obscurity, without dragging a lifetime of possessions along.

That's something my mother taught me.

But I have a lot of baggage now... literally, figuratively... and I'm not entirely sure how it'll all fit into our new life. Dozens of cardboard boxes clutter every room of the house, most of them still empty. It's been a few days since we made the decision to move, and I feel like I've been packing constantly since, but I've barely made a dent in any of our belongings.

Truth be told, Naz has accumulated a lot of shit.

Although, okay, whatever, I guess I have, too.

I used to be able to fit everything I owned in three boxes, but now I need more than that for just shoes.

Standing in the den, my eyes scan the massive bookshelves packed full of Naz's books. He's sitting at his desk, half-dressed, a pair of black slacks and a white dress shirt. It's barely buttoned, not tucked in, the sleeves of it shoved up to his elbows.

He looks exhausted.

He probably is.

He walks around here, quiet, stoic, distracting himself by cleaning, scrubbing the same shit over and over. It's rare I catch him sitting down, like he is now, but even off of his feet, he still manages to look busy. How the hell does he do that? He's flipping through the newspaper, not paying me any attention, as I stress about how to pack up his books.

"You're stressing," he says, not looking at me, his eyes never averting from the newspaper.

"I'm not."

I'm lying.

"You're lying."

Ugh.

"It's just... this is a lot of books."

"I know."

"We're going to need, like, a billion more boxes."

"What for?"

What for?

What kind of fucking question...?

"For the books," I say. "You have a lot."

He slowly sets his paper down as he looks at me. "Doesn't matter. I'm not taking them."

"What? Why?"

"Because they're not necessary."

Somewhere out there, a bookworm's head just exploded. "How can you say the books aren't necessary?"

"Easily," he says. "They're not."

"I just... I don't even know what to say to you right now."

He laughs lightly, sitting back in his chair to regard me. "There's no point in taking most of it, Karissa. It's all unnecessary... it's just things. I started over from scratch once, and I'm more than happy to do it again."

"So, what, you'd just leave everything?"

"Not everything," he says. "I'd still consider taking you along."

"*Funny*." I resist the urge to stick my tongue out at him. "What would we do with it all?"

"Whatever you want."

"What did you do with everything last time?"

"Burned it."

I scrunch my face up at that. "What a waste."

He shrugs. "We could toss it, or sell it, or donate it, or just leave it. I'm not planning to sell the house right now. It can all just stay where it is."

The thought of it all staying here, collecting dust, oddly makes a pang in my stomach start to grow. It's one thing to pick up our lives and relocate them elsewhere, somewhere far away from here... but it's another to just walk away without it all, to leave who we were behind.

"Look," he says, standing up and strolling toward me. "Say the house is on fire, and you've only got a minute to grab what's important to you. What's *irreplaceable*. What do you go for?"

"This sounds kind of philosophical," I point out. "You're not going to quiz me about this later, are you? Make me write a paper or something? If so, I'm totally gonna fail this. Can I phone a friend?"

A smile tugs his lips. "Just answer the question."

I think about it for a moment. What would I grab if I only had a minute? "Pictures. I don't have many, but I'd like to, you know, keep a few."

He nods. "Understandable."

"Killer," I say. "I'd want my dog."

His cheek twitches. "I'm not surprised."

"You... do you count?"

"No, I'll get myself out."

"Then that's it, I guess."

"Photos and the mutt," he says. "That's what we take along."

I scrunch up my nose at him. "What about you? What would you grab?"

"Nothing."

I look at him incredulously. "Nothing?"

"It's all replaceable," he says, stepping toward me, his hands finding my hips. Leaning down, he kisses me, softly, sweet little pecks.

"Except for me?" I murmur against his lips.

I can feel him smiling against my mouth. "Even you."

Rolling my eyes, playfully scoffing, I shove away from him when he says that, but he keeps a hold on me. Laughing, he gazes down at me, one of his hands drifting from my hip and skimming along my stomach. He presses his palm flat against my shirt, over my belly button, as his eyes shift that direction.

He doesn't say anything, but he doesn't have to.

I can see the flit in his eyes, the spark, the restrained excitement. He's trying like hell not to get his hopes up. Naz isn't the kind of guy who lives his life in a cloud of optimism. He looks at the world and sees the darkness shrouding it. But light is peeking through the cracks in his armor, and it's warming some of that bitterness he's held onto.

"We should get going," he says quietly, "get this all over with so we can move on."

Frowning, I push away from Naz. "I'll get my shoes."

"Good."

"You should probably wear some shoes, too, this time."

"I'm already on it."

Ten minutes later, we've both got our shoes on, the two of us in the car, on the way to Manhattan. I've put it off as long as possible, but the time has come to go in and give my official statement about the attack with the cab. The lawyer told Naz if I didn't show up this afternoon, tomorrow they'd be at my door, prepared to escort me in.

That's the last thing I want.

The police station is busy when we get there. The lawyer is already waiting, a necessary formality, or so I'm told. They lead me back to the homicide division, to a small interrogation room, where Detective Jameson and Detective Andrews already wait.

"Mrs. Vitale," Jameson says, smiling in greeting as I sit down across from him, the lawyer right beside me. "I appreciate you taking time out of your busy schedule to come talk to us today. I know you've probably got more important things to do."

I almost tell him he's welcome, thinking he's genuine, when the lawyer clears his throat, chiming in. "Cut the passive aggressiveness, Jameson. She's here. Get on with it."

Jameson shrugs it off, turning to me. "Let's go over it again. What happened that day? Start with you getting in the cab."

"I got in the cab to go home, I wasn't really paying attention... we were driving for a while, and when I looked up, we were going the wrong direction."

I go through it, leaving out big chunks, but repeating exactly what I told them happened the day in the park. As soon as I finish, Jameson shakes his head, leaning back in the chair, as Andrews scoffs. "You're leaving something out."

"I'm not."

"It doesn't add up."

I go over it three more times. They've got me so flustered I almost slip up. The lawyer realizes it, I think, because when they start to hound me again, he speaks up. "She's told you what she knows. She's given you her statement. We're done."

Jameson reaches into his file and pulls out a blank piece of paper, sliding it across the table. He sets a pen on top of it. "Write it down."

I do.

I write it down.

My hand is cramping and my head is pounding by the time I'm done. I sign the paper, confirming it's all true, before walking out. Naz is sitting in the lobby, impatiently drumming his fingers on the arm of a chair.

He stands up as soon as he spots us.

He knows right away I'm upset. "What's wrong?"

"Nothing, I just..."

I don't know *exactly* what's wrong.

I feel like I've been raked over some coals.

I want to cry.

Ugh, I'm so damn emotional.

"Typical Jameson and Andrews," the lawyer chimes in. "You know how they are."

We leave, and I'm quiet on the drive back, leaning against the door and closing my eyes, wishing my head would stop pounding. We're almost to the house when the silence is shattered, a song ringing out.

Naz's phone.

He grabs it, looking at the screen, his brow furrowing. I watch him as he hesitates before answering. "Hello."

The call lasts only a minute.

He barely says anything except for a strained, "I'll be there."

When we reach the house, he pulls into the driveway, putting up the garage door, but he doesn't pull the car in. I know it right away. I know he's leaving.

He walks me inside, though. He lingers for a moment. He waits until I'm settled in the den before he drops it on me.

"I've got something to take care of," he says quietly. "You'll be okay here by yourself?"

I hesitate. "Sure."

"If you need me for anything... *anything*... don't hesitate to call me," he says. "I'll have my phone on me, and I mean it, Karissa... *anything.*"

"I'll be fine." I smile reassuringly. "I'm just gonna pack, maybe start piling some boxes up in the garage so they're out of the way."

"Just don't overdo it."

"Yes, sir."

He nudges me before walking away. I hear Killer faintly

growling in the kitchen where he's been sleeping as Naz passes through, but it's feeble, like the dog's not sure if it's worth the effort to give him hell today.

It's ten, maybe twenty minutes later, when I hear the side door from the garage open. The growling picks up almost instantly, but this time the dog pours his heart into it.

That was definitely quick.

"Relax, Killer," I say, walking into the kitchen. "It's just Na—"

Naz.

Not Naz.

Holy shit, it's not Naz.

It takes only a second for that reality to strike me. The kitchen is dim. It's a cloudy afternoon. It's a man, massive, with broad shoulders and a husky build. He's probably six and a half feet of solid muscle. His leather jacket clings tightly to his biceps, like the seams around the arms are going to burst. He's twice of me and not at all my Naz.

It was supposed to be Naz.

Not whoever the hell *this* is.

He's maybe six feet away from me, not close enough to reach me yet, but he's still too close... too damn close... close enough for me to smell him.

My nose knew something was wrong before my eyes did.

The scent is strong, like he's wearing piss that's been bottled as cologne, a woodsy chemical odor that makes my nose twitch. I get a good whiff and oh god, it's disgusting. It nearly takes my breath away.

My chest burns as panic sweeps through me so fast, so intense, that I almost gag, trying hard not to breathe it in.

I stare at him. One second. Two seconds. Three. He knows I'm here. He's already spotted me. He doesn't seem to be at all feeling the panic I'm feeling. His scruffy face is etched with a nasty kind of calm, his eyes a dark pool that lead to no soul. Some monsters hide in plain sight, wearing a mask around others, but I suspect this guy is the kind of monster that doesn't mind that everybody sees his true colors.

He's not even fazed by Killer's growling as the dog viciously bares his teeth.

A few more seconds... ten, maybe twenty... before he takes a step toward me. That's the only warning I need to send me into motion, fight or flight kicking in. There's no way I could ever take down that hulking figure, so I'm going to get the fuck out of there.

I run.

I turn and sprint from the kitchen, my heart racing wildly, thumping so hard it's vibrating in my ears. He's right behind me, running, looming, as Killer starts barking, lunging at the man. It all goes down too quick. I don't know what's happening. Killer's biting, snapping, attacking the man, but it's not enough to stop him.

Fuck. Fuck. Fuck.

He keeps coming.

I make it to the front door. The son of a bitch is locked up tight. I fumble with the chains and deadbolts for a second, but there's not enough time to get out that way. I dart a different direction. Back door's also locked, I know. I'll have to go back around to the side door, making my way out the garage.

I run. I fight. Hands grab me, tearing at me, throwing me around to try to get me to stop. He says not a goddamn word. He's grunting and growling in anger, trying to subdue me as he fights off the dog. A kick to the side sends Killer whimpering, but he doesn't retreat, lunging once more. Teeth clamp down on the man's leg, forcing him to let go of me.

He grabs a hold of Killer instead, throwing him across the room, into a living room table, knocking a lamp off. It crashes to the floor, and gives me enough of a distraction and dash out of the room. I run, as fast as my legs can carry me, but I'm no match for his strides. Two steps later, he's on me, grabbing my shirt, yanking me around by it, fisting my hair. I feel a tug on my neck as the chain on my necklace snaps.

He pulls me through the kitchen, limping, and opens the garage door, dragging me outside. Twisting me around by my hair, I flinch, pain ricocheting around my skull, as he forces me to look at him.

"You gonna play nice with me, little lady?" he asks.

I sneer. "I wouldn't *play nice* if you were the last man on earth."

The second I say it, he pulls out a red handkerchief and shoves it right in my face, covering my nose and mouth. I inhale sharply. Oh God, it burns. It reeks.

That stench.

That's it.

I struggle, I fight him, I try to breathe, but nothing I do can stop the darkness.

I can feel it.

It's coming quickly.

Chapter Eighteen
Ignazio

The pink-trimmed house is locked up.

Seems they found a body inside of it just the other night. It managed to grace the newspaper, barely getting a small blurb. Another hoodlum murdered in Bensonhurst.

Nobody seems to care anymore.

It was curious, though... they called it **unoccupied**. The house was empty when the police arrived. According to them, nobody had lived there for a long time. Lorenzo had moved out fast, right under people's noses, just like he'd move into it without raising any alarms.

Sounds like Lorenzo.

The black BMW isn't anywhere in the neighborhood. I park across the street and get out of my car, but I don't approach the house, standing on the sidewalk instead, waiting.

He'll show his face.

After all, he's the one who called me here.

"Shame, isn't it?" a voice says behind me. "I liked that place."

Turning my head, I spot Lorenzo as he appears on the stoop of an adjacent townhouse. The white cookie-cutter building looks like half the others on the block. "Seems as if you've already moved on."

He glances at the townhouse behind him, shrugging. "Actually had this one first. But that one across the street? I thought it was charming. Nobody was using it, so I figured, hey... *why not*?"

That, in itself, says all you'd ever need to know about Lorenzo. He takes whatever he wants, and he uses it, and abuses it, and then he walks away when it serves no purpose to him anymore.

"It was too pink for my liking," I tell him.

"It wasn't pink... it was peach," he says. "You must be colorblind."

"Must be."

He steps down onto the sidewalk, coming to a stop right beside me. He's got an orange in his hand, and he casually runs his fingertips along the thick rind. "Did you know oranges show up in something like twenty-two scenes in *The Godfather* saga? They're symbolic."

"For what?"

"Death," he says, holding his orange out to me. "Violence."

I stare at it for a second before turning away, looking back at the other house. "That makes no sense."

"I think the point is things are what we make of them." He shrugs off my snub and starts peeling the orange. "They mean what we want them to mean. We see what we want to see. Signs are all around us... you just have to pay attention."

"If there's some kind of threat in those words, I'm not hearing it."

He laughs. "No threat. Just making small talk."

"I don't like small talk."

"You never did."

"So why don't you get to the point," I tell him. "I doubt you called me here to share movie trivia."

He laughs to himself. "No, you're right... I called you here to help you out."

"And how, exactly, are you planning to help me?"

He seems to consider that... maybe *reconsider*... as he throws some of his peel to the ground. "I got a call from a friend down in

Florida. He told me something interesting."

"What's that?"

"He's been working with these guys down in Cuba, you know... the import-export business. Started a long time ago, back when my stepfather was still around. They'd smuggle things in, anything there was a market for, and they'd store them at the grove for safekeeping. Made a pretty penny off of it back then."

I know all this.

He's telling me nothing new here.

"These days, there's not such a demand. They still do it, you know, still bring it in, but the way the economy is, nobody wants to pay. But this friend of mine, he's still got a few lucrative clients, guys willing to shell out the cash for something special."

He pauses to eat a piece of his orange.

"You got a point here?" I ask. "If I wanted a lesson on economics, I'd go to business school."

He ignores my comment and waits until he swallows before continuing on. "There's this one particular guy, he's got this thing for cigars... and not just any cigars. He wanted the top of the line, these special Montecristo ones. He was willing to pay a couple hundred bucks each. So my friend, he's been bringing them in every few months, making a killing."

"Good for him."

"Good for me, too," he says. "He still runs it all through the grove, so I get a piece of it... and dare I say, I think it's good for *you*, too."

"Are you trying to recruit me? If so, you're wasting your time."

"This isn't a sales pitch."

"Then get to the point."

He shakes his head, eating another wedge of the orange. "This client of his lives here in New York. Old guy, high profile, been smoking these particular cigars for years, since back in the day, when he got them from my stepfather. He's a bit of a recluse, though, doesn't like to go out, so he sends someone else to pick them up for him and deliver them straight to his house in Long Island."

As soon as he says that, I know exactly who he means. There's only one man around who would sell his soul for a decent Cuban. "Genova."

"Bingo."

He stops there, like any of this even means anything. So, what? His cigars are illegal? What about the man's life isn't? "Well, I appreciate the info. If I ever want to buy him a gift, I know where to get it."

I turn, annoyed, and take a step toward my car. I don't have the patience for this. He's wasting my time.

"Whoa, you're not going to ask the magic question?" Lorenzo looks at me, cocking an eyebrow. "Not going to ask who he sends to pick them up?"

"Okay, I'll buy it... who?"

"A big guy, I'm talking massive. My friend says he's got a memorable name, like that guy in some sitcom, but he goes by the nickname of—"

"Fat Joe."

Son of a bitch.

Again, he smiles. "Bingo."

I wish I could say I was surprised, or even that I was disappointed, but this is right up Genova's alley. The bastard has been toying with me.

"I need a favor, Lorenzo."

"I just did you one."

"I need another," I say. "I want a meeting with the five families."

"And you think I can help you with that?"

"I think *you* think you can," I say, "and that just might be enough to make it happen."

He considers that as he tosses some of his peel to the ground. "I'll see what I can do."

I knew he would.

Curiosity will always win out when it comes to Lorenzo. Besides, I'm sure he enjoys the challenge. That's why he's here, after all, why he even made the move to New York City. He does what the world tells him is impossible to do. Maybe it's just a game at this point, or maybe he's out to prove something to himself. To prove he's not one to ever back down.

It isn't going to end well for somebody, that's for certain.

I don't want to stick around and watch it play out.

But people, they're making it hard for me.

They're making it hard for me to live my life.

"So," Lorenzo says after a moment. "What do you want this meeting for?"

I glance at him. "I guess you'll find out."

Sudden noise breaks the silence. My phone. I pull it out of my pocket and glance at it, my muscles tightening. Her name is flashing on the screen. Karissa.

I press the button to answer and bring it to my ear. "Karissa? What do you need, sweetheart?"

Silence.

It's deafening.

It screams louder to me than any words.

"Karissa?"

Still nothing.

All at once, I know it's not her. It's like a feeling wafting through the line, the air wrong, too tense, too heavy. Someone is there. I can sense it. Someone's listening, someone's breathing, someone's existing on the other end of this call.

But it's not her.

Not again.

"Who is this?"

I don't expect anyone to answer me.

And for a moment, they don't.

But after a strained breath, a long exhale, I hear the words.

277

"You're lucky I don't feel like killing anyone today."

The line goes dead.

I pull the phone away, staring at it as the call ends. *You're lucky I don't feel like killing anyone today.* I know those words. I've said them. I can feel the blood drain from my face, can feel it rushing through my body, bitterly cold, replaced by an ice in my veins.

"Ignazio, you okay there?" Lorenzo asks. "You're looking kind of pale."

My vision blurs. Everything goes black around the edges.

I sway, damn near passing out, as it all seems to hit me at once.

Anger. Fear. *Adrenaline.*

It rushes through me, a toxic cocktail of emotion that nearly knocks my feet out from under me. Lorenzo reaches out, grabbing a hold of my arm, but it's too much. He's touching me. His tainted hands are on my skin.

I snap.

Grabbing him, I throw him back against the townhouse so hard he gasps from the surprise of it all. The orange drops from his hand, rolling along the sidewalk, as I pin him there. He doesn't fight. He doesn't struggle. He just stares at me, his expression blank, like he's not bothered at all.

"So help me God, Lorenzo, if this was all you..."

I can't even finish those words.

If this was all just a game.

A ruse...

I shove him again, knocking him hard against the brick, before I turn around and walk away, moving as fast as my legs will carry me. By the time I reach my car, I'm already at a sprint.

I drive home, speeding through the streets. It's dreary out, middle of the afternoon, but the darkened clouds make it feel much later. Everything is cast in gloomy shadows. It makes the hair on my arms bristle.

Everything feels hollow, more silent in the dark.

I pull the car into the driveway when I make it home, and throw it in park before pausing, my hand gripping the key in the ignition.

The garage is wide open.

The side door is, too.

My hair bristles even more.

Cutting the engine, I reach under the seat, feeling around for *War & Peace*. I get a grip on it, pulling it out, and flip the pages open, grabbing the concealed gun.

The first thing I notice, when I step into the garage, is the blood on the concrete. *No. No. No.* It's not much, a few drops, but it doesn't belong here. It's not mine, and I hope like hell it's not Karissa's, but the alternative is there's somebody else here bleeding.

And I don't like that just as much.

I step through the side door, right into the kitchen. The second I do, I hear the faint growling. It's weak and strained, over in the corner. My eyes dart that way, my stomach dropping when I see Killer.

He's cowering there, blood on his face. I don't think he's injured—not seriously, at least. He seems to be in one piece, but somebody else might not be. Carefully, I reach into the cabinet, quietly grabbing a few treats. I toss them to him, and he quiets to a whimper, but he doesn't eat them.

Not this time.

"Stay in the kitchen," I tell him. "Stay quiet."

Will he listen? I don't know.

I don't even know if he understands.

But if there's a chance anyone else is still in the house, I'm not ready to alert whoever it is to my presence.

The living room is wrecked. A lamp is knocked over, lying on the floor. Scanning the area, something shiny catches my eye, and I step toward it, looking down at it.

My world stops.

A necklace.

Karissa's necklace.

The one I gave to her.

The chain is snapped, the round crystal pennant reflecting the little bit of light streaming into the room. She never takes it off. She wouldn't take it off. She certainly wouldn't leave it here, broken, on the floor.

Not unless she didn't have a choice.

Reaching down, I pick it up, holding it up by the chain to eye the thing.

Carpe Diem.

I grip the necklace tightly, fisting it, as I tear through the house, looking for her. There's no more blood, and the rest of the house is in order, but there's no sign of her anywhere.

No fucking sign of her.

My hands are shaking. Anger merges with fear until the red I see turns blue. I feel *cold*. A shiver tears down my spine.

They're not going to take another life from me.

They can't have my wife.

They can't take her.

They can't steal my happiness.

I'm not going to let them.

Not now. Not ever.

Not again.

Not again.

"What happened?"

The sudden voice behind me makes my back stiffen and my grip on the gun tighten, but I don't turn around. I don't look at him. I didn't hear him sneaking up, but I'm not at all surprised he's here. Not surprised that he followed me.

"My wife," I say, my voice strained. "Somebody took her."

"Uh-oh."

Uh-oh.

Lorenzo says 'uh-oh', like that's an adequate response to what I just said. He'll be lucky if I don't give him a 'boo-boo' in the form of a fucking bullet to the head.

"For the record," he says, "it wasn't me."

"So you say."

Tucking the gun into my waistband, I pull out my phone, hoping like hell Karissa's is still on, wherever it is, so I can locate it.

"Look, Ignazio," he says. "I don't know how many times I've got to say it. I've got no reason to target you, or your father, or your wife, for that matter. It's not *me*."

The phone connects, and I look down at it, staring at the address.

It's an address I know... a place I've been to before.

"You want me to believe you, Lorenzo? You want me to trust you?" I start toward him, pausing right in front of him. "Then get me my meeting, like I asked."

I shove past him, hearing him call after me, following me out of the house. "Where are you going?"

"To get my wife back."

"How do you know where to look?"

I hold my phone up. "I've got a map."

"A map?" He laughs. Laughs. "You ever feel like Admiral Ackbar with the Death Star plans?"

I look at him, brow furrowed.

"You know... *Return of the Jedi*? It's a trap!"

I shake my head.

"Really? Nothing?" He scrunches up his face as if I disgust him. "How are we even friends?"

"We're not."

"Look, I'm just saying—"

"You're saying it's a trap."

"I'm saying this is awfully convenient, so either you're dealing with a bunch of idiots, or yeah... it's a trap. And these guys... they're

281

not exactly brilliant, but they're not stupid, either."

He's saying nothing I'm not already thinking.

But it doesn't matter... I've got no choice.

Trap or no trap, I've got to go.

"Just get my meeting, Lorenzo."

He nods, walking out. "It's as good as got."

Killer tries to follow me when I leave, but I lock him in the house. If he gets loose, if I let something happen to him, Karissa will be distraught when she gets home.

Because she's coming home.

She is.

I'll destroy the whole world to make sure it happens.

And I know where to start.

Chapter Nineteen
Karissa

It's dark.

So dark.

But the darkness wasn't gradual.

It was a sudden plunge into blackness, like the light was siphoned from around me. Gone. I was at home, terrified, fighting, then blink, and I'm here.

I don't know where here is.

The terror still flows through my veins.

Where the hell am I?

Scarce windows surround me, covered with old bars, the glass so grimy they might as well be tinted. I can't see out of them, and I know it's just as impossible for anyone to see in. I woke up lying on a cold concrete floor, pressed against a wall in the darkness.

It's like being trapped in a void.

A dirty, disgusting void. Ugh.

My vision is fuzzy.

The air smells funny.

My head is pounding like a fucking bass drum.

I came to just a moment ago... or maybe an hour ago, I don't know. It's all a big haze. Forcing myself to sit, I blink, and blink, and blink some more, trying to make sense of my surroundings, trying to push back my fears, but it's not helping.

Nothing is helping.

I'm confused.

"You must be confused."

The voice across the room startles me and I flinch, letting out a gasp of air, a shuttering breath. My chest burns, and I inhale sharply in response, as my eyes trail the sudden movement across the room.

A guy.

The guy.

The one who was in my house earlier.

He stands in the shadows on the opposite side of whatever room this is, watching me. *Oh God.* He looks like a beast. He's staring me down, awaiting some sort of response to what he just said, but I can't get my voice to work yet.

Fuck, I can barely *think.*

He gives up waiting on me to answer and takes a step in my direction, his leg almost buckling as he does. "Don't hurt yourself trying to remember what happened. If you want to know, all you've got to do is ask."

"Who are you?"

My voice cracks, the question quiet when it leaves my lips on a shaky breath. He hears it, though, and limps even closer. He's injured. There's blood on his ripped khaki pants. Killer tore into him good.

Killer. Oh God, I hope he's okay.

"Let's just say I'm a friend of Vitale's."

I slowly shake my head, my vision blacking out around the edges, as I whisper, "he has no friends."

He's told me that, and I believe him, most definitely, if these are the kind of people who call themselves his *friends.* We certainly define friendship differently.

With friends like these, who needs enemies?

He laughs at that, still advancing toward me, that strange smell wafting through the air. It's sickly sweet. Acidic. My nose scrunches up, my lip curling instinctively as he crouches down right in front of me, close enough that I can see his eyes are bloodshot, like the blood vessels have burst.

Tears burn my eyes.

I look away.

His hand reaches out toward me, and I press my back against the wall, cowering away, but that doesn't deter him. Rough, red patches coat the skin around his palm and fingertips, rubbed raw and bleeding, like a chemical burn. He grasps my chin, roughly tilting it, squeezing my face to force me to look at him. A cry bursts from my chest, unable to be restrained, as tears start to flow from my eyes.

His calloused thumb wipes them away as a smile touches his lips.

He's enjoying this.

I try to pull away, to move away, but he's too strong and fuck, I'm weak. I'd drop the second I got to my feet. My legs are shaking, my head swimming. Even at my best and him at his worst, I couldn't outrun him.

"Please," I whisper, "just let me go."

His smile grows.

There's a spark in his eyes.

I think he likes it that I'm begging.

Ugh, sick fucker.

"Please," I say again. If it buys me time, if it buys Naz time to realize I'm gone, to come for me, I'll do it. Because he'll come for me. I know he will. He's promised, time and time again. *I'll always come for you.* "I don't know who you are, or what you want, but I've done nothing—"

His smile dissolves into a full-blown grin as he again laughs. This time it's sharp and loud, cutting off my words, as he grips me tighter. "You really think your innocent act is going to work on me?"

285

"It's not an act."

"Oh, but it is. You married a monster, little girl. Don't act like you don't know what he is, like you don't know what he does. He murders, in cold blood, and he makes it *personal*. That's why he uses his hands, why he uses a knife... why he suffocates, and strangles..." The man lets go of me and leans back, drawing his fingertips across his neck. "Why he slits throats."

My blood runs cold at those words.

"He likes to be up close," he continues. "He likes for you to look at him, for you to know who is stealing your final breath, like it makes him some sort of God, some angel of death, casting judgment while he stares you right in the face. He doesn't just kill, little girl... he robs you of your dignity, of your strength, of your self-respect. He takes it all as he toys with you. He takes it all for himself. And then he kills you, after you've got nothing left. So don't act like you're innocent, like you're ignorant, because I know who you are. We *all* know who you are. You were one of the hunted. He was going to do the same thing to you. He wanted you to suffer, too. And you know that... you know it, yet you gave him your heart, you gave him your cunt, and now you have the nerve to act innocent about it, like you've done nothing to get yourself here?"

I look away from him again.

I feel like I'm going to throw up.

"I know he's not a good man," I say quietly, "but he's not a bad one, either."

"*Bullshit.*"

He spits the word at me. Literally. He spits it. I grimace, gagging, feeling the saliva hit my cheek, inhaling that acidic odor that surrounds him for some goddamn reason. It's disgusting.

I can even smell it on *me*.

He stands back up and stares down at me. I still don't look at him, but I can feel his eyes. I can feel them pecking at me, boring into me, judging me the same way he says Naz does when he takes someone's last breath. And I've seen the look before... seen it on Naz's face, seen the cold, callous cruelty in his eyes. The day in the den, when he choked me on his desk, a day I know he could've easily killed me, a day I realize part of him *wanted* to. I've met the part of Naz that is a monster, but that isn't all of him, and I refuse to let anybody tell me differently. Maybe it's unhealthy, loving a man like him, staying with someone so dangerous, but I'm not his prey, and he's not my predator, and this man is fucking insane if he thinks he can poison me against him.

"He's different," I say. I'm wasting my breath. I know I am. But I need more time. I need a distraction. I need a way out of this. "You just can't see it."

"Different?" he asks incredulously. "Let me tell you something... there's nothing *different* about that man. You can capture a lion and teach it to do tricks, but you'll never change the nature of the beast. It'll still rip your fucking head off if you poke it the wrong way."

I start to respond, to refute those words, when a flash of light cuts through the room, illuminating the filthy concrete walls surrounding me for a brief moment before shutting off again. *Headlights*. My stomach clenches as the man glances toward the nearest window. "Looks like company is here."

Company.

More men.

More guys like him.

"Why are you doing this?" I ask, my voice shaking. "What do you want?"

He glances at me. "What do I want?"

I nod.

"I want your husband dead."

I inhale sharply.

The answer doesn't shock me, but it hurts. It fucking *hurts*.

"But it doesn't really matter what *I* want," he continues. "What matters is what the boss wants."

The boss.

Of course he's working for somebody else.

They always are, aren't they?

"So what does your boss want, then, if he doesn't want him dead?"

"Oh, I never said he didn't want him dead, but the boss? He's taking a play out of your husband's handbook. See, me? I'd make it quick and easy. Shoot up your house, kill him without ever getting out of the car. I like a good drive-by. It's *timeless*. But I guess somewhere along the way, this turned personal, and the boss wants Vitale to get a dose of his own medicine. Steal his pride, his hope, his dignity. Then after he's got nothing left, we take his life. Because without the rest of those things, it's not really worth living, is it?"

He turns to walk away, limping a few steps.

"So that's what Lorenzo wants, huh? To toy with him?"

He pauses, glancing at me, genuine surprise flashing across his expression. "Lorenzo?"

"That's your boss, isn't it? Lorenzo Gambini."

I've caught him off guard. I can see it in his eyes. He stares at me like he isn't sure how to respond. The man obviously likes to talk a lot, but I've rendered him speechless.

"Lorenzo Gambini," he echoes before shrugging and turning to leave again. "Doesn't ring a bell."

I scowl at the door when he opens it and shuffles outside, leaving it open a crack so he can peer back in and keep an eye on me. It's the only way in and out that I can see. To escape, I'd have to go right through them.

I don't know how many of them there are.

I hear a few voices, fragments of a conversation. I can only make out part of what they're talking about, but very little of it makes any sense to me. They talk about trees and Park Enforcement, like any of that is relevant, before someone mentions a crime scene and something sparks inside of me. I look around the room I'm in, feeling like I'm going to be sick.

The park near the East River.

Could it be?

They keep on babbling as my captor periodically glances back in at me, like he thinks he's going to catch me in the act of doing something. I'm not sure what the hell I could do in this situation. It's so damn dark and my head is still pounding and I'm so woozy it's taking everything in me just to sit up straight. I hear more words, something about cigars and borrowing a lighter, before someone yells to douse a fire before they blow us all to smithereens. I don't know... it's all beyond me... until I hear them say his name.

"Anything from Vitale?"

I don't know the voice that asks that... have never heard it before that I can recall. But it's the hulking man who responds.

"I called him on the girl's phone. Shouldn't take him long."

My phone. *Of course.* It won't take Naz long to track me using it, and it seems they're banking on that fact. I don't know what to do with that information, though, if I'm supposed to be hopeful, or if I should be terrified this is all a trap. I try to remind myself that Naz is smart, too smart to let them have the upper hand, but he's just a man... a flawed man... a man that probably doesn't even have a plan.

How the hell are we getting out of this one?

They talk some more. I don't know about what. Endless babbling that goes in one ear and out the other, as my eyes scan the small space around me. I see headlights again eventually as the car leaves, the door opening, my captor waltzing back in.

Ten.

Nine.

Eight.

I count in my head as I close my eyes, trying like hell to stay calm, to keep my heart from racing. It feels like it's going to give out on me any second. Each inhale brings about a swell of nausea as bile burns my throat. There's something wrong. I can feel it deep in my bones. I feel intoxicated, yet suffering from the worst hangover... dizzy and desperate, my head damn near explosive.

I don't know what the hell the man did to me to get me here, but it can't be good.

It can't be good for the baby.

I wrap my arms around my stomach, holding myself together one lungful at a time. Inhale. Exhale. Just keep breathing.

I remember those words.

Remember Naz repeating them.

You'll be okay... just keep breathing.

The man paces the room in the darkness, his hands shoved in his pockets, his knee buckling every few steps. He's in some pain, I can tell it, and he's getting nervous.

He should be nervous.

He's right, maybe... and maybe Giuseppe was right, too. A leopard doesn't change its spots. That's what he told me. That's what they all say. For everything that is undoubtedly different about Naz these days, a few things will never change.

Naz won't give up.

He won't give in.

He's not going to let anyone bully him.

He's not going to let somebody else *win*.

The old Naz will come for me.

I have no idea what the hell he's going to do to get us out of this, but I don't doubt for a second that somehow, he will.

He has to.

Inhale.

Exhale.

Just fucking breathe.

My eyelids are heavy from exhaustion. My body is screaming for me to lie down, for me to go to sleep. The offensive smell keeps haunting me, surrounding me, like it's seeping from my pores the same way it clung to him.

Him.

He continues to pace, muttering to himself. I don't know the man's name. Not that it matters, really. I probably wouldn't recognize it, just like I don't know the face. He's a stranger to me. He's in over his head, and I think he knows it, with the way his eyes keep darting toward the windows, with the way he seems to be jumping out of his own skin. I wonder if he's second-guessing this plan of his, if he's realizing just how stupid going after Naz is. I wonder if it's not too late to try to convince him that letting me go is still an option.

I wonder.

I wonder.

I fucking wonder.

But there's nothing I can do about it.

Because my mouth is dry, my throat is burning, and if I try to speak, I know I'm going to lose it. I'm going to lose the last shred of my composure, and he's going to know he's got me. He's going to know he broke me. He'd love nothing more than to hear me beg again, and I just can't give him that.

Don't let him win.

I don't know how much time passes. I blink and blink. Inhale. Exhale. Breathe. I think I pass out, because a second later I'm lying down, startled by a loud bang... loud enough to vibrate the concrete floor beneath me. There's a commotion outside. Someone shouts. There's rustling around the building, frantic enough that the chaos creeps through the cracks in the concrete, and I know it then.

I know it.

Naz is here.

My breath catches. I've got to keep breathing, but at the moment, I can't. Terror freezes the blood in my veins, everything blurry when I sit back up and stare at the door. The man does the same, stopping a few feet to the right of me, so still in the darkness it's like he's ceased to exist from the weight of this whole thing. I count in my head; I don't know what number I get to... I keep fucking it up as

I stare and stare and stare.

The door swings open, and I nearly black out from the shock of adrenaline surging through me. My eyes meet Naz through the darkness as he calmly, casually, steps inside.

The fucker just walks right in.

A few seconds pass. I expect the chaos to follow him, but it doesn't. Nothing follows him.

No one.

I don't know what that means; I don't know what the hell happened outside or what's about to happen in here. All I know is Naz is in front of me.

Naz.

My Naz.

Oh God.

He's holding a knife, fisting the handle of it, the tip pointing to the floor. I catch a gleam of the metal. I exhale sharply, a worried cry, as I stare at him. The noise catches Naz's attention, his eyes seeking me out. It sets my captor into motion as he darts my direction, yanking me off the ground.

I almost do it again. I almost black out. It's only a few seconds, as I slump in the man's arms, damn near hitting the floor. He grips me tightly, though, and grunts as he forces me onto my feet, shaking me like that'll keep me conscious, but it only aggravates my queasiness.

A massive arm is snaked around me, forcing me on my tiptoes. Naz doesn't look at the man right away, his eyes on me, studying me, making sure I'm okay.

Am I okay?

I see it as Naz's nose twitches, his posture stiffening, his grip on his knife tightening. *Maybe I'm not.* After a moment, he glances past me, above me, looking at the man for the first time.

Something suddenly sets Naz off, almost like he's in a panic. He takes a few steps toward us, his expression darkening, when the man reaches into his pocket, pulling something out. At first I think it's a knife as I catch a gleam of metal, but as I cut my eyes that direction, I see it's a lighter.

A silver Zippo.

The man flips it open and holds it up in front of me, his thumb on the wheel. Naz pauses suddenly. It's like he hit a brick wall. Something flashes in his eyes, something I'm not used to seeing on him.

Fear.

The darkness seems to melt away as his eyes seek me out again. This isn't the cold, calculating monster the man wanted to draw here. In front of me stands a terrified man. I can tell it from the look on his face.

I see him breaking right in front of me.

Naz's voice is low, threatening, as he says, "You wouldn't dare."

The man responds right away. "Try me."

I expect Naz to do just that, but he doesn't move an inch. He does nothing. **Nothing**. He stands there, clutching the knife, staring at me, desperation shining through. Holy fuck, he's seriously scared. What the hell is happening?

"Let her go," Naz says.

"Drop the knife and I'll think about it."

I almost fucking laugh. **Yeah, right**. Like Naz is going to do that. But all at once, without a second of hesitation, he opens his hand and the knife clatters to the concrete.

He listens.

He drops the goddamn knife.

Whatever is making me foggy must be **seriously** fucking with me, because none of this is adding up.

Why would he do that?

"Kick it over here," the man orders, and again, Naz listens. He kicks the knife right at us. It comes to a stop by my feet.

"Let her go," Naz repeats, his voice borderline pleading. "You want me, you got me. Just leave her out of this."

"Naz," I whisper. "What's happening?"

Naz looks at me but he doesn't answer my question.

My captor, on the other hand, is eager to chime in. He pulls me tighter to him, waving the lighter in front of my face. "Do you smell it? I know Vitale does. It's on me, and on you, and since he walked in, it's probably on him now, too. It's all over the room, it's in the air, and it's clinging to our clothes, but especially yours. You're coated in it, little girl. I made sure of that. And all it needs is one little spark, one flick of my thumb, and you'll go right up. Whoosh."

Do I smell it?

I do.

I've smelled it since the second I saw him.

"What is it?" I ask, the words coming out as a strangled cry. Holy shit, he's going to burn me. He's going to *burn me alive*.

"Ether."

It's Naz that answers that time.

Ether.

I've taken enough chemistry in school to recognize that word. I couldn't tell you what it's used for, but I know without a shadow of a doubt, ether is highly flammable.

"No... I just... *No!* You can't!" I start to struggle as tears start streaming from my eyes. "It's on you, too. You can't do it. You'll go up in flames."

The man leans down, closer to my ear, as he whispers, "So?"

Jesus Christ, he doesn't care.

No wonder he was so anxious.

It's a suicide mission.

"Let her go," Naz says for the third time, his voice louder, more threatening.

"Why should I?" the man asks.

"Because she's pregnant."

The man laughs at that. He laughs, like it's *amusing*. Like me being pregnant makes this all the more entertaining. And I know it then. I know he's not going to let me go. He's not going to just let me walk out of here. Maybe there was some second-guessing, but it was never about me. It was just self-preservation. But it's too late for that now. He wants to kill Naz but more importantly, he's here to torture him.

He's going to torture him by torturing *me*.

No. He can't do it. I can't let him.

This can't be happening.

Something snaps inside of me then. I can *feel* it. It's like the walls holding me together start crumbling, the panic pushing its way through like an overflowing river. Headlights flash in the windows yet again, drawing the man's attention, distracting him long enough for me to do something. Terrified, I lash out, struggling in his arms, my arm thrusting back, my elbow going straight into his gut. Hard. His grip on me slips and he loses hold of the lighter. The man goes to retrieve it, and I react in the moment.

I *have* to.

Reaching down, I grab the knife, the one Naz brought with him. I recognize it.

It came straight out of our kitchen.

One second it's firmly in my hand; the next second I'm swinging the damn thing. I don't stop to think about what the hell I'm doing, because if I do, I might hesitate.

There's no time for hesitation, not when our lives are at stake.

I hit him, I think, somewhere in the leg. I'm surprised by how easy the knife goes in. I always thought it took brute force, but the blade slides right through the skin. He grunts, fucking growling as I twist out of his arms and pull the knife back out, blood spurting from the gash.

I drop the knife as I run.

I run straight to Naz. He's already advancing toward me. I throw myself into his arms, trying to hold myself together, but I'm crying. Naz's hands frantically explore me, like he's trying to make sure I'm okay, and his lips find my forehead a moment later. It's a soft kiss, a quick kiss, before he pulls away.

He looks me right in the eyes.

I watch as his terror fades away.

Something else takes over.

An anger.

A hunger.

The monster.

"Run," he says quietly.

I cling to him, eyes widening. "What?"

"Get out of here," he says, pulling me off of him, as he pushes me toward the door. There are car doors slamming outside. People are approaching. *Oh God.* No. No. *No.* "Run and don't look back."

I want to argue.

I want to tell him he's a fucking fool.

There's no way I'm leaving here without him.

Till death do us part.

I want to stay here, stay with him, but I know, deep down inside, there's no way he'll let me.

Because it's not just me now.

It's me and a baby.

His baby.

Our baby.

He gives me another look, and I know I can't hesitate. Closing my eyes, I look away from him, running for the exit just like he told me.

Yanking the door open, I burst outside, my head still pounding. I feel *sick*. My chest burns, as I break into a sprint, unable to help myself as I do it... I look back.

It's only a second, as I stare at the closing door.

A second of hesitation.

Oh God. *Naz.*

I keep running, though, nearly fucking tripping, stumbling over my feet before crashing right into something.

BAM

Hands grab my arms, keeping me from falling on my ass. My

head whips back around, and there I see him.

I see that face.

Lorenzo.

The sight of him is like being punched in the gut.

It's crippling.

I'm crumbling.

Falling to pieces.

"Sunshine," he says casually. "Figured we'd find you here."

"Of course you did," I whisper through my tears, trying to yank away from him, but he just grips my arms tighter. Men surround us, maybe half a dozen. I don't count them. I don't give a shit about them. They all look the same.

Dressed in black with ski masks on.

They blend in with the darkness.

"Where's your husband?" he asks, but he doesn't wait for me to answer. Swinging me around, he shoves me back into one of his men, looking at the guy pointedly as he says, "Take her. Make sure she doesn't get hurt. You know the drill."

The man starts to drag me away as Lorenzo pulls out a gun, holding it firmly in his hand. He heads toward the concrete building, and a scream bursts out of me. A scream of sheer terror, of utter desperation.

Oh God, he's going to die.

He's going to kill him.

"No!" I shriek, fighting the man who's holding me, kicking and punching, trying to break free. "Naz! Please! Naz!"

I scream his name, praying he hears me, praying he's ready, praying he walks away from this okay. I can't do it without him. I need him.

I *need* him.

It takes three of them to subdue me, to shove me in the back of a car that's only a few feet away. Two climb in the back with me, while the guy he passed me off to gets behind the wheel. I fight with all my might, grabbing masks and pulling on them, scratching faces, trying to take out their fucking eyes.

Anything to escape.

I scream and scream and scream, his name the only word I can now conjure. *Naz. Naz. Naz.*

I don't know if he can hear me.

I don't know if it's too late.

I punch a guy straight in the nose before trying to break out a window, beating on it with my fists, but it's not buckling. I use my foot when they try to pull me away from it, hauling my leg up and kicking the glass, angry that it just won't fucking break.

Why won't it break?

It takes damn near a dozen times before the glass fractures, splintering and cracking, falling to pieces. My foot goes right through it then, and I hiss as the jagged glass slices the skin near my ankle.

Fuck, I start bleeding *everywhere.*

"Jesus Christ," the driver yells. "Get her under control!"

I hit, and I hurt, but it gets me nowhere. The two guys pin me down in the backseat of the car as they start driving away. We don't make it very far, just through the park, before a bang rocks the area, loud enough that it vibrates the windows in the car.

A flash of light illuminates the sky.

I don't have to see it to know what happened; I don't have to look to know how bad it is. The man driving raises his mask, resting it on his head, as he glances in the rearview mirror, looking back.

Don't look back.

He lets out a low whistle.

I'm sobbing, hyperventilating, trying to breathe, but I don't think I can survive this kind of pain.

As the building explodes, my world implodes.

Everything around me goes up in flames.

Chapter Twenty
Ignazio

I've always been fascinated by how the body works.

How a fist-sized muscle deep in your chest is responsible for keeping you alive every day. It steadily beats, every second of every hour, pushing blood through your arteries then back to it through your veins. And you do nothing to make it happen. It just does it, all on its own. Doesn't matter how you're feeling, what you're thinking, if your fucking heart is breaking... it keeps on beating, a hundred thousand times a day.

But someday, it'll stop. Someday, it'll beat for the last time, and then there will be nothing.

Nothing except for death.

I don't know if there's an afterlife, but if there is, what awaits me won't be pleasant. Because I've stood there and watched as well over a dozen hearts stopped beating, and rarely have I ever felt anything more than *fascination* about it.

Maybe, in some other life, I could've been a doctor. A cardiologist. Instead of stopping hearts, I could've got them started again. But in this life? I'm nothing more than a man with a fascination, watching as yet another heart makes its last beat.

The door behind me opens.

I don't turn around.

I don't really have to.

Call it intuition, but I know already who it is.

I knew he wouldn't be far behind.

Lorenzo strolls over to stand beside me in the middle of the room, his gun in his hand. He's not going to need it, and he realizes that right away. He lets out an exaggerated sigh. "Well, that's anti-climatic."

I glance at him. "You sound disappointed."

"I am," he says, slipping his gun into his waistband. "I was kind of looking forward to shooting someone today."

I shouldn't laugh, but I do.

The son of a bitch probably means it.

"You can still shoot him," I say, motioning toward where Fat Joe lays on the concrete floor in a pool of blood, his heart no longer beating.

"No point," he says. "You already killed him."

"No, I didn't." Reaching down, I pick up the knife. "Karissa did."

She doesn't know, though.

She has no idea what kind of wound she inflicted.

She stabbed blindly, aiming to incapacitate, to get away, but she hit him at the perfect angle. I couldn't have done it better myself. The blade went into his inner thigh, slicing right through the femoral artery, and then she twisted it.

She *twisted*.

As soon as she yanked it back out, I knew he was a goner. He was on the ground, gushing blood, his heart making its last beat in under a minute.

"Huh." Lorenzo steps closer, surveying the guy. "He smells like we need HazMat for clean up."

"Probably do," I say. "It's ether."

He looks at me with surprise before turning back to the guy, hesitating when his eyes find the silver Zippo. He picks it up, shaking his head. "What an idiot."

That's one way to put it.

"We should get out of here before the police show up," I say, turning to head for the door, carrying the knife with me. It's got her fingerprints on it. "I give them twenty minutes, tops."

Lorenzo follows me. I hear him clicking the lighter open and closed as he walks. The fresh air is welcoming when I step outside, after breathing in those ether fumes the past few minutes.

It's got me feeling queasy.

I can't even imagine how Karissa must be feeling.

I don't have time to dwell on that, though.

I turn toward Lorenzo and start to speak when I see him flick the wheel of the lighter with his thumb, igniting it. *Son of a bitch.*

He tosses it behind him, back into the building, before running.

BOOM

I barely have a chance to duck before the windows blow out, glass shards flying, as the inside of the building goes up in flames. My ears ring from the explosion, the concrete walls keeping most of it contained. Fire burns, though, hot and heavy, catching the fumes and following them straight to the body, the highest concentration of it. Lorenzo rubs his ears with the palms of his hands as he grimaces. "Better make that ten."

The heat radiating from the building is intense.

I can still feel it as I approach my car, concealed over among some trees. I'm about to get in and leave when Lorenzo follows me, slipping into the passenger seat.

"Where are your men?" I ask, annoyed.

"Already left."

"Too bad," I tell him. "Find your own way home. I've got to find Karissa."

He ignores me, settling into the seat. "My place."

"I told you, Lorenzo. I've—"

"Got to find Karissa," he says, cutting me off. "Heard you loud and clear. And if you want to go out there and tear the city apart looking for her, be my guest, but it'll be much easier just to, you know, go to my place."

Reaching over, I grab ahold of his shirt, yanking him toward me. "What the hell did you do?"

"Relax," he says, holding his hands up defensively. "Just had my men take her there for safekeeping."

Safekeeping.

There's no such thing as far as Lorenzo is concerned.

I barely make it out of the park before I hear the sirens, red and blue lights flashing in the distance, heading straight for the fire. My heart pounds ferociously at the barrage of police cars passing us. I wait for one of them to stop. Wait for one of them to recognize my car.

But we get through without incident, and once we do, I start to speed. I weave through traffic, heading out of Manhattan, right to Bensonhurst. Lorenzo says nothing the whole way there, staring out the window, his posture casual.

None of this bothers him.

I park right near the abandoned pink house and follow Lorenzo across the street, to the townhouse. As soon as we step inside, I hear the chaos. His men are everywhere, scrambling and shouting.

It stirs up a bad feeling in my gut.

"Whoa, whoa, whoa," Lorenzo says, strolling down the hallway. "What's going on in here?"

A guy turns to him, pinching a bloody rag to his nose. "The bitch *punched* me!"

Lorenzo's eyes widen as I freeze, staring at him. Did he really just say what I think he did? "And which bitch would that be?"

The guy looks at me, just now noticing I'm here, too caught up in his own circumstances to realize what's going on around him. The color immediately drains from his face, turning him a shade of white I'm not sure I've ever seen before on someone still living. "I, uh... I mean... nobody. I didn't mean..."

He's stammering, starting to sweat, as he blinks rapidly, like he's about to pass out and lose consciousness. *Huh.* Figured a man who worked for Lorenzo would have more balls than that.

"Yeah, so she broke your nose," Lorenzo chimes in, reaching over and grabbing the guy by the nose, roughly squeezing it. The guy screams as blood starts soaking through the rag. "Suck it up, buttercup. If you'd rather, I'm sure Ignazio would be happy to put you out of your misery."

I nod. "More than happy."

Lorenzo shoves the guy away and he drops. He hits the floor right away, the carpet doing nothing to soften the fall. He fainted.

Unbelievable.

"Incompetence," Lorenzo grumbles, shaking his head, as the others scramble to pull the coward to his feet. "I'm beginning to understand why you prefer to work alone, Ignazio."

"You can't count on anyone," I say, turning around, glancing through the house. There's no sign of Karissa anywhere that I can see.

"Right," Lorenzo says, stepping toward me, hitting my chest with the back of his hand as he strolls past. "Except for me, of course."

"Not even you."

He ignores my remark as he strolls back the way we came, instead focusing his attention on his men. "Take me to her, Number One."

Number One.

You've got to be kidding me.

I watch as a guy clambers after Lorenzo.

He gave them *numbers.*

The guy rushes straight toward a door in the hallway, hesitating with his hand on the knob. He looks at Lorenzo, then me, then back at Lorenzo, like he's afraid to open that damn door for some reason.

Like he's afraid of what we're going to see.

Anger and impatience stirs inside of me as I push past them, knocking the guy out of the way to open the door myself. A basement.

It's dark, pitch black. I can barely make out the pair of wooden stairs leading down into it. It's mostly silent, until I strain my ears, hearing only the faintest cry.

It's a sound that's familiar to me.

A gasp for air, a devastated whimper, the sound of Karissa trying her hardest to be strong, but it's not working. I don't hesitate. I head right down those flimsy stairs, down into the darkness, frantic to get to her... to find her... to see her. To let her know it's okay, that she's okay, that we're going to be okay.

I swear it, we will, we'll make it, even if it's the last thing I do.

I'll give her the happiness she deserves.

No more of this grief.

No more of these goddamn tears.

She's huddled in a corner, her knees pulled up, her head down, shielding her face. Hands fist her chaotic hair, clinging to it like her life depends on it, like holding on is what's holding her together. She's rocking and shaking, oblivious to my presence, so lost in her head, so overwhelmed by her heartache, that she didn't even hear me.

I stare at her, for just a second, taking her in as she collapses into herself in the darkness, feeling a deep ache in my chest. Feeling the pain I know she's been feeling. Her heart is broken, but the fucking thing is still beating. Second after second, it continues to keep her alive.

I take a step toward her, then another, before she breaks out of her trance, realizing she's not alone. Her whimpers cease as she inhales sharply, steeling herself like only she can. Her head darts up, piercing, angry eyes cutting through the darkness, seeking out whatever she heard. Her gaze meets mine, and I watch as the rage fades away, melting straight to that goddamn heartbreak.

I hate it.

I hate seeing it.

But fuck, she's beautiful.

Happy. Sad. Angry. Terrified.

She's the most beautiful thing I've ever seen.

She's beautiful because she's strong.

Beautiful because she's fierce.

Beautiful because, even when I hesitated, she didn't.

She fought.

She fought *hard*.

And goddamn if that's not beautiful to me...

Her mouth moves, but no words greet me.

She's shell-shocked.

She stares at me, silent tears falling down her cheeks.

She's not moving, not even blinking, like maybe I'm just a figment of her imagination and she's afraid the darkness is going to erase me if she surrenders to it.

"I told you," I say quietly. "I'll always come for you."

That does it. That's all she needs.

A cry echoes through the basement as she forces herself to her feet, shoving off of the floor, barely able to stand, let alone walk, but she's strong enough to throw herself at me, knowing good and well I'll never let her fall. I wrap my arms around her, pulling her to me, holding her tightly, relishing in her warmth. She's on her tiptoes, clinging to me.

"I thought you were dead," she whispers, her voice cracking around the words.

"Come on," I say, stroking her tangled hair. "You really think I'm that easy to kill?"

She laughs, but it's not a happy sound.

There's nothing funny about any of this.

Footsteps register behind me then, just a moment passing before a harsh overhead light flicks on across the basement. Squinting from the light, I set Karissa on her feet and loosen my hold, but she winces, clutching ahold of me. My instinct is to look at her, my eyes scanning her, alarmed when I see the blood coating her dirty, bare foot. "What happened?"

My question is lost on her as she starts to panic. Her breath quickens, body shaking, as she frantically clings to me, her attention across the room. *Shit.*

I turn my head, looking right at Lorenzo, his apparent number one little soldier standing guard by his side. The guy looks nervous.

"What happened to her foot?" I ask, motioning toward it, a touch of anger in my voice.

He starts to stammer.

What is it with these guys?

"She, uh... well... she did it to herself."

I look at him incredulously. "She did it to herself."

"Uh, yeah," he says. "She kicked out the car window."

"She kicked out the car window."

"And the glass, it shattered. Cut her, I guess. She was fighting us, you know? Wasn't anything I could do about it. Like I said... she did it to her—"

Before the guy can finish saying 'herself,' Lorenzo reacts, reaching into his waistband and pulling out his gun.

BANG

A single shot, right to the temple, lights up the basement. It blows his fucking head apart. The guy drops instantly. Karissa lets out a scream, startled, and I pull her to me tightly, holding her as I glare at Lorenzo. "Was that necessary?"

"Of course," he says, slipping the gun back away. "All I heard was *blah blah blah I didn't follow instructions so just kill me already.* Why? What did you hear?"

"That you're a lunatic."

Karissa tenses. She's terrified.

But Lorenzo? He laughs.

Unlike everyone else, he finds this all funny. Life, to him, is nothing more than a game. Product of his upbringing, maybe, but it wouldn't surprise me if it were merely coded in his DNA. He never knew his real father, but the Gambini name is one of the worst. Cold, calculated mass murderers. He was raised an Accardi, though, which arguable isn't much better. His stepfather was an abusive alcoholic with a hot temper and an itchy trigger finger, the kind of man who would beat a child unconscious and not bother to call an ambulance until after he fixed himself a drink.

Another of those reasons I had to kill the man.

"Naz," Karissa whispers. "We've got to get out of here. I can't... I can't do this. He's going to kill us."

"Relax. He's not going to kill us. He's—"

"A friend," Lorenzo chimes in, looking almost smug about it as he does.

Karissa's face contorts at the word. *Friend.*

"He's not a threat," I tell her. "Not to me."

Not right now, anyway.

Tomorrow is another day.

"How can you think that? He... he was there! With the cab driver, and the man, and oh God, just right now! He did it... he's one of them. And you expect me to trust him?"

"No," I say, turning toward her, my hands cradling her face as I look at her pointedly. "Never trust a word he says. He'll lie right to your face."

"I'm right here, you know," Lorenzo says.

I ignore that.

"But trust *me*, Karissa. Can you do that?"

She nods, although she looks at me like I might be losing my mind. But I don't have it in me to try to explain it right now. I'm utterly exhausted, and she needs to see a doctor as soon as possible.

"Can you walk?" I ask her.

"Uh, yeah... of course."

I take her hand, turning to Lorenzo. *Don't make a liar out of me.* "We're leaving."

He steps aside to give us a path to the wooden stairs, but he says nothing. I lead Karissa over toward them, letting her go up first, and cast another look at Lorenzo.

He's watching me curiously. "You still want that meeting?"

"You know I do."

He nods, looking away. "I'll be in touch."

We find no resistance leaving. The men are still scrambling around, too preoccupied to even notice us. They heard the gunshot. We slip out the front door, and I help Karissa straight to my car, waiting until she's settled before getting in beside her.

She's still trembling.

"Hey," I say, reaching over, stroking her cheek. "It's going to be okay, baby."

"You promise?"

I stare at her, wiping away a stray tear as it falls. "I swear it, Karissa. We're going to be fine."

She smiles, a sad kind of smile, as she reaches up and places her hand over my hand. She lets go after a moment, turning her head to gaze out the side window at the quiet neighborhood.

I start to drive away, and she stays quiet for a while, before she lets out a deep sigh. "Did you kill him?"

"Who?"

"The man in the building. The one... tonight."

I pull up to a red light, sitting there for a moment, before quietly answering, "Yeah, I did."

She closes her eyes.

She expected that answer.

She still doesn't like it, though. This world isn't for her. The violence, the bloodshed, the murder... it's just not her. She struggles accepting that I end lives.

She'd never forgive herself if she knew *she* killed that guy.

I hate lying to her. I hate it. But I lie to her this time.

I lie to her to spare her.

Because no matter what he did, or what he would've done had he not been stopped, he was still a human being to Karissa.

He had a beating heart.

"We should get you to a doctor," I say, changing the subject. "Head to the closest hospital."

"No." Her voice is sharp, almost panicked, as she reaches over, placing her hand on my arm. "No hospitals. Hospitals mean police which mean *questions*. Questions about where I was, questions about what happened, questions about you, and me, and I'm just tired of answering questions. I just... I want to go home."

"But I need to make sure you're okay."

"What about that guy? Dr. Carter?"

"He's a veterinarian, Karissa."

"So? That didn't stop you from calling him when you were shot."

"Don't be ridiculous. You need a real doctor."

"For what? A few stitches on my foot? I can sew it up myself."

I wait until we reach another red light before I respond. She's being absurd. I know it's because she's scared, but I can't risk it.

"You're pregnant, Karissa. It's not just *you* I'm worried about."

"I know, but..." She lets out a deep sigh. "How is it going to help us if you get locked up? You killed someone tonight, Naz, and the building... it blew up. What are they going to think if I show up at the hospital, smelling like a fucking meth house?"

There's no winning this argument.

I can already tell it.

She has tears in her eyes, and I can't push her right now, not when she's already so traumatized. Sighing, I pull out my phone, looking through it for Michael Carter's number. He answers on the second ring, his voice hesitant. "Hello?"

"It's Vitale. I need you to meet me at my house."

"Is it an emergency?"

"I wouldn't call you if it wasn't."

With that, I hang up.

I told him to be there, so I know he'll come.

"A compromise," I tell her. "Dr. Carter will look you over, but if he's concerned, if he thinks there might be a problem, we go straight to the hospital."

"Fair enough."

As soon as we get home, we head inside, and the first thing Karissa does is call out for her dog.

Killer comes right away.

Ears laid down, tail wagging, tongue out, he jumps up on her, and I go to stop him, but Karissa takes it in stride. She slips right down to the floor, plopping on her ass in the living room, and hugs him as she again starts crying.

I give them a moment, excusing myself to the kitchen. I splash water on my face from the sink before staring at my hazy reflection in the window, running my hands through my hair.

Please be all right.

Carter isn't far behind us. He pulls into my driveway, squealing tires, driving like a bat out of hell. As soon as I open the door, he looks me over, stepping into the foyer, carrying a black medical bag. "What's wrong with you?"

Hell of a question.

Wouldn't even know where to begin answering that.

"It's actually Karissa," I tell him, pointing toward the living room where she's still sitting. "I need you to take a look at her."

Confusion clouds his expression as he heads that way. Right away, he fixates on her foot. "Ah, why don't you come to the kitchen and we'll get you fixed up?"

Karissa stands up, making her way toward the kitchen, with Killer protectively right on her heels. I stall in the doorway, leaning against the doorframe, giving them space. Karissa climbs up on the counter, washing her filthy foot right in the sink. Carter grabs her by the calf and surveys the gash.

He doesn't ask any questions about how she got injured. He knows better than to pry. Wordlessly, he opens his bag and starts digging out supplies. "You're going to need a few stitches. I didn't bring anything to numb the area, because, well, Vitale never wants it, so if you've got any liquor around here, now's probably the time to break it out."

She clears her throat, and I can barely hear her when she says, "I can't."

Carter looks at her peculiarly. "Oh, right... not old enough, huh?"

"No. Well, I mean, you're right, but that's not why." She pauses. "I'm pregnant."

He freezes, eyes widening, like that shocks him. He doesn't comment, though, as he turns back to his supplies. "It'll hurt a bit. Feels like someone pushing a needle and thread through your skin, because, well, that's pretty much what I'll be doing."

He lets out an awkward laugh.

He's nervous, working on her.

I figured he would be.

The man sews me up all the time without issue. He happily takes my cash in exchange for subpar medical care. He does it, knowing I don't expect perfection, knowing his silence is what really matters to me. I've been through hell and back, dragged myself out of the pit more than a few times, toying with death because I don't fear it.

But her? She's different.

He has to take extra care with Karissa.

"It's okay," she says quietly. "I'm sure I've felt worse."

Before me, she hadn't. She'd been coddled. People were careful. But I introduced pain into her life. Don't know that I'll ever forgive myself for that.

Carter does what he needs to, getting down to business, giving her five stitches right on the side of the foot. The second the needle goes in, Karissa grimaces, but she doesn't make a sound even though I know it stings.

As soon as he finishes, he takes a step back, eyeing her. I know he can smell the ether. It's a potent stench. Once you smell it, it's a smell you never forget. Reaching into his bag, he grabs a stethoscope, warming it before pressing the metal to her chest.

He's not an idiot. That's why I employ him.

He can figure out the real issue here.

"How far along are you?" he asks, listening to her heartbeat. His voice is casual, like he's just making conversation, but I know he's taking this serious.

"Eight weeks... or, uh, I guess maybe nine now."

He motions for her to turn her body as he moves to her back, pushing her shirt up, using the stethoscope to listen to her lungs. "Deep breaths for me."

Karissa obliges.

He seems satisfied after a moment and puts the stethoscope away. "No cramping, no bleeding, no other issues?"

She hesitates. "My head is killing me."

"We can do something about that," he says. "Anything else?"

"No," she says. "Nothing."

He smiles softly, laying a hand on her shoulder, patting it. "You're going to be just fine."

She looks relieved, as she closes her eyes briefly, returning his smile as she hops back down off the counter, carefully not to hurt her foot more. "Thank you."

"My pleasure."

"I'm going to go take the longest bath known to man now, wash off this stink."

"You'll want to be careful not to get your stitches wet for the next forty-eight hours," he calls after her. "They should come out in about two weeks."

She nods, acknowledging she heard him, as she limps past me. Killer follows, as usual, giving me a wide berth as he leaves. Carter starts to pack up his things as I stroll further into the kitchen.

He glances at me. "I'm guessing congratulations are in order."

I pause beside him. "Give it to me straight."

"I always do," he says, turning to lean back against the counter, crossing his arms over his chest. "Like I said, she'll be fine. A couple Tylenol and a good night's sleep and she'll be good as new by morning."

"And the baby?"

He hesitates.

Hesitates.

"It's so early on, there's no way to know. Ether effects at a cellular level, and at nine weeks, the cells would be rapidly changing. So much can go wrong at this stage. Chances are, it'll all be fine, but if it isn't, well... not even the greatest doctor in the world could do anything to change it."

That's about what I expected to hear.

"I appreciate you coming," I say. "Before you leave, I need you to do me one more favor."

"What's that?"

"Check to make sure the mutt is okay."

He looks at me peculiarly. "What's wrong with the dog?"

"Let's just say he went up against the same opponent as Karissa and he didn't fare any better."

"Ah." He motions toward the doorway. "Lead the way."

Killer is lying in the hallway, right at the top of the stairs. He growls when I approach, but he lets Carter crouch down and look him over, not trying to get away.

"He seems all right," he says after a moment. "A little banged up, maybe a broken rib or two. The blood on him, well..."

"It's not his."

Carter looks at me as he stands back up. "I can tell."

He's got questions he really wants to ask, questions about what the hell happened tonight, but I'm not going to answer them for him and he knows it.

"He should probably be brought in for some X-rays," he continues. "Otherwise, he'll be okay."

"Take him with you, check him out," I say. "I'll come by later and get him back."

"Sure thing."

I stand there, watching as he leaves my house with the dog. I'll pay him whenever I pick Killer up.

I make my way down the hallway, toward the bathroom, finding the door cracked open. Quietly, I push it open further, pausing there as I look in.

Karissa is in the tub, covered in bubbles, her injured foot propped up along the side, out of the water. She turns her head, sensing my presence, and smiles softly, like she's happy to see me.

"Good news," I tell her. "The mutt's going to live."

"That *is* good news," she says. "And what about you?"

"What about me?"

"Are you going to be all right?"

Something about the way she asks that stalls me.

People in my world only care about what you can do for them. *Friends* only need you until they don't need you anymore. But Karissa asks me that like my answer matters, like whether or not I'm going to be okay makes a difference to her.

I shouldn't be surprised about it. She loves me, after all. But it's been a very long time since somebody else gave a damn about how I was feeling. A very long time since someone asked me those words.

"My heart's still beating," I tell her. "That tells me I'm going to be just fine."

Chapter Twenty-One
Karissa

A cold front moved in.

That's what this morning's newspaper told me.

I found it crumpled up, tossed in the trashcan beside Naz's desk in the den, hastily—*angrily*—thrown away. He was sitting at his desk, staring at his books in silence. I had no idea what he was thinking, but I didn't ask. Instead, I fished out the newspaper and glanced at it, seeing the front-page headline: **Corlears Hook Park Murders**

I skimmed the article, my stomach dropping when I encountered my name. *Karissa Vitale.* Lone survivor of the first attack. That was all it really said about me, but looking at Naz, I knew that was already too much.

The cold front had come overnight, the temperature dropping into the fifties instead of the usual seventy-five this time of year. I could feel the cold deep within my bones, like if we don't do something quickly, I may never again be warm.

"I'm ready," I told him, throwing the newspaper away again.

He tore his gaze from the books, meeting my eyes. "You're ready."

I nodded carefully. "I'm ready to go."

An hour later, here we are, sitting in his car as he drives through the city, in no hurry to get anywhere. It's not like we really even have somewhere to be, anyway. Time to wrap up a few loose ends before we can leave the city.

We're starting over. A clean slate.

When we reach Greenwich Village, Naz pulls over, swinging into the entrance of the parking garage beside the old dorm I used to call home. He puts the car in park but leaves the engine running.

I look at him, surprised. "What are we doing here?"

He nods toward the building. "I figured you'd want to see her."

My gaze drifts that direction, and I see her. *Melody.* She's standing in front of the building, leaning back against it, shivering. She's wearing shorts and a t-shirt, like she thinks it's still summertime, refusing to embrace the cold. *Of course.* She looks like she's waiting for something, or someone... I don't know... but I can guess. For now, though, she's just standing there, quiet, all alone.

I watch her for a moment.

I don't move.

I never gave much thought to this part of it all.

"Should I?" I ask quietly. I'm just not sure. "Wouldn't it be better to just... disappear?"

Naz doesn't answer that right away, the car still running, his gaze out the windshield. I'm not sure if he even knows the right answer.

"Someone she loved disappeared once," he says finally. "It shouldn't happen again."

Paul.

It took her a while to recover from that heartbreak, although I know some part of her probably never truly will. The *what ifs* broke her, fracturing off a piece of her soul. Melody always lived a life of privilege, where everything was beautiful and nothing hurt. She didn't know pain and suffering. She never learned what it was like to have to let go. Love, to her, was innocent and pure. It wasn't until

Paul that she realized that sometimes, no matter how hard you fight it, love is just going to *hurt*.

It's hard to get over something when you don't know what happened, when you don't understand what went wrong. Without closure, the wound remains open, and it's hard as hell to get it to heal.

I get out of the car then, wrapping my arms around my chest. I'm wearing a scarf and a sweater with a pair of black leggings, my usual getup, but I couldn't put on my boots.

Hurt foot and all that.

So I'm wearing a pair of black slippers, the padding softening the blow from my footsteps on the sidewalk. *Ugh*. I look absurd. I shuffle over toward Melody, and she looks up when she senses me, plastering a smile on her face. It's genuine. Nothing about her is fake. Quirky as she may be, Melody wears her heart on her sleeve.

"Kissimmee!" She pushes away from the wall, looking me over, her smile dimming when she spots my feet. "Oh my God, are you sleepwalking?"

I pause in front of her. "Nope, definitely awake."

She meets my gaze, horror twisting her features. Instantly, her hand darts out, smacking me right in the forehead. "Jesus, girl, do you have a *fever*? Are you delirious? This is Manhattan and you're going all *People of Wal-Mart* on us, wearing slippers out of the house!"

Laughing, I shove her hand away. "I hurt my foot, so it was either this or go barefoot."

"Barefoot," she says right away. "You could pull off the whole bohemian hobo chic look. But this? Nobody can pull off *this*."

She looks seriously distressed, like she's going to burst a blood vessel over my choice of footwear. Rolling my eyes, I playfully shove her. "Yeah, well, unlike you I choose comfort over style."

"I know." She sighs dramatically, her smile returning. "It's your only flaw."

My only flaw.

Yeah, right.

"So how'd you hurt your foot?" she asks.

I hesitate for a moment before answering. "Kicked out a car window."

That horror is back on her face before she cracks. She thinks I'm joking... or maybe she just *hopes* I am. "Seriously?"

"Yeah," I tell her. "Thought I was being kidnapped."

"Really?"

"Really. But Naz came and got me, took me home... called a veterinarian he knows, who sewed me up with a needle and some thread. Hurt like a bitch."

"Wow." She shakes her head. "Sounds like you had one hell of a night."

"You don't know the half of it," I tell her. "You see, before I *thought* I was being kidnapped, I actually was. So they kidnapped me from my kidnapper, who I'm pretty sure was actually just suicidal. He was going to blow us all up."

She laughs. "Wow."

"Right?"

"So... how'd you really hurt it?"

I pause, smiling softly, looking down at my foot. "I cut it on some glass."

She stares at me for a moment. She's still smiling, but there's concern in her eyes. She's trying not to let on, but she's worried. "But you're okay?"

She's not talking about my foot, not directly. Melody knows so much more than she wants anyone to believe. If they think she's oblivious, that means she's not a threat. She avoids scrutiny. It keeps her safe. But I know her well by now, and she's proven time and again how smart she is.

She probably had this all figured out before I even did.

"Yeah, I'm... okay."

I realize I mean it as I say it.

I'm okay.

Things aren't perfect, and I'm more than a little scared, but I'm okay. It's going to be okay.

I believe it.

"Well, that's all that really matters," she says, scrunching up her nose. "And I guess I'll forgive your fashion faux pass, since you obviously just don't know any better. I mean, two years later and you're still wearing that damn scarf."

"I like my scarf," I say defensively, reaching up and stroking it. "At least I'm not running around half naked with a cold front moving in."

She makes a face. "Don't hate the playa."

"Hate the game."

"Exactly. See! Finally, you're getting it! There might be hope for you yet."

I laugh. Unlikely. I'll never be someone I'm not.

"Anyway," I say, turning around, glancing at the idling car. "I should probably get going. Naz is waiting. I just wanted to stop by, to see you, to…"

To say goodbye.

Fuck, this is hard.

Melody looks past me, straight at the car, and I can see her expression change. Somewhere, deep inside, she knows.

She knows what this is.

Call it intuition, or the bond between friends. She can sense the shift in the atmosphere. Everything's changing all around us as we stand here. The world is shifting on its axis, the magnetic poles pulling us apart, slowly but certainly. It won't be the same anymore.

I used to sense it with my mother.

I guess that part of my mother lives on in me.

"You're moving on," she says. "Is that what you're telling me?"

Yeah, it is.

"It's just… *time*, I guess." I don't know how to explain it. "After everything that's happened and with everything that's going on, it just feels right to get out of New York for now."

"For now," she says, "but not forever, right?"

"Do you think I could actually leave forever?"

"No, I wouldn't let you."

That's what I thought.

I don't have a chance to respond to that, as she pulls me into a hug, wrapping her arms around me tightly, almost painfully.

"Promise you won't forget about me," she whispers.

"I promise," I say right away. "Don't have to worry about that."

"I'll call you seventy-six times a day," she says. "I'll write you letters with those smelly glitter gel pens like they had back in middle school. I'll draw you pictures in the margins. BFF's and all that gushy shit. I'll even dot my i's with hearts."

She pulls away, smiling, although I can see there are tears in her eyes. She's trying to hold them back, to take this in stride, but like I said... goodbyes are hard.

"And I want to hear all about that baby," she says. "I want to be there, I want to know him... or her... Oh God, especially if it's a *her*. She's going to need Auntie Mel to teach her all about patterns, about fabrics, and how to coordinate without being matchy-matchy. She's going to need me to teach her all about fashion because God knows you can't do it. You'll have the poor girl wearing socks with sandals."

"Okay, I'm not *that* bad."

"Come on, your husband owns a turtleneck sweater. You need me, Karissa."

"Don't worry. You'll know her... or him."

"I hope it's a her."

Me? I don't care. I just hope the baby is okay, whichever it is, boy or girl.

"So yeah," I say, motioning toward the car. "I should go now."

She nods, pulling me into another hug. "Take care of yourself."

"You, too."

"I'm going to miss you."

"I'll miss you, too, but it'll be okay." I take a step back, and then another, pausing as I smile. "Through every dark night, there's a brighter day."

Her expression lights up. "Just me against the world."

Who needs 'goodbye' when you've got Tupac Shakur?

Turning, I walk away, shuffling back to the car. I climb in the passenger seat, clipping my seatbelt on. "Thank you for that. I didn't realize how much I needed it."

"You don't have to thank me," Naz says. "Besides, you should always say goodbye to your friends."

I stare out the window, stare at Melody, as she leans back against the building again, continuing to wait. It's less than a minute later when Leo shows up. The second Melody sees him, she throws herself at him, wrapping her arms around his neck as she buries her head in his shoulder.

She's crying.

I can tell it, with the way her body's shaking, the way she's clinging to him like he's her plank. Tears burn my eyes at the sight of it, my chest aching.

Leo just holds her.

I don't think he even questions it.

I want to think he's a good guy. I want to believe he'll never get her hurt. But it feels like I'm leaving her in the hands of monsters, like I'm walking away as my friend unknowingly plays with wolves.

"I can't tell her, can I?" My voice shakes as I ask that. "I can't tell her where we're going."

"No," Naz says. "You shouldn't."

I knew that, deep down, but it still hurts to hear it confirmed. I spent my entire life running. *Hiding*. I know the rules. I've *lived* the rules. Any threads left intact connected to your past can be followed straight through to your future.

What's the sense in leaving if you just let them all follow?

"Do you think she'll be okay?" I ask quietly as a tear slips down my cheek. I just want her to be happy, to live the life she deserves.

"With him... Leo. Will she be okay?"

"I'm sure she'll be fine."

"But maybe I should've told her. Maybe I should've *warned* her. He's... I mean, his brother... she should know how dangerous that world is."

"It wouldn't make a difference," Naz says.

"How do you know?"

"Because you had all the warnings in the world, Karissa, and it didn't make a difference to you."

Naz pulls the car out of the garage then and drives away. I watch them, as we drive past, then stare at them in the side mirror until they disappear.

Goodbye, my friend.

I won't ever forget you, that's for sure.

⁃⁃⁃

I expect us to get on the road to go pick up my dog, but instead, a little while later, we end up in Hell's Kitchen.

The deli is busy in the middle of the afternoon. I can see a crowd inside, enjoying lunch, as others filter through the door. Business seems better than ever, and something feels different about it all. It feels strange. It takes a moment for it to strike me what's changed.

There's a new sign above the green awning, replacing the generic words 'Italian Delicatessen'.

Vitale's

It's simple, just the letters, nothing except for the name, but it's more than I've seen before. *Holy shit.*

Naz isn't looking at it, but I don't doubt that he noticed the second we pulled up. The man notices everything. His hands are still clutching the steering wheel, the engine still running. He looks conflicted, like he's locked in a silent debate.

To say goodbye to his father or not...

"You should go in," he says after a moment. "I'm sure he'd like to see you."

I frown. "Why don't you come with me?"

He glances past me, at the deli, his eyes fixing on the new sign. "I have something I need to take care of, the last loose end I need to tie up."

I get it then, why the engine is still running.

He's just dropping me off.

"It shouldn't take me long," he continues. "There's nobody else I'd trust to leave you with. My father... he doesn't take anything from anyone. You'll be fine here while I'm gone."

That's not what worries me.

I'm not worried about my safety.

I know I'm going to be fine.

But I don't know what he has planned, what this loose end is, and knowing Naz?

It can't be good.

"You'll come back?"

His eyes shift to me when I ask that, his expression serious. "You know I will."

I don't want to let him go but I know he wouldn't leave me, not right now, unless he thought it was unavoidable. So wordlessly, I nod and get out of the car, making my way to the door of the deli, pausing there, but I know he won't leave until I go inside.

Hobbling in, I pause, hearing the friendly chatter, listening to the cheerful whistling. I don't know what the tune is, but it's the same one every time.

Giuseppe is wandering around, cleaning off tables, smiling at people, obviously in a good mood this afternoon. He turns my direction, grinning, but his expression quickly falls.

Intuitive.

Like father, like son.

"Karissa," he says. "What's the matter, girl?"

I ponder that question for a moment before shaking my head. "Nothing."

His brow furrows. He doesn't believe it. "Nothing?"

"Absolutely nothing," I say again. "You see, I just found out I'm going to be having a baby, so even if I could complain, I'm not going to."

Those words, they hit him hard, just like I knew they would. They were the last words my mother ever said to him before she disappeared from his world. And he knows that, as he stares at me. He knows exactly what they mean. They run deeper than just on the surface.

They cut him deep.

His expression shifts, from shock to sadness to acceptance, as he puts a smile on his face again, sucking it up, forcing those emotions back. He reaches over, placing his hand on my arm, and nods his head toward a nearby table. "How about some cookies? I made them fresh this morning."

I take a seat, and he disappears to the kitchen, returning a moment later with a plate of Snickerdoodles. He's whistling again as he sets them on the table and slips into the chair across from me.

"What song is that?"

He hesitates for a second, like he's got to think about it. "Johnny Ray. *Just Walkin' in the Rain*."

"Never heard of it."

"Ah, it was well before your time. Hell, it was almost before *mine*. My wife... it was her favorite. First song we ever danced to."

I smile at that as I grab a cookie. He spends his days whistling the song he danced with his wife to for the first time. "That's sweet."

"Yeah, just reminds me of simpler times. *Better* times. When Ignazio was young, she used to sing it to him. I'd come home from a long day here at the deli, and they'd be dancing to it in the kitchen, and she'd be singing her heart out, and he'd be grinning like a fool." He pauses, laughing to himself. "He was a good kid... a happy kid. Wish I knew where we went wrong."

"You didn't go wrong with him," I say, taking a bite. They're perfection, as usual. I'm so hungry my stomach sounds like it's trying to pick a fight. "He's not a bad man, you know."

Giuseppe gives me a look like I've lost my fucking mind as he stands up. "You're starving. Let me make you a sandwich."

I don't have a chance to argue with that. He's gone, disappearing into the kitchen again. By the time he returns a few minutes later with an Italian special, the cookies are all gone.

"I'll get you some more," he says, reaching for the empty plate, but I snatch it up before he can.

I motion toward his chair. "Come on, relax... keep me company."

He plops back into the chair, relaxing back in it as I eat. He laces his hands together behind his head, watching me and whistling.

"Were you being serious?" he asks out of the blue.

"About Naz not being a bad man? Absolutely."

"No, I know you're full of shit about that. But earlier, when you showed up, you said you were having a baby."

"Oh. Uh... yeah."

"Yeah?"

"Yeah."

He stares at me some more, his expression blank. I'm not sure how he feels about what I'm telling him.

A baby.

His grandchild.

"You know yet what it is?"

I shake my head. "Still too early."

"You know what you want?"

"Doesn't matter as long as it's healthy."

He laughs, his expression softening. "That's what they all say, but me? I wanted a boy. No question about it. A son. Someone to carry on the Vitale name, to make us all proud."

"You got what you wanted."

"Yeah, well, the jury's still out about that."

"You should be proud of him," I say. "He's made some mistakes... okay, he's made *a lot* of them... but he's strong, you know... he's tenacious. He's a survivor. And one of the greatest things about him is he's a man of his word. If he says he's going to do something, he does it. He's never broken a promise to me."

"You just need to give him time."

"And *you* need to give him a chance," I counter. "You shouldn't hold his mistakes against him forever. It does neither of you any good."

"That's nice of you," he says, "standing up for him like that, but Ignazio would be the first one to say that he doesn't need you to stand up for him. He knows what kind of man he is."

"Yeah, a stubborn man, just like his father."

I don't think he finds that amusing, but he doesn't lash out. He rocks his chair back on its hind legs, regarding me peculiarly. "You remind me of someone."

"My mother."

"No, you look like your mother," he says, "but you remind me of my wife."

Whoa.

"She used to tell me that all the time," he continues. "She was optimistic, always saw the best in that boy. Didn't matter what he did, she never lost hope in him."

"Smart woman."

"So, where is he?" he asks. "Waiting out in the car?"

"He had something important to take care of."

"Of course he did."

"Don't worry, though," I say, "he'll come back. He always does."

Chapter Twenty-Two
Ignazio

Cars surround the brick mansion in Long Island, a sea of black sedans with darkly tinted windows. It's rare seeing so many together in one place at one time. Usually, when that happens, it means someone's in serious trouble.

Today's no exception.

There's going to be hell to pay.

"You sure you know what you're doing?"

Lorenzo stands behind me, dressed in a pair of ripped jeans with a plain white t-shirt. He asks that like he's curious about the answer, like he's actually worried about anybody but himself.

"Don't I always?"

"Not sure," Lorenzo says. "Heard your wife once poisoned you. That true?"

"Not at all."

"Really?"

"I was drugged, not poisoned," I tell him, "and besides, she wasn't my wife back then."

"Ah, that's just the fine print. Song remains the same, my friend."

My eyes scan the house for a moment before something strikes me. I turn around, looking at him. "How'd you know about that?"

He raises his eyebrows, surprised by my question. "What?"

"I never told anybody she drugged me," I say. "How'd you know?"

He stares at me.

He's thinking about how to answer.

That tells me I'm not going to like whatever he has to say.

There are only so many people who were aware of what happened, and I'm not sure any of them would run their mouths to him. Hell, most of them haven't lived long enough to get the chance to do it.

"My brother heard it from his girlfriend. Guess your wife told her about it."

"I don't believe you."

Karissa told nobody about drugging me.

Nobody except for her parents…

He tries to keep a straight face but it doesn't happen. Cracking a smile, he shakes his head. "Yeah, you probably shouldn't. Truthfully, Ignazio? I heard it from Carmela."

That answer surprises me, although I refuse to let it show. "Carmela."

"Yeah, seems she got desperate. This was back before you killed her, of course."

"Of course."

"Guess she didn't get the memo all those years ago about what happened… guess she didn't know you killed my stepfather because of what he did to me."

I cut in. "I killed him because he crossed me."

"You can say that all you want, Ignazio," he says, "but you'll never convince me it wasn't because of what he did to my face."

I say nothing.

He's partially right.

The man would've eventually killed Lorenzo if he hadn't died himself. To spare his little brother, Lorenzo willingly took the brunt of the abuse. He'd put herself right in harm's way, no matter the consequences. I respected that about Lorenzo.

"Anyway, so Carmela sought my stepfather out, looking for help. She found me, though, told me all about everything. Told me you were still at it, hunting them. Told me you'd killed Johnny and that she was next. That's when I decided it was time to finally make my way to New York."

I do the math in my head. "You've been in New York that long?"

"On and off," he says. "Wasn't until after you decided to take Ray out that I saw my opening."

"I didn't decide anything. It was self-defense."

"Isn't it always? When it comes down to it, it's always either you or them."

He's got a point there, although I'm not going to admit that. I'm not giving him any more credit than I have to. If any more ego squeezes into the narcissistic brain of his, nobody will be safe.

"Almost two years," I say, "and you wait until now to say hello?"

"Eh, what can I say? I wasn't sure what to make of you. The man Carmela spoke of sounded a hell of a lot like the friend I remembered, the one who saved my ass, but the guy I saw when I got here? He was different. So I kept my distance, because quite frankly, I was trying to decide what to do about it."

"I'm assuming you've decided."

"We're here right now, aren't we? Besides, it would've been a pity to have to kill you."

"You really think you could've?"

"Maybe," he says, casually shrugging a shoulder. "Glad we didn't have to find out."

The conversation is over at that.

I glance at my watch. A few minutes before noon. I'm standing here in broad day, wearing my favorite suit. The sun is shining, but it's doing nothing to provide warmth. It won't be long now until winter is upon us, blanketing New York with snow.

I'll be long gone before that happens, though.

Long gone.

Although, a small part of me is worried this is a mistake.

I shouldn't be here.

I shouldn't do this.

I should just go.

Run.

But I don't have it in me.

People who run are being chased.

I'm not going to let that happen.

Not now, not ever.

So maybe, this time, I don't know what I'm doing, but I do know I have to do it.

There's just no other way.

I fix my tie and smooth my jacket before setting my focus on the house. It looks quiet, still, but looks are deceiving. There's nothing benevolent about this place today.

At exactly twelve o'clock, the front door cracks open. They're watching, waiting...

I don't expect it any other way.

"Go time," Lorenzo says, waltzing right past me, practically glowing with excitement as he heads toward the porch. He's going to enjoy every second of this. I know he is. There's a bulge at his hip, his oversize shirt mostly concealing it. I only know it's there because, well, it always is.

Some things just never change.

Go time.

I follow Lorenzo right up to the house. A man stands there, wearing all black, guarding the door. He lets us in without a word. A few men are gathered around, coming together to lead us down the hallway, toward the thick set of doors. They stop there, but Lorenzo keeps going, shoving the double doors open and strolling right in.

Four men sit inside, at the long wooden table, each of them

dressed in their best suits. The heads of the four remaining crime families in the city have gathered together yet again for little ol' me.

A fifth chair is still empty.

Guess that one now belongs to Lorenzo.

They don't seem happy about it as he plops down in it, not awaiting an invitation, not offering any sort of greeting, like there's no question about his importance. Official or not, he's one of them. He's earned that spot. He leans back, kicking his feet up on the corner of the table, crossing his legs at the ankles.

Genova looks like he wants to shoot him right in the face.

I've been acquainted with the man for about two decades. He's hostile, and bitter, and about as selfish as you'd expect him to be. He doesn't do dirty work, though. No, that's what his men are for. His own little bloodthirsty army. He's a ruthless general.

He doesn't like it when others try to invade his space.

Stepping into the room, I close the doors behind me, reaching over and locking them. Always lock the doors. The men are too preoccupied by Lorenzo's antics to even notice what I'm doing.

"Weapons on the table," Genova demands, his voice bordering on a growl as he tries to contain his animosity.

I step forward and stand there, right in front of the table, reaching into my pants pocket, retrieving my same black ink pen. I set it on the table, but Genova pays me no attention.

He knows I've got nothing else.

He's not talking to me, though.

He's looking right at Lorenzo.

Lorenzo, who treats his gun like American Express. *Don't leave home without it.*

Sighing dramatically, Lorenzo reaches into his waistband, pulling out the Colt M1911. He waves it in the air, as if to say 'you got me', before setting it down on the long wooden table.

Seemingly satisfied, Genova finally looks at me, but Lorenzo clears his throat, interrupting. "Weapons on the table."

Genova glances back at him. "What did you say?"

"I said *weapons on the table*," Lorenzo says. "Come on... don't even try to pretend that I'm the only one in this room packing heat today."

"This is my house," Genova says. "I'm in charge here."

A smile turns Lorenzo's lips. "Got me there."

Genova tries to veer the conversation. "Vitale—"

"*But*," Lorenzo chimes in, stressing the word, as he drops his feet to the floor, suddenly sitting straight up. "Correct me if I'm wrong—"

"You're wrong," Genova says.

Lorenzo ignores that. "But these things, these meetings, are governed by a set of rules, rules put in place long before you took over... long before these meetings were held in your house. You don't just make this shit up as you go. Even the president has gotta follow the Constitution."

Genova shakes his head. "This isn't a fuckin' democracy."

"So I've been told," Lorenzo says. "Word around town is you're a bit of a *dick*-tator."

That sets Genova off. I can see him tense, his anger flaring. Before he can react, though, the others interject, pulling out their guns and laying them on the table.

Rules are rules.

We all have to follow them.

Begrudgingly, Genova pulls out a gun from a concealed shoulder holster. He sets it right in front of him, still within reach, as he glares at Lorenzo, not liking that the man one-upped him.

The smile returns to Lorenzo's lips.

His feet go right back up on the table.

"Now, if there aren't any more objections," Genova says pointedly, "I'd like to get on with this meeting. I'm not getting any younger here."

Lorenzo laughs under his breath.

"You find something fuckin' funny about that?" Genova snaps. "What are you even doing here, *Scar*?"

Lorenzo hates that nickname. I can tell it by the look on his face. His lip twitches, the rest of him betraying his smile. It's frozen on his face. "Honestly? I don't know. All of this, if you ask me, is total bullshit. You're just whacking yourselves off under the table, getting off on the theatrics, like we're on fucking Broadway. Dance, little soldier, *dance*. It's a *joke*. I'll never understand it. But Ignazio here requested a meeting, and what kind of friend would I be if I didn't show up?"

He's got the others completely thrown off. They're so used to order, used to people just falling in line out of fear, that they don't know how to handle Lorenzo. He brings chaos, the kind they don't like. He's not afraid of them. They don't matter to him.

Seems Genova has nothing to say to that. His gaze yet again seeks me out. He wants this over with. He wants Lorenzo out. "What do you want?"

He's done playing games.

Done dealing with all of this.

He's just... **done**.

"I've been thinking about what you said to me a few weeks ago," I say. "About loyalty, and honor, and knowing who your real friends are."

Genova relaxes just a bit. "Is that right?"

"I've come to realize, thanks to you, that I can't just sit around anymore and expect things to happen... I need to go out there and go after them. I need to *fight* for them. And I need to show those around me what their friendships mean to me. So I'm ready now."

"You're ready?"

I nod. "I'm ready to finally see this through."

With those simple words, it's like the last five minutes are erased from Genova's memory, his irritation and impatience gone. He's getting what he wanted.

Or so he thinks.

Leaning back in his chair, he regards me with a sort of awe. "So you're ready to join us, huh?"

"I've never been *more* ready," I say, "to finally leave my mark."

A smile lights his face as he holds his hand out. He's reaching toward me, extending his hand, like it's an olive branch, like a simple shake is going to erase all of the hostility in the past. I look at it for a moment. I look at his stubby little sausage fingers wedged into all those gold rings. He's got no callouses, no scars, no marks... he's got blood on those hands in the figurative sense, but literally? He's probably never even shed any blood.

Reaching across the table, I take his hand. His grip is firm, forceful, like he's trying to intimidate me, like he's reminding me of exactly who here is boss. I tolerate it, tolerating his show of force, until he goes to pull away.

And that's when I'm done.

I'm done with the lies, the games, and the backstabbing. I'm done with the petty bickering, the egos, and the *cowardice*. I'm done with men who demand you honor family but in the next breath order the death of the ones you love. I'm done with it all, every bit of it.

I'm done with this life.

I'm ready for another.

I move fast. I don't give him a chance to react. The second he tries to let go of my hand, I squeeze it tightly, yanking his hand and twisting his arm. My free hand snatches up the pen, and I fist it. Swinging with all my might, all the force I can muster, I shove it right into his neck, stabbing him with it.

It knocks him off kilter, as I let go and instead grab the back of his head. I slam his face into the table, as blood spurts from the hole in his neck.

BAM

Reaching over, I snatch up Lorenzo's gun. The others I'm not so sure about, but his? It's loaded. He knows it needs to be when you're outnumbered.

BANG

BANG

BANG

It's like fireworks going off. The dim room lights up with the gunfire, and the three other heads of the families drop. A single shot right to the forehead, close enough blow their brains out the back of their skulls. They barely have time to even know what hit them.

Because men like them, with their cushy jobs and positions of power? They never expect anyone to be brave enough to actually take them out. Because there are rules, rules we all must follow.

You never kill a boss without permission from the others.

Genova lifts his head up, trying to react, but he's dazed from the blow, blood still pouring from the wound. He scrambles for his gun, his eyes meeting mine. Terror like no other shines from him.

He knows he's fucked.

"You owe my father ten-thousand dollars," I tell him, "but I'll take payment in the form of your life instead."

BANG

"Now *that's* what I'm talking about!" Lorenzo shouts, his voice tinged with a sick sort of excitement as he drops his legs to the floor and sits up. "I knew you still had it in you, Ignazio!"

I turn to him as soon as he says that, as soon as the man starts to stand up. I grab him by the collar of his shirt and throw him right back down so hard the chair tips over. I shove him backward, onto the floor on his back, and hover over him. I point his own gun right at his face, my finger on the trigger, lightly pressing against it.

He goes deathly quiet, not even breathing, as he stares me right in the eyes. In his face, I see nothing. No emotion at all. There's no fear to be found. No worry. No alarm.

It isn't because he doesn't think I'll do it.

He knows I will.

He knows I won't lose a moment of sleep over taking his life.

It's just he's empty.

He always has been.

He's a shell of a man. There's no soul left inside of him. I'm not saying he's unredeemable, that he isn't capable of love... that's not my place to judge. But darkness long ago consumed him, a familiar darkness, one that I used to know. I know what it's like to be ravished by that kind of hunger, to have a one-track mind for bloodshed. There's no room left inside of him for him to see the light, not when he's so overrun by the dark.

There's a banging on the locked doors then. Chaos is erupting in the house. None of the men have any idea what is happening, but they've been trained to always protect their boss. They're shouting, and shoving, trying to break inside. The world is crumbling all around them.

Unlike Lorenzo, they aren't calm.

"I'm out," I tell him. "You wanted New York? You wanted the power? It's yours. But I'm done, Lorenzo. I'm walking away from it all. And so help me God, if you ever try to follow me, if you ever try to stop me, if you ever try to pull me back in, I'll kill you... I will... and I'll take away everything you love before I do it. Do you hear me?"

"Loud and clear," he says.

I stand up and set his gun down on the table before extending my hand toward him. He doesn't hesitate to take it. I pull him to his feet, and Lorenzo reaches over, snatching up his gun right away. My muscles stiffen from alarm. I don't trust Lorenzo. I can't. I can't trust anybody.

But I need him, and that makes him the closest thing to a *friend* as I've got.

I need him to keep people off my trail. I need him to do exactly what it is that comes natural to him... *create havoc*. I need him to be such a nuisance that I play second fiddle to the hell he causes. I saved his ass once... now it's his turn to help save mine.

I may have taken out the heads of four families, but I did nothing to bring this to an end. The callous hunter simply killed more lions.

It won't be long before more Kings, *new* Kings, come in.

Lorenzo slips his gun back in his waistband as he looks around the room, his gaze trailing along the four bodies. I don't look at them, my focus at the door. It's bucking from the force of someone banging against it.

"You know this will never *really* be over, right?" Lorenzo asks, strolling over to stand beside me. "These things don't ever end. Nobody's going to just forget about you and what you've done, especially after this."

"I know," I say, looking at him, "but I'm banking on the fact that they'll be so busy with you that by the time they come for me, I'll have lived my life."

"And your wife? Your baby?"

My eyes narrow. "How do you know about that?"

"Got it from my brother. Guess your wife told his girlfriend." He cuts his eyes at me. "For real this time."

Huh.

"They'll be fine," I say. "I'm not worried about them."

"Why not?"

"Because I seem to remember us having a deal, Lorenzo... you said you'd make sure my wife didn't get hurt, and I'm holding you to that."

"Touché."

"Besides, I was one of the worst out there... I was out for blood, and it was personal... but when it came down to it, even I couldn't do it. Even I couldn't take out my enemy's kid. So they'll come for me, someday, sure, and when they do, they'll probably get me. But Karissa, she's under your protection, and that's the only reason I'm letting you live."

"Not the *only* reason."

"Yes, the only reason."

"Come on." He steps around me, to stand in front of me. "After all this, you still can't admit we're friends?"

"I'll tell you what, Lorenzo," I say, looking around him, at the door. "You get me out of here unscathed, and then I'll consider telling you how I really feel about you."

"Oh, that's easy." He makes a face, like I'm unnecessarily worrying, as he reaches into his pocket. "I've got a grenade."

I look at him incredulously. "You've got a grenade."

A grenade.

He's carrying a fucking *grenade*.

And not a smoke grenade, like logic would say he meant. The son of a bitch pulls his hand out of his pocket, and he's clutching a round green grenade. It's small, maybe the size of a golf ball, but there's no mistaking what it is.

"What, like you've never carried one before?" he asks.

"Can't say I have."

"Ah, well, they come in handy," he says, shrugging me off. "Just pull the pin and *ka-boom*, bye-bye problem."

I don't even know what to say about that.

I don't know where he got his hands on it.

Cuba, probably, like everything else.

"And how is a grenade getting me out of here? Preferably with all of my limbs."

"Easy," he says. "Just watch."

Lorenzo turns around and heads straight to the door, flipping the lock before stepping back. I move away from him, back toward the table, and reach over, snatching up one of the guns still lying there. I check it, finding it loaded, and turn back to the door in just enough time for it to fly open.

Men appear.

There are only three of them. The rest, I figure, probably fled the gunfire. They burst in, wielding guns, and I point my weapon right at one of their heads, my finger on the trigger.

Lorenzo holds his hands up in front of him before they can think to fire, before they can see the bodies, before they even have time to riddle out what happened. He holds the grenade with one hand, a finger from the other slipped through the pin, ready to pull it.

"Gentlemen," he says loudly, "unless you want blown to fucking pieces, I suggest you vamoose."

Panic seizes them. Two run. The last one just stands there, staring at us. The loyal one. No, he's not afraid to die, not if it means he takes us out long with him.

He points at Lorenzo.

He's going to shoot.

I aim right for him, pulling the trigger, round after round.

BANG

BANG

BANG

All three bullets hit him. He squeezes the trigger as a reflex, firing off a round, damn near hitting Lorenzo, who doesn't have enough sense to duck. As soon as the guy drops, Lorenzo looks down at him. Two bullets struck the guy in the chest, the third hitting his temple. "Nice job, Han Solo. Always knew you shot first."

I have no desire to figure out his nonsense.

I'm stepping over the guy and out into the hallway in the next breath, heading right for the door. Lorenzo follows me without a word. I can hear his hurried footsteps racing to keep up.

I veer a different direction, taking the back exit instead, not wanting to be seen. I step out into the back yard and look around, turning toward Lorenzo, about to say something, when I see it.

I see him.

I see exactly what he's about to do.

Clutching the grenade, he squeezes the safety, his finger snaking around the pin. *Son of a bitch.*

Not again…

"Lorenzo," I growl, but that's all I have a chance to say, before he pulls it.

He pulls the pin.

Motherfucker.

I turn and run through the yard, run away from the house, as he tosses the grenade right in the back door. Four seconds. That's all the time we've got. I throw myself down into the grass, covering my head and holding my breath.

BOOM

The ground shakes as it explodes inside the house. It's not enough to take it down or even do that much damage, just enough to destroy the walls around it, blowing out a few windows. Lorenzo lands in the grass right beside me, laughing.

I glare at him as I climb to my feet. "You know, sometimes I *really* hate you."

He glances at me. "Only sometimes."

"Most of the time."

"But not always."

I don't dignify that with a response.

Turning around, I walk away, making a speedy escape from the yard, slipping around a few neighboring houses, to make my way to my car. Neighbors are out, gathering in the street, panicking about the ruckus, about the explosion that rocked the brick house. I know they had to have felt it. I slip through the crowd, keeping my head down, refusing to make eye contact with anyone. Lorenzo jogs to catch up with me, making a point to smile and greet people.

"You shouldn't draw attention to yourself," I tell him, pausing beside my car. "Makes it easier for the cops to identify you."

"I'm not worried about the cops."

"You ought to be."

"Nah, not when I've already got a few of them in my pocket."

I shake my head. "Good luck, Lorenzo."

"Hey, wait," he says when I start to get in my car. "Can you give me a ride?"

"Walk," I tell him.

"It's like, eight miles. It'll take me forever."

"Then jog."

He mutters under his breath before stepping away. "I'm gonna miss these adventures of ours, Ignazio. You sure you won't reconsider, stick around, maybe help me run this city?"

"I'm sure."

"Pity."

"Piece of advice, Lorenzo? It's not the titles that honor the men... it's the men that honor the titles. It'll do you good to remember that."

He stares at me. "You're quoting Machiavelli to me?"

"What can I say? It's my favorite."

Getting in my car, I start the engine and drive away without looking back.

He wanted control of the city. He wanted to be the boss.

I just hope when it's all over, the kingdom is still worth having.

Stepping into the deli, I pause, turning my head to stare at the door. *Silence.* Ever since I was old enough to walk, stepping inside this place was always accompanied by a noise, the obnoxiously loud jingling.

Today, there's nothing.

The door closes when I let go of it. Still nothing.

The bells are gone.

Huh.

My eyes scan it for a moment before I turn back around and look through the deli. Guess the sign out front wasn't the only change he made. Most of the place still looks the same—tables and chairs aren't any different, neither is the counter, and I imagine the kitchen hasn't changed, because I know the man would be peculiar about that, but there, along the far side of the wall, is something I've never seen before in here.

A television.

I blink a few times at it.

You see, my father never saw the point of television. He always said it did nothing but rot the brain. My mother, she was more lenient. After all, she loved her soap operas. They only ever had a television in the house so she could watch them.

Over at the deli? Strictly off limits.

But there one is, hung up on the wall, tuned into the twenty-four-hour news station, utterly silent but still playing away. *Strange.*

Shaking it off, I look around, seeking Karissa out. She sits at a small table in the middle of the deli, across from my father, the two of them chatting. What they're saying, I'm not certain, but I can make a guess that the conversation is probably about me. Because as soon as they notice my presence, all conversation ceases.

Karissa smiles, relief shining in her eyes, as she calls for me. "Naz!"

Slowly, I approach, pausing beside the table. I reach toward Karissa, cupping her chin, tilting it, as my thumb strokes her cheek. Leaning down, I kiss her softly. "Sorry it took so long."

"Oh, it's fine," she says, her cheeks flushing as I pull away. She waves across the table. "Gave your dad and I a chance to chat."

"About?"

Karissa starts to speak, her mouth opening, but my father beats her to it, uttering a lone word: "Memories."

Memories.

"Interesting." I look at him. He doesn't look very happy. He never is when I'm around, but usually it's anger and disappointment I sense. Today I see exhaustion. "Care to share any with me?"

He leans back in his chair, regarding me for a moment, before nodding. "I got one for you."

I motion for him to go on.

"It was twenty years ago," he says. "You were still a teenager, barely eighteen, just a kid yourself."

Eighteen.

Worst year of my life.

Memories from that year are cast in a haze of pain and loss. It's hard to remember the sun even rising back then, hard to remember a day that wasn't dark.

I almost tell him not to bother. Almost tell him not to go on. But whatever he has to say, I'm going to let him say it; I'll let him say his piece and then I'll be gone.

"I remember the year well," I say. "Kind of hard to forget it all."

"Then let me tell you something you might not know," he says. "One morning, on the way to the deli, I ran into Raymond Angelo. He told me his daughter was expecting a baby, that he was going to be a grandfather. Now, I wasn't a fool... she was your wife then, so I knew the kid was yours. I congratulated him, since that was what he wanted. And I went home that night, and I told your mother the news."

Okay, he's right... I've never heard this story.

I'm not sure I like where it's going, though.

"Your mother, she was ecstatic. She said you'd be a great father, because you learned from the best there ever was. I agreed with her, you know, because she was your mother, but I didn't believe it. You see, by then, Angelo already had his claws in you, and judging by his reaction, he wanted his claws in that baby, too. Figured the kid was doomed."

From my peripheral, I can see Karissa squirming.

She isn't so sure about this conversation, either.

"But, you know, what happened happened, and twenty years later, here we are... another baby. Your mother's not around now, not here for me to share the news, but I know what she'd say if she was."

He pauses, staring at me.

He doesn't say the words, but I know what they are.

You'll be a great father, because you learned from the best there ever was.

"I've got a memory for you," I say. "I was twelve or so. It was the summer you brought me here to work."

He nods. "I remember it."

"You taught me how to use a knife. I spent all summer in the back, chopping everything up for you. I loved it, you know, but I needed more practice. The knife slipped sometimes when I lost my focus. One day, the last day you let me back there, I made a mistake and cut my finger. Blood was everywhere, all over me, all over the table, all over everything I'd been chopping that morning. I thought I was bleeding out. I felt woozy. I yelled for you, and you ran back there. You took one look at me, and do you remember what you said?"

He just stares at me. Of course he remembers.

"You said, *God damn you, Ignazio, you're ruining my food*! Point is, based on that, my parenting's probably going to need some work."

His expression cracks when I say that. A small smile plays on his lips. Shoving his chair back, he wordlessly stands up, leaning over and kissing Karissa on the cheek. "If you ever need me, you know where I am."

He steps toward me then, pausing in front of me, and reaches over, squeezing my shoulder. It only lasts a few seconds, as he looks at me with the closest thing to pride as I've seen in his eyes since that summer years ago.

Letting go, he shakes his head, muttering as he walks away. "Get out of here, Ignazio, and for everyone's sake, don't ever come back."

I just stand there as he walks away, disappearing into the back. My gaze shifts back across the deli, toward the television. I'm instantly greeted with a peculiar headline. It's scrolling across the bottom of the screen: **Fatal Attack in Long Island**

Leave and never come back. That sounds about right.

"You, uh... um..." I look at Karissa when she talks, stammering a bit. She's motioning toward my chest, pointing with her finger. "You've got grass on your shirt."

"Oh." I look down at it. "Yeah."

"Do I want to know?"

"Probably not."

"Well then." She stands up, pushing her chair in. "How about we get out of here?"

Chapter Twenty-Three
Karissa

"Got everything you want?"

Naz's voice is quiet as he asks that question, standing behind me, in the doorway to the den. A duffel bag lay at my feet, my pictures stashed in it, along with enough clothes to probably last me a week. Killer is running around out back, home from the vet, feeling much better. Nothing was broken.

Is that everything I want?

I'm not sure.

But I certainly don't need anything else.

"I think so," I reply, not wanting to lie. "Honestly, I don't really know."

"Take your time," he says. "We'll leave whenever you're sure."

Whenever I'm sure. If that's what we're waiting for, we'll both die of old age right here in this room. I've never been sure about much, really, except for him.

I'm sure about *him*.

He might boil me alive before it's all over with, but I'm here, with him, because I'm sure this is where I belong.

"You really don't want to take any of these books?" I ask, glancing around the packed room. Nothing looks out of place. It's all just there, where it has always been, maybe where it'll always be, unless we come back for it. "Like... none of this?"

He lets out a resigned sigh. "No."

I turn to him. He's got a duffel bag, too, but it's only filled with clothes and shoes. "Not even The Prince?"

He smiles softly at my question. His favorite book. "It's got a bit of water damage, remember?"

"Ugh, don't remind me," I tell him. "I still feel bad about that. I almost bought you another copy for your birthday, but I figured it probably wouldn't be the same."

He doesn't agree, but he doesn't deny it either.

"Don't feel bad. Besides, I don't need it anymore. I've told you before, it's all up in here." He taps a finger to his temple. "Everything's up here. All of my memories, good and bad. I forget none of it. I don't have to take this stuff along with me to remember any of it. Memories are all that matter."

Ironic, really, since some of my memories I'd love to forget. Naz, though, embraces it. He doesn't let his memories define who he is. While I always envied Melody's resilience, it's really Naz's tenacity that I wish I had. Nothing ever holds that man down.

"I think I'm sure, then."

He laughs. "You *think*?"

I turn to him, turning my back to the bookshelves, and smile. I know how ridiculous it sounds. "Yeah, I fear that's as good as I'm getting."

"Well then." He reaches into his pocket. "Before we go, there's something I want to give you."

Stepping closer, he pulls something out, holding it up. It catches the bit of light streaming in through the windows, the shiny metal sparkling.

I recognize it right away.

My necklace.

"I found it the other day. It was lying on the floor, the chain snapped. I took it and had it fixed. Figured you'd want it back."

A smile touches my lips as tears burn my eyes. I looked for it, when I made it back home, but the thing was gone. I thought I'd lost it forever.

I've never in my life been so happy to be wrong.

Wordlessly, I turn around, pulling my hair up, out of the way. Naz slips it around my neck, his rough fingertips brushing against my warm skin.

"There's just something about you, Karissa," he whispers, "something I've sought for a very long time."

Jesus Christ. *Don't cry*. He's about to turn me into a blubbering mess. The swell of emotion that consumes me is intense. "Is that right?"

"It is."

Leaning down, Naz kisses the nape of my neck, before I let my hair drop. I go to turn around, to look at him, but instead he wraps his arms around me, pulling me back into him. I relax into his touch as I reach up, toying with the sparkly pendant. "I love you, Naz."

"Not as much as I love you."

"Pfft, *yeah right*." I let go of the necklace. "I don't think that's humanly possible."

He doesn't argue with me.

Neither of us says anything for a while.

We just stand there, reveling in the silence, enjoying the moment. Is this what *forever* will feel like? Just me and him...

And the baby, of course.

Our own little family.

A fresh start. A new beginning.

"Do you wanna, you know, play around one more time before we leave?" I ask, slipping around in his arms, gazing up at him. "Go out with a bang, so to speak?"

There's a twinkle in his eye as he looks down at me. "What do you have in mind?"

"Maybe you can fuck me like you hate me again."

He reaches up, nudging my chin, his thumb grazing my lips. "I think that kind of play will have to wait... for another couple months, at least."

I smile, feeling the blush on my cheeks. "Darn."

"I can, however, give you something even better."

"What's that?"

"I can show you how much I love you."

"Hmm, I like the sound of that."

He leans closer, pausing just a breath from my lips. "Thought you would."

Instead of kissing me, he pulls away, grabbing my hand to lead me from the den. I follow him upstairs, my heart pounding hard in my chest, my skin prickling from anticipation.

As soon as we're in the bedroom, he shuts the door, even though it's pointless. Killer is outside. Nobody's going to burst in the room.

"So beautiful," he says, pulling my shirt off. I raise my hands in the air, making it easier for him. He tosses it to the floor, like its nothing, before reaching around and unhooking my bra, getting rid of it.

Kneeling, Naz unbuttons my jeans, tugging down the zipper, before his hands slip in. He cups my ass, slipping inside my panties, and pulls it all down at once, shedding me of them. The second I kick my pants off, leaving me naked, Naz's mouth is on me.

Holy shit.

My knees nearly buckle.

He licks and sucks, his tongue working magic, as he pins me there in front of him. Tilting my head back, I let out a shaky breath, spreading my legs wider, making it easier for him. My hands somehow find their way to his head, and I stand there, legs trembling, gripping tightly to his wavy hair, as he makes love to me with his mouth.

Jesus Christ, he *ravishes* me.

I can barely take it.

Can barely handle the sensations flowing down my spine.

It's a jolt of electricity, a strike of lightening.

It almost takes me down.

I'm moaning, gasping. It's heaven. It's *torture*. Just when I'm on the brink of losing it, Naz picks me up, moving me over to the bed.

He throws me down on it, not wasting even a second, his lips trailing down my stomach before finding my sweet spot again. He works magic, the kind of magic only he's capable of. In less than a minute, I'm writhing, crying out his name. "Oh God, Naz... *Oh God...*"

Orgasm rips through me. My back arches. My body shakes. It takes my breath away for a second before I gasp for air. As soon as the sensations start to fade, he moves up in the bed, his lips trailing up my stomach, kissing and caressing, before he finds my mouth.

I kiss him deeply, desperately, as I paw at his clothes, and he tolerates it for a moment. Just a moment. Long enough for me to unbutton his shirt. In a blink, his hand snatches ahold of my wrists, pinning them together, pinning them down to the bed above my head. Pulling back some, he looks me in the eyes.

He says nothing.

He just stares.

Studying me again.

It's almost a minute, as I count the torturous seconds in my head. It should been awkward, but it isn't. It's erotic. His gaze penetrates me, effectively fucking my soul.

He lets go after a moment, sitting back on the bed. He strips then, taking it all off, leaving him stark naked.

The second he's back on me, he's stroking himself, finding his way between my legs. I feel him, hesitating at my entrancing, pausing there.

He pushes in then, slowly, deeply, stroking a chord inside of me. My breath hitches. *Oh God.*

"I love that sound," he whispers, his voice gritty. "It's the best

349

music in the world."

I wrap my arms around him. "Maybe that should be your ringtone, then."

He laughs, his face nuzzled into my neck. "That wouldn't work."

"Why?"

"Because then others would hear it. That sound belongs only to my ears."

He makes love to me then, like only Naz can, alternating between slow and deep and rough and hard, sending me into a tailspin. It's a breath-catching, skin-slapping, soul-capturing kind of love. The man owns me. He consumes me. Every part of me was made for every part of him. It's the kind of love I can't imagine ever living without. It's raw, and real, and it's ours.

It's *ours*.

It goes on forever.

Life flashes before my eyes.

We're old and gray and happy. We're *happy*.

Nothing is going to get in our way now.

He shows me that, and I feel it, as he holds me tightly, making love to me. I'm sweaty, and exhausted, by the time it's over. My body is spent from orgasms, and my heart feels like it goes to explode. I say nothing, though, afraid to speak, afraid to offer him any words. Because if I do, I might spew a fucking rainbow. I might spout out the kind of nonsense found in Napoleon's romance novella.

Naz lies on top of me for a moment after he finishes before finally pulling out. He stands up, gathering our clothes, tossing mine to me as I lay on the bed.

"I'm sure now," I manage to say, as I watch Naz getting dressed.

He turns to me. "Yeah?"

I nod as I sit up, clutching a hold of my necklace. "I've got everything I want."

Epilogue

I'm going to tell you a story, a story about a hunter that killed a powerful lion not long ago. The hunter gave no thought to the consequences, gave no thought as to how it would affect the future.

You see, the hunter only cared about one thing... *her*.

To him, nothing else mattered except for her safety. He would've slaughtered entire prides, caused mass extinction, if it meant saving the one he loved. Because while the hunter might've learned his lesson, while he might've ultimately put down his gun, there's something innate about survival.

Something instinctive about protecting her.

I stand on the second-floor terrace at the back of the beach house, facing the dark blue ocean. The water blends into the night sky, a wall of darkness accentuated by crashing waves. This stretch of beach is quiet, very few strangers ever wandering this way. It's isolated, most of the neighboring houses vacant, used sparingly for vacations.

It's like our own little world out here.

Karissa stands on the beach, barefoot, no longer pregnant. She's wearing a pair of cut-off jean shorts and a flowery bikini top tied around her neck. She's beautiful, her long brown hair whipping in the wind. Even with sand clinging to her sweaty body, stretchmarks marring her tanned skin, she's still the most beautiful woman I've ever seen.

I can hear her laughter the whole way up here. It's light and carefree. *Happy.* She never used to laugh that way. Not *before.* She's throwing a tennis ball down the beach and watching as Killer excitedly chases after it, showing no fear as he dashes toward the water.

She glances up at the terrace, smiling, as she pushes her hair out of her face. The beach house is two-stories, open and airy, the entire back wall made of glass. We can sit in the living room and look out at the ocean, can lie in bed and stare up at the starry night sky.

Karissa stares at me from her place on the beach, and I stare back, taking in the sight of her in the moonlight. I almost want to go down and join her, but a noise behind me, in the house, rules that out.

Turning, I make my way inside, out of the main bedroom and across the hall, carefully heading into the only other bedroom. It's dim, only a small lamp on, illuminating the white wooden crib by the door. I step to it, pausing as I look down in it.

Looking right at *him.*

He's wide-awake, his big bright blue eyes open, zeroing in on me the second I appear. He looks a lot like his mother, I think, although Karissa claims he's a miniature version of me. He's quiet, maybe unnaturally so, rarely ever crying.

Happiness seems to radiate off of him.

Fabrizio Michele Vitale

He's three months old today.

He's perfect.

"Hey, little man," I say, reaching toward him. "Shouldn't you be asleep?"

He smiles at the sound of my voice, flashing his toothless grin, and grabs a hold of my pointer finger, wrapping his fist around it.

Picking him up, I cradle him in my arms as I walk through the house, rocking him to sleep.

It's so quiet in here.

It's almost too quiet.

I find myself humming.

What can I say? He likes it.

I hear Karissa come inside, hear her approaching. I stop humming and turn to her when she enters the kitchen where I am, but it's too late.

She heard me.

"Just Walking in the Rain."

"Yeah, my mother—"

"I know," she says, tracking sand all over the floor. "Your father told me."

Huh.

Killer runs inside then, coming right into the kitchen, dropping his tennis ball at Karissa's feet.

He turns to me.

He starts growling.

Sighing, I reach up in the cabinet, grabbing a treat and tossing it at him. He silences, eating it.

Karissa laughs. "He's totally got you trained."

"I'm pretty sure it's the other way around."

"Is it?" She raises her eyebrows as she steps toward me. "Come on, Naz, he's been living with you for a while now. He's had plenty of time to acclimate to your presence, but he knows, if he growls, you'll give him a treat."

She reaches up on her tiptoes, kissing me, before snatching the baby from my arms, setting off to feed him. I stand there, considering that, as Killer finishes his treat. As soon as it's gone, he glances up at me.

He starts to growl again.

Son of a bitch.

I've lied, and stolen, and cheated. I've taken lives and assaulted men. I've gotten what I wanted through coercion, through intimidation, using force when necessary. I always win.

But a goddamn mutt managed to outsmart me.

Unbelievable.

"I'm on to you," I tell him, walking away. "Get your own fucking treats now."

I make my way to the bedroom, finding Karissa lying in bed, holding the baby. I stand there in the doorway, watching, feeling my chest tighten with emotion.

Her and *him*.

My life.

My second wind.

I'd take on the world for them.

And I promise you... I'd *win*.

Acknowledgements

This book wouldn't exist if not for you, the readers. I'm truly humbled and honored by your love of Ignazio. He was born out of frustration at a time when people were telling me my writing just wasn't marketable, that nobody would ever pull for the kind of guys I write. Thank you, from the bottom of my heart, for proving those people wrong.

Sarah Anderson, what can I say? You are extraordinary. You make me see the worth in my words when the voices in my head tell me they're utter rubbish. Despite what self-doubt might tell you, you are one of the most naturally talented writers I've ever met. Never stop pursuing your dream. I believe in you. Nicki Bullard, the greatest best friend in the world, I don't know what I'd do without you. Thank you, times a million, for always being there when I need someone, for letting me talk through this with you and trying your damndest to help me even though I was practically shrieking that it was beyond help. Look at it now, actually a book and shit, ha!

To my family, for being so supportive, and to my book friends, for being so damn amazing, and to my readers... wow... you guys are one of a kind. I'm lucky. Very lucky. Know that I appreciate all of you SO much. To the many bloggers out there, big and small, for giving the time of day to my work. Your love of books is inspiring.

Made in the USA
Coppell, TX
26 May 2024

32825225R10208